I wou... ...ing your choice tonight

Her inner animal wanted loose. She felt her cheeks
heat because normally she had better control over her
impulses. Knowing that everyone else had the same urges
didn't keep her blush from deepening either. She felt
like he could read her thoughts. He had a demeanor that
suggested he was more perceptive than the average guy.
Defiantly in more control than most. A ripple of sensation
went across her skin and she smiled, enjoying the response
because it was so intense. There was something about the
guy that just made her want to fling the rule book aside.
No worrying about repercussions or anything lurking in
his past.

DANGEROUS TO KNOW

DAWN RYDER

St. Martin's Paperbacks

This is a work of fiction. All of the characters, organizations, and events portrayed in this novel are either products of the author's imagination or are used fictitiously.

DANGEROUS TO KNOW

Copyright © 2016 by Dawn Ryder.
Excerpt from *Dare You to Run* copyright © 2016 by Dawn Ryder.

For information address St. Martin's Press, 175 Fifth Avenue, New York, NY 10010.

ISBN: 978-1-250-07521-5

Printed in the United States of America

St. Martin's Paperbacks edition / March 2016

St. Martin's Paperbacks are published by St. Martin's Press, 175 Fifth Avenue, New York, NY 10010.

10 9 8 7 6 5 4 3 2 1

For Monique Patterson and the Team at St. Martin's. Thanks for believing in me and all the help along the way.

CHAPTER ONE

"Do I need to remind you that your father considers this man a friend?" Colonel Decains asked.

Bram Magnus stared straight back at the colonel. "I've grown up with him as an uncle."

Pain crept into his tone, despite his efforts to remain poised in front of his superior officer.

The colonel leaned back in his chair, but he took an eight-by-ten picture of a downed helicopter with him. His eyes narrowed as he looked at the charred remains of three servicemen.

"That intel was sent through my passcode," Bram said.

"You were hacked, son," the colonel said. He frowned at his own use of a familiar term and tossed the picture down. "We'll have the culprit tracked down soon enough. No one gets off this post unless I clear them."

"That's only half the problem," Bram argued. "I've traced the intel to my sister's house."

"Which means she might be the buyer."

Bram tightened his fingers until his knuckles popped. His superior officer didn't miss it, either. Decains flattened his hand on the desktop.

"I appreciate your feelings, Captain, but we need to maintain our perceptive." Decains tapped the picture. "Your father's record and yours are both impressive. I don't doubt that your sister comes from the same stock, which is why we're going to do this by the book."

"Zoe will check out," Bram said firmly. "It's got to be Tim. He's the only other person who has access to my sister's house."

"Sure about that?" the colonel asked. "She's plenty old enough for a boyfriend."

"Check her out all you want," Bram stated firmly. "Zoe will stand up to your worst."

The colonel's face tightened. "Glad to hear it. Your father is a friend of mine. I'd hate to have to tell him your sister is going to disappear."

"You won't have to," Bram answered. "Zoe is no traitor, and she certainly wants both me and my dad home safely. I could have been on that helo."

Decains looked back at the picture. "These men deserve justice."

Bram nodded.

"I'm turning this over to a special branch of intelligence. Completely off the radar. They'll send in a team to get evidence. They specialize in catching their prey with their hands on the smoking gun. We'll back off on our leak here and give him a little bait intel to pass along. I'm going to leave your old access code active, no need to let him know we're on to him. Besides, we can't be outdone by one of the stateside teams. I want to catch this traitor with his hands on the cheese."

Bram drew in a stiff breath but didn't argue. It had to be done the way the colonel was doing it. His insides were knotted and he was half afraid he was going to puke from the knowledge of what his sister was going to endure. But he kept his composure and cut the colonel a salute before making his way out of the man's office.

He itched to pick up the phone and call his sister.

He couldn't.

Which pissed him off. Tim had been his father's buddy longer than Bram had been alive but there was no doubt in Bram's mind who was responsible. And it pissed him off knowing he couldn't get his hands locked around Tim's neck. At least not personally. Still, part of him was enjoying knowing Decains was setting a team on Tim's ass that was going to tear him apart, bit by bit.

Exactly what a traitor deserved.

"The Magnus family has a good reputation," Kagan said.

"They do," Colonel Decains confirmed. The connection was scratchy, the distance between Afghanistan and the States showing up as background noise. It was the most detailed thing about the moment. The office Kagan sat in was stripped of anything that might be considered personal. The phone he was using was a landline that would be disconnected the moment the operation was finished. "That's why I'm calling you. Make sure your team does a good job. When it gets to mopping up, there is going to be a full-bird colonel looking mighty close at the details."

"You know my men are going to see the daughter as a possible suspect," Kagan advised Decains.

"No way around it," Decains agreed. "I'll handle the heat over that point."

"I'll be in touch." Kagan cut the connection.

There was little else to say. He lived in a world of shadows because that's where he was most effective at catching the scum who did business there. The information was spread out over his desk. He considered it before picking up his phone and selecting a contact to reach out to. Agent Tyler Martin answered on the second ring.

"I have an assignment for you." Kagan didn't waste any time.

Tyler Martin liked his job.

In fact, it was his life.

Which was why he was going to make sure his future was a bright one. One thing about working shadow operations, it left a stink on a man. Once you were in deep, there really was no leaving, so it was best to ensure a long, profitable career. Sometimes, that meant doing some dirty work for powerful people.

Tyler considered the case Kagan had just assigned him. It was a gift really. A perfect little present dropped in front of him. One he'd been waiting for. That was another thing about shadow operations: the hard fact that just when you thought you were safe, fate would circle back around and bite you in the ass. He'd been waiting a long time to get in some payback. But today, that wait was over. Saxon and Vitus Hale were about to get a king-sized serving of it. It was going to be Tyler's pleasure to dish it out. He'd been waiting for just the right case to take them down. Tyler looked over the details of the information Kagan had sent over and grinned.

It was perfect. Classified intel. Dead servicemen. All the components needed to blacken someone's name forever. Since the leak was already plugged, there was no reason not to twist the operation to suit his own agenda. All he had to do was find the man on this side before anyone else did.

He didn't spare a thought for the Magnus family. They had friends for certain but no other family, which made them an even stronger candidate for what he needed. They could be buried. They'd end up with full military honors or branded as traitors. He really didn't care so long as they were dead and silenced. Tyler had his future to secure and it wasn't going to come cheap. He'd always known that. But it was his blood or someone else's, because the men he was negotiating with played for keeps. He couldn't afford to get picky about the means. The opportunities would be few and far between. His own future had a price tag on it, one he had to pay if he didn't want to end up dead himself. It was a dog-eat-dog world.

He selected a contact from among his teams and punched it. Time to assign Saxon Hale to the last case of his career.

And life.

Tyler didn't let his conscience get in the way. Congressman Jeb Ryland might be a whack job of an overprotective father but the man was in the right position to offer Tyler a secure future. So if Jeb wanted the Hale brothers taken out for pissing on his turf, Tyler planned to make it happen. A nice little treason case was the perfect answer. As for the Magnus family, well, it wasn't personal.

* * *

"Now, he is hot."

Roni rolled her words and ended up sounding like she was purring. Zoe glanced over to the man in question and wished she hadn't.

Hot was an understatement.

She'd never known his equal, much less experienced what it must be like to have such a prime animal in her bed. Sensation prickled along her skin instantly, deep, carnal awareness twisting through her belly. The swiftness of the response sent her looking away with a shrug designed to protect her emotions from being spotted.

Roni was a master at sniffing out Zoe's true feelings. It made her a great friend and major pain in the ass when life decided to deliver a punch to her solar plexus. Which was the perfect definition of a best friend. Zoe nodded, earning a husky chuckle from her pal.

"Lickable," she agreed.

The guy really was a double shot of whiskey. The kind you wanted to take straight up then slam down the empty glass while you felt the burn smoking your insides.

Mega hot.

She looked down at her drink suspiciously. Maybe the bartender was just doubling up in the hope his bar would get a reputation as a great pickup joint.

"Oh Lord." Roni jabbed her with an elbow. "What's the point of hanging out at a bar if we don't do a little window-shopping?"

"Point taken."

Zoe lifted her drink and watched the man in question over the salted rim of the glass. He was wrapped in black leather, which made him doubly delectable. The jacket hung open, giving her a glimpse of a T-shirt that hugged a torso defined and tight. Dark hair and eyes gave him a slightly sinful, badass look, and combined with the black leather, he was like dark chocolate.

Premium window-shopping, for sure.

"I'm going to ask him to dance." Roni slid off her bar stool with a click of her heels. "Wish me luck."

"He's not a dance-floor kind of animal." Zoe wasn't sure where the justification for her opinion came from, only that she was firmly sure of it. The guy was suited to shadows and thrived there. The only thing capable of scaring him was being predictable. Confidence radiated from him so thickly, it felt like he just might be worthy of the arrogance his stony expression declared.

"He'll turn you down," she muttered while setting her glass down. She was no longer interested in numbing her wits. Not when there was such a feast standing near enough to enjoy. Nope, she was going to enjoy the moment. Completely.

Roni fingered the strand of silver beads hanging around her neck. "You might be right; you're definitely spot-on about the fact that he's an animal . . . One I'd like to let play with me, no taming required. He can run wild . . . anywhere he wants to go." Roni made a sweeping gesture with one hand up and down her body.

Zoe laughed at her friend. "You're not normally the 'toy' type. Sure your modern woman can handle the hit to your pride? That man isn't going to let you walk him on a leash."

"Never let it be said I backed down from a challenge," she declared in a husky whisper. "Besides, I fully intend to play as good as I get played with."

"Matching collars, is it?"

Roni made a low sound in the back of her throat. "If I'm lucky."

With a wink her friend made her way across the worn planks of the barroom floor, drawing stares from the shadowy booths lining the walls of the place with the sultry sway of her hips. It was really a whole-body thing, one that Zoe admired as much as she detested. Her friend's ability to mesmerize the male population fit nicely with her flirtatious persona but tonight, Roni was focused on the man leaning back against the bar. He'd bought a longneck beer of some sort but had only taken a single sip of it. It sat next to him, forgotten as he scanned the room.

Another prickle of sensation went down Zoe's back. The beer remained on the bar while those dark eyes landed on every single soul in the place. He looked like he was assessing them, cataloging them; like nothing was more important than sizing up the occupants of the room.

He sure wasn't interested in the beer.

He reminded her of her brother, every motion controlled and his position selected for the best angle of defense. He was military-trained. No doubt about it, the guy had served time in something more than general ranks, if she was any good at judging body language.

Nosy . . .

The word floated through her mind, but she shrugged it off. Hell, if she was going to read anyone's body, his was infinitely top-grade. Besides, she wasn't up for a quick hookup. The main point of the evening was to ride shotgun for Roni and indulge in girlfriend time.

She wasn't being nosy. He'd come into the bar, and bars were places to be seen.

Right . . . Now I'm justifying my spying.

True. But that didn't make her thinking wrong. Zoe took a slow sip from her drink and peered over the rim of the glass at the subject of her thoughts. Her lips curved as she took another sip.

This guy's body language said a lot more, too. Her eyes narrowed, the lids feeling heavy as she watched the way his hips worked when he moved. The sight set off something deeply sexual inside her. Heat was spreading gently across her skin and it was just too enjoyable to resist a few more moments of indulgence.

So what if he caught her staring?

It was a bar after all. Everyone in the place was there with sex on their minds. Maybe that was a blunt way to put it, but it was still true. Really, really true. One look at the tight jeans and short skirts was all you needed to confirm that fact. The groups of people crowded around the tables were there to connect with someone else, the drinks in their hands nothing but liquid courage. Even Military Man, animal that he was, had to be looking for companionship in some form. He'd be off on his own if he wasn't in the mood for company. Loneliness had a way of reducing everyone to pitiful piles of need. Of course a man like him wouldn't have to work very hard to gain a little company.

I wouldn't mind being your choice tonight . . .

Her inner animal wanted loose. She felt her cheeks heat because normally she had better control over her impulses. Knowing that everyone else had the same urges didn't keep her blush from deepening, either. She felt like he could read her thoughts. He had a demeanor that suggested he was more perceptive than the average guy. Definitely in more control than most. A ripple of sensation moved across her skin and she smiled, enjoying the response because it was so intense. There was something about the guy that just made her want to fling the rule book aside. No worrying about repercussions or anything lurking in his past.

He glanced at her, sending a jolt of awareness down her spine before Roni reached him, angling his head to look down from his six-and-a-half-foot frame. A bare half inch of black hair covered his head, the lights above him shining off the neatly sheared surface.

Yup . . . military. She'd bet on it. Lust teased her again, so she decided to bask in the glow of the heat. Window-shopping did need to be enjoyed, after all, especially if she wasn't willing to lay down the price of making a try at touching the merchandise.

Why not? Why let Roni have all the fun?

Her inner voice was becoming more daring by the second, the heat gripping her body and urging her to abandon her common sense.

Yeah, well, impulsive sex came with too many risks for her peace of mind. It was a fun idea to toy with but that was as far as she was going. She needed to stick to her ideals because the leather-clad god across the room wouldn't be the staying kind.

Oh, but the things I could enjoy while he was around . . .

Which would be followed by a guilt trip that would cost her too much self-confidence for her comfort. Besides, she wanted more than just hot sex.

Ha! Not at the moment I don't . . .

Zoe lifted her margarita and took a long drink, but the fruity taste didn't mix with the sight of Mr. Untamed

Temptation. She set her glass down, craving the hard bite of whiskey.

Yeah, I want hard . . . that's for sure.

Roni did her best to get him onto the dance floor. He shook his head and reached for his beer instead. Roni propped one hand on her hip and pouted at him but he only tipped the bottle up, using the beverage like a shield. Roni didn't give up; she continued to talk to him in a tone that was too low for Zoe to hear over the band.

Zoe reached for the bowl of peanuts sitting on the table and broke one open. She was bored. The music was good but the bar scene just wasn't her thing. Roni thrived on the fishbowl experience. Her friend was turned out in a mini-skirt and loose tank top, looking like she belonged up on the stage. She fit next to the brawn king, looking relaxed as she flirted with him. Another man leaned over and a moment later Roni was on her way to the dance floor with him.

Zoe grinned. Roni began dancing with a flair that made Zoe envious. Her body curved and moved with the skill of a belly dancer, only with a much more modern rhythm. Roni turned around and shot Biker Boy a look that made it clear she was performing for his enjoyment.

"Looks like you've been abandoned."

Zoe got a glimpse of blue eyes and short-cut blond hair before the stool next to her was occupied. The guy set his whiskey tumbler down and considered her.

"I'm a big girl," she responded while fighting the urge to look back at Mr. Untamed. The guy sitting across from her wasn't second-class by any means. In fact, he was clean-cut, wearing a buttondown shirt with the collar unbuttoned and the cuffs rolled up.

"I noticed," he said as he contemplated her. He reached for his whiskey and took a sip but almost as an afterthought, because his blue eyes were fixed on her.

"Saxon." He offered her his hand across the small pub-style table.

"Zoe." She was shaking his hand out of reflex.

Mr. Untamed wouldn't shake my hand.

It was a majorly unfair thought and really bitchy of her but there it was. Gut response. Honest and brutal. Saxon didn't deserve it but she doubted he needed to be jerked around, either. He was looking for company and she wasn't interested. Not a bit. All she wanted to do was turn back around and stare at the leather-clad animal stuck in her brain.

Another peanut crackled between her fingertips before Zoe's cell phone buzzed to rescue her. She didn't bother to check the caller ID; it was better not to look a gift horse in the mouth. Even if it was a telemarketer, she was taking the call. It beat throwing a pity party.

"Excuse me." She slid off the bar stool.

"Hello?"

"Hey, sis."

Zoe pushed the front door open and hurried outside where she could hear her brother's voice better. "Bram? It's been bloody forever since you called."

Her brother snorted on the other end. "Been working. I assume you recall just how often we servicemen get separated from our loved ones while we're deployed? After all, you grew up with the same active-duty dad I did."

"Yeah, yeah, I know the drill. How are *you*?" There were rules when she talked to her brother, "no serious questions allowed" sort of rules. Keep it light and friendly because it just might be the last conversation they had. Guilt could be a razor-sharp bitch.

"How are you?" Her brother's voice was firm and serious.

Zoe frowned and leaned against the exterior of the bar. "Fine. Why are you asking in that tone of voice? As well as redirecting the conversation?"

There was silence on the other end of the line. Static crackled while she waited for her brother to respond. He finally offered her a dry laugh that drew every muscle she had tight with tension.

"I'm just thinking about you," he muttered. "Keep your guard up, sis."

"Why?" The word was out of her mouth before she remembered who she was talking to. "All right, forget I asked that."

There was a deeper chuckle on the other end of the line, one that almost put her at ease, but not quite.

"You know me a little too well, sis. Keep that intuition sharp and make sure you watch your back. Call me if there's anything suspicious happening, even something small. Leave a message."

"Is that all the information I'm getting?" she said, her voice filled with frustration.

"For the moment." Bram laid down his decision with every bit of arrogance she'd just decided Biker Boy had. "If you don't notice anything, there is nothing to worry about. Don't hesitate to call."

"I won't," she groused, far from satisfied with the lack of details.

"That sounds like my brat sister, nosy to the core," Bram accused her with amusement in his tone, enough to make her throat tighten because it had been too damn long since she'd heard it.

"Got to go." Bram's voice had chilled and hardened, tightening her neck muscles once again. "Remember, leave a message. If all I see is a hang-up, it will concern me."

The line went dead and she worried her lower lip. Her brother was on another continent. If there was some kind of trouble, there wouldn't be much he could do to help her. But she sure as hell wasn't going to do anything to distract him while he was crawling around God knew where.

"Bad news?"

She jumped, fumbling the phone, and ended up with it pressed to her cleavage to keep it from falling to the ground. Mr. Untamed was watching her with eyes as black as his hair. This close, the term *Biker Boy* didn't fit.

He was all man.

Still a few paces away, he managed to strike her as huge. She wasn't used to feeling delicate, but the wide expanse of muscle-coated chest sent a shiver down her spine. He put her on edge, for no other reason than she knew he was stronger. It was a primitive idea, one that rose above every bit of faith she had in equal rights. She was staring and he was watching her do it.

"Ah . . . not really," she forced out before tearing her gaze off him. He was too distracting.

I mean too tempting . . .

Behind him, on the other side of the front doors, was a motorcycle. It was coal black but clean enough to pass a white-glove inspection.

"I guess it's a good thing you didn't finish your beer. It doesn't look like you brought a designated driver."

His lips twitched and she regretted making the joke

because the guy was even sexier when he was grinning. Still arrogant but it looked good on him. Just a hint of playfulness.

That could be so much fun . . .

Crap, she must look desperate. She felt like it sure enough. Her breath was caught in her throat, anticipation sharpening her senses.

"You're perceptive." He shrugged, the motion looking impossibly sexy. Behind her loose top, her nipples contracted. His gaze dropped to the hard points and his lips thinned. "I didn't come for the liquor."

He closed the gap between them and leaned against the building with one shoulder while watching her. Sensation shot through her, tingling and filling her with an intense awareness of him. She had to fight the urge to allow her gaze to slip down past his six-pack to see what his leather pants offered her to admire.

"Why did you come?" His voice was husky but his gaze sharp. He was still leaning against the building as if he didn't have a care in the world, but the look in his eyes didn't match his lazy posture. He was intimidating but it struck her as a challenge. At last she was able to grasp her wilting self-control and master the surge of lust flooding her. She wasn't going to simper in the face of his brawn.

"I came with a friend, who's off dancing now. Nosy."

He studied her, looking like he was gauging just how solid her resolve was. Another jolt of awareness hit her but it annoyed her as much as it thrilled. She would not melt at his feet.

"Maybe I got the impression you wouldn't mind me being nosy." His gaze slipped back down her chest to where her nipples still raised the silk of her top. When he made eye contact with her again, heat simmered in those dark orbs.

Maybe . . . I should just let my impulses rule . . .

"Yeah, well, maybe I should recall the pepper spray my dad gave me for my twenty-first birthday." She was poking him with a stick now but at least she sounded confident.

One dark eyebrow rose in response to her threat. "Pepper spray works better when you don't warn your target."

"You've got a point," she agreed, trying to sound amused. Unconcerned. It was a lie, though. She was rattled. Her belly queasy with nerves. The guy was setting her on her ear without even trying.

Pathetic. Yet really interesting because it's never happened before.

He studied her for a long moment. "I've always preferred to experience those boundaries instead of just being told where they are."

What an experience he'd be, too . . .

She looked past him to the motorcycle, an image of him clasping the mean-looking machine between his thighs surfacing. "I believe you."

"Does that mean the pepper spray will stay in the bottom of your purse?" he asked in a slow drawl that made her shiver again.

She laughed, the sound husky and full of heat in a way she couldn't recall feeling in a very long time. There was no buildup, no warning from her better judgment to establish a stronger foundation for trust. There was just need, hot, burning need. She wanted it satisfied. Now. It was the intensity of her reaction to him that made her dig her heels in. A protective instinct rising above the flood of pheromones trying to drown her common sense.

"Nothing personal but we're strangers."

His gaze lowered to her chest and came back up. "Why don't we change that? Let's go for a ride. As you noticed, I'm still sober, and not interested in dulling my wits." His eyes narrowed and homed in on her lips. "I'm in the mood for highs that don't require mind-numbing chemicals."

Oh hell yes . . .

Her mouth went dry and her body pulsed with excitement. Lust chiseled away at her resolve, pushing her toward the impulse to do exactly what she wanted without a care for the regrets that might show up at sunrise.

"Ah . . . I shouldn't."

But I sure as hell want to . . .

His grin was gone, pure intent shinning in his eyes. "Why not? It will be more fun than standing here waiting to drive your friend home. I promise you that."

And his voice dipped down, loaded with suggestive possibilities. Ones she was all too tempted to entertain.

"Careful," she warned him. "I don't desert my friends."

He lifted his hands in mock surrender. "I can respect a lady who keeps her word." His voice dipped down again while something flickered in his eyes that looked like victory. "But you're no baby and neither of us came out tonight because we wanted to drink. I think your friend would understand if you altered your plans. She struck me as confident enough to arrange a cab ride home all by herself."

"So why not be impulsive?" Her darker side was gaining the upper hand and the words spilled out, part of her longing for any excuse to just give in and indulge. To challenge the boundaries around her and be wild.

"Exactly."

His tone deepened, becoming something almost too

decadent to resist. She gave in to the urge to look down the length of the man teasing her. Below the six-pack, his leather pants outlined a bulge promising her exactly the sort of ride she'd been thinking about.

A deep chuckle pulled her attention back to his face. He reached out and stroked her cheek. She shivered in response, the feeling of his skin against her own nearly explosive.

"Like what you see, baby?" His hand moved to cup her nape, gripping it just enough to send another ripple of need through her. "I do."

He planted his free hand on the wall next to her head as he maintained his grip on her neck. The lights from the parking lot were blocked out when he leaned over and kissed her.

Oh hell . . .

She twisted in his embrace, overwhelmed by the intensity of the moment. No kiss had ever affected her so deeply. He followed her, pressing a hard kiss against her mouth. More than a kiss, it was a challenge, but that only drove the heat index up another few notches. It shouldn't have. She'd never been a fan of overbearing men, but a moan surfaced from her chest as she reached out for him.

No sweet, sedate, agreed-upon kiss had ever set her blood on fire, either.

His chest felt as good as it looked: a feast for her fingertips. She moved closer, kissing him back with the same intensity his mouth was applying to hers. Lust became need, her body begging for less clothing and more skin. He pressed her lips apart, and the tip of his tongue teased her lower lip before slipping inside her mouth.

She shivered, her body alive with a thousand different points of awareness. Her nipples contracted and her clit throbbed with need so intense she pushed him away. She reached up and shoved her hand between their lips to separate them. It was a desperate motion, one driven by the knowledge that she was in way over her head.

"Just . . . back off a second." She didn't recognize her own voice; it was too sultry, too needy to be hers. Mentally toying with being reckless was far different from doing it. Consequences were often 100 percent unforgiving. She needed to think but her brain felt frozen.

"Why?" His hand slid down her neck, across her shoulder, and down her chest until he cupped her breast. He thumbed one hard nipple without hesitation, sending a little jolt of hard pleasure down her core.

Shit!

How in the hell did his touch make her feel so good? She should have taken a swing at his face. Instead she bit back a husky sound of enjoyment. His gaze homed in on her lower lip, victory flickering in his eyes.

"You're just as interested as I am, baby. Let's take a ride and feed our appetites. No games, no meaningless chit-chat. Blunt . . . honesty."

She actually thought about it. The passion smoldering in his eyes was too hot to ignore. He teased her nipple with his thumb, sending a rush of heat through her belly. It was so intensely carnal her hips jerked, moving without any sort of decision. Part of her really wanted to know just how the ride might be with him, for no other reason than that she was pretty sure she'd never been so turned on in her life.

"That's right." He slid his hand farther down until he was cupping her hip. He moved in closer, pressing against her lower body while his mouth landed back on top of hers. "It will be explosive," he whispered against her lips. "Better guilty of being impulsive than missing out."

She opened her mouth to say something but her mind went blank. There was only the touch of his lips against hers, the scent of his skin filling her senses, and the pure desperation to get another taste of him brewing inside her.

This time she was overwhelmed. The wave of desire washed across her and swept her into its powerful surge. He guided her hips closer to his, until the hard bulge of his erection was pressing against her belly. Her clit pulsed and her passage ached. Sex had never been so necessary before. Tonight she actually hurt with yearning. Her body quivered with it, hunger ruling her as he thrust his tongue down into her mouth. The hold he had on the back of her head was harder than she liked, or thought she liked, because that little taste of his strength sent her common sense flying in favor of following her impulses. Her pride didn't care for it but the intensity of her desire was like a drug she was addicted to. She'd do anything to experience the high.

"Let's get out of here. I need to get you naked."

His voice had a ring of authority that didn't sit well with her. It was the splash of cold reality she needed to grasp at the shattered remnants of her self-control.

"Look . . . I'm sorry . . . but . . . no."

She wished she sounded more convincing. He'd stepped back from her but frowned and made to close the space between them again.

"I mean it . . . no, I'm not that kind of girl."

But I am tempted . . .

She planted one hand in the middle of his chest. She

really didn't have the strength to hold him off if he decided
to kiss her again, but he flattened his hands on either side
of her head, caging her but granting her enough space to
hold on to rational thought.

Maybe.

"Married? Boyfriend . . . lover?" His voice was low and
rough with frustration. "If you were devoted to him, you
would be in his bed instead of here. If he was smart, he
wouldn't be letting you roam. Or leaving you hungry."

I have an appetite all right.

There was a flicker of something in his eyes that looked
like jealousy. And no matter how absurd it was, she felt a
tingle of respect for him. The guy wasn't a douchebag.

"My reason doesn't matter. I told you to back off."

His lips twitched up but it wasn't a pleasant expression.
"It matters, all right." He cupped her nape again, massaging
it, and sent ripples of sensation down her body instantly.
"Do you really want to play the dating game? Neither of
us is a teenager."

She pushed harder against his chest, but he only lifted
one dark eyebrow. Her temper flared up; he was too damn
smug. "That doesn't mean I jump into bed the second a
guy snares my attention. That's also a result of no longer
being a teenager. It's called self-control."

"Bull." He delivered the word like a whip crack. He
threaded his fingers through her hair and closed his fist
until she felt the delicate strands pull just enough to send
prickles of pain across her scalp. But he somehow managed to keep the pressure perfect, leaving her balanced
on the edge of true pain. It fanned the flames of lust again.
His smile grew before he leaned toward her and tilted his
head so she felt his breath against the side of her neck.

He is an animal . . . deadly when he decides to claim what he wants.

"What do you really want, baby? Honesty?" His lips grazed the delicate skin of her neck, sending ripples of pleasure down her length. "The honest truth is, you turn me on. My cock got hard the moment I saw you, and you couldn't keep your eyes off me, either."

He lifted his head and released her hair. A second later he stepped back, giving her the space she'd demanded, but no relief showed up. Instead disappointment sliced through her like razor blades.

"Sexual arousal isn't enough—"

"Enough to trust me? If I wanted to rob you, it would be done." His eyes narrowed. "Same thing goes for rape. The music is loud and you chose a dark corner to take that call in. I'd already have used you and been done if that was how I got my rocks off."

His tone was blunt and cutting, his eyes full of confidence in his ability to overpower her. The fact that he was boldly letting her know he was aware she was at his mercy made her tremble. The problem was, she wasn't afraid of him and she really should have been.

As in, really, really should have been.

Foolish . . .

He stepped back farther and pulled a pair of riding gloves from his pocket. They were black leather and he shoved his hands into them with hard motions before tugging the tension cord around the wrist tight. No Velcro to announce his movements. The man was definitely lethal.

He extended his right hand toward her, palm up, the invitation clear.

Well, challenge actually.

"I'm not into bars, so if you want to get to know me, let's go someplace we can explore personal details about each other." Arousal flashed in his eyes. "I'm real interested in doing that. The hard points of your nipples tell me you are, too."

They'd be naked before she learned his full name.

She wanted to.

Hell, she felt like she needed to. The heat was still swirling around in her belly so intense, it felt like her skin might blister. But she shook her head.

"Sorry, it's still not my style."

His gaze lowered to where her loose top was just revealing the very tips of her hard nipples. She shivered again because he had such a commanding presence; it was so tempting to let him call the shots. Bending beneath that arrogance would be a very convenient way to sidestep guilt.

Zoe straightened her spine; she made her own choices and shouldered the load. She wasn't going to turn into a woman who blamed her lover for everything. When she had sex, it was her choice. No excuses. No playing the blame game.

"Not tonight," she insisted.

He frowned, looking like he wanted to argue, but he pulled a key from his pant pocket.

"Later then."

A tiny chill touched her nape. He didn't sound like he was saying good-bye to her, which didn't make any sense because she could see the hunger blazing in his eyes. Hunger she wasn't going to be satisfying.

A man like him wouldn't have to search very far to get what he wanted. But there was something in his gaze that made her think she'd see him again. He walked toward the bike, taking a moment to strap on a helmet before swinging his leg over the machine and kicking the kickstand up. He revved the thing only once before letting the sleek machine glide across the parking lot.

He was an animal.

Zoe took a deep breath and felt her desire turning into an unsatisfied ache guaranteed to hound her for the rest of the night.

I could have gotten lucky . . .

She scoffed at her inner voice. Yeah, she could have thrown caution to the wind but she hadn't. Maybe it was the wiser choice but she felt like cussing.

"Oh, tell me you did not let that man get away?"

Roni's heels clicked on the walkway. Zoe felt her friend's gaze on her face and watched her eyes narrow.

"I am so jealous," Roni announced with a huff. "How did you get a kiss out of him so fast? I could barely get a once-over from those devil-dark eyes. He must taste delicious."

"He didn't . . ." Zoe rolled her eyes when she realized she was trying to cover up. What was she? Sixteen? "So he did. Big deal."

Roni chuckled. "Oh, that man was a big deal, and I'll just bet he is big everywhere it matters."

"Maybe."

Her friend clicked her long fingernails together, warning Zoe that Roni was in the mood to pick apart her responses.

"Don't start, Roni. Even you have to admit riding off with a guy whose name I don't know isn't a bright idea."

"Oh man . . . he offered to take you for a ride on that machine of his?"

Among other things . . .

Zoe dug in her pocket for her keys. "That's it, we're leaving. We are rapidly exiting reasonable, logical thinking land. You know, that place where we"—Zoe gestured to the pair of them—"live because we're not pathetic enough to need to score with intoxicated dudes."

Her friend only laughed at the disgust in her voice.

"Yeah, right, you did the *sensible* thing but damn he was *hot*."

Zoe offered her friend a smug look. "He kisses really good, too."

"Bitch."

"What? No score, Mercer? I'm shocked."

"I scored a lot closer to the bull's-eye than you managed." Mercer watched his commanding officer arrive. Saxon had pulled on a leather jacket for protection before riding away from the bar, but his legs were still only covered in denim because they'd needed to look different. It had been good-cop, bad-cop time and their target had gone for the leather.

She liked bad boys. Part of Mercer enjoyed knowing it. Okay, enjoyed it a lot.

The other part of him was a little wary of just how much he enjoyed the knowledge. She was a target.

Saxon frowned. "She would have warmed up to me."

"Face it, she wasn't interested in you, buddy." Mercer smirked.

"Doesn't look like she's interested in you, either. Back of your bike is mighty empty."

"She was interested. Just cautious," Mercer stated with full confidence and Saxon cursed.

"Doesn't count if you couldn't get her on the back of your bike. The operation requires one of us to have her trust. If you don't have the stomach for the job, I'll call in Maddox."

Mercer revved his bike. "I've got her attention; the assignment is mine. Giving her space will build trust faster than storming through her defenses."

Saxon considered him, his expression hard. "Don't take too long, lives are on the line."

"I'll complete the mission within the time frame. I wouldn't be on this team if you didn't trust me to follow through. What did Greer uncover at her place?" Mercer asked.

Saxon's expression tightened. "Her home system is encrypted so complexly, we'd be risking watching all evidence fry if we try to trace the intel back to source through it."

"Shit."

"Exactly," Saxon agreed. "Which means we need to hook her."

"I'll do it."

Mercer pulled away, leaving his team leader behind. He didn't need Saxon drilling him or doubting him. The mission objective was clear enough, even if he didn't personally care for the method of achieving their goal. But he didn't have a better suggestion, so he'd follow the plan.

It was still just another mission. One vital enough to have Saxon's team assigned to it. He needed to keep his mind focused on the fact that men could lose their lives if he didn't succeed. Just because he was operating in civilian territory didn't change that aspect of the mission.

Either Zoe Magnus was an innocent being used as a mule by her brother to move classified information into the hands of the enemy or she was his accomplice. If she was innocent, he was her only chance at clearing her name.

He pushed the bike faster, enjoying the feeling of his body flying through space. Zoe's face invaded the moment. Looking into her eyes had shaken him. At first glance, they were brown, but up close, when he could smell the fresh scent of her hair, those orbs were a kaleidoscope of brown, green, and topaz. Full of life. As if the woman inside was rarer than he'd ever suspected possible. He'd seen his share of attractive women. Honestly, his reaction to her didn't make any sense. He should be able to keep her under the label of "target" and hold the mission line in his head. Instead, he was recalling the way her lips curved when she was calling his bluff.

Bitterness filled his mouth, and he pushed the bike faster.

It wasn't the first time he'd been challenged by a mission, even if it was the first time his duty had included cozying up with a civilian woman. If she was a spy, he wouldn't care if she got hurt. That was the risk she took by involving herself in espionage.

It was obvious he had more experience with sex than she did. But doubt gnawed at his resolve to see the mission through.

Her kiss had lacked practice, lacked the calculated motion he'd encountered in professional female spies. Part of him didn't care for overwhelming her, even when he suspected she had it coming. Zoe Magnus didn't use her body like a weapon. Of course, that might be a clever ploy. One employed by her brother—choose a mule who was sweet and innocent. That much better to cover up his crimes. If she was a mule, Mercer might end up feeling bad.

Try feeling like shit.

They had plenty of suspicions but no real evidence yet. Once he thought again about getting in her bed, that bitterness rose again. Part of him was trying to come up with another option. He needed to be in position to obtain the data, both physically and mentally. Bugging her system wouldn't be too hard but they needed more. Needed to hear personal conversations that might just hold the key to unlocking the case. There was a chance he'd prove her innocent, too.

But that didn't stop him from feeling like crap over the method. He wrestled with the problem but still came up dry of other solutions. If Zoe was guilty, it was possible she had her hard drive rigged to dump every megabyte of evidence the second someone failed to navigate her security. So someone had to witness her retrieving the stolen information. Saxon liked his cases airtight, and so did Mercer.

Yeah . . . well, the facts weren't helping him detach his feelings. Zoe was a military brat. Her family well respected. It was striking too close to the heart. But that was more of a personal problem. Being an operative on civilian ground meant taking the risk of colliding with emotional entanglements. Fancy, polished words that did little to soothe his guilt, though they did reinforce his dislike of undercover operations. He grinned ruefully. Circumstances had decided he wasn't going to be on the front line any longer. But he wasn't going to just hit the civilian world and settle in, either. Honestly, he wondered if he was headed straight toward being just another veteran who failed at returning home. Joining Saxon's team was an attempt to find his feet now that he was back on

American soil. A place where he could still be himself, because locking his gun up in a safe wasn't his style.

Give him a straight-out fight any day.

Getting into Zoe Magnus's bed? Well, that was going to be a walk through fire.

The hallway light came on when she pressed the garage door opener. By the time Zoe pulled into the three-car garage and turned off her engine, her father's parrot was squawking at her from his cage in the kitchen.

"Yes, Harley. Your sister is home."

The scarlet-winged macaw parrot shook his head and fluffed his feathers now that he had light to see with. He lifted one foot and waited for her to dump her purse on the kitchen table. Then she opened the door and offered him her arm.

Ignoring him was out of the question. As in very-bad-idea sort of decision. Harley never let inattention go without giving her a piece of his mind. In terms of sheer volume, parrots could be heard for nearly a mile. Harley was definitely in the category of overachiever.

But he was also a big cat at times. Once in her arms, he purred softly as he turned and nuzzled against her chest. Zoe rubbed him as she walked over to the answering machine sitting on the kitchen counter. The message light was blinking. She pushed it and continued to rub Harley as the messages played.

She ended up frowning at the modem noise coming from the machine. It would cut off after thirty seconds, and then the next message would start up with the same annoying nonsense.

Telemarketers.

She held down the DELETE key before moving back toward Harley's cage. He gave her an opinioned squawk.

"We have a full day tomorrow," she told him.

The parrot wasn't very interested in anything that didn't involve a long cuddle session. Zoe turned off the kitchen light to get him to step off her arm and into his cage. Parrots didn't have the ability to see in the dark. Harley clicked his beak at her but settled in for the night as she locked the cage door, checking the lock twice to make sure it was secure, and covered the cage. One of the kitchen chairs bore the marks from one of Harley's escapes. The lower leg was gnawed for a foot. She kept his cage well supplied with toys to feed his chewing need, but there was nothing like the forbidden fruit of the furniture as far as the parrot was concerned. Escape was always on his mind.

She made her way upstairs, checking every room before going into her own. Her father's house rules, which she kept even though she was on her own now.

" 'Night, Dad," she muttered as she passed the picture of him hanging on the wall in the upstairs hallway. Her brother's picture was there, too, both of them looking stern in their service portraits. She went toward the two smaller bedrooms the upper floor offered. One was her bedroom and the other her home office. Something was on the floor of her office. She peered through the doorway at the lump. On closer investigation, it was her jacket, the one normally draped over the back of her chair. Suspicion prickled along her neck as she picked it up.

I'm just jumpy because of Bram's call.

That was likely so. She might have knocked the jacket off the chair when she left. Just because she didn't remember doing it, didn't mean she hadn't.

Mr. Untamed had gone to her head.

She smiled on her way across the hall to her bedroom. It felt a little emptier tonight.

Ha! He'd have cleared out before sunrise.

Definitely not something she needed to deal with. An encounter like that would be mind blowing and it would also leave a huge crack in her self-esteem. All the self-directed lectures about making her own choices would be worth about two cents if her "choice" for the night wasn't interested enough in her to stick around.

It would suck donkey balls.

Ah yes, the flip side to being a modern, professional woman who didn't need a man to make her happy. Sometimes that meant she had to make the choice to be alone.

She settled into the bed and turned the lights out. Her lips tingled, the memory of blistering-hot kissing following her into slumber.

Well, it had been a night to remember.

"Yummy."

"Can it, Thais."

Thais pouted at him. The woman had an unfair knowledge of how to affect the opposite sex. Every motion she made was alluring. From the way she shifted her eyes to the motion of her lips. Nothing was ever normal with her. She oozed sex appeal. "Why the shutdown? Shouldn't I be allowed to admire you on your way to charm another female? You deserve some attention for your effort after all."

Mercer reached down, clasping the femme fatale by her forearm and pulling her off the arm of the sofa she was perched on. She appeared delicate and feminine, which normally touched off all the right impulses inside him. Today he was remarkably unaffected, which gave him the opportunity to toy with her. "You're not the target, honey, and I'm a little too busy at the moment to indulge you."

Thais didn't lose her composure so close to him; there wasn't even a slight widening of her eyes to betray uncertainty. Instead she trailed a lazy finger along the open collar of his buttondown shirt, sending a tiny ripple of sensation across his skin with a perfected touch. For all that she felt delicate in his embrace, he knew she was anything but. Her lean body was trained to lethal perfection. Thais could knock him senseless with more than her feminine wiles. One moment of inattention and he'd wake up on the floor with a splitting headache.

"Off to the grammar school for a parent–teacher conference?" she mocked. Thais drew her hand down his forearm before moving away from him. The caress was perfect, too, but it just didn't unleash the same amount of sensation he'd sampled last night. In fact, he was a little annoyed by her pushing into his space.

Obviously he was focused on Zoe, because Thais could arouse a marble statue.

"That little shirt-and-slacks combo is sure to win points with the carpool moms." Thais swept him from head to toe before shaking her head.

"I need to work on the trust angle with our target."

"So you put your leather away? Pity," Thais muttered. "From what I saw last night, you were making progress with your bad-boy persona. She was . . . sniffing the bait. Tasting it."

Her voice had turned husky and he felt the back of his neck heat.

Mercer turned on his CO. "I didn't need surveillance last night, Saxon."

Saxon dropped the touch pad he'd been holding. "This is a team operation. As in, no 'I' in team. The target is a female, you're on point, and Thais got surveillance detail."

Saxon surveyed him with a look Mercer knew too well. His commanding officer was calculating the mission. Assessing Mercer's word against what he'd seen on his data spreadsheet.

"This case won't be solved so quickly. Why'd you bring me in if you can't handle waiting a few days for me to establish my position? This is a little different from crossing a hostile zone with fifty pounds of gear on my back to set up my position for a kill shot. She's not an easy mark. If she were, she'd be callous enough to separate sex from emotion and inserting me into her bed would be a waste of time."

"Some men like that in a girl," Thais purred, earning herself a hard look from their team leader. She blew him a kiss in response. "Relax, boss man, I'd be little use to this team if I had any delicate sensibilities. Even a trace of them."

Thais knew how to disguise her emotions, but there was a faint hint of disgruntlement in her tone from the slap of reprimand no one in the room missed. She made her way to another desk and sat down, providing Saxon with her back. Their team leader stared at the back of her head for a long moment, awarding the point to Thais.

The tension in the room increased while their only female member ignored the intense stare of her boss. Thais filled the void with the faint sound of her typing. She knew

Saxon was watching her. Thais had an uncanny ability to get under Saxon's skin, but their leader proved his worth by ignoring it. When it came to Saxon, he kept business separate from personal matters at all times. Still, Mercer was betting on Saxon's patience running out at some point. There were cracks appearing in their solitary team leader's shell. Part of him wanted to see the explosion.

Part of him wanted to be nowhere near it.

Saxon turned on Mercer with a hard look that warned him against watching him and Thais. Just a momentary flicker in his eyes before his expression became guarded again.

"I'm not giving you past the weekend. Get into her bed or I'll let Maddox take a shot. We need to witness the interception of the next shipment of data. Intel says the buyer is moving cash, that something is incoming."

Mercer felt his muscles tense. Getting his mind back on the facts was the way to go. Sometime during the night, Zoe's face had invaded his dreams. He needed to shake that emotional response off. She was the target. Allowing himself to label her any other way would interfere with clear thinking.

Something like that could get a man killed.

The sort of intel being sold from Zoe's brother's location was the kind people died over. Locations of bases and operations. One shoulder-held surface-to-air missile could take out an entire unit if the enemy knew the flight path of a mission. Apache helicopters went out as air support on all missions so the enemy had turned to using small, one-man missile launchers that could be buried in the sand when they knew where a mission was going to land. Ambush-style warfare with modern missiles. Mothers were getting flags and someone was raking in the money earned with the blood of Mercer's comrades. Guilt aside, Zoe was the most likely point for that information to be smuggled out of her brother's secured location.

"I'll get into position. Tell Maddox to stay wherever he is." He was overstepping by telling Saxon what to do, but the team wasn't purely military. They fell into a gray area, which was a large part of the appeal. He liked being able to operate without regulations crushing him. Rules had their place, but there were plenty of criminals who had figured out how to use the law to protect themselves.

A sense of anticipation swept through him and he frowned on his way out of the house they were using as a base of operations. It was set up on a hillside, overlooking the California coastline. Outside he heard the surf as he climbed into a four-wheel-drive Jeep. The back was open, allowing the air to blow around the cab as he guided it onto the narrow streets of Malibu. He left behind the bike, parked near several other vehicles the team used. They were all different, all resources for the team depending on their case needs, from a dented-up two door, two-decade-old beater to the armor-plated limo. He wasn't in the Jeep to enjoy the afternoon breeze, he was in it to maximize his chances for success.

Target. That's all she could ever be.

Shit.

"I can't tell you how grateful we are that you came out today." The administrator of the children's hospital rubbed her hands together. "It means so much to the kids."

"Wouldn't miss it. You know, call Tim and I'll be here. My dad sends his apologies," Zoe replied.

The administrator nodded. "Your booking agent is always moving things around for me, and we greatly appreciate it. Some of our kids just don't have time to wait and they
love Harley. Your dad, too. I've never met a man who en-
joys being a pirate so much. Are you sure he's in the navy?"

"Sometimes I wonder," Zoe admitted. Her father was
notorious for doing children's events dressed like a pirate
and sporting an eye patch along with Harley and a very
over-the-top accent.

The administrator turned to address one of the other
entertainers attending the afternoon celebration. Zoe
struggled to pull one of her cases from the van while her
star performer let out an impatient squawk.

"Patience, Harley. Sis needs to get your perch out first."

The large scarlet macaw parrot eyed her while clinging to the side of his travel cage. People were arriving by
van loads, kids running over to the face-painting booth to
have glitter applied to their cheeks. Parents pulled out
money as popcorn began filling the area with its delectable aroma. There was a grinding sound as the snow cone
vendor pushed blocks of ice through his shredding machine to the delight of a little girl who had a pink head-
band on her chemotherapy-induced bald head.

Harley flapped his wings impatiently. Once the small
stage was set up, Zoe opened the travel cage and transferred
him to his perch. The crowd shifted and cameras appeared.
Zoe adjusted her safari hat and dug in for the six-hour event.
She coaxed Harley through his performance with cashews
and peanuts. The afternoon passed in a blur of sugar-high
faces until at last the crowd began to thin.

Which allowed her the chance to see *him*.

He was still hot.

Even in a striped cotton shirt and khaki pants, there was still an edge radiating from him. She'd bet he was just as intimidating buck naked.

Oh . . . yeah . . .

She looked away, the idea of him in the buff undermining her ability to think. It was as if the man held the magic combination to her sexual appetite. She hadn't blushed in years, but she could feel him watching her and it increased her awareness of him.

It was completely frustrating.

And totally exhilarating.

She looked back and he was gone. Zoe scanned the crowd but there was no sign of him. A tingle touched her nape. That same sense of unease that had interrupted the red-hot passion between them last night. There was something about the way he was . . . well, stalking her. Maybe it was just who he was.

Maybe she was imagining things.

Yeah, maybe Roni was right about her life being too mundane.

Definite possibility.

The evening breeze was blowing clouds in for the night. The wild birds were beginning to chirp, sensing the approaching darkness. Cleaning personnel began sweeping up the remains of arts and crafts while Zoe packed her parrot stage.

"Do a lot of charity events?"

Zoe turned around too fast, startling Harley. The parrot extended his wings and flapped. His clipped wings didn't allow him to take flight, but she'd already released his leash and he went gliding across the parking lot. Her mystery man reacted instantly, his body snapping into action the moment the bird moved.

The second he realized the bird wasn't intent on attacking him, he launched himself after the animal. Harley turned and lowered his head, his beak open with wings spread in challenge.

"Harley bites," she warned. "Deep."

"I can tell." But that didn't keep her mystery man from sizing the bird up and moving closer. "Come on, buddy, let's not tangle before dinner."

"He's stuffed. He only performs for food rewards." Zoe chased after Harley. Mercer stuck his arm out in a blockade to keep her behind him, nearly clotheslining her.

"Now, don't be jealous, honey, I'll have time for you just as soon as I catch your parrot."

He actually grasped her biceps and set her back several feet. It was done effortlessly, his strength stunning her. But his grip didn't hurt; instead, his control was perfect, the contrast of so much power mixed with a gentle touch flooding her with sensual heat that went straight to her core.

It would be amazing in bed . . .

Zoe shook her head. "What you'll be doing is heading to the emergency room. Macaw parrots have enough strength to take off fingers. Even overgrown ones like yours . . . buddy."

"I guess it's a good thing he isn't hungry."

It should have been illegal for anyone to have so much confidence and not strike her as a fool.

It should disgust me to be turned on by it . . . Where is my inner confident, modern woman?

Zoe stood back, annoyed with the way her gaze traced

his movements. She was fascinated by him, just as she had been the night before, and now there was no margarita to blame.

Harley snapped his curved beak in warning, but that didn't stop the advance of her company. He moved in, lowering his body and extending his forearm. Zoe smiled as she witnessed the way he kept his fingers in a tight fist.

"Come on, fella . . . that sun is setting fast."

Zoe's eyes widened when Harley lifted one talon and climbed up onto the offered forearm.

"That's impossible; Harley is a one-man bird," she declared, astonishment flashing through her.

"Don't you mean one-woman?"

Zoe shook her head. "No. Harley belongs to . . ." She snapped her mouth shut and lifted her arm, but Harley was busy climbing up to the guy's shoulder.

"Who?"

She propped her hands on her hips. "Look, I don't even know your name, so my personal information is none of your business. And letting him stand on your shoulder is a bad idea. He thinks you're submissive to him."

As if such a thing were possible. The guy didn't have a bendable bone in his body, much less anything that could in any way be considered submissive.

"Mercer." He reached up and scratched Harley. "But I enjoyed the personal nature of our interaction last night. You'd have learned my name if you'd taken a ride with me."

There was such a double meaning to the word *ride*. She shot him a suspicious look. "Is there a reason you're trying so hard to invade my space? I'm feeling a lot like Omaha Beach."

He choked on a fit of laughter.

"You've officially crossed into the creepy zone."

His expression changed instantly, his eyes losing their glint of amusement. "Is there a reason you're assuming I came here today to see you?"

Maybe she was being presumptuous, but there was something about the way he was watching her that started an alarm blaring somewhere in the back of her brain. It was centered in the memories of her dad questioning everything. He'd raised her to be no one's fool and to remember that the world was full of bad guys.

"Yeah, there is." She reached out and Harley stepped onto her forearm. She brought the bird close, stroking his back gently. "These free events attract single parents looking for something to do with their kids that won't cost them a small fortune, and families out to keep their budgets tight. You are neither."

"You're a suspicious one, Zoe."

She turned around from putting Harley in his carrier to find Mercer only two spaces behind her.

"The newspaper covered the event, had your name, city of residence, and telephone number for those interested in booking parrot parties. Your friend happily gave me your name last night."

"All right. Fair enough, still slightly creepy. I hope you enjoyed the afternoon." Her emotions were churning inside her, part of her fascinated with the raw magnetism he gave off, while the other side of her grew more suspicious. He was pressing her.

"I'd enjoy it more if you'd have dinner with me."

"Why?"

Mercer slipped his hands into his pockets. On most men, the pose would have looked relaxed; on him, it appeared calculated. The man just seemed too controlled not to have every move thought out.

"I think I'm about to call you fickle, Zoe. You didn't want to throw caution to the wind last night, so I'm here doing the respectable thing and asking you to dinner. Which way do you want it?"

Her lips went dry at the challenge.

"Maybe I don't want it at all."

His hands were out of his pockets in a flash. A second later he had one flattened on the closed rear door of her midsized SUV. Sensation prickled along her limbs, raising goose bumps. The man even smelled sexy. Some faint hint of soap lingered, but it was his own unique scent that seemed to speed up the rate of arousal inside her until it was hard to ignore.

She felt like she was suspended between breaths, that he could see exactly what effect he was having on her as their gazes fused.

The damn world felt off balance, the pair of them stuck in some crazy moment between dimensions. She was getting high on him.

"The attraction between us isn't common, Zoe. It felt like the article in the newspaper was written just to get me another chance to see you. You're right, this isn't my normal scene, but I wanted to see you again." He leaned closer, his warm breath teasing the delicate skin of her lips. "So I'm asking you to dinner, like a *nice guy*."

"You're nothing of the sort," she accused softly, her voice gone husky.

His eyes narrowed and his other hand cupped her nape. "Like I said, you're perceptive." His voice dipped lower until it was hypnotic. "Something I like a whole lot. Makes me wonder how spot-on your intuition would be once we get past the trust barrier."

He pressed a firm kiss against her mouth, sealing her reply beneath his lips. She'd never enjoyed kisses so much. Mercer's tasted good. She should have been able to push him back but she just didn't want to. She reached for him, the need he'd unleashed last night rising up as if it had never cooled. Her clit began to pulse and she felt as if her vagina was empty. She gripped his shirt, pulling him closer as desire tightened every one of her muscles. His kiss turned harder, pressing her to open her mouth. When she did, his tongue swept over her lower lip before thrusting inside to stroke hers.

Harley let out a screech, sending Mercer back a step. He grasped her around her waist and lifted her before she realized he was moving. She ended up behind him before he recognized the sound was coming from the parrot.

"How long have you been out of the service?" she asked.

"Not long—" His features tightened, as if he'd responded without considering his words. His eyes narrowed for a scant second before he shrugged. "I guess it shows."

"Yeah." Harley was throwing a fit inside the back of the car. "I need to get him home. Parrots can't see in the dark, so he's going to get wigged out by the fading light."

Mercer captured her forearm in a solid grip. He pulled her closer, so close his body heat wrapped around her again. With the sun setting, it was warm and inviting. One glance into his dark eyes sent heat spiking through her at the hunger glittering in the dark orbs.

"Dinner," he insisted in a husky tone. "One hour."

"Um—"

He pressed a quick kiss over her protest. Just a short

taste of what she craved before she was free and he was striding across the half-empty parking lot, yelling back that her only other option was to chicken out.

Oh hell.

"I'll tell him I'm tired."

Harley only stared at her as she paced in front of his cage.

"I'll tell him . . ."

The doorbell rang, startling her.

"You're early."

She spoke while opening the door, which was a good thing because coherent thinking became impossible—instantly. Mercer had changed back into his black leather. The man embodied the animal she'd labeled him last night and it excited the hell out of her.

And there went all ideas of chickening out. Heat was zipping along her veins, making her bold.

"Your hour started in the parking lot, not when you got home, honey." His tone sent a shiver down her spine because it was edged with a demand she recalled very clearly from his kiss.

She'd be an idiot to go out with him, it went against every rule of safe dating, but her body just didn't give a rat's ass. Her nipples contracted, making her sorry she'd slipped into a soft jersey top.

He held up a leather jacket. "Come on . . . are you really worried about me turning into a psycho?"

"I should be." But she wasn't. It was time to enjoy the moment and leave the regrets for tomorrow.

He chuckled and curled one finger, beckoning her forward. "I already told you my name, baby, and besides, your parrot likes me."

"No he doesn't. Harley only likes one person on the face of this planet. The rest of us exist to serve him."

One dark eyebrow rose. "I'll just have to work on stroking him the right way."

He held the jacket up for her to slip her arms into the sleeves. It was heavy and pressed against her hard nipples, sending little zips of awareness across her chest. She fumbled the zipper before succeeding in pulling it up to her neck; all she could think about was his hands stroking her.

"Or maybe I'll demonstrate my skill on you and you can recommend me to the bird."

He curled his fingers around her wrist and tugged her toward him. She ran into the solid wall of his chest, but that only pleased her in ways she hadn't believed possible. He was hard and she wanted to touch every inch of him. She stroked his chest, the ridges of muscles thrilling her on some previously unknown primitive level. But it was there and intoxicating pleasure went through her and took hold.

"Oh hell . . ." she muttered, food the last thing on her mind.

"I was thinking the same thing . . ." He reached up and grasped the zipper. He jerked it down so the night air brushed her chest. Anticipation sizzled along her nerve endings but she stiffened, suddenly scared. Only she wasn't frightened of him, just of the way she was responding to him.

He seemed to know how to reach a deep place within her. It was unsettling to say the least, but exciting on a scale she'd never experienced. It was a whole new realm of sensation, like discovering color for the first time.

He yanked the zipper back up and clasped her wrist to pull her through her front door. He'd somehow managed to take her keys from her hand while she was trying to draw in enough breath to jump-start her brain. There was a click behind her as he locked the door and tried it to make sure it was secure.

"Let's take a ride."

His bike was in her driveway, looking mean and somewhat misplaced there in front of the oh-so-mundane tract-home garage door. The cream edging and gray stucco said *responsible* while the Harley screamed *rebel*.

He swung his leg over the bike and looked back to see what she'd do. He tossed her a helmet before putting one on himself.

Throwdown.

Total and complete. The challenge was in his eyes. A flash of anticipation sparked off a need inside her, and she was on the back of the bike before she really thought any further.

Big surprise. Thinking isn't something I do around him . . .

Nope. But feeling was.

And boy, was she feeling now.

He was hot and hard and . . . *delicious*.

Zoe wrapped her arms around him, scooting up against his back so that her thighs were hugging his hips.

Decadent.

Sinful.

Totally mind blowing.

The vibration of the bike sent a jolt through her clit. It was bluntly sexual and she decided she liked it.

A lot.

He pulled out of the driveway, giving her a moment to adjust her hold and mold her body to his. Mercer did a slow zigzag down her residential street as she learned how to flow with the motion of the bike. How to cling to him and move in unison with him.

It was mind blowing.

But the word that seemed to describe the experience best was . . . carnal.

The sun was gone, the moon rising on the horizon. The perfect complement to the moment. The air was cooler, making her more aware of the warmth she was hugging. Although, *hug* seemed too casual a word. Too sedate. A whole new meaning was blossoming inside her brain.

Mercer was at the center of that definition. Guiding the bike through the streets with a hard, determined purpose. Traffic didn't slow him down. He just went around it.

Going after what he wanted. That was at the heart of his personality and at the moment, she was enjoying it hugely.

He drove out of the city, up into the hills. There was less light and Zoe liked that, too.

Darkness suited Untamed.

They were leaving behind the prime, clifftop ocean-view lots and heading where the landscape wasn't maintained. There was scrub brush and local plant life. The road had potholes, the edges crumbling from weather. Ahead there was a flash of light that grew into a tin-roofed building with weathered boards on its exterior and about a hundred bikes parked in front of it.

Once Mercer killed the engine, music filled the air. A hard, classic-rock sort of music that suited the dozen or so bearded men smoking on the porch of the establishment. They wore leather and boots, had tattoos and piercings. There was more than one shaved head. They stared right at Mercer and her without a care for polite behavior. Direct, calculating looks. She was sized up from head to toe, a couple of snorts coming her way.

"Let's eat."

Mercer pulled her past the smoking group as he gave them a warning glance. The grip on her hand didn't go unnoticed, either. It was a territorial declaration.

The inside of the place matched the outside. More weathered wood and tin siding. There was a fence running across a corner of the place from floor to ceiling with a band playing behind it. She got the feeling the fence wasn't there to keep the band in.

"Tough venue?" she asked.

Mercer pulled her into one of the booths whose sides went all the way to the ceiling before he nodded. "Trial by fire. If the audience doesn't like your sound, they'll be sure to let you know."

"Think I'll stick with my day job."

"What you drinking?" a waitress in a leather vest and skirt asked as she came by the table. She was all woman and looked like she just might double as a bouncer, her arms defined and tattooed. A brazen amount of breast was on display that she had no trouble aiming toward Mercer.

Mercer tossed a couple of twenties on the table. "Bring us what's cold and goes with the special."

She scraped the money off the table and tucked it into her cleavage. "Sure thing." She looked at Zoe and her heavily lipstick-coated mouth curved mockingly before she glanced back at Mercer. "Let me know when you get tired of playing with baby dolls."

Zoe managed to hold in her snickers until the waitress was far enough away. Mercer eyed her with a raised eyebrow. She interlaced her fingers, propped her elbows on the table, and put her chin on her fingers. "Baby dolls." She mimicked the waitress's words as she fluttered her eyelashes.

Mercer spread out on the other side of the booth, propping one foot on the seat so that his knee was bent and he was lounging in the corner. "She's not too far off the mark. Surprised she didn't card you."

Zoe didn't exactly care for the assessment. "So that's how I strike you? A real babe in the woods?"

His eyes narrowed, like he was rethinking his opinion of her. She stared straight back at him, making it clear she wasn't going to buckle. He let out a half laugh that was an admission of sorts. "Maybe you just look sweet and innocent."

Something in his tone touched off a tingle on the back of her neck. But the waitress returned, dropping off two longneck bottles that had frosty surfaces and a glass of water that she plopped down in front of Zoe with a flourish of her manicured hand.

"How thoughtful of you," Zoe said, earning herself a cutting look before the woman turned around at the sound of a bell being rung.

"If she spits in your food, it'll be your fault," Mercer observed.

"Not likely." Zoe fingered the neck of the beer. "You're lounging across the booth like a serving of cream in a silver saucer. Little wonder she wants to encourage me to shove off."

He snorted. "Can't wait for you to take a lick."

Zoe took a swig of her beer instead. It might not have been the wisest thing. Her wits were already buzzed on pheromones. "Guess you're going to have to wait . . . since we're in public and all."

His eyes narrowed. It lasted only a moment. He actually looked surprised for an instant before he recovered his nonchalant expression. "Tease."

There was a double ring on the bell on the counter between the kitchen and the restaurant as Zoe took another sip from her beer. "Maybe I'm adjusting to my company."

His lips curved approvingly before the waitress was back with a couple of plates that she slid onto the table. She was gone as someone whistled at her.

"You're playing some sort of game." Zoe wasn't really sure where her suspicion was coming from or why she felt the need to voice it. But it was there.

Mercer lowered his leg and sat up to the table. He grabbed the steaming sandwich crowned with glassy onions and took a bite. Zoe picked up a fork and started eating her food with the utensil because there was no way she was going to fit the thing in her mouth.

"I always thought dating was a game, too."

"Smart-ass." She pointed her fork at him. "You're up to something."

He'd taken another bite and was chewing it. He opened his hands in an innocent gesture.

Zoe wasn't buying. Mercer wiped his lips before answering. "I wanted to find a way to get you to wrap your thighs around me. Had to settle for you doing it with your clothes still on." His eyes narrowed. "This time anyway."

"Very funny."

"The waitress probably thinks it is," he answered.

Zoe laughed and took another bite to avoid talking. She

needed to think but couldn't really decide just what it was about the situation that was bugging her. Part of her wanted to say it was the guarded look that surfaced on Mercer's face from time to time.

Yeah, well, it's not exactly like he knows me any better than I know him.

Point for the "making too much out of nothing" team. Or as Roni would say, *Live a little. This isn't a dress rehearsal.* Either she was interested in tasting life or she could just head on home and get started on being a crazy cat lady.

"Dog or cats?"

Mercer's eyes narrowed in confusion.

Zoe shrugged. "Getting to know each other? Right? The nice-guy thing? So what's your style, dogs or cats?"

He claimed his beer from the tabletop with a slow motion of his fingers that made her breath catch. "That's a trick question."

"How so?"

He pointed at her as he placed the bottle down. "You're a bird person."

"No, I'm just domestic staff for a parrot," she clarified.

He offered her a half laugh, his gaze lingering on her lips. She still didn't know very much about him but the space between them felt like a small canyon. Zoe laid her fork down. Mercer's expression tightened, need flickering in her eyes. He slid out of the booth and captured her hand. The waitress shot her a cutting look as they crossed the restaurant.

That's right. He's mine tonight.

Maybe just tonight, but she'd worry about that tomorrow. It was a really long time away.

* * *

Greer McRae turned around from the bar, pulling his phone from his breast jacket pocket. He typed in a message before tossing down some bills and walking toward the door. Men turned to look at him, sizing up his ability to fight by the way he moved. Greer admitted to enjoying it. He liked a good fight and always had. His grandfather said it was in his genes. Maybe so. Greer had seen his share of fighting men and even among their ranks, he found an enjoyment in brawling that just might be better suited to the Highlands of Scotland a century ago. About the only thing he didn't like was the way his blond hair showed every drop of blood. Someone always called over a damn medic when what he really wanted was a shot of whiskey.

Mercer was already on the back of his bike, their mark slipping on behind him with a hesitant smile on her lips. A blind man wouldn't have missed what was on her mind.

Greer wished he could have. The details of the operation were leaving a dirty taste in his mouth. Sure, he knew it came with the territory, understood that sometimes you had to roll through the gutter to find the criminals who did business there.

Still, the Magnus family had an impressive service record. Honor was earned and the Magnus family had done their time and duty. If her father was innocent, he was going to be pissed. Rightfully so.

But the evidence was there. Saxon wouldn't have been assigned the case otherwise. Greer shook off his guilt. It was rare but not unheard of for a man like Zoe's father to get tired of being paid only in respect. Personally, it turned Greer's stomach to think of the man going bad, but it happened.

Greer started up his bike and headed out, tailing Mercer through the winding hill roads. He needed to focus on the mission. Regret would show up later.

It always did.

Mercer kissed her before she got off the bike using a handful of the leather jacket to pull her close.

It was a hungry kiss, his mouth claiming hers, and no matter how impulsive it was she kissed him back just as hard.

She wanted to know what he tasted like.

"Let's get inside . . ." His voice was sharp and his words clipped. He lifted her right off the back of the bike with one hand, dropping her on her feet with an ease that made her breath catch again. Somehow, in the nice, civilized world that surrounded her, she'd never really come face-to-face with just how much stronger a man was than herself.

It was both alarming and sexy, the two sensations mingling to produce an edgy sort of anticipation that made her steps clumsy on the way to her front door.

Mercer was right behind her. Shoving the door shut and slipping one arm around her waist with the other one beneath her knees, he swept her off her feet in one sure motion.

"A little over the top, carrying me off to bed . . ." She wasn't entirely sure what she meant. The truth was, she was grasping at the remains of her control.

He took her right up the stairs without missing a beat. "Not planning on giving you time to consider reaching for that pepper spray."

He spun her loose in her bedroom, the light from downstairs illuminating him. She was being so impulsive but it felt too damn good to stop.

"I'd rather keep you besotted . . ."

"You're mighty sure of yourself."

He stripped off his own jacket and the shirt beneath it. Her mouth went dry. His torso was far more impressive bare than she'd thought it was covered by his T-shirt.

"I'm sure of how we react to each other, double sure I want to see how much more intense it can get."

His voice was hypnotic, and the way he moved set chills down her body. Right . . . wrong, she didn't give a damn at the moment. She wanted to know how much deeper the sensation might go.

She wanted to wrap her bare thighs around his equally bare skin.

She chucked the leather jacket aside and reached for the hem of her shirt but Mercer beat her to it. He ripped it up and over her head with a satisfied grunt.

"Your nipples have been driving me crazy." The soft cups of her bra proved no barrier for him. He slid his hands down over the tops of her breasts and beneath the beige fabric. She shivered when he curled his fingers around each globe and lifted them above the lace edge. There was so much sensation flooding her, just standing took too much effort.

"Beautiful rosebuds." He brushed each peak with his thumbs while backing her up against the foot of her bed. "I bet they taste delicious."

Her bed didn't have a footboard. Mercer grasped her waist and tossed her onto the mattress. She bounced a few times and actually giggled.

"That's it, honey, let loose a little. Let's play, like adults."

He crawled up onto the bed, every muscle in his arms visible. He just looked too damn male. Her belly tightened with anticipation, her humor evaporating. Heat consumed her. Need ate at her like a living force. She wanted to scratch and bite. She wanted—to take. Just . . . take.

But Mercer pushed her back, hovering over her like the predator she'd decided he was. He nuzzled her belly before moving up her body to where her breasts had slipped back behind the cups of her bra. He still found her nipples with his mouth, sucking one through the fabric of the undergarment. She gasped, her spine arching to make sure he maintained his hold on the sensitive tip.

He chuckled but it sounded dark and dangerous. He found the waistband of her jeans and popped the button open. Pleasure mixed with the need burning inside her until he released her nipple, sending a little jolt of frustration through her. She reached for his shoulders but he rose above her and flipped her over. Her hair went flying and her face sank into the goose-down comforter.

"I don't think I ever enjoyed unwrapping a present more than I am right now."

He unhooked her bra and slid his hands down to her hips. A moment later her jeans went slipping down her legs and onto the floor. She half turned to see him sitting on his haunches, magnificent torso illuminated by the entryway light. But what made her hesitate was the look on his face. The raw expression of hunger. It glittered in his eyes and drew his features tight. Her body filled with a longing that hurt. The ache centered in her channel, making her almost desperate to have him inside her. It frightened her with its intensity, but it also made her want to lunge toward what she craved.

Wild abandonment . . . no holds barred.

She suddenly had a new understanding of the phrase. The urge to chicken out pricked her, illuminating the fact that all control was about to be ripped from her hands. She'd never done anything so rash, so utterly impulsive.

I'm not a kid anymore . . .

Which made it so damn tempting.

"Show yourself to me, baby. I want to see you."

Mercer wasn't asking, he was demanding. Anticipation took command of his features and she turned over, amazed at her power to captivate him.

"You're stunning," he muttered before his hands hit the bed and he began to crawl back up her body. "Unbelievably beautiful."

He paused over the triangle of her panties. Her clit gave a crazy twist of excitement as she felt his breath against her folds. It was stunning just how sensitive her body was. She couldn't recall ever feeling such an abundance of need and sensation. Sex had never felt so damn good before, or so incredibly necessary. A tiny sound escaped her lips.

"We can do better than that." His hand landed on top of her pubic bone, pressing down on the soft flesh with just enough pressure to send a bolt of need through her. "A whole lot better."

He slid his hand lower, rubbing against her entire slit. She gasped, shivering as the need to climax became almost unbearable. She grasped the bedding and lifted her hips for the next downward motion, but it didn't come. Instead Mercer grabbed the thin straps of her panties and snapped them.

"Still not enough," he announced before pushing her thighs wide. "I want to hear you scream."

His last sentence came out between clenched teeth. Zoe wasn't even sure it made sense to her because she was so focused on the need burning her alive. Her eyelids closed but she didn't need to see; touch was the only important thing.

Mercer didn't waste any time fulfilling her need. He leaned back down and caught her folds between his lips. Sandwiched between the delicate tissues, her clit responded to the pressure with a crazy spike of pleasure. It ripped into her belly, sending a moan past her lips.

"That's more like it."

He separated the folds before returning to her spread sex. "But there's room for improvement."

Zoe opened her eyes but squeezed them shut a second later when his tongue swept over her clit. The sensation almost qualified as pain but it was completely mind blowing, taking her past a threshold she hadn't realized was there inside her. Conscious thought ceased; all that remained was response. She twisted beneath the motions of his tongue. Her hips lifted, seeking more pressure, just a little more to send her over the edge into release.

Mercer didn't leave her hanging. He thrust two fingers deep inside her sheath at the same time his lips closed around her clit. The combination sent her body spiraling into climax.

"Oh sweet Christ!" Pleasure snapped hard and sharp along her nerves. It drew her muscles tight while she strained toward the source of pressure giving her release. The moment felt like an eternity, and when her brain began functioning once more she was gasping because she'd forgotten to breathe. Perspiration dotted her forehead and her limbs ached from the ways she'd been straining. Another first. Climax had never been such a whole-body experience before.

"Much better."

Mercer growled, his fingers still gently working in and out of her sheath.

"But . . . you didn't enjoy that . . ."

One dark eyebrow arched. "Didn't I?"

His voice was coated with satisfaction. "Don't doubt I enjoy making you respond, baby."

She curled up, propping her elbows behind her so she could stare at him. "You sound so controlling and smug."

His lips curled into an arrogant grin that flashed his teeth. "And you loved it."

He pushed back onto his haunches and opened the front of his pants. Her mind stopped functioning on a rational level again, her attention drawn to the hard flesh he pulled into sight. His cock was rigid. Long and thick, it was crowned with a ruby head. Despite the satisfaction still rippling along her body, her vagina demanded a taste of it.

"In fact, I think your last few boyfriends have been too complacent to suit your needs, Zoe. Great sex is sometimes hard and demanding."

He reached out and grabbed her hips. The bed rocked again, letting out a squeak when he tossed her over onto her belly. He grasped both sides of her hips and pulled her up onto her knees, sending a spike of anticipation through her.

She whimpered when he rose up behind her, the sound of a condom wrapper crinkling before the head of his cock slipped between the folds of her sex. He leaned down, covering her back with his length, his skin hot against her own. His breath brushed the side of her neck, on that tender spot that was so vulnerable. She quivered, caught between helplessness and anticipation. Mercer didn't give her time to dwell on her feelings. He pulled free and plunged back into her with a solid motion.

"You need to be taken sometimes, Zoe, admit it." His grip tightened on her hips. "You want to feel my strength. It makes you fucking hot, doesn't it? Admit it."

"I'm not into slave play." But her voice was husky and needy. The head of his cock was now only teasing the entrance to her sheath, tormenting her with how hard and thick it was. She pushed back, trying to impale herself, but he held her steady. He leaned back down and captured her earlobe between his teeth. It was a tiny bite but the sensation rippled down her body, fanning the flames of desire, making her skin hot.

"Does that mean you're sorry you submitted to me tonight, Zoe?" He thrust forward, only a few inches, but it drove the head of his cock into her pussy, stretching her sheath. A strangled sound escaped from her lips, need and anticipation threatening to drive her insane.

"It feels like you're as pleased as I am that we aren't sitting in some restaurant trading details of our lives while trying to ignore just how much we'd rather be fucking."

"You're being an asshole," she snarled. The response startled her but Mercer chuckled.

"So be a bitch." He straightened up and thrust forward until every last inch of his cock was lodged inside her. "Tell me what the hell you want and refuse to take any shit from me."

Her body liked that idea. Loved it. Her clit pulsed, demanding to be pressed against his rigid length, but he held tight to her hips, keeping her on her knees.

What I want?

"Fuck me." She didn't recognize her voice. It was far too sultry. "Hard."

Satisfaction coated his words. "Yes, ma'am." He growled at her again, savage and primitive, but it fed the need eating her.

"Now."

She didn't need to prompt him but she liked doing it. He was already in motion, keeping her in position with a grip that almost hurt, but she barely noticed because she was too absorbed with the way his cock felt moving in and out of her. Pleasure slammed into her every time she felt his balls against her slit. She couldn't recall being so full before, the walls of her pussy aching just enough to tell her she was being stretched. She pressed backward, matching his rhythm, and heard him snarl with satisfaction.

"Take what you want, Zoe, and to hell with what anyone else thinks is right. Go with your feelings."

Being lured away from convention had never appealed so much. He leaned down and teased her ear with his breath. "I want to see what kind of fire you have in your belly."

"Turn me over."

She needed more friction; her clit was pulsing with need again. But she wasn't the only one craving release. Mercer pulled free and sent her rolling with one push on the side of her hip. She hadn't truly landed on her back when he pressed his weight down on her. Someone groaned but she wasn't sure who. He pushed her thighs wide, returning his length to her pussy.

"Then again, I like having you on your back . . . *a lot.*" He growled softly.

This time she felt every inch of his hard flesh pressing against her clit with each thrust. She twisted, unable to decide how to release all the pleasure contained inside her. There was no thought, only response. He slammed into her and she rose to meet each thrust. Her fingers curled into talons on his shoulders, digging into the skin, but it only gained her an increase in pace. Pleasure exploded, shooting up into her womb. White-hot and uncontrollable, it sliced through her. Mercer snarled something before he buried his length and she felt the shudder of his release. It increased the pleasure, deepening it, and left her battling to remain conscious. She heard him roll over and the bed groan when he landed on his back, but her body was too flooded with satisfaction for her to do anything but lie there. She opened her eyes in surprise when he rolled back toward her, one arm securing her against him. He was solid and warm, everything she had no right to expect. She floated off on the ripples of delight, without another thought for how wise it was to fall asleep with a near stranger in her house.

Because the moment felt perfect and she just didn't have it in her to argue with perfect. Disillusionment could fucking wait.

Mercer fought the urge to pass out. His balls ached, proving he'd come harder than he had in a long time. It shouldn't have felt so good, shouldn't have become so consuming. His thinking was clouded with satisfaction now. He wanted to sink down into the afterglow and forget the details of how he'd come to be in Zoe's bed. She fit perfectly against him. Hell, he even liked the scent of her skin. It wasn't a perfume, just her own musk. One that struck him as sexy.

But emotions had no place in his mission.

Shit.

He sat up and his head spun. A deep breath banished the feeling as he stood and tossed the comforter over her. Zoe was sleeping, her breathing slowing as she relaxed. All he wanted to do was lie back down next to her. The urge was so strong he had to fight it.

He had a mission and it didn't allow for emotional reactions to sex. Discarding the condom, he closed the front of his pants. He retrieved his shirt and jacket from the floor and went into her office. He didn't flip the light on to keep the parrot from blowing his cover. He checked the tiny camera set up to film the computer screen before dialing Saxon.

"You in?" Saxon's voice cut with how sharp it was.

"Yeah, are you getting a clear shot?"

"Yes. Thais wants the cell phone."

They couldn't get into her files but at least they'd be able to see whatever she had up on her screen. The camera would provide a double service, giving them the information from what she was working on as well as providing irrefutable evidence that she had been the one receiving the classified files. Zoe's sweet face wouldn't keep her from being convicted once they had the video footage.

He felt like shit.

The emotion stunned him and he sat back in the chair for a moment while he tried to shift through his response.

It was sex. Nothing else. It couldn't become anything

more. Zoe Magnus was knee-deep in military espionage. It was his duty to gather enough evidence to convict her. Their contacts had traced the link to her brother and the point of entry into the United States as her phone lines.

Or she was innocent and he was a complete asshole for using her. At least it would beat being convicted of treason. Somehow, he doubted she'd be very happy either way.

The main problem was he couldn't think of how she might be unaware of the intel crossing through her computer. The system was locked up tighter than a prison. She had to have a motive for protecting her files so well.

He had to move forward with the team plan. Even if he was going soft, there were still the men in the field to consider. Someone was selling out positions, and men died when that happened. His bruised feelings would have to take a backseat to preventing more bloodshed.

Sitting back up, he dug into his pockets and retrieved the bugs he needed to plant. Pushing the chair back, he crawled under the desk to make sure every last byte of information coming into the office also transmitted to Saxon's network. The last thing he did was pull her cell phone out of her jeans.

Mercer slipped the phone into his pocket. Planting a mobile download device into it would require specialized tools and knowledge of micro-electronics he didn't have.

He glanced at Zoe, studying the way she slept, innocence showing on her face. He turned away, forcing his attention to his mission.

Zoe fought her way free of slumber. It wasn't what her body wanted. Her mind refused to surrender easily, wanting to remain in the dream world. But something needled her, some pressing thing that refused to allow her to sleep despite how much she was enjoying it.

She rubbed her eyes and sat up. The room was dark but she couldn't recall turning the downstairs light off. Memory returned swiftly and with a sharp edge that cut through her drowsiness. Reaching out, she discovered the bed empty.

Well . . . what did she expect?

Standing up, she froze when a pinch of discomfort rippled through her passage, marking where Mercer had been.

And now he was gone.

That bothered her more than it should have. There had been no promises, not even small talk. She stood up and rubbed her eyes to kill the urge to cry.

She wasn't a teenager anymore.

But it still stung that he hadn't stayed past midnight. She could smell him on her skin, and her body tingled with renewed passion. She kicked her jeans on the way to the bathroom and flipped the shower on. With only the closet light on, she stood beneath the slightly warm water to wash the scent of her impulsiveness away.

He wasn't her lover.

Nope. She worked the soap bar across her skin. He'd been hot and looking for sex, but she had higher standards for someone she called a lover. Mercer was . . . well . . . she wasn't sure of exactly what he was.

Except gone.

CHAPTER TWO

"Did you get the data from her desk camera?"

"I did my job," Thais muttered to Mercer, holding out her hand for Zoe's cell phone while pulling a magnifying lamp in front of her. She laid the cell phone on the surface of her desk and picked up a tiny scalpel to begin opening it.

Mercer yanked a chair around and straddled it. "So why the bitterness in your tone, Thais?"

She never looked up. "We're teammates, Mercer. The only thing that matters is my performance. You're out of line evaluating my personal feelings."

He propped his forearms across the top of the chair. "Really? It sounds to me like you give a damn about the target, which is definitely territory any team member has the right to intrude on because it might compromise the entire mission."

Anger flashed in Thais's dark eyes. "Since I'm not in direct contact on this mission, you don't need to worry."

"You're backing me up, that makes it my business."

Her expression turned knowing. "It sounds to me like you're pushing that mission objective protocol pretty hard. We're still lacking hard evidence." She returned her attention to the cell phone, her delicate fingers perfect for working with the tiny components.

"And you don't like knowing there is a chance of there being no evidence?" he questioned.

Thais looked up at him, locking gazes. "If you're that comfortable, Mercer, I've misjudged you."

"Stop picking on Thais and get your tail into my office, Mercer."

Saxon was in a pisser of a mood. Thais waved good-bye to him with a knowing look in her eyes that sent a chill down his spine. Mercer tightened his hold on his feelings before crossing into Saxon's territory.

"I'd think you'd be in better frame of mind, since I managed to complete my mission objective," Mercer announced from the doorway.

Saxon looked at him over the top of a laptop. "Nothing's complete. One of the packets of intel was moved, but since I can't navigate her system, you missed an opportunity to possibly allow us to catch it last night by not getting her on the back of your bike."

"You're being a hardass."

Saxon's lips finally twitched up into a grin. "Thanks. I consider it one of my best attributes." He studied Mercer for a long moment. "Is she getting to you?"

Saxon had an uncanny ability to sniff out a lie. Mercer bit back the urge to deny it and shrugged. "Nothing I can't handle."

"Done," Thais announced from the other room.

"I'd better get that back. She sleeps with the thing," Mercer said. He felt crowded, which should have raised a red flag inside his brain; instead, all he could think of was getting back to Zoe. Part of him knew damn well it had nothing to do with his assignment.

Saxon shook his head and pointed at the chair in front of his desk. "She logged into her email account forty-two minutes after you left. Let her think she put it into the jacket you put on her. Brief as it was, she'll be pissed because you left. Figure out how to deal with her injured feelings."

"Fine."

Mercer was on his way out of the office before Saxon found an excuse to dig at him. He took the cell phone from Thais on his way out the door of the command center. The Spanish-style house they were headquartered in was spacious and open, but he felt caged.

She knew he'd left.

That knowledge dug at him despite all the reasons why it shouldn't matter. At least not beyond the needs of the operation. He should be focused on how to approach her now that she'd woken up alone.

He needed a plan. Zoe might be inexperienced when it came to heavy flirting, but beneath that failing he'd discovered a core of solid strength. The knowledge left a bitter taste in his mouth because it was a small bit of evidence, telling him she could be hard if she wanted to be. He'd begun to doubt if the woman entertaining sick kids with a parrot had what it took to sell men out. Beneath the fragile sexual awareness, though, was a woman who wasn't a complete pushover. He'd sensed, practically tasted it in those moments when she'd abandoned everything except what she craved.

Maybe that was the real problem. A pushover wasn't his style. Zoe had grit, too much of it for him to shield his emotions, which only brought him around to regretting how they'd met. If she was innocent, it was a sure bet she'd never want to see him again.

His buddy Vitus was right: He needed to stop working on special cases. The rush was addictive, but it was the innocents who could eat a man alive.

If Zoe ended up being not guilty, he had the feeling he was going to see her face in his nightmares for a very long time.

Like forever.

But there were already faces there, in the one place he couldn't avoid. The faces of his buddies. The ones who hadn't been lucky enough to walk away from the ambush he'd survived. Sometimes, he seriously questioned who was the lucky one among their number. He was alive but not really living. The past had a stranglehold on him, one that was the driving force behind his involvement in the operation he was engaged in. Just one shoulder-held air-to-surface missile and the intel to tell the enemy where to be. That was all it took. He had to hold on to that knowledge when he was looking into Zoe's eyes.

His mother sure hadn't raised him to use women, no matter the reason.

But his buddies' mothers were all new recipients of American flags. He was in position to keep other mothers from the same fate.

So why didn't he feel better about it?

The answer was simple.

Zoe.

If she was hiding a black heart, she was a master of deception.

Mercer walked out the door because he couldn't dismiss the possibility of her being exactly that.

Zoe woke up tired the next morning. There wasn't enough coffee in North America to improve her mood, either. Her workday crept by like a lame tortoise in the cold.

She tied on her running shoes and took off the moment it was close to quitting time. Running took her focus off her thoughts. She didn't return home until her legs were threatening to cramp. Her hair was slick with sweat, and most of the anxiety that had been needling her throughout the day was gone.

But she froze when she found Mercer back on her front porch.

"You look surprised to see me, Zoe."

She brushed her hair back and became frustrated with the urge to improve her appearance for him. "Since you left at just about the same moment you finished getting what you wanted, I am surprised to see you."

Peevish? Maybe. But she was going to call it as she saw it.

"Would have called you but you left your cell in my jacket pocket."

He held up her cell phone and wiggled it. She hesitated before reaching for it. Recalling last night wasn't a problem. Images replayed across her mind with a crystal clarity that aroused her despite her temper.

Only she didn't recall putting her cell phone in the pocket of that jacket.

"Yeah, well . . . thanks for bringing it back. I wouldn't

have noticed it missing until I was packing for my next party."

Mercer frowned. "You have more than one cell phone?"

She plucked the phone out of his hand and slipped it into her lightweight sweatshirt's pocket.

"Most guys ask for a girl's cell phone number." She fit her key into the front door and heard Harley greet her. She turned and blocked the doorway. A ripple of apprehension traveled along her nerves because even standing on the top step, she still wasn't eye level with Mercer. Keeping the man out of her house wouldn't prove easy.

Yeah, try impossible . . .

"But you didn't ask for my number and you neglected to leave yours, so thanks for returning my phone. Good night."

She backed up and moved to close the door only to see his booted foot lodged firmly where she'd stood half a second ago.

"Don't start sounding like a teenager who's pissed off at her prom date, Zoe." He pushed the door open but stood in place, watching her with his dark eyes. "I'm really beginning to like you, so don't ruin the moment. You're not the only one surprised by how strong our reaction is to each other. I didn't show up at the bar looking for anything more than a cold beer and some stress relief. I just got back on American soil and half my mind hasn't finished the journey. Fun, I was out looking for. You're complicated. I needed to think about that."

He struck a chord inside her, in the same place she was nursing injured pride because she'd woken up alone. But she knew full well what her dad and brother looked like when they made it back home. Post-traumatic stress was no joke. It was very possible he didn't trust himself to sleep next to her. She'd be a complete turd to forget how deep the unseen scars of combat ran. They weren't exactly close enough for her to expect him to blurt out the fact that he was having night terrors.

"All right, fair enough."

His lips curled up into a grin, but the look in his eyes never softened. The fingers he had curled around the door frame were white. "So invite me in."

"What are you, a vampire?" she asked.

His grin became wider until his teeth showed. "Tell me, baby, wasn't my skin hot enough last night for you to notice I'm not a member of the undead community?"

It sure was . . .

Zoe blushed. It was a humiliating response and he didn't miss it. His gaze homed in on the telltale spots of color brightening her cheeks.

"I'm waiting for the confident woman who told me exactly what she wanted last night to invite me in."

She turned away, wrestling with the weakness. Trying to shove it back down, beneath the foundation of her confident, modern-life persona. The supportive daughter and sister who was proud of her family members in the service, up to the challenge of holding down the fort while they were away. Mercer reached out and cupped her shoulder, turning her back to face him and punching right through her good intentions.

"Every relationship begins with raw magnetism. Anyone who says otherwise is just trying to slip into your bed while you're busy believing in fairy tales. Call me what you will, Zoe, but I'm more honest than you're being. We made each other hot, that's what happened, and I'm standing here because I think we have something worth taking to the next level."

So tempting . . .

Her resolve was starting to crumble. "Good point."

He considered her for a long moment. "But you don't know just what you think about me being right."

She ended up snorting. "Didn't your mother teach you not to trust girls who don't behave?"

He lifted a shoulder and shrugged. "Want me to be a good boy?"

Absolutely not . . .

The thought was instantaneous and it made her arguments invalid.

"Please come in." She tossed out the invitation in a tone rich with the frustration that had eaten at her since she'd woken up alone. "Don't think this means I'm allowing you into my bed again."

Good luck with that one . . .

Mercer followed her into the kitchen. "It's not very sporting of you to be pissy when you were just as hot as I was last night."

Zoe filled a glass with water and took a long drink from it before answering. "You're the one who encouraged me to be a bitch."

She regretted the barbed comment almost instantly. Mercer didn't take offense. Instead his features became a mask of sensual enjoyment.

"I don't regret it," he said firmly with hunger glittering in his eyes. "That's a woman I'm interested in getting to know better."

Heat snaked through her belly and her gaze dropped to his package. The moment she realized she was staring at the bulge his cock made behind his fly, she jerked her attention back to his face. But it was much too late.

He was smirking with victory. "Now who's at fault for turning the conversation back to sex?" He reached out and stroked the surface of her cheek. "Not that I'm complaining. I think I could become used to you deciding what we're doing on our dates."

"Christ!" She slammed the glass down on the counter, not sure if she was madder at herself or him. "This isn't the way healthy relationships form."

One of his eyebrows rose, warning her he was preparing to shoot a massive hole through her argument. "According to statistics, lack of satisfying sex is the number one reason couples cheat."

His voice was edged with razor-sharp confidence once more. It was as if the heat transferred between them and magnified. Zoe stepped back when her mouth went dry and she witnessed the recognition of his victory in his eyes.

She ended up laughing.

And it felt good. Like he was best-friend material as well as smoking hot. His lips curled up and they stood there, locked in a moment of shared amusement. It was uncharted territory, both of them freezing when they realized how much in common they had.

"I need a shower," she announced.

"But you want something else."

Zoe stopped on her way out of the kitchen, heat licking at her as she felt Mercer watching her. She felt grimy and unkempt but that didn't stop her from noticing that he was watching the sway of her hips as she moved. It was an unrealistic way of thinking, a self-absorbed way of looking at the situation, but she looked over her shoulder to find Mercer staring at her, his eyes glittering with hunger.

"I want dinner, too."

She was lying, flat-out. But it felt good to see surprise register on his face before she rounded the corner and went up the stairs to clean up.

Duty and temptation were complete opposites.

But Mercer found himself trying to combine them.

It wasn't working. Duty was slipping out of his grasp, leaving him noticing just how enticing Zoe was. Her skin was creamy and looked good with sweat on it. A woman had to be damn sexy to look good fresh from a run.

Zoe had.

His cock was rock-hard and making him focus on getting another taste of the supreme satisfaction he'd sampled in her bed last night. It had just been a sample. They'd both been too hot to linger over the finer details of toying with each other.

But he recalled exactly what her skin felt like pressed against his.

He chuckled, trying to stay in the kitchen as he heard the shower turn on. She was nude and one set of stairs away. His leg muscles twitched with the urge to close the distance between them so he could get another chance to taste her cream.

He was a beast.

Maybe *jerk* was a better word, but he wanted back into her bed with a need that was beginning to worry him. It was too intense, too sharp to be healthy. Obsessing over a woman had never been his way, and when it came to one who was a team target, he should not change.

Shit.

He wanted to. The desire was just there, fueled by the way Zoe laughed with him, her eyes full of merriment.

He pulled his cell phone open. Saxon answered on the first buzz.

"She has another cell phone."

"Shit."

Harley squawked from the front room, drawing Mercer to the doorway of the kitchen. A practice stage was set up next to the cage the parrot lived in. The colorful logo of Zoe's parrot party caught his attention.

"Shit."

"Yeah, I just said that," Saxon remarked.

"She said Harley was a one-man bird."

"Who's Harley?" his CO demanded.

"The parrot and there's a different cell number on the company logo. Find out who owns the bird company and we might have our link."

"So why do you sound pissed?" Saxon inquired. "She's a target, you knew the details going in."

"Never mind how I sound. I'm doing the job, that's all that matters."

Mercer snapped the phone shut while Harley eyed him. He moved closer to the stage, inspecting it with a critical eye.

He was being damn defensive with his CO.

Insubordinate even.

He needed to focus before he let someone get the jump on him because his head was spinning.

The shower shut off and he cussed. Why did she have to be the one woman in the state of California who didn't take long showers? He needed to find the phone but it would have to wait.

Coward.

Zoe fluffed her bangs but couldn't escape the fact that she was looking for excuses to avoid returning to face Mercer. Her insides felt like a bowl of Jell-O, souring her mood.

Why was she letting the guy make her jumpy?

Her attention landed on the bed and she swallowed roughly. Okay, the guy was a pistol and that was what was making her hesitate. There was no getting a grip on her feelings when he touched her. He reduced her to pure response.

Some women dream of connecting with a guy so strongly . . .

Yeah, and she was one of them, but that didn't make it any easier to trust in something so sudden. She dropped her hairbrush, determination settling her insides. There was no way she was going to waste her opportunity on jitters.

She went down the stairs and turned the corner to find Mercer leaning against the counter and watching the doorway.

"I guess my apron was a little too girlie for you."

He grinned, and the expression made him too attractive by far. "I don't cook."

"Every Special Forces course includes basic cooking."

He laughed. "Only if you like flame-blackened squirrel."

His lips curved to offer her an expression that wasn't so serious, but it didn't dispel the suspicion brewing inside her.

"You're not being on the level with me." It wasn't the

wisest thing for her to say while the guy was in her house. Her father's voice instantly rose inside her head, reprimanding her for being so stupid. She should have made an excuse to get him out of her house before calling his bluff.

"We haven't had any time to level with each other, Zoe." His eyes narrowed and lowered to where her nipples showed through the fabric of her top. "We keep getting distracted."

He pushed away from her counter, and her belly tightened. It was frustrating the way she responded so quickly. "That doesn't explain why you looked like you were mad that I noticed."

He didn't stop until he was leaning over her, his hands planted on either side of her. Desire slowly heated inside her, moving along her skin and chasing the chill from her shower away.

"You're right."

He leaned in and placed a kiss against the side of her neck, the two words his only concession.

"Right about what?" she demanded, attempting to push him away before he added any more kisses.

"Both points. I just got home and the last thing I want to talk about is where I've been stationed. So I'd rather you didn't notice." He lifted his head and locked stares with her. "Your brother ever show up looking like he forgot what life was for?"

"Yeah . . ."

He framed her face. "Good. You understand more about me than you realize."

Whether or not she agreed slipped right out of her head. His lips pressed down on top of hers, driving the topic of conversation too far away to be recalled. Pleasure awoke in a hundred different points along her body. Need nipped at her, sending her seeking what she'd craved from the moment she'd opened her eyes alone.

Zoe reached for him, slipping her hands beneath the hem of his T-shirt.

"That's it, baby."

She didn't much care what he said; it was his husky tone that sent anticipation zipping along her nerve endings. There was dark promise edging his words, and her memory offered up solid evidence to support the fact that he was a man who kept his word.

She stroked upward first, teasing the iron-hard muscles of his six-pack before dragging her hands back down to his waistband.

"*God*." He arched backward, his jaw clenched hard enough to cord his muscles down the length of his throat. "Claw me."

She stroked all the way to his nipples before curling her hands into talons and raking them down the satin-smooth skin covering his abs. He sucked in a harsh breath, raising her confidence. It was a crazy rush of self-esteem, like a pure shot of fire. She suddenly felt on par with him, a lover equal to the task of driving him as insane with need as he did her.

She didn't stop at his waistband, but sent her hands gliding over the worn denim to tease the bulge of his erection.

"That's it . . . take what you want."

It shouldn't feel so good . . .

Mercer gritted his teeth, his balls tightening. Zoe's touch was barely noticeable but his cock twitched, every nerve ending more aware than he could ever recall. His fly felt too tight. Savage enjoyment surged through him when she hooked her hands into the waistband and popped the button open. Relief speared into his cock when the front of his pants opened.

"No underwear. Should I accuse you of being presumptuous?"

"Call me whatever the hell you like, so long as you keep touching me."

She didn't disappoint him. But she did threaten to drive him insane. She teased his dick with just a glancing stroke from her fingertips, up and down and back up again. He wanted more, needed more. His cock was painfully hard and her toying only brought more blood flowing into the already swollen flesh.

"Bitch," he growled.

"Be careful what you ask for," Zoe leaned forward and pressed a kiss against his rock-hard abs. "I might be a demanding one."

"Don't worry baby, I can handle your fire."

He looked too damn arrogant and she liked it too much. Her heart was racing but she felt in control, so firmly in command of the moment that it was exciting her beyond anything she'd ever felt. Her clit was throbbing, the folds of delicate flesh surrounding it growing moist from the fluid escaping her pussy. But she was in no hurry to ease the hunger. Instead, she wanted to feel it grow, tighten, until the need for release became so powerful, it overrode her desire to push Mercer to the same limit.

She wanted to challenge him, see who broke first.

Her next kiss was lower and then she passed his belly button. She parted the sides of his open fly, allowing his cock to straighten. He drew in a harsh breath as she bent her knees and sank lower, until she knelt on the floor. Wrapping her fingers around his length, she looked up.

His expression shocked and thrilled her at the same time. Savage enjoyment shone from his eyes; it was so powerful, a little zip of fear went across her mind because he was too strong for her to defend herself against. She knew she wanted him, which required a leap of faith.

Or a stab at taking control of the moment.

"Holy Christ!"

Mercer planted his hands on the edge of the tile counter. Zoe ran her tongue around the crown and through the slit.

"Suck it, baby."

His voice was low and rough, proof that she was doing exactly what she wanted. Pushing him. Zoe licked the head of his cock again, closing her hand around the staff and working it all the way to the base.

"Bitch," he growled.

"You already called me that."

But she enjoyed hearing it again. She really wasn't interested in what he said, only the way his words sounded, forced out between clenched teeth. She knew that desperation, could feel it nipping at her pussy now. She wanted the hard length of flesh deep inside her, but she opened her lips and let her mouth sheathe it instead.

"Oh . . . hell yeah."

His hips jerked, driving more of his cock between her lips. She took it, moving her head and toying with the sensitive spot on the underside of the head with her tongue. She maintained her grip on the length outside her mouth, working her hand along it. His breathing became rough as his hips drove back and forth. She reached the base of his dick and rotated her wrist to cup his balls.

"Shit!"

He grabbed a handful of her hair and pulled out of her mouth. Frustration speared through her.

"Let go of my hair, Mercer. I'm calling the shots right now." She glared up at him, unimpressed with the savage glow in his eyes. But it sent a ripple of need through her clit, so acute she gasped.

"I never promised you fair play, baby," he warned her.

Her hair was free in a second, but Mercer didn't give her the chance to renew her position. He hooked his hands beneath her arms and lifted her off her knees.

"I only promised I could handle you."

He cupped the sides of her face again, tilting his head so their mouths would fit together perfectly. His kiss was hard, almost vicious, but it fed the need boiling inside her. He kissed her for a long moment, numbing her brain and leaving her thoughts nothing but a vapor. She was twisting against him, clawing at his shirt as she tried to pull him closer. She was desperate for him, exactly the thing she'd feared, and yet now she purred, enjoying the raging sensation. He lifted his mouth away and grasped her hips. The hold sent a jolt of need through her pelvis.

He lifted her off her feet and deposited her on the countertop.

"Damned if I didn't want to handle you the moment I stepped up to you outside that bar." He grabbed the waistband of her lightweight jersey pants and tugged them over the curve of her hips. She tightened her grasp on his shoulder while he stripped the garment off her. "When you turned me down, I thought about pushing you back into that corner outside the bar and kissing you until you melted. Spreading your thighs and shoving my hand into your pants to rub your clit until you begged me to satisfy you."

"I should throw you out for a comment like that," she said, but she so didn't mean it.

He cupped each knee, watching her with glittering eyes. "Why? Because it isn't candy-coated?" A dry laugh followed as he massaged each of her thighs. "What's between us isn't soft, baby. It's hot and combustible, and you don't want me to beg you for a ride between your thighs."

He drew his fingers down her thighs, setting off a hunger that made her heart accelerate. But he took a moment to dig into one pocket and pull out a condom. Normally, the delay of dealing with safe sex was a turn-off. Not with Mercer. The action promising her the satisfaction she craved.

"Part of you loves the fact that I push you." He cupped her knees again and spread her legs while holding her gaze. "Just as I love every second of you trying to reduce me to a quivering idiot."

She felt her lips lifting into a smile of satisfaction. Reaching out, she cupped his balls once more while he sheathed his cock. "I'll get you next time, Mercer, that's a promise."

"I guess now's a good time to tell you how controlling I can be when it comes to making sure my lover is as satisfied as I am." He leaned closer but instead of using the hard head of his cock, he teased her with the tips of his fingers, gliding them between the slick folds of her sex until he settled them over her clit. Pleasure spiked through her as hard as a spear.

"Stop toying with me, Mercer," she warned.

One eyebrow rose and his fingers remained exactly where they were, gently circling her clit. It sent her to the edge of climax but denied her enough pressure to actually tumble into the vortex.

"Weren't you just telling me how much it bugged you, not knowing anything about me?"

She slapped his shoulders. "That doesn't mean I want to talk now."

He pressed a little harder on her clit, sending a bolt of need up her passage so hard, she arched backward with it. She would have smacked her head on the cabinet if he hadn't caught her nape with one sure hand.

"I couldn't agree more, baby."

She grabbed his shoulders, feeling a wildness surging along her limbs. The first touch of his cock sent past her lips a primitive sound she'd never made before.

But it felt perfect.

"I love the way we communicate." His voice was harsh, almost unintelligible. But he gripped her hips and sent his dick tunneling inside her.

"And I love the feel of your pussy clasping my cock."

Her eyelids were heavy, and all she wanted to do was sink into the feeling of being stretched by his cock. But she forced herself to look into his eyes, and the hunger blazing there was worth the effort. It mirrored her own, adding more fuel to the inferno.

"Faster," she demanded, her thighs tightening around his lean hips. "I thought you claimed to be a man of action."

A soft slap landed on the top half of her bottom cheek. "Want to test my worth? I can arrange that, baby."

He felt larger than before. The walls of her passage were stinging but not enough to detract from the insane rush of delight each thrust gave her. She really was a bitch; she could feel the animal inside her clawing and biting its way past civilized behavior. She didn't want to be his equal, she wanted to be fucked. But more than that, she wanted to match his pace, and she moved her hips in time with his, lifting to take each forward thrust. Pleasure tightened in her belly, twisting and contorting until she jerked forward, grinding against Mercer while her climax tore away every last shred of awareness. There was only the blinding, white-hot flash of enjoyment so intense, every muscle strained toward it.

Mercer growled, low, deep, and savage. It suited the moment and the way he gripped her hips while driving his cock as deep as possible. A second ripple of pleasure jolted her when his climax produced a scathing outburst of profanity. Her eyes flew open, a moan escaping her lips. But speech was beyond her grasp because she'd forgotten to breathe. She drew in deep gulps of air to fend off the waves of dizziness threatening to drag her down into the pool of satisfaction her climax left behind.

"Christ . . . that was intense . . ."

Mercer flattened one hand on the countertop, his body shaking like hers was. But he kept a solid arm around her, holding her securely while they both recovered.

"My neighbors are going to call the cops," she groused when she regained enough strength to open her eyes and discovered she could see through the kitchen window. With only a half curtain, privacy wasn't really ensured.

Mercer smirked at her. "I guess I don't need to apologize

for keeping my pants on. Let them wonder if we're really doing what it looks like we're doing."

Zoe groaned and pushed him away. "Easy for you to say, you don't have to deal with them at homeowners' meetings. Some of them are mighty free with their opinions."

He closed his fly before bending down and retrieving her pants.

"Considering how impulsive we are, maybe a full curtain is in order."

He was teasing her, his voice rich and edged with amusement while he nuzzled her neck.

Zoe blushed because her underwear was still lying on the tile. But she threaded her feet into her pants while Mercer stole her breath with a tiny bite. He lifted her hips so she could finish pulling her pants up but he didn't back off to allow her off the counter. "Is that some kind of promise that I'll see you again? Because your performance record isn't very exemplary to date."

"If that window had been open, your neighbors would be able to testify as to just how good my performance record is—"

The kitchen window shattered with a pop. A second later she was facedown on the floor, Mercer's weight heavy on her back as he pressed her down.

"Who's shooting, Zoe?"

His tone had gone razor-sharp and as cold as a glacier. His knee was in the center of her back and his hand on the back of her neck.

"What the hell are you talking about? Some kid likely threw a rock because he saw us." She kept her voice even because newly returned servicemen were often a bit jumpy. "It wasn't a gunshot."

She expected him to ease up; instead, he ground his knee into her back. Pain shot down her spine and she began to struggle. Post-traumatic stress disorder was no laughing matter. She had to get his mind back in the present, fast.

"Get off me. This isn't . . . wherever you just got back from." She pushed against the floor but he remained unmovable. "My neighbors don't have guns, Mercer."

But he did.

She froze when a turn of her head brought her nose-to-muzzle with a handgun. The thing was coal black and wrapped securely in Mercer's hand.

"Where in the hell did you have that?" she demanded.

"What? Did you think I was going to be an easy kill?" He pressed the muzzle of that weapon against her skull with a confidence that chilled her. "Don't move."

Shock held her still, the muzzle of the gun too real to dismiss. In a detached, this-can't-really-be-happening way she was slightly curious, having watched scenes like this on television, but the cold tile beneath her cheek made her shiver because it confirmed that no commercial break was going to show up to save her.

Mercer flipped open a cell phone. "My cover's blown. Someone just took a shot at me through the kitchen window."

"What do you mean your cover?" she demanded.

Another pop sounded, followed by several more. The window past the cabinets shattered in a wall of falling glass.

"Still want to tell me no one's shooting at me?" Mercer accused.

The sounds were echoing in her ears while she stared dumbfounded at the broken glass coating her kitchen title. It fell from the countertop in little, tinkling waterfalls while the horrible reality sank in.

"They're shooting at both of us."

Someone kicked in her front door but Mercer wasn't waiting for their assistance. He yanked her up and sent her rolling through the kitchen doorway. He came up on one knee, his gun level, and fired off three rounds without hesitating.

He looked like a complete stranger.

Harley was screaming. Whoever had come through the door ran past him and on to the kitchen. There was suddenly a second man crouching on her tile and firing a gun. She scooted away, full of disbelief. She banged her knees on the hard floor but it wasn't enough to keep her from getting to her feet and running out the opposite door of the kitchen. Her thoughts were jumbled, racing too fast to make sense of, but Harley was still screaming so she went to his cage and opened the door.

The parrot jumped at her, digging his talons into the soft jersey of her top.

"Where the hell do you think you're going?"

Mercer grabbed her biceps and jerked her around to face him.

"Someplace where there isn't gunfire," she snarled. His grip was painful and the confidence with which he held the handgun scared the crap out of her. "Let go, you're hurting me."

"Too bad."

His tone was glacier-cold once more. He jerked her around and Harley gave a squawk of displeasure.

"Get rid of the bird."

"Like hell. I'm not telling my dad I left his bird behind in a firefight."

She intended to say something else but the sight of Mercer's shoulder silenced her. Bright-red blood was dripping unchecked down his arm. A groove was cut through the thin fabric of his T-shirt, and the remaining sleeve was saturated.

"You're hit." Her voice was a shocked whisper.

He propelled her toward the garage. "Congrats, but it will take a better shot than that to put me down. We're clearing out."

His last statement was for the other man who had kicked in the front door. He was every bit as powerfully built and his eyes had the same cold look in them when he glanced at her.

"Why did you say 'congrats'?"

She was already in the garage when she managed to get the question past her lips. Everything was happening too fast. It didn't seem real, couldn't be, not when she was inside her own home. All around her were the trappings of her life, but then she caught the scent of fresh blood and looked at Mercer's shoulder. The wound slapped her with just how real it was. Someone had tried to kill him in her kitchen, and he believed she was in on it.

"I had nothing to do with—"

"Get in. We'll all be dead in another few minutes if we stay here." He shoved her toward the van, which was still loaded with the parrot party stage. His friend had yanked the sliding door open and she tumbled through it while trying to control Harley. The parrot extended his wings and fluttered with outrage. Zoe rolled over, trying to maintain her grip on his body, and heard the door slam.

"Make it good, Greer. They've had time to reposition," Mercer growled to his companion.

"Not that much time, we might make it."

The *might* in his response chilled her blood.

Greer punched the accelerator the moment the garage door was high enough. The van swayed dangerously, the tires skidding when he took the turn into the street too fast. The crazy, drunken pitching of the vehicle didn't faze him any. He used his muscular arms to yank the steering wheel around as the engine roared from how hard he pushed on the accelerator.

"What the hell are you doing?" she demanded as she was flung against the portable cage, Harley hanging on to her for dear life. His talons were digging into her skin, drawing blood. His beak was sunk into the center of her bra.

"Trying not to get killed by your partners."

Zoe got a look at Mercer around Harley and his expression was hard. The gun was tucked into the front of his waistband, low enough to conceal it from anyone driving past them. Greer had eased off the frantic pace and settled into the flow of traffic.

Fear slammed into her, intense enough to nauseate her. It sent her looking around the van, seeking escape.

Mercer carries a gun.

She shivered, the memory of her suspicion rising above her growing terror. She should have given the impulse more credit.

A phone buzzed and Mercer picked it up. "Yeah . . . we're clear."

"He needs a medic," Greer announced loud enough to be overheard by the caller.

Her attention returned to Mercer's arm. At some point, he'd grabbed a towel and wiped the blood away so it wasn't so noticeable. But she could still smell the metallic scent of it.

"Who are you?"

Mercer turned to stare at her. There wasn't a trace of the man she'd gotten to know in the last two days. All that faced her was a hardened man who condemned her with his stony expression.

"You've been made, Zoe. You and your family members are going to stand trial for treason."

"You're insane," she announced.

She needed to think but her brain felt frozen with shock. Hadn't she just been having sex with Mercer? Hadn't her life been normal and gun-free?

But the van engine surged forward, confirming the reality of the situation. It still seemed surreal. She could see the tops of larger vehicles passing by the windows. Harley was holding on to the outside of his travel cage now and glaring at her.

Why had she packed the back of the van so tightly?

The rear doors were useless for escaping, which left the large sliding side door. She sat up, trying to gain an idea of where they were but, more important, hoping for a traffic light that might stop them long enough for her to make a break for it.

"Down."

She snapped her face around to see Mercer leveling the pistol at her. Disbelief held her still while she searched his face for any hint of the man she'd so foolishly let become her lover.

"I'll put a slug through your leg the second you reach for that door."

There was no hint of hesitation in his tone; even Harley mumbled in response. She reached out and stroked the parrot.

"Yeah, Harley, he is an asshole."

But one with a gun.

"You're out of your mind."

Or she was stuck in a nightmare. Possibly both.

Greer didn't seem to be interested and only continued to strong-arm her up the driveway of a plush Malibu home. A security gate slid closed behind them, sending another bolt of fear through her. The house built into the hillside sported tinted windows like most of its neighbors.

Only today, Zoe didn't think that tinting was to shield against the powerful California sun.

"Where the hell is your badge?" she demanded. The shock was wearing off.

She turned on Greer, calling on every bit of coaching her father had given her. He underestimated her and she sent a palm strike directly at his unguarded throat. Recognition of what she was doing registered on his face and he threw himself backward to lessen the impact, but she still broke free while he was cussing.

But she ended up facing two more men. One raised an eyebrow, clearly warning her, but in his hand was a badge. She had to look at it for a long time because it wasn't a familiar shield, like local police. The word FEDERAL showed quite clearly, though.

She turned around to find Greer reaching for her. His throat was turning red. "Try that again and I'll break your arm."

"You failed to identify yourself; I have the right to defend myself against kidnappers." She faced off with him, her entire body rebelling. "What is going on here?"

"That's what you'll be telling us," Greer informed her. There was a glint in his eyes that sent a chill down her spine. It promised her he was a man who got what he wanted, no matter the method needed to achieve his goal.

Well . . . he's in for a disappointment with me . . .

"Not without a lawyer," she muttered, but she did turn and start walking.

She looked back at the house. The thing looked like it was looming over her now that she was closer to it. The security team behind her only completed the feeling of being trapped.

From the outside, the house looked imposing enough, but across the threshold it became worse. There were gun racks running along the walls near the door. Resting in those organizational units were high-powered rifles. There were also handguns and spare clips, all loaded. Large flat-screen televisions were just about everywhere, displaying scenes of the exterior of the house and even one that had a shot of her desk. Her jaw dropped as she blinked but the picture didn't change. It was her desk, all right, her morning coffee cup sitting right where she'd left it.

Greer pulled her along and into what looked like a high-tech lab of some sort. Part of her expected a director to show up any moment to yell *Cut*, but no one came to her rescue. Instead, Greer tugged her past tables with electronic tools and components on their surfaces. Nothing was messy; it all looked organized and precise.

Which only added to her growing alarm. There was a realism that just couldn't be faked.

"Sit down, Ms. Magnus. I want to know why one of my men got shot in your company."

Zoe looked toward the doorway that led to the kitchen. The man standing there looked misplaced because he wasn't the homey type at all. She also recognized him from the bar. Saxon's face was lean, the sort of hardness that went along with prime conditioning.

Just like Mercer . . .

Her eyes narrowed as her mind latched onto the fact that she had been worked over. Her pride wasn't just stung, it was on fire.

"Your man? Your man is the one who brought a gun into my life, and people who carry guns tend to attract the same sort. So you can explain to me why my kitchen just got shot up." She tossed her hair over her shoulder. "Right after you show me your badge and provide me with a legal representative."

"Nice try, Zoe, but Saxon isn't going to bend under your innocent act."

She turned around to find Mercer leaning in a door frame that led somewhere else in the house. Pain slashed through her, startling her with its intensity. He looked quite at home.

I'm a goddamn idiot.

"You're supposed to be with the medic," Saxon replied. He had the same arrogant authority in his voice, but the men in the room all responded to it.

"Thais did her worst and pronounced me 'going to live.' It's just a graze." Thick gauze was wrapped around his shoulder, and a new T-shirt covered his chest now. Relief mixed with the pain still tingling inside her. Zoe looked away before he read her emotions off her face.

"Nice to know I can appreciate a botched job from time to time. Better timing on their part and you'd be bleeding out on her kitchen floor," Saxon muttered before moving farther into the room. He tugged something out of his pocket and tossed it across the room to land on the table nearest her. Backed on a solid piece of leather, the badge looked exceptionally shiny. She picked it up, studying it.

"Special agent can mean a whole lot of things," she said before dropping it back onto the table. She found herself fighting the urge to look at Mercer but realized she was doing it because she didn't want to see him flip out a badge. "Besides, you're supposed to identify yourselves before shoving me into a vehicle."

"You were under fire, which makes it a protective motion," Saxon informed her. "If you want to incriminate my team, get the charge right."

"Fine, your men are my heroes." She fluttered her eyelids a few times, earning herself a scowl from Saxon.

"My man was undercover."

Undercover. She cringed. There was no way to remain unmoved. Her emotions burned too hot for that.

"What the hell is that?"

Saxon looked beyond her, and Zoe turned to find one of his men carrying Harley's travel cage.

"He's my parrot," Zoe hissed. She reached for the handle of the cage, and the man gladly gave it to her.

"You said he was a one-man bird."

There was a note of incrimination in Mercer's voice. "Who is Harley's man? Your dad or your brother?" His eyes were still cold. "Which one is your accomplice? Or is it both?"

"I'd accuse you of being irrational but I actually think you're just plain insane."

"Looks like the passion has gone cold." Saxon took command of the situation with a single sentence.

Harley let out a squawk, a loud one that the parrot emphasized with a flap of his wings.

"I don't like the bird," Saxon informed her.

"Well, he doesn't like you and neither do I," she announced.

Maybe it was a childish answer but Zoe held the cage close, the knowledge that she was completely at the mercy of the man studying her slamming into her. He lifted one eyebrow but Mercer let out a sharp bark of laughter.

"I really hate getting shot, Zoe, so drop the innocent act and spill your contact information before we have to get creative."

Greer jerked the cage out of her hand while she was staring at Mercer, seeking any hint of the man she'd allowed to become her lover.

Not lover.

Sex partner.

She forced herself to swallow the term.

Sex partner . . .

She really had to get a wall up between her personal emotions and the charge of being a traitor. Fast. Before she made an idiot of herself by letting her injured feelings be seen. Business first.

"I already told you, the only person I seem to know who

carries a gun around is you." She forced her voice to be devoid of emotion. Pain ripped into her but she drew confidence from it. "Which makes me a fool . . ." Her eyes narrowed. "And you a gigolo."

"Cute."

Saxon interrupted but not before she got a look at Mercer's temper flickering in his eyes.

"Sit your ass down and stop whining about the method. You weren't a virgin."

Zoe turned to glare at him and fought off the urge to squirm. She wasn't the one out of line. "That doesn't excuse your actions. You've got a nerve setting me up like this."

Saxon appeared only mildly amused by her temper. "I save my concern for the men who end up dead when greedy people like you sell their positions out. There's not a hell of a lot I wouldn't do to succeed in bringing you down."

His expression was hard and certain, but she still struggled to believe what he was saying. Zoe stared at him in astonishment because whatever reality he was talking about was just not soaking in. It threatened to scare her to death because it was all focused on her.

"Sit, or I'll have someone duct-tape you to that chair." He tossed out his options in a bored tone.

"Why duct tape? Did you misplace your handcuffs, Mr. Federal Officer?"

Saxon shook his head slowly. "Nope, got them right here." He pulled a pair off his belt and dangled them from one finger. "But duct tape hurts a hell of a lot more when I rip it off."

"You're a turd." But she dropped into the office-type chair, still wrestling with the mental concept of espionage.

There was a degree of intense seriousness in the room that chilled her blood. But her confidence wasn't dead yet. She knew she was innocent. It was time to prove it.

"We got a second laptop, it was part of the parrot stage . . ." Greer appeared in the doorway, taking Saxon's attention away from her. "Thais is checking it."

"I only use it for pictures." Her mouth went dry when Saxon looked back at her. There was a flicker of victory in his blue eyes. "So look through it until you're satisfied . . . I am not a spy."

"Then your brother is. Testify against him and we might be able to keep you away from the firing squad."

Cue the intimidation tactics.

Zoe shook her head. "You're dead wrong about Bram."

"Dead? Who's dead are men who had their positions exposed for the right price." Saxon leaned forward. "I'll go to a lot more extreme measures than just sending one of my men into your bed to blow the cover off this operation. Tell me who your contact is or I'll introduce you to the side of my personality that isn't so nice."

"I want a lawyer to be present for any further questions."

Saxon smiled at her, sending the temperature of the room down a few more degrees. "In case you missed it, we're a special unit. An issue like this requires immediate response. Which means we cut through the bullshit."

The urge to look toward Mercer had her turning her head, but she froze before she did. Her temper flared up, killing the chill that had taken control of her. Zoe gripped the plastic armrests of the chair and leaned forward, choosing to face Saxon with the aid of her temper instead of shivering in a huddled ball.

Confidence.

Anger was only an advantage to an opponent.

Zoe drew in a deep breath.

"What you are is a special brand of jerk. Who gets high off intimidating people. I'm not a traitor and you're messing with the wrong family when it comes to questioning our loyalty. My brother and father are out there, too, so you can bet your ass I'm not selling out their positions."

Saxon held her stare, doing his best to break her, but Zoe didn't back down. Someone began pulling a length of duct tape off the roll, the tearing sound as sharp as nails on a chalkboard, but Zoe held her ground.

"Someone's moving intel . . ."

Saxon looked away, his attention on the woman in the other room. "How the hell is that possible?"

He was out of his chair and across the floor before he finished asking the question. Mercer cleared out of the doorway, his eyes narrowed.

"Someone's on her home system."

Saxon leaned over Thais, reading the information coming across her computer screen at the same time she did. Everyone turned toward the surveillance flat screens, but the one in her office had switched to a black-and-white sandstorm.

"Who's your partner, Zoe?"

Mercer asked the question. His voice was low but full of incrimination. It hurt, stabbing into her.

"No one." She looked at the floor, furious with herself but unable to banish the sense of betrayal.

A hard hand cupped her chin, raising her face so Mercer could witness every boiling emotion showing in her eyes.

That physical contact was her undoing. Her skin rippled with sensation, her insides tightening, and she just lost it completely.

How could she respond to him?

"I don't have a fucking partner!" She kicked him, exactly the way her dad had taught her. Her knee came straight up and the bottom of her foot went crashing into his tender parts. He cussed and stumbled back, one hand covering his crotch out of instinct. Zoe was out of the chair before he could stop her.

"And if you want to know who's using my computer . . . call the damn cops to see who's in my house because *I'm here!*"

She'd underestimated Saxon's use of the word *team*. Greer grabbed her from behind before Mercer shook off the pain. She was deposited back on the chair, the spring protesting at how hard she landed. The duct tape ripped again, a flash of silver reflecting the light as Greer looped it around her body. He taped her to the chair with amazing speed.

"You can't do this."

Her mind was having trouble absorbing the situation again. It defied the boundaries of her life. It was the stuff of movies and murder-mystery paperbacks, not her benign existence.

"We can do anything necessary to close this leak, Zoe." Mercer cupped her chin once more and she hissed as a familiar jolt pierced her. He frowned and released her, almost as if he felt the same thing.

Which was impossible, because the guy had only been doing his job when it came to getting into her pants.

His job . . . nitwit.

"I got that part already."

She offered him the same cold stare he'd been aiming at her. The duct tape ripped some more but she refused to allow it to terrify her. By all rights, she should have been scared to death, but the pain of betrayal seemed to be fending off everything else.

Well . . . she'd take what she could get.

"Ease up, Greer. She won't get the jump on me again."

Another loop of silver tape went around her body. "I'd just as soon not sample any of her work; that kick was dead-on. She's Daddy's little girl, all right."

"Leave my father out of this."

"Either your brother or your father is a traitor," Saxon announced on his way back into the room. He scanned her, the sight of the duct tape binding her to the chair causing not even a hint of emotion from him. He went back to his chair and sat down.

"Maybe all three of you."

"Yeah, well how do you figure in the fact that someone is using my computer after taking a shot at us?"

"I think you made Mercer, and your contacts wanted to take out my team to wipe any trace of guilt off your name. I sent him in to catch you red-handed. We already have enough evidence to take you to trial, but I like my cases airtight."

"If I'd figured out he was working a case, I never would have . . ." Words failed her as her cheeks turned hot. Saxon homed in on the weakness.

"Let him screw you?" he asked bluntly.

"Don't be vulgar."

There was a hint of something in his eyes that looked like appreciation but he covered it quickly. "You've missed the fact that you're duct-taped to a chair and very helpless."

"You seem to have missed the fact that whoever you're looking for is currently in my home," Zoe fired back. "If you're waiting for me to start bawling, better get comfortable."

His expression hardened. Words really weren't needed to convey the message his stony features sent her. This man could be ruthless, no doubt about it.

"She might be telling the truth," Mercer put in.

Saxon didn't like what he had to say but the team leader looked past her to his man. "Meaning what?"

"It's possible her brother isn't involving her in the deal. We haven't found the money and she doesn't live beyond her means." Mercer studied her. "She's either really good or a mule."

"My brother isn't a traitor," Zoe insisted.

Mercer was back to leaning in the door frame. "Then tell us who is, because we followed a trail to you, Zoe. Information is moving, money, too, and all through your computers. Let's not forget that someone just took a shot at me. You're the one who told me your neighbors don't have guns. Who else has access to your house?"

She opened her mouth but shut it without saying anything.

Saxon leaned toward her and she felt the stares of his men on her. "Nothing to say? That's a first."

"Spit it out, Zoe," Mercer urged her. She turned to glare at him, wanting to refuse him on principle, but there was a challenge in his eyes she just couldn't ignore.

"Tim." She hated saying it, detested hearing the name of someone she considered family crossing her lips under the circumstances.

"Tim is . . . who?" Mercer pressed.

"He books the parrot parties for my dad . . . or me, when my dad is deployed," she said, her mouth dry with horror. "He has a key and the alarm code so that he can deal with Harley if I get stuck somewhere overnight."

"Convenient," Saxon shot back at her. "What a nice scapegoat. Bet the guy didn't count on being set up when he signed on to be a good business partner."

She bristled. Saxon raised an eyebrow at her. "Cat got your tongue at last?"

He was prodding her. She knew it but just couldn't stop herself from rising to the bait.

"I was going to call you all a bunch of assholes, which is still true, but you're a dedicated group of jerks." She looked at Mercer. "I recognize the mission mode. But I also know I wouldn't be sitting here if you had any solid evidence, which means you're all making assumptions. The only true thing you've told me is that you don't have an airtight case, so you're trying to intimidate a confession out of me."

She'd surprised him. It flashed through his eyes and left a small spark of guilt behind.

"And you're dead wrong. My brother is no traitor. That goes double for my dad. That's the only reason I recognize the level of intensity in you. Besides, I was on that countertop, too, which means I could have been the target. I'd expect a team of this caliber to recognize facts when they hear them."

It would be a whole lot simpler if she didn't understand their motives. She could curse Mercer and his asshole of a boss, but deep down in her gut she knew her brother would have done the same. They were going to extremes to protect their fellow soldiers.

But that didn't keep her from feeling used.

"Bet Colonel Magnus will have a meltdown when he discovers what you're up to."

Tim jumped. Tyler Martin simply stared at him for a long moment. "It's your lucky day. I want a cut and I can make it all land on the girl."

Tim wasn't happy. "Why should I trust you?"

Tyler moved his shirt, exposing his badge. "Because if I didn't want a piece of the action, you'd already have a toe tag. Your contact on the other side has been made. There are cameras all over this house now. I know, it's my team that's on the job."

"So why am I still breathing?" Tim mumbled.

Tyler shook his head. "When I was looking over the case, I knew what was driving you. Years of working under Magnus's thumb when you were enlisted and now that you're a civilian? You jump when the good colonel calls, too. The girl has too much of her daddy in her to be the one selling intel. You, on the other hand, you're just the help."

Tim grunted. "Maybe you just want me to give over the name of my buyer."

Tyler shrugged. "Could get that without taking the time to set it up so you could get in here while the colonel's little princess is neatly out of the way and under suspicion. I'd just have to haul you in. Half an hour with a bowie knife and you'd sing. I'm no Boy Scout. Never have been. I like my job because I don't have to be a good guy. I can get my hands dirty." Tyler finished up with a grin.

Tim drew in a deep breath and relaxed. "I can do business with that sort of man." His pallor was returning to normal. "Providing you bring something to the party."

"I can bury the team that has the girl and knowledge of someone else picking up that intel. As far as the report will read, they were all gunned down by their buyer." Tyler shrugged again. "That's the risk of dealing with terrorists, don't you know. It will be such a shame that my team got caught in the cross fire. I'll have to make sure their relatives get their service medals."

"Yeah, real shame," Tim agreed. "Don't forget Bram. We used his clearance code. Got to cap him or he'll keep singing about the fact that it wasn't him."

Tyler grunted. "You're a mean fucker. Know that? You're going to leave Bryan Magnus with no family."

"Payback for a lifetime of licking his boots," Tim cut back.

"Thought he called you friend."

"Friend?" Tim snarled. "In the way a man calls his fucking butler *friend*. I was burning shit while he was wearing an officer's uniform when we served together. Had to fetch his goddamn ass wipes for him."

"Wasn't his fault you were enlisted."

"Yeah? Well, it was never anyone's fault that my life was a pile of shit. One foster home after another because my alley-cat mom had the right to keep me waiting for her when the bitch couldn't keep her ass out of prison long enough to play parent. By the time I was eighteen, the only choice I had was serving. Just another way the system screwed me over while men like Bryan Magnus had a home. Well, I'm getting a slice of that pie and I'm going to enjoy it. About fucking time it was my turn to sit at the big table. You want part of the money? That's the deal."

Tyler stared at Tim for a long moment, letting the man think he was debating the issue. He wasn't, but Tim wasn't bright enough to realize he was being used.

"Soon. I need to let my team leader make the mistake of trying to come back in here."

"And if he doesn't move on that option?" Tim questioned.

Tyler grinned. "He will. This guy is a Boy Scout. He'll melt under the weight of Zoe Magnus's pretty little face. Won't have the stomach to send her through processing without a solid evidence trail. Just make sure you bring me enough to cover dealing with the paperwork of waxing half his team. That's a lot of goddamn public funerals to stand through looking like I give a shit."

"My buyer will cough it up," Tim assured him.

Tyler nodded. "My car is in the garage. Get in the back-seat. I'll get you out of the area."

Tim looked uncertain but moved toward the garage after a long moment of contemplation. He didn't have a choice. Tyler didn't really care about the guy at all. Not beyond the fact that he could be used to pay Congressman Jeb Ryland what the congressman wanted. The money would make a nice little evidence trail leading to Saxon Hale. That was, right after Tyler set up an account in the agent's name and had Tim transfer the funds. Tonight's little sniper attack would be easy to lay on Saxon, a lot easier since his entire team would be dead by the time everything was sorted out. Tyler got into his car and drove out of the neighborhood.

"She's right."

Mercer watched his boss, but his attention was on Zoe. She was still taped to the chair and left behind in the living room while they had withdrawn to the back room. He took solace in knowing she was secured, because she needed protecting. He was sure of it. Saxon shot a look that made it clear his team leader didn't agree.

"Since she was on the countertop, it's reasonable to wonder who the sniper was aiming for. She wouldn't be the first mule slaughtered for the sake of making a clean getaway," Mercer said.

"Any decent sniper can time a shot precisely," Saxon insisted. "He was aiming for you, Mercer."

There was a long silence as they both considered the facts. "That would stink of bad brass," Mercer said at last.

Saxon snorted. "And the little princess of parrots might not be innocent." He was thinking it through, weighing the details. "But the intel was moving through her home system with its minefield of passwords. So . . ."

"We still need a witness or we've proven nothing. The perpetrator will move his information through another location."

"What are you suggesting?" Saxon demanded. "Going back in there? You've been made."

"She needs to be cleared."

Saxon rolled his eyes. "Knew you didn't have the guts for this sort of operation. You can't go falling for the bait."

Mercer stared straight back at Saxon. "I signed on because you always struck me as the sort of man who wants to see justice done. No matter the means. Even when you don't like the way the facts line up."

Saxon grunted, conceding the point. Mercer didn't dwell on the surge of emotion it gave him. He needed to focus on getting Zoe's name cleared.

"Send her back. I'll sneak in and cover her."

"You're injured," Saxon cut back. "She can cooperate to clear her family name. I'll post a team two blocks down."

"If she is an innocent, she needs a shield," Mercer added. His boss shot him a hard look, one Mercer wasn't willing to buckle under. "I've had enough innocent blood spilled during my missions to last a lifetime. If her name is on an elimination list now, I plan to make sure no one crosses it off. You knew how I worked when I signed on with you."

Tension was building in his gut but it wasn't because of the scowl on Saxon's face. Mercer knew himself too well to make that mistake. Failing to understand your own emotions was a fault more than one man had died for.

Besides, he had gone from feeling like shit to something a whole lot closer to guilt. He wasn't leaving Zoe's side. Period.

"Greer can take point," Saxon decided.

"Don't test me." Mercer sent his commanding officer a hard look. "You know damn well a switch will tip off our delivery man. I admit I'm questioning whether or not Zoe is guilty of anything more than having a dirty family member, but that won't affect my performance."

"Fine, you're right . . . we need something more to close this case now that intel moved while she was here with us. Tim might be our man but that still leaves her brother involved."

"And she's the only link we have," Mercer finished.

Saxon didn't like it, but Mercer was more concerned with the surge of victory traveling along his insides. It was too hot, too intense for just the satisfaction of knowing he was going to get the chance to bring down a traitor.

It was personal.

The sort of emotional tie he didn't have time for. It was also the kind of thing that got men killed because they lost the ability to be objective. Saxon recognized it. His CO was mentally running the facts through his brain, trying to formulate an alternative plan. Saxon let out a soft word of profanity before he nodded. It was a bittersweet victory, because going back in just might get them both killed. Mercer followed Saxon into the living room where Zoe was strapped to the chair.

He'd deal with it. Somehow, some way. Nothing had changed about the mission, and he'd just have to bury his feelings deep enough to keep his guard up.

That was the part he was going to need his luck for.

Because when it was over, Zoe would be dealing with him.

Personally.

"We need to talk."

Saxon sat down in front of her again.

"So remove the duct tape." Zoe wanted to sound more forceful, but the silence had taken a toll on her resolve. Left alone, she'd battled to ignore her rising sense of helplessness.

"We'll talk first." The jerk took out a pocketknife but only flipped it over a few times. "My offer is for you to cooperate fully with my team."

"In exchange for what?" Zoe asked bluntly.

He flipped the knife a few more times, his expression stone-hard. "The chance to prove your innocence."

"You mean my family's."

Saxon leaned closer and opened the knife with his thumb. He did it with such ease, never even looking down. "Better worry about yourself."

He slid the blade beneath the tape and jerked it upward.

"Do you honestly think you're the only one who understands team values?" she asked him.

Her barb hit a soft spot. Saxon snapped the blade back into position and shoved his chair away from hers.

"What I know is you'd better think long and hard before trying to take my team out." His eyes darkened.

Zoe refused to accept that.

She yanked the tape off. Several pieces of her hair went along with the silver mess, drawing a snarl from her.

"Mercer is your partner, and your superior," Saxon informed her.

"Like hell he is." She tried to throw the ball of tape but it clung to her fingers and she had to settle for scraping it off on the side of a table. Very unsatisfying.

"He'll sneak into your place tonight. Hopefully whoever was on your home system will think you're alone."

"He can sit on the curb and wait for me to call him in," Zoe countered.

"You'll miss me too much," Mercer replied.

Zoe gave herself a little push, sending the chair rotating around so she could stare at him.

"Like a wart."

She stood up, relief flooding her and pissing her off at the same time. She resented having to be grateful for her freedom. Resented it because it made her realize just how fragile normalcy really was. Things she took for granted were actually privileges that she'd been overlooking the value of. Some asshole was really close to taking those basic rights away; her personal privacy had already been trampled. She ended up looking back at Mercer, bitter over the facts. She'd thought him out of her league but didn't really care for the sting of discovering she was nothing but an assignment.

"Greer and Maddox will be backing you up, along with other members of my team," Saxon interrupted. "You won't see them unless I want you to. So don't try anything stupid. Run and they'll catch you."

There was a hard warning in his voice, and he backed it up with a look designed to make her knees quiver. Zoe refused to buckle.

"Fine," she agreed. "What's my part?"

Her firm poise earned her a flicker of respect in his eyes, but his expression never softened.

"Get back to your place, wait for Mercer. We'll see if you can find a way to convince me you aren't in on the transfer. Let's see if your dad's buddy makes a try at connecting with you."

Part of her really hoped so.

Part of her was horrified at the very real possibility that Tim was a traitor. That knowledge was going to shred her dad. Her too. A lifetime of trust was going up in smoke as she realized that Tim was very likely guilty. That, or some wacko had access to her house. Both left her feeling like she needed to kill someone.

"If your team is watching me so closely, I don't need Mercer along for the ride," she argued.

"If you're telling the truth and you aren't in on this, you damn well need me watching your back, Zoe, because you can't prove anything if you're dead." Mercer stepped between her and Saxon. She caught a glimpse of Saxon rolling his eyes before the team leader turned his back on them, making it clear he'd made his decision.

"I don't need you."

But she was too damn aware of Mercer, which was just another point in favor of leaving him behind. Arousal warmed her skin even as her memory offered up the feeling of his gun against her neck.

Nitwit . . .

"Yes you do." Hard, curt, and without a shred of mercy, his words didn't draw any attention from his team members, either. They seemed perfectly willing to let the drama unfold without any involvement.

She'd be an idiot to expect help from any of them. Their jobs were to gather enough evidence to send her to prison. She refused to allow that to happen. She was her father's daughter, after all. Her daddy had raised her to be tough, and she wasn't going to disappoint him.

But thinking of her father made her recall Harley. The parrot was quiet, which was never a good sign. He hated his carrier, too, so the silence had her sweeping the room in search of him.

Mercer grabbed her arm and brought her around to face him again. Surprise registered on his face. "What's wrong?"

His question brought the other team members' gazes to her, but Zoe wasn't interested in their concern.

"Where's Harley?" She pointed at Mercer. "If you hurt

my dad's parrot, he'll make you wish you were dead. Harley is never quiet in his carrier." She rolled her shoulder and dropped her arm on the other side of his hand to break his grip. Yeah, she was her father's girl, all right, and knew a thing or two about handling herself. Fury appeared on Mercer's face the moment he recognized what she was doing. The knowledge came too late to keep her from gaining her freedom.

"You know, never mind worrying about my father . . . Harley is my responsibility while he's gone. I'll kick your lying ass myself if there is even one feather out of place on that bird."

She turned and began to cross the room, looking for the carrier.

"I put the bird in there . . . he's fine. How much trouble can a parrot be anyway?" Greer pointed her through the doorway to another room, an amused look on his face. Zoe ground her teeth but froze in the doorway, her temper evaporating the second she got a look at Harley.

"More trouble than you think," she muttered.

Her father's prized parrot was busy destroying Mercer's leather jacket. Harley purred as he chewed on a sleeve, which already sported too many punctures and tears to count. She looked back at Greer.

"You forgot to check the door latch. Macaw parrots are very intelligent. One that's Harley's age will check to make sure the door is locked."

His eyes narrowed but Mercer had followed her and let out a growl. The sound brought the rest of the team forward to investigate. Zoe hurried ahead of them, scooping Harley up. Mercer yanked his jacket out of the parrot's grasp, earning a squawk of outrage. The tattered sleeve made her laugh. Harley had made good use of his free time.

"Gee, for a team of guys who seem to think themselves so on top of details, I've got to say. I'm less than impressed."

She ran a soothing hand down Harley's back. Her father's pet wasn't appeased. He let out another screech and clicked his beak at the jacket.

Mercer aimed a deadly look at the bird. "This is a custom-made jacket. It's going to be a bitch to replace."

Yeah, he wasn't a normal size. Not with those shoulders . . .

Not anywhere else, either . . .

Zoe shook her head but heat still touched her cheeks.

"I like the bird," Saxon said.

Mercer turned and growled at Saxon. The team leader was sporting a genuine grin for once, but his eyes glittered with warning.

"I bet I'd like him even better with barbecue sauce."

CHAPTER THREE

"The rush job will cost you."

Zoe made a sound that wasn't really a word but the window repair guy grinned, smelling a larger commission. He sniffed a few times and made a show of inspecting the window framing. "Might be bent . . ."

"Can you get the job done or not?"

Mercer appeared on the other side of the kitchen, keeping to the shadows but sending the repairman a look that meant business. The workman instantly abandoned his lazy mode of operation. "Sure can, got the glass on my truck."

"I need it in my kitchen. Name your price or we'll call the next service in the directory."

The repairman turned and scribbled across a work order. Zoe reached for it but he took it to Mercer, leaving her nursing her pride. The second Mercer signed it, the guy was out the door.

"I didn't need your help to get the house fixed."

Mercer still had his sunglasses on, preventing her from seeing what emotion was in his eyes.

"You needed my help, and you need more of it, Zoe." There was a hard edge on his tone.

"Not a chance. I'll be happy to show you and your buddies the error of your ways without a shred of assistance from you."

One dark eyebrow arched above the gold rim of the shades. He moved toward her, sending prickles of sensation across her skin. It was the way he moved; she was intently aware of it. She noticed things about his body that normally didn't register.

"I get that, Zoe." He didn't stop at a normal distance but pressed her up against the hallway wall. The night breeze was coming through the window that lacked glass to keep it out, but it didn't cool off her cheeks. "What are you planning to do the next time bullets start flying?"

She flattened her hands against his chest and pushed but gained only a tiny grin for her effort. "I'll improvise."

"You'll end up bleeding out on your own floor," he told her gravely. "You need me."

"Shut up." She tried to punctuate her comment with a stiff knee to his groin but he blocked it expertly. He hooked her ankle with his foot and pulled her right leg across the floor so he could press his thigh between hers.

"You only get one crotch shot, baby."

She struggled, failing to master the urge despite knowing damn well he had her pinned. His hold wasn't painful but she could feel the iron strength.

"Don't count on that."

His eyes narrowed. She reached up and yanked the shades off his face. It was the only way she could strike out against him, but it backfired because she got a glimpse of his eyes. Hunger was brightening them, battling against the suspicion. She felt an answering tug at her own insides.

How can I? The guy should nauseate me. I've been an assignment. Where the hell is my pride? The attraction should be fizzling out as my temper strangles it.

"You haven't proven you have the right to be mad, Zoe. I'm here to help you do that."

She shoved at his chest again. "Just because they drill confidence into you during special ops training doesn't mean you've become infallible. You're wrong about my family."

"Maybe." His voice deepened into the tone she recalled too well from more intimate moments. "But that would only double my confidence in the fact that you need me watching your back. Whoever is guilty is nearby and has every reason to take you out to cover his tracks. I didn't show up without a reason, Zoe—an evidence trail led me to your doorstep. Like it or not, you need to trust me."

"Not a chance in hell of that happening."

Fury flickered in his eyes. "Your father should have taught you that adjusting to the situation is key to survival. Liking me isn't necessary."

The workmen came back through the front door. Mercer stepped back, freeing her, but not before she noticed something in his expression that hinted at misgiving.

Good! I hope guilt is chewing a hole in your gut.

She turned her back on him, knowing without a doubt she couldn't handle seeing any hint of true concern for her in his eyes. She'd be sunk if she did. Her heart would end up on her sleeve in a matter of hours.

Someone else knocked on the open front door. "Deli delivery."

Zoe started through the doorway but a hard grip on her arm jerked her back a pace.

"We need to discuss the rules, Zoe, because you're going to get yourself killed if you try taking point without a weapon. Don't trust anyone. We're here as bait, baby. Try not to get eaten."

He whispered against her ear, holding her against him. It earned them a smug look from the two workmen struggling to replace the kitchen window. She dug her elbow into his ribs but he captured her wrist with the hand that was draped around her back. He held her for only a moment, but it felt like the longest few seconds of her life. She was keenly aware of him, the way he smelled, the way his grip felt against her skin. There was a flicker of arousal in his eyes that unleashed a curl of lust in her clit.

All accomplished in so short a span of time, as if she were suspended between heartbeats. Mercer was moving past her before she managed to drag enough breath into her burning lungs to protest.

She decided to save her breath; the guy was already halfway across her living room but he stopped before he got too close to the windows again, inviting the delivery guy in with a jerk of his head.

"Thanks for coming out," Mercer muttered while digging his wallet out of his pocket.

"Twenty-four-seven, that's our motto."

Mercer handed the guy a few bills and received a plastic bag in return. The scent of hot tomato sauce and cheese drew a rumble from her belly.

"I'm starving, too." Mercer put the bag down and dug

out two carryout containers. "Let's eat while they finish the window."

Zoe stared at him, trying to decide if her pride was worth suffering through a bowl of cold cereal while the scent of hot Italian food tormented her.

It wasn't.

"Fine."

She picked up the container on the top and grabbed a plastic fork.

"Where are you going?" Mercer demanded.

"Upstairs," she muttered. "You get the sofa and the window bill. Partner."

The look of frustration that appeared on his face brought her a measure of satisfaction at last. She just wished it hadn't dissipated by the time she reached the top step. A tingle of dread began chilling her. Her windows weren't the only thing shattered; so was her confidence in her home. The place felt colder and less inviting now. An urge to look over her shoulder at the capable vision Mercer provided tugged at her but she forced herself to keep going until she made it into her bedroom.

Fine, she was scared. But there was no way in hell she would ever let Mercer see it.

Mercer had to kill the urge to follow her. Forcing himself to stay put while she disappeared into the master bedroom. It took an amazing amount of discipline.

It shouldn't have.

The place was wired and bugged to perfection. Saxon had ordered him to keep enough of a leash on Zoe to make sure they didn't lose her but also give her the slack to think she wasn't being watched too carefully. Just a few loopholes, like making it look as though he was being nice enough to allow her the privacy of her bedroom.

There was nothing private about it now. Greer and the team had seen to that before Zoe finished dealing with her window. If she made a move to warn her family members, they'd know it and have their evidence.

The dinner he'd been salivating over suddenly tasted like sawdust. He ground his teeth, frustration turning his stomach.

Idiot.

The plan was clear and necessary. Men had died and it was his duty to intercept the people responsible.

So why wasn't he enjoying his dinner while his target was so neatly in a position to close the case?

Because he doubted she was guilty. It was more than a tickle now, it was a full feeling that they'd followed a very well-laid trail. Zoe was more than just a mule, she was also intended as the scapegoat. A plan that worked a whole lot better if she was dead and unable to defend herself.

He just hadn't figured out how yet. Saxon would accuse him of being a softhearted idiot, but he wasn't able to shake the feeling. Zoe had better adjust her attitude soon, because it might become necessary for them to stick a whole lot closer to each other.

Eating didn't take long. Zoe found herself beginning to pace, but the wood floor of her bedroom seemed to echo each footfall. She kicked her shoes off but still heard the floorboards creaking.

She just didn't want Mercer to hear her. He was too sharp to not figure out what she was doing. Another silly impulse but she wanted to hide her anxiety. Her bed didn't feel as comfortable as it normally did. She looked at the remote control but never reached for it. Her desire for drama was nonexistent. In fact, anything but *I Love Lucy* reruns struck her as unpalatable. The fear and stress of the last few hours played across her mind with enough clarity that she felt sweat on her forehead.

Someone had tried to kill . . . her . . . or Mercer . . . maybe both.

Her dinner suddenly wasn't sitting so well, and her body was exhausted. She fell asleep on top of the covers, her dreams a nightmarish mixture of recollections from the day.

She jerked awake, sure it was her dream that had startled her. Her hands were curled into talons, gripping handfuls of the comforter while her heart hammered inside her chest.

Her cell phone buzzed again and she sat up. The thing was sitting on her nightstand, illuminated with an incoming call from a classified number.

Zoe reached for it out of habit.

"Where were you today?" Her father's voice was peppered with static. "Don't tell me Tim booked you a party on a regular workday."

"Hi, Daddy." Her voice cracked as the day's events rushed at her like a tsunami. She drew in a quick breath and got a grip on her composure before she let the cat out of the bag. "Don't worry, Tim didn't mess up." She left it at that, hoping her father wouldn't ask again. Lying to her daddy was a bad idea. Bryan Magnus would call her on it.

"How's my baby bird?"

Zoe smothered a short bark of laughter. "Harley is almost thirty now."

"Just a baby, like you, and don't forget it, my girl," her father insisted.

"Harley is . . . Harley. He chewed up an expensive custom leather jacket today." Just saying it lightened her mood but it brought Mercer back to mind.

"Whose jacket?" her father demanded.

Busted . . . Daddy's radar is working great.

"Someone who wasn't alert enough to notice a bright red-and-blue bird slipping under their nose. Harley is very much . . . the same bird you left with me," she said playfully. It was a lame attempt to lighten the mood and lull her dad into thinking she was just fine and didn't want to worry him while he was on assignment. The military family code.

Still, it was dishonesty, and her dad was going to call her on it. She had no doubt.

"I love him, every last opinionated squawk," her dad drawled at last.

Zoe smiled in the dark. "Yeah, well, the neighbors aren't so happy about those. You need to encourage Tim to book more morning parties because Harley wakes up at first light."

"Another reason I love that bird," her father said. "Keeps better time than anything man-made."

Her hand began to ache because she was holding the phone so tightly. Tears stung her eyes, the need to reach out to her father so great, it felt uncontainable.

But she held on to her determination. Her father was working on a top-secret project and didn't need her adding to his stress level. The phone was always on her nightstand because she never knew when he'd find a few moments to call. She liked to think he made contact with her when he needed to remember why he was out doing his duty.

So she wouldn't be letting her daddy down in his time of need by adding to his worries.

"Got to run, baby girl, tell Harley Daddy will be home soon."

The line went dead, leaving her to rub her forehead after laying the phone aside.

"Why didn't you unload on him?"

Zoe stiffened, every muscle drawing tight enough to snap. The first time she'd seen Mercer, she thought he was more suited to shadow than anything else. He was hanging back in the hallway now, blending in as he watched her.

"I know the home-front rules."

Zoe put the phone back on the side table and found Mercer. He was just a dark shape in the hallway but he moved, coming through the doorway and stopping at the foot of the bed.

"My dad doesn't need to worry about me while he is deployed." She moved to the side of the bed, feeling far too exposed on its surface. Memories were rising fast and hot from the moments they'd shared in the room.

"And Harley belongs to your dad. Which makes Tim his partner."

Zoe stood up, outrage piercing the enjoyment of the call. "They do parrot parties for little kids together. My dad's way of blowing off the stress of his job. He and Tim served together."

She went to brush past Mercer, intent on getting a drink of water. He hooked her around the waist with a loose arm, but she knew how hard his grip might become if she resisted.

That idea made her quiver.

"So why are you shaking?" He asked the question next to her ear, the hand resting on her hip gently stroking it.

"Not because I'm worried you'll find any dirt on my dad."

"I didn't ask why you weren't shaking." He guided her closer to his body. "I asked why you were."

She quivered once more, the scent of his skin teasing her senses. It was almost impossible to resist the urge to raise her face. Her lips tingled with anticipation while she fought the impulse to seek out his kiss.

It wasn't real. At least not on his end. But it felt so necessary to reach out to him.

"Because Tim has been a part of my life. He's like my uncle, my dad's best pal."

He cupped her chin, lifting her face. Part of her rejoiced, grateful to have what she wanted without having to commit to the motion. Grateful to have him reach for her. Maybe that was naive, but he was all she had at the moment.

"Someone's guilty, Zoe."

"I know."

It wasn't easy to get her mind to function. She didn't know if it was the darkness or the chill of the night, but something made his body too inviting to ignore. She wanted to press up against him, melt into the warmth he offered while no one else was watching. Take shelter in his embrace. Just let him hold her and soothe the ache that was making her feel like her entire world was coming apart at the seams.

Mercer was lowering his head, tilting it so their mouths might fit perfectly. Giving her what she craved.

The bedroom window shattered, spilling onto the floor in a thousand pieces. It was almost a gentle sound, like water flowing over smooth stones. Zoe jerked her attention away from the floor as the door at the end of her hallway splintered.

"Get down!"

Mercer didn't wait for her to understand him; he pulled her down as two more bullets sliced through the air. They whistled above her head, sending adrenaline surging into her bloodstream.

"Goddamn snipers," Mercer growled. "We have to move. Now."

He was in action as the words came out of his mouth. There was no way to resist and she didn't really want to. The steady command in his voice was a welcome sound as the drywall below the window frame was punctured several times.

She yelped as something burned across her calf.

"Shit. He's going to cut us to pieces. Bastard was just waiting for us to be close enough together to get us at the same time," Mercer snarled.

He hooked his hand into her waistband and hauled her up. "Run. Now. The other end of the hallway. We'll go out the window . . ."

Zoe tripped over her discarded shoes. She slammed into the floor, her knees taking the brunt of the fall. Pain spiked through her as she gathered up the footwear while trying to go where Mercer wanted her. She was an awkward mess while he ran for his life with precision.

"Go now! The bastard's got a heat scope."

Mercer shoved her through the doorway as more bullets buzzed through the air, going through the space she and Mercer had just vacated.

Time slowed down. She must have been in shock because she was aware of every inch of ground they covered. She noticed details as if she had time to study them, the way her knee bent as she lifted her foot from the floor and straightened when she transferred her weight.

"Goddamn it, Zoe . . . run!"

"I am running!"

Mercer pushed her ahead of him, the bedroom door showing several new holes as they ran into it. He must have turned the doorknob because she was still hugging her shoes against her chest. They tumbled into the room, Mercer shoving her down before he grabbed a chair and swung it at the window.

The glass shattered and this time she didn't find the sound pleasant. It was jarring, feeding the horror rising inside her. Her hands shook as she tried to push her feet into her shoes. One went on fine but she stopped before tying the laces on the second one. The street lamp shone in, the light glistening off her pant leg.

"It looks clear . . . we have to make a break for it."

"Huh?" Zoe looked up, her fingers still holding the laces of her shoe. Even in the dark she could see Mercer scowling at her.

"We have to make a break for it, Zoe. That shot was aimed at you, I saw it this time." But his attention lowered to her leg. Unlike her, he didn't hesitate but reached right out and touched the wet material.

"Shit." He closed his hand over her calf. "It's just a graze."

"Good."

It wasn't good but she was still caught in the grip of shock. She tried to tie her shoe and ended up with a huge knot, her hands refusing to perform the simple task. She stared at the mess, trying to figure out how she'd bungled the job. Bright light illuminated the area around her face. Mercer held out a lighter and calmly set the flame against the curtain.

"What are you doing?"

Fire began licking its way up the length of fabric, the scent of burning material tickling her nose.

"Making his heat scope a little less reliable." Mercer grasped her chin and raised her face so her attention was on him. "Listen to me, Zoe, it's do-or-die time."

His voice was steady and she leaned toward him, needing the security he embodied.

"We're going over the windowsill, out onto the garage roof, and then we're going to drop down onto the driveway."

"What—" Her mouth was suddenly bone-dry. She swallowed. "What about your backup?"

"Since they haven't gotten a single shot off, we have to assume they're down."

The grimness of his voice sent a shiver down her spine. His fingers tightened around the side of her jaw momentarily, the light from the spreading fire allowing her to glimpse his expression. He was every bit as focused as he'd been earlier that day, but the chill was missing from his eyes.

"We're going to get on my bike and make a run for it. If

something happens to me, go to the police, don't tell them anything, and call your dad the second you can. Got that?"

"Yeah."

Dark smoke was beginning to swirl around the ceiling, creeping closer to where they huddled. The entire valence was ablaze, bits of smoldering ash floating down onto them. The paint bubbled as it gave off a burning-plastic smell.

"We're going, before he repositions."

Mercer started toward the window. Fear flooded her, the silence intolerable. She dug her fingers into his waistband, pulling him back.

"What if there's another one on this side of the house?"

"We'd be dead. Drywall and wood don't stop a heat scope. The guy is repositioning. This is our only chance."

"We could call the cops . . ."

"And they'd have a great double homicide to investigate by the time they showed up." Mercer reached down and wrapped his hand around her forearm. "We have to help ourselves, baby. Trust me."

He went over the windowsill first. The moment she was alone in the house, terror filled her. Every tiny sound heightened the emotion. Mercer reached back for her and his hand was the most welcome sight she'd ever seen. There was no contemplation of running from him, only pure response.

Zoe placed her hand in his and pushed her body through the open window. The stone tiles covering the roof crunched beneath her shoes. They made it to the edge and she sucked in a harsh breath as she looked down. The house had never seemed so tall when she was looking up.

Mercer made the jump with a sure motion. He didn't

stand all the way up but remained crouched while scanning the surroundings. His confidence both drew her toward him and made her think of running back into her house. Indecision pulled her in both directions.

Did she trust the man she'd allowed to be her lover, or hope the local law enforcement might keep her alive?

Her leg burned, reminding her how close she'd already come to becoming a morning news flash. The fire was glowing red and she felt the heat searing her back.

Mercer looked up and waved her down. Fear tingled along her limbs but she did her best to mimic his jump. Pain ripped through her leg the moment she landed. She stumbled and ended up on her butt, trying to suck in enough air to keep from passing out.

"We've got to keep moving."

Mercer pulled her up and she brushed her hair out of her face to see his bike.

He swung his leg over the back of it with ease and fit the key into the ignition.

"Trust me or die, Zoe."

There was a hard certainty in his tone that sent her forward. She was torn, the idea of needing him now battling against the fresh betrayal of knowing he'd seduced her to get at her family. But she slid onto the bike behind him and wrapped her arms around him because there wasn't really a choice. Sniper or him, those were her options. Life majorly sucked.

He took off down the street the moment she was secure. In the early-morning hours, the city was quiet, almost eerily so. The wind whipped her hair about and chilled her cheeks. A fire engine had its siren on somewhere nearby as they left her neighborhood.

But what truly turned her blood cold was the way no one followed them. Greer and the other team members were nowhere to be seen.

Mercer pulled up two blocks from her house. "Put the helmet on so we don't get pulled over."

He reached behind her and pulled two helmets off the back of the bike. The flashing lights of the emergency vehicle rounded the corner before it turned again and headed toward her dad's house.

"Aren't you going to call your boss?"

"Cell phones have location chips in them. I left mine behind," he muttered before lowering the visor. "Now that the fire department is here to rescue your dad's bird, I know a place we can go to fall off the grid. Hang on."

Her arms tightened around him out of instinct, which was a damn good thing because she was frozen with shock.

He cared about Harley?

Hell. That put a hole in her ideas about him being nothing but an asshole.

A big hole.

Mercer pulled the bike up to a residence that looked like a biker hideout. She could see a dark-colored house but only the top of the windows because the bushes were so tall. There wasn't a single welcoming thing about it. If the cops showed up with their sirens blaring and hauled some muscle-bound guy sporting multiple tattoos out of it, she wouldn't be surprised.

Mercer drove around the side and stopped. He reached over and pressed his thumb against something hidden behind a couple of inches of nondescript shrubbery. A moment later the garage door opened, but not upward. The thing slid sideways, only a quarter of the way.

Mercer guided the bike inside. He was going on memory, had to be because there wasn't any light and what lay inside the building was a dark mystery. She clung to him, his body the only solid thing in the world at that moment. The door slid shut behind them.

The lights came on the second the door was closed.

"You better have a good reason to be getting me out of a warm bed at four in the morning."

The man was wearing only a pair of worn jeans, which showed off the perfection of his chest. Every muscle was toned and sculpted. His hair was shoulder-length and light blond. He peered at her with blue eyes, sweeping her from top to bottom and lingering on her calf.

"She might be a good reason, depending on why you've got her." He looked back at Mercer. "Might also be a good reason to kick you off my property. I don't need heat coming down on me."

"She's a good enough reason for me, and there will be heat," Mercer said. He removed his helmet but didn't get off the bike. When Zoe began to lift her foot he reached back and flattened his hand against her thigh. She could feel the two men taking stock of each other, Mercer remaining on the bike while their reluctant host eyed her. With a grunt he nodded.

"Stay. I'll get the medical kit for your passenger." The man disappeared into the dark shadows of the garage.

"Who is this guy?"

"A buddy I can trust." Mercer didn't sound as certain as she would have liked but she got off the bike and gasped when pain went zipping up her leg the moment she tried to use it.

Mercer was on a knee next to her before she finished catching her breath. "Sit." The word was short. Zoe obeyed without considering why she was letting him boss her around. Maybe it was the fact that she could smell her own blood, and he sounded like he knew what to do about it.

Of course, such a skill must be handy when he carried a gun around.

There was a flash of light off the blade of a pocketknife. Mercer wielded it expertly, flicking it out and slipping the tip of it beneath the ribbed cuff of her pants. A quick jerk of his wrist cut the fabric and he kept going until he reached her knee.

"It looks like we're both members of the 'lucky' club today."

Their host returned, a sort of beat-up-looking tackle box in one hand. "Glad to hear she isn't going to bleed all over my garage and leave me with the chore of disposing of her carcass. It's a little harder to buy bags of lye in this state. Not enough farms."

Zoe gasped, unable to contain her horror.

"Relax, Zoe. If Vitus were serious, he'd have told me it was my job to haul away your body," Mercer said ruefully.

"Seems fair enough. You showed up with her."

Vitus dropped the box near Mercer and hooked his hands back into his waistband. He'd shrugged into a shirt but hadn't bothered to button it.

"I thought you were working a case."

Mercer opened the box and lifted the top tray so it exposed all the ones beneath it. He searched out what he wanted before answering.

"She was my target," Mercer answered.

Zoe narrowed her eyes. "Only because you're stupid enough to doubt my family."

There was a soft snort from their host. "You pulled a real gem, Mercer. Almost makes me sorry I wasn't available. I enjoy feisty women."

Mercer smeared something that stung like hell over the open gash in her skin. She dug her hands into the padded chair seat.

"A little warning would be nice," she groused while a wave of pain sent her vision black for a few seconds. When she could see clearly once more, she found herself being studied by Vitus. The blue of his eyes reminded her of Saxon but the long hair seemed in direct conflict to the team leader's clean-cut look. Still, the resemblance was uncanny. It was in the shape of his jaw and cheekbones, too.

"Are you related to Saxon?" she asked out of impulse. She felt the need to prove she wasn't so intimidated she wouldn't voice what was on her mind. And that she wasn't slow on the uptake.

"Half brother. Which means I didn't inherit the stick up my ass."

She smiled, unable to help herself. Mercer began binding her leg, which sent another dull shaft of agony through her.

"Saxon has the right goal, even if he sometimes has to dig a little to get at the truth."

Suspicion still coated Mercer's words. Zoe looked down at him to find his dark eyes focused on her. Conflict flickered in those dark orbs, and she discovered a similar feeling twisting her gut.

Maybe tonight was a clever ploy to regain her trust.

She shivered, her emotions too tender to deal with the idea.

"She looks a little shocky. Better bring her into the house," Vitus muttered casually, as if they weren't talking about a gunshot wound.

Mercer offered her a hand. Zoe looked at it suspiciously before placing hers in it. Maybe he was just trying to worm his way back into her confidence. If that was so, she needed to learn to play the game better than he did. Her family honor was on the line.

Vitus led them through a darkened section of the garage, but it didn't smell musty. The garage was clean, every corner and shelf. There was an entire wall of tools, Peg-Board running up the wall, and every single item was in order and shiny, a contrast with the exterior of the house.

They walked through the backyard and up to a single door that led into the house. Every window was covered by dark curtains, making the place look as inviting as a tomb.

Inside was a different matter.

The scent of coffee lingered in the kitchen, a pot of dark java resting inside a coffeemaker. No white plastic model appliance for Vitus; this one was stainless steel. The countertops were granite, and there wasn't a speck of grease or a crumb in sight, only a ceramic mug.

"You know your way around, Mercer. Tuck her into bed and come see me."

Zoe frowned. "You have some things in common with your brother."

Vitus turned to consider her. "Yeah, I like staying alive." His attention lowered to her newly bandaged leg. "Something you seem to have a little challenge with at the moment." He winked at her. "Don't worry, darlin', you've come to the right man."

Mercer slid an arm around her waist, moving her forward while his buddy offered her a grin that was sexy as hell.

"She came in with me."

Vitus shrugged. "I can handle sharing." His lips thinned, taking on a sexual look that made her mouth go dry. "I wonder if she can."

"Don't," Mercer snapped.

Vitus grinned, looking completely unrepentant. If anything, the man appeared to be offering her a dare. Mercer steered her away and through an open bedroom door.

"He's testing you. Trying to see how well you deal with stress."

"Lovely," she muttered, trying to decide why Mercer was so full of informative comments all of a sudden. Suspicion wrapped around her like a blanket while she watched him take care of her personal comfort.

Mercer pulled a drawer open and rummaged around for a moment before pulling out a pair of sweatpants. "It looked to me like you were mesmerized by the idea of a ménage à trois."

She grabbed the pants from him. "And you sound kind of jealous for someone who keeps calling me a target."

She went into a small bathroom and shut the door on him. When she emerged with the sweatpants on, Mercer was leaning against the iron footrail of the double bed that dominated the room.

"Someone's got you marked as a target, Zoe. I'm your best bet for avoiding the toe tags they've got picked out for us."

"You inserted yourself into this, so don't think I'm going to feel sorry for you."

He shrugged. "I guess if you'd rather be dead and headed for a cold-case file because the local cops have no clue why someone would want to shut you up, fine by me. Go ahead and keep nursing that injured pride because I got into your bed." He pegged her with a hard stare. "It wasn't one-sided, baby. Not even close."

He was smug.

But right.

She leaned against the wall. "I appreciate your help tonight." She had to force each word out. Acceptance flickered in his eyes briefly.

"There're some painkillers on the bedside table." A glass of water was waiting for her, too.

"You're the one who keeps calling me a target. How the hell do you expect that to make me feel?" She crossed in front of him, hating how much effort it took.

His hand snaked out and captured her wrist. "Maybe I'm having trouble deciding which side you're on, Zoe. Are you really so clean, or has your father taught you more than your innocent eyes tell me?"

He bent her arm at just the right angle to keep her close.

Too close for her comfort, because it allowed her to feel his warmth. His scent teased her senses, unleashing a need to lean on him, actually reach up and kiss him. Part of her really wanted to take shelter in his embrace, just for a bit anyway.

"Damn it, Zoe." He turned her around and gave her a push that landed her on her butt on the bed. It bounced slightly but didn't give so much as a faint creak. "We're in deep now."

"*We're*? When did this become a *we* thing?" She slapped his hand away from her. "I thought you just introduced me as your target. Why don't you go call your boss and let him know where I am? You can ride off scot-free the moment you do that."

"I should."

Two little words had never impacted her so harshly before.

Fool.

"Well, fine by me," she snapped.

She wanted to hurt him or at least insult him. But there was a flicker of heat in his eyes that stopped her from continuing. She recognized that flame. It wasn't something she might explain her way around, either. It touched her, deep down inside where instinct ruled. Arousal flared up in all the spots he'd made tingle so intensely.

She was a damn fool, all right.

"That part of the operation is over." There was a hard certainty in his voice.

"Oh, great. Thanks for sharing that bit with me."

He leaned over and hooked her around the waist with one solid arm. With a quick motion he had her secured against his body, not even a millimeter between them to help her maintain any level of composure. Her senses went into overdrive, soaking up every delightful sensation.

"You're welcome, Zoe." He cupped her nape, not even granting her the freedom to turn away. She wanted to. The need to hide was strong.

But there was something else, too, enjoyment of his strength and the demand his imprisoning embrace conveyed. His confidence offered shelter from the fear of the unknown.

"And since we're past the business stage of this relation-ship, I'd like to enter into the next stage with very clear intentions."

"I don't—"

His mouth cut her off, sealing her protest beneath a kiss that was as demanding as his embrace promised. She withered, unable to remain still. Pleasure ripped into her, shredding every reason she had to ignore how much she enjoyed his lips sliding across hers.

It was too pleasurable for rational thought . . .

She made a soft sound of protest, one she didn't fully understand, but it gained her no mercy. Instead his lips pressed hers to open, his tongue teasing her lower lip and sending enough delight across her nerve endings to draw a gasp from her.

Mercer took instant advantage, thrusting his tongue deep. She shivered, her passage heating and begging for a hard thrust, too. It was so deeply sexual, so intense, she gripped his jacket lapels, wanting him closer. There was too much sensation filling her to remain still and her hun-ger became consuming. She kissed him back, meeting his demand with high expectation. For a moment the kiss flared hot enough to be called a firestorm, their mouths moving in perfect rhythm.

"I'm here to stay, baby. Get used to me."

Mercer captured a wrist and pulled her arm straight down. She heard a tiny click and felt the cold kiss of metal against her skin.

"Are you serious?"

Her thoughts were still muddled with arousal. She didn't want to think about anything beyond the need twisting in-side her. But the guy had handcuffed her.

Mercer surveyed her with a determined glint in his eyes. "I'm making sure you don't do something stupid while I'm talking to Vitus."

She looked down and stared at the set of handcuffs binding her to the iron headboard. The elegant swirls of leaves suddenly lost their serenity as she recognized just how solid it was.

"I'll be back," he muttered on the way to the door.

"Stay gone, I don't need you back to mess with me. Just leave the key," she insisted.

He turned around in a motion that instantly reminded her of how deadly he might be. For some reason she kept forgetting.

Like while he was kissing her . . .

"Where are you going to go, Zoe?" He came back toward her, stopping close enough for her to touch him. She wasn't sure if his aim was to intimidate her or challenge her. In any case, she wasn't taking it. She shot him a hard look, making it clear she wasn't backing down. Mercer didn't care for it. He braced his hands on the footrail of the bed.

"Who do you trust now, if not me? I don't need you sliding out the window because you get some notion into your head that the police are somehow your friends. Saxon's superior signed the order for us to move in on you. Remember that before you go thinking any branch of law enforcement is going to be interested in helping you clear your name."

"That sounds like a bunch of bullshit designed to keep me clinging to you like a lost kitten." She wasn't helping herself get free by asking, but there was something about his boldness that demanded she stand up to him with the same brass-balls attitude. "Regular cops aren't as insane as you and Saxon. They actually recognize a civilian when they see one. One call to my dad and I will be fine."

His eyes flashed with warning.

"The information is moving through your computers. If the local cops dig up that trail, they might decide to charge you."

"That's bullshit!"

"Is it?" His voice turned deadly calm. "If the guilty party disappears into the night, leaving your computer with evidence on it, what's to stop them from deciding you're guilty? We've got nothing on Tim and everything on you. If you and I were dead on that hallway floor, the report would have my name listed as your partner. Why do you think the bullets started flying the moment we were together?"

He might be right.

She hated him for it but . . . he might be right.

"What have you got then, Zoe?" he said, digging into her while she was undecided.

Zoe shut her mouth, desperately trying to think of a logical argument. She was trapped, a noose tightening around her neck. He had her. That was the long and short of it.

Mercer nodded. "You're pissed but you're not stupid. That's something I like about you, Zoe. Feeling emotion for you stirring inside me isn't something I like. You were my target and I won't apologize for how we met. It was my duty."

"So take these things off me and let me take care of myself. Go back to your team and wait for the next set of orders that include whoring yourself out for the good of the team."

He surprised her by grinning. "You care about me, too."

"Not that . . . deeply." It was the best denial she could manage without flat-out lying. It did bug her that he'd wormed his way into her bed on assignment, and the idea of him going to another target turned her stomach. "Should I trust you? I mean, really?" She detested how wounded she sounded. Where was her temper when she needed it?

He shrugged, leaning against the bedroom door instead of opening it. "Why don't you think about that while I'm gone. But I'll tell you this, Zoe: Your chances of beating this thing without me are pretty low."

"Words like that lose their charm when coming on the heels of you handcuffing me."

He grinned again, too damn smug for her taste. "Like I said, Zoe, your chances are better with me because I know how to play dirty, and the man responsible for selling intel is definitely playing for keeps. Go against him without me and you'll earn that toe tag he wants to tie on you. He's left enough of a trail on your email accounts to get the powers that be to believe you're the guilty party—and if you're dead, there won't be any argument. That's his plan. Don't doubt it."

His lips pressed into a hard line, all traces of amusement fading from his eyes. "I enjoyed being in your bed, Zoe, and it goes deeper than the mission plan."

He turned and pulled the door open while she was stunned into silence. She ended up staring at the closed door, still trying to think of a good retort. Sitting on the bed was the best she could do. The pain pills drew a suspicious look from her while she battled to decide what she wanted to believe.

Was Mercer someone she should trust? Or should she suspect Saxon of planning the sniper attack? One thing she'd noticed was that Saxon and his team were all deadly serious when it came to carrying out their mission.

Shooting at them wouldn't be too far a stretch. Not if it drove her back into Mercer's arms. Cultivated trust between them.

But that left her handcuffed and at the mercy of a man she didn't know.

Shit.

"Where is the Magnus girl?" Tyler asked the second Saxon picked up the phone.

Saxon was used to his superior's direct attitude when it came to calls. No greeting, just cut to the point. "Running from the bad guys."

"I need her brought in." Tyler laid down his order. "Immediately. I want that hard drive decoded. Use any means necessary to get her cooperation."

The line went dead.

It was a coldhearted order. One Saxon wasn't unfamiliar with receiving. The game they were playing paid out in blood. So a lot of the time the only way to win was by spilling blood on the other side. Nothing was amiss or abnormal, and yet he leaned back in his chair trying to decide what was bugging him.

Tyler Martin had been his superior for years. Questioning the man went against the grain. But it was still there, chewing on his insides, combining with the scar that was left from the way Tyler had handled his brother Vitus.

That was a wound that still leaked resentment, as well as causing misgivings about Tyler's command style. Maybe that was all it was. A specter rising up from a situation Saxon felt was handled unfairly. If so, he'd have to get over it.

Life wasn't fair.

CHAPTER FOUR

"Do you know what you're doing?"

Vitus was leaning against the kitchen counter, his fingers wrapped around a mug of coffee. He still hadn't buttoned up his shirt, and his hair was only tucked partially behind his ears. He looked lazy, but anyone who knew the man understood the deadly power hidden beneath the blasé exterior. His hair was growing out, sort of a calendar, marking the amount of time he'd been off special assignment.

Mercer didn't care for how much he noticed that detail or how great an impact it made. Vitus had been one of the best and he'd been taken down for nothing more than one man's pride. Or maybe one woman's. It was still unclear whether it had been Congressman Jeb Ryland or his daughter Damascus who had wanted vengeance when their relationship soured. Frankly, Mercer didn't give a shit. Stripping a man like Vitus of his shield over a roll in the hay was low. Plenty of special assignments included them. Living on the edge drove people together in a quest to keep in touch with life.

A fact that also just might be influencing his own thinking, but he honestly didn't give a crap. He was sticking close to Zoe and that was the end of the discussion.

Mercer walked over to the coffeemaker and poured himself a measure before turning to face his buddy. "Tell me again, Vitus, why is it you haven't signed back on with Saxon?"

His words were slow and measured but they hit their mark perfectly.

"Because I don't like anyone telling me to ignore my gut instinct, especially when I'm right. It paid off. My target would have been dead without my action." Vitus glared at him over the rim of his coffee mug before answering.

Mercer tilted his head. "Exactly. I'm feeling the same way right now. My gut says she's a mule; the evidence, on the other hand, is cloudy."

"Which brought you to my door."

Mercer stared his buddy straight in the eye. "If you want me gone, say so."

"Or I could call my baby brother and turn you in before you screw up your performance record. I listened to my gut and lost my shield over it. Maybe I should prove I've learned my lesson."

Mercer growled. "Don't disappoint me, Vitus. You're an asshole most of the time but I can't rightfully accuse you of being a dick. Which is why I call you a friend. I'd hate to be proven wrong on that count; friends are hard to come by. Besides, I'll take losing my shield over her blood on my hands."

Vitus offered him a soft grunt. Mercer watched the man take a few more sips of coffee while he contemplated the situation. It was time for Mercer to think things through himself.

His neck was on the line, or it would be if he didn't call in soon.

"You're welcome to stay but my baby brother might remember you call me a friend."

"I know."

Vitus raised an eyebrow. "Sounds like you're counting on that."

Mercer nodded. "Best place for me to call in from is your house. It will make falling off the grid a lot easier. Besides, when it comes to walking away clean, you're the master."

"Yeah, well, the skill comes in handy from time to time." There was still a trace of bitterness in Vitus's tone. A ghost left behind that was slowly eating away at one of the best agents Mercer knew. Jeb Ryland and his daughter could choke on their petty revenge. Vitus was a man without a cause now, and Damascus Ryland would be dead if it hadn't been for him.

"If you decide to drop off the grid, make sure you have a good reason, buddy." Vitus gave him a hard look. "Make sure she's worth it. From where I'm standing, you don't look completely sure about what you believe."

He rocked back on his heels for a moment. "You're right; I'm still on the fence," Mercer admitted. "But my gut tells me she's innocent. I'm sure about one thing—I'm not willing to live with her blood on the pavement when I know I could do something to prevent it. This case stinks of bad brass."

Vitus raised an eyebrow and took another sip from his coffee as he contemplated Mercer's words.

Then he tossed a cordless phone to him. "As I said, be

very sure, buddy, because that feeling might be the only thing you're left with once it all washes out. That package you rolled in with didn't look like she was sure about you. That's something I'd advise you to think about. It's hell losing your position and then having the girl leave you, too."

Vitus left the kitchen, his feet making only a faint sound before Mercer couldn't hear him at all.

Zoe didn't trust him.

It was the fact that it bothered him that kept him sipping coffee instead of dialing Saxon.

He wouldn't care about anyone who was a traitor.

That thought was solid and firmly rooted in his gut. Going after Zoe hadn't bothered him, but too many facts weren't adding up. He set the mug down and picked up the phone.

"It's about time you called in," Saxon growled.

"I've been busy avoiding snipers. What the hell happened to my surveillance team?"

Mercer heard Saxon mumble something under his breath. "A couple of the new kids had relieved Greer. They never saw the shots that took them out."

Mercer felt the harsh reality bite into him. "He was aiming for Zoe this time. I'm certain of it."

"It could just as well be a very clever ploy to make you sympathetic."

Mercer was quiet for a moment, trying to listen to the wisdom in Saxon's words.

"My gut tells me otherwise."

"Don't listen to Vitus, Mercer. He made the mistake of falling for his target and she left him after he scrapped his career to cover her ass. The coldhearted bitch walked away clear without so much as a fucking Christmas card for what it cost him. Which was his shield, in case you've forgotten."

There was raw fury in Saxon's voice. It was by far the most emotion Mercer had ever heard him express about his half brother, not that he would have expected anything less.

"Don't make the same mistake. Bring your target in and let the team perform its job. Tyler wants her here, to decode the hard drive. That has always been the mission. Stay focused," Saxon urged.

It was the sensible thing to do. The one that would polish his record, maybe even earn him a commendation. Saxon was calling Zoe a target to help desensitize him, but it wasn't erasing the feeling burning in his gut.

He didn't want to be separated from her.

"I know what I saw. That sniper wanted her dead. She's a mule and one who's been classified a liability. They will do anything to silence her, and maybe your boss will feel bad after it's all mopped up, but that won't change the fact that she's dead. I need to keep her hidden."

Zoe wouldn't be the first mule caught in the cross fire, either.

"Mercer, you're one of the best, don't chuck it out the window for a woman you've known less than a week. She's getting to you because these guys know how to choose their mules. Bring her in so we can set up her accomplices."

"I can't do it. Someone's dirty and I'm not coming back in until they're neutralized. You can't ensure safety for her. Whoever is running this show has top clearance."

"Listen to me, Mercer," Saxon insisted, "Tyler isn't going to budge on this one. He thinks your brains have sunk into your cock. He'll make me issue a dead-or-alive order if you don't bring her in. He's my superior, nothing I say is going to protect you."

Mercer felt the feeling intensify. A protective urge enveloped him, filling him with resistance to everything Saxon was trying to get out of him.

"That only makes me more determined to keep Zoe out of his hands. Tyler's got a hard-on for this that isn't normal. I was under fire and called in within three hours. Why is he so hopped up?"

"Is there something wrong with your hearing?" Saxon growled into the receiver. "Dead or alive, and you know it's a hell of a lot easier to bring you in dead. Tyler is only as committed to the operation as he was when he set us on her to begin with. Don't let the trip to her bed blind you to what began this."

"Yeah, I know the logic. But I also know bringing Zoe in is exactly what the traitor wants. That sniper was aiming for Zoe and me. He didn't want to take a chance on either of us walking away. Once, I could write off, not twice. He could have dropped her or me fifty times over but he waited until we were both in the line of fire. They sure didn't need to cap my backup to get to her. Something's off. The intel that's moving is classified. That smells like bad brass is involved somewhere. You need to watch your six."

Saxon was quiet, the line still open. "You raise a good point, Mercer. Let me see what I can find out. Stay off the grid until I contact you. I'll tell Tyler it was my call to send you bugging out."

His superior's tone was grudging to say the least, but beggars couldn't be choosers, Mercer decided.

"I need one more thing . . ." Mercer said.

"What?"

Mercer felt his mood lighten just a fraction. "Take care of Harley, in case her father's clean. I'd hate to piss off a full-bird coronel."

"Son of a bitch," Saxon cursed. "The fire department took him to animal control. I'm not a bird-sitter."

"So tell Thais to get in touch with her feminine side. I hear macaws are like kittens with feathers."

There was a snort on the other end of the phone. "I just might do that and tell her it was your suggestion."

Mercer chuckled as the line went dead, the holes in his jacket keeping the grin on his face for a few more seconds. But reality returned and killed his enjoyment. His gut told him Zoe wasn't dirty, but she didn't trust him. Which classified him as a fool for going out on a limb for her.

Still, he knew a fact when it was staring him in the face. That sniper had wanted them both. They were both wearing targets now.

He wasn't entirely sure what he was going to say to her to sway her opinion, either. Only that he wasn't willing to walk away. It might leave him as bitter as Vitus but hell, ending up with a scarred heart was the least of his worries with a sniper on his tail. The only luck he'd had so far was that the guy had lousy judgment when it came to timing.

It wasn't the first time Lady Luck had kept him alive. He drained his coffee mug and squared his shoulders.

Zoe wasn't going to like it, but she was stuck with him. They'd end up dead together or vindicated.

At the moment, the odds were stacked against them.

"So . . . you've decided to start torturing me?"

"Ha-ha," Mercer responded from where he was adjusting a wig with the help of the bathroom mirror. Shoulder-length, the strands were black. "This isn't my idea of fun, either, sweet cakes."

She snorted at him. "Actually, you look like you're having a grand time."

"Don't mistake confidence for enjoyment, Zoe. I'm just doing the job right, because there won't be a second chance."

She hated the way her muscles tightened in response. It was instantaneous. Pure reaction to the sharpness of his tone and the glint in his eyes. Mercer turned to look at his appearance again. He eyed the fake tattoos adorning his arms with a critical eye. A sleeveless muscle shirt allowed her to see every inch of brawn, and she turned back to her disguise to hide her blush.

I can't trust him . . .

Yeah, well that little tidbit didn't seem to be interfering with her responses to him.

"It's not that bad."

Zoe jerked her attention away from the dress to discover Mercer standing only two paces from her. Her cheeks burned brighter as she realized she'd been lost in her thoughts.

"It's indecent," she muttered while pulling the dress over her head and down her body. Made of a soft jersey, it had a plunging neckline and was small enough to hug every curve she had.

"Exactly." His tone had a touch of heat in it that sent a tingle down her body. His eyes swept over her from head to toe and his lips curved with approval. She shouldn't have felt complimented, it was way misplaced under the circumstances, but hell, the guy liked what he saw and there was no missing it.

"You need more eyeliner but the wig looks splotchy enough," he decided.

"I look like a streetwalker," she groused. On her head was a wig sporting patches of dark red dye. Coupled with the too-tight dress, the better part of her breasts on display, and the spike heels on her feet, she looked cheap.

Trashy is more like it . . .

"Vitus is arranging our transportation but he's going to dump us off in a questionable part of town. We need to fit in."

There was a rap on the bedroom door. Mercer pulled it open to reveal Vitus. Saxon's brother had undergone a transformation, too. His long hair was missing, buzzed away.

"Didn't see that coming," Mercer said.

Vitus shrugged. "Seems I'm back in the biz." The long hair had hidden something about him. Something polished and respectable. The baggy clothing was history, too, a pair of jeans and tucked-in shirt replacing it.

"You clean up nice," she said.

She ended up drawing the attention of those blue eyes. Vitus considered her for a moment from behind an unreadable expression. "Don't get my buddy killed. I'd take that personally."

A chill touched her nape. The guy meant every syllable. "I'll do my best. Can I have a gun?"

Vitus grunted, the sound making it clear he lacked anything even close to confidence in her ability to add anything of value to the team.

So what am I going to do?

That was a damn good question. One she really needed to get busy pondering. Deciding she didn't trust Mercer was all fine and dandy but until she had a solid plan, she'd be pretty stupid to leave him.

Disjointed scenes from the night before flashed through her mind. There was no overlooking the very real nature of those gunshots. Mercer might be carrying one of his own but that could come in handy considering her circumstances.

"What are you thinking, Zoe?"

She jumped, then looked away when Mercer tried to lock gazes with her. "Nothing."

He caught her chin. "Like hell. I can see the wheels turning in that head of yours."

Zoe stepped back, pulling away from him. "Just . . . about last night."

"Good," Vitus said. "Might remind you not to do anything stupid." He jerked his head toward the hallway. "Like handling a gun and trying to protect yourself."

Zoe offered him a get-real look. "My dad taught me how to handle a firearm."

Vitus shot her a look that said he was less than impressed. "Mercer's assignment. His call." He jerked his head toward the front door.

Zoe followed him out of a lack of alternatives. Mercer came behind her, making her feel small in the compressed space. This time, it wasn't just a matter of physical superiority. She felt like she didn't understand how to play the game. Not the way the two men did.

Her brother's phone call came to mind.

It felt like someone had smacked her with a two-by-four. Bram might be the king of tight-lipped-ness when it came to classified matters but he'd still reached out to warn her. She just hadn't realized it.

Okay, so just what was she going to do now?

The answer was to crawl into the back of a beat-up sedan. One fender was a different faded paint than the rest
of the car. There was duct tape holding the driver's seat
headrest together and the backseat groaned when she
sat down, the springs clearly ancient. The scent of time
and past take-out meals clung to the interior. But the engine purred like a kitten.

That figured.

Everything in Mercer's world was disguised. On the
surface, the car was a clunker. Under the hood, it was a
powerful beast. She should have looked at the tires. Bet
they were in good repair. She needed to adjust her thinking. Learn to look for the pertinent information. Yeah,
maybe if she had done that a little sooner, Mercer wouldn't
have sideswiped her so completely.

Or easily.

Vitus pulled into traffic and headed into the heart of
downtown Los Angeles. The lanes were narrow, the over-
passes sporting artistry from the 1940s that modern construction lacked. They joined the hordes of people making
the morning commute. Trucks in every shape and size
mixed in with high-end sedans and sleek sports cars. Driv-
ers defied the hands-free law and held their cell phones
while piloting their vehicles with one hand as the traffic
crept along at thirty miles an hour.

"Your next ride is in an hour. You'll need it to cross the
inner-city blocks and make it up to the other side of the
Staples Center." Vitus pulled off the interstate and punched
the radio on at the same time. A blare of rap music spilled
out of the dented speakers.

"Are you laying out the torture now?" she asked.

Vitus flashed her a peace sign as he slouched in his seat and worked his head in time with the beat. "Got to set the scene."

At some point he'd pulled on a jersey hoodie cap that had dreadlocks dangling from it. He steered his way around double-parked delivery trucks and avoided pedestrians before sliding up to a curb. Pigeons scattered when Mercer pushed his door open and yanked hers. She stepped over garbage and made it to the sidewalk while trying to tug her hem down to mid-thigh.

"Leave it." Mercer looped an arm across her shoulders and guided her into the flow of pedestrian traffic. "And try to look like you like me."

Slipping her hand around his waist seemed like mission impossible. She reached up with her left hand and clasped his fingers where they were cupping her shoulder. Two cops passed them on bicycles. Zoe found herself staring at them.

"Tempted?"

She bit her lip but Mercer squeezed her fingers. "Maybe." Her admission hung between them.

"Going to tell me the plan?" She wasn't exactly sure why she asked.

"Getting off grid isn't easy in a society with so many cameras. We need to double back and loop around a few times to confuse anyone trying to follow us."

He guided her into a shop and into a dressing room. A few minutes later she emerged in a skirt-and-blouse combo, wig, and false pregnancy belly. Mercer headed out of the shop, leaving her to follow behind him.

She slowed down as she passed a pay phone.

Tempting.

And yet she still didn't have any sort of plan. At least Saxon had agreed to let her try to clear her family name. Escape might be alluring but she really needed a place to go. At the moment, she had no home.

She passed the phone, feeling trapped by circumstance.

"Keep walking. Greer is waiting on the other side of the intersection."

Mercer turned at the next light, crossing the street away from her. She waited for the light to change and followed. When she stepped up onto the pavement again, there was no sign of Mercer's fellow agent. She trudged on, sweating under the layers of clothing and padding. A homeless man tugging a granny cart was shuffling along in front of her. Wearing multiple layers of dirty clothing, he was talking to himself. Zoe went around him.

"Waddle a little, you're pregnant."

She jumped when Greer's voice hit her. A moment later, the rambling began again. All around her, the city was moving. It felt surreal and yet her heart was racing. She fought the urge to look around, trying to spot . . . well . . . something.

All she ended up doing was admitting how little she knew about shadow games. The admission left her feeling exposed, like a sitting duck. Okay, duckling. One that didn't know how to identify the dangers around her.

A cab slid up to the curb in front of her as she waited to cross the next street.

"Get in," Greer muttered behind her.

She lifted the handle and slid into the front seat. Mercer pulled the car around the corner, heading back down the way she'd just walked.

The hours passed by in a haze of wigs, clothing changes,

and vehicles. By the time she ended up in a car that headed onto an interstate, she was mentally whipped.

"Hopefully that will keep anyone tailing us off our asses," Mercer said at last.

He meant it as good news. The only problem was, it left her relying on him.

Mercer drove out of the city and up into the mountains. They changed cars twice before leaving civilization behind. The twinkling lights of the city were the only reminder that there were any other souls on earth. The road became winding, the sun set, and Mercer kept going. At least the last car came with an ice chest. Zoe happily dug out sandwiches and chips. She peeled back the wrapping and handed one over to Mercer.

"I could take a turn driving," she suggested out of a desire to be congenial.

He took the sandwich and shook his head. It was an immediate response and one that drove home his lack of trust in her.

It shouldn't have stung.

She focused on the tingle of suspicion teasing her nape while she chewed on the sandwich. Time passed, her belly satisfied but her mind full.

"Home, sweet home," Mercer announced at last. He pulled off the road and onto a small access road that might be called a driveway. But only if one was being generous. It wasn't well maintained. The trees lining it had branches that stuck out into the road. Mercer had to slow down as they brushed against the sides of the car.

"Don't look so worried, Zoe. We're not roughing it completely."

"I'm pretty sure even if a five-star lodge appears in front of us, I'm still going to be worried. Life's been a tad complicated since you showed up."

He chuckled beside her, his attention still on the road. "Nice to know you need me, baby."

"Don't call me that." The words were out of her mouth before she thought about what she was going to say. She bit her lip because she didn't like him knowing he'd struck a tender chord. She had precious few things left to her at that moment and felt like she needed to defend herself.

Mercer cut her a glance, one that set her heart beating faster. There was a promise brewing in his gaze. "I'm sticking my neck out for you, Zoe."

He sounded sincere and she hated it.

"Yeah? Well, maybe you and your team are just setting me up again. Maybe that whole sniper attack was just a clever way of driving me back into trusting you again because you came so gallantly to my rescue."

He surprised her by flashing her a grin. "Not bad, Zoe. Even Saxon would appreciate that angle of thinking."

"Because it's ice-cold?" she asked.

Mercer nodded and turned the car onto another narrow access road that she would never have seen in the dark.

"Saxon keeps his mind on the operation. Maybe you're pissed at the moment, but recognize the service he's doing for men like your brother and father. Even if you're innocent, someone is guilty. Saxon intends to catch them. People like that don't play by the rules and they aren't nice. You have to think like them. Act like them to box them in."

Her anger died in a sizzle of harsh reality. The kind that would manifest into gratitude for people who were willing to keep her from becoming the recipient of folded flags at the graveside of her loved ones.

"Guess I'll have to upgrade your boss's title from 'Asshole' to 'Hardass,'" she conceded.

"He'll be touched. Good timing, though, he's taking care of Harley."

"That better not involve a bottle of barbecue sauce and a basting brush," she warned him.

Mercer snickered. "I'm not saying Saxon wouldn't be above showing the bottle to Harley. Maybe even uncapping it and sniffing it—"

"You are talking about my baby brother," she said indignantly.

Mercer slid her a disbelieving look. Zoe folded her arms across her chest. "My dad has me make a hatch-day cake for Harley. Make. Not buy. We're talking family member status. When this is all cleared up, if that bird even looks stressed out, my dad is going to make someone pay. In a very creative fashion, mark my words."

Mercer lifted his hands in mock surrender. "Just remember, I told Saxon to go pick Harley up from animal control."

"He was at the shelter?" Zoe gasped. "My dad will flip."

"It will be worth suffering his wrath, just because we're alive to see it."

Tension renewed its grip on her. But there was a lingering glow inside her that refused to be banished. He couldn't be all bad if he'd told his boss to get Harley. He just couldn't be. But she had no idea what to do with that bit of knowledge.

Some sort of structure came into view. Mercer pulled something out of his pocket and pressed it. A door slid open in front of them, making her realize that the "un-kempt" road was actually left that way on purpose. There wasn't a single branch in the way of the sliding door.

Mercer drove inside and the door slid shut behind them. Just like Vitus's garage, the inside was immaculate. She got out as Mercer killed the engine. There were tools and camouflage clothing hanging from hooks on the wall. Boots were neatly lined up by the back door with two backpacks hanging above them, looking full. A pair of dirt bikes were there, off-road tires on them, and helmets hanging from the handlebars.

"Bug-out gear," Mercer explained. "Last resort."

He opened a door that led to a covered walkway. Ten feet away was a cabin. There was only the moonlight to see it by. It had an A-frame roof with twin brick chimneys on either side. Mercer clicked the remote again and the door clicked. He reached out and opened the door for her.

"Sorry, no Internet."

Zoe couldn't stop a smile from lifting her lips. The exhaustion that had been threatening to break her for the last couple of hours seemed worth it now. She hadn't realized how exposed she felt. Having solid walls around her drove it home, though.

"Peace and quiet seems . . . perfect," she said. "Um . . . thanks."

Their gazes met for a moment. His eyes had dark shadows under them, telling her how tired he was. She ended up offering him a tentative smile in gratitude. His lips curved in response a second before she lost her nerve and looked around the cabin to avoid dealing with her personal feelings.

There was a small living room with a sofa in front of

the fireplace. But set inside the brick opening was an electric furnace.

"No smoke," Mercer explained. "As far as anyone else is concerned, no one's home unless we want them to know we're home." He jerked his thumb toward the windows. There were boards in them, like something out of the Blitz. She moved closer to look at the construction. It was an actual box, like a window in a storefront. The curtains were hung in front but the wood came out to ensure that not even a tiny crack of light made it through to the outside world.

On the other side of the doorway was a kitchen.

"There're some amenities." Mercer opened the dated refrigerator and scanned the contents. "The bathroom should have hot water and something else for you to wear."

Zoe was already heading through the tiny living room. A door opened into a bedroom that had honest-to-goodness harvest-gold shag carpet in it. A dresser sat there looking like something Lucy Ricardo might have owned. But Zoe was far more interested in what sort of clothing it might yield. She pulled on the brass knob and was rewarded with a selection of jeans. Another drawer had tops; there was even clean underwear and flannel pajamas.

Bliss.

Or at least it would be once she got a hot shower. The bathroom kept to the theme of the rest of the cabin. It was like a time capsule back to 1972. Honestly, the lack of cable suited the overall effect. She stopped to fiddle with what looked like an old radio. Upon closer inspection, she found an iPod connected to the back of it.

A little tingle touched her neck again. She was way out of her league. Mercer was playing for keeps. She was going to end up with a crushed heart if she couldn't keep that fact in the front of her mind.

Except that there were times when he just touched something inside her. Like telling his boss to get Harley. She snorted as she pictured Saxon's face during that conversation.

Yeah, there was something about Mercer. Something she was flat-out chicken to put a name on.

She selected one of the playlists at random, the silence of the cabin grating on her nerves. The shower might have been made out of small squares of faded blue tile, but the water was hot. The application of shampoo and soap did wonders for her outlook on life. By the time she made it out of the tiny bathroom, the scent of dinner was drifting into the room.

The mountain air made her wet hair cold. She put on some layers before opening the bedroom door. The kitchen table was set.

She paused in the doorway.

"There's no mouthy waitress." Mercer tempted her from where he was stirring something on the stovetop.

"Just you."

Zoe wasn't sure if she was saying it for him or herself, but her options were limited. She slid into a chair and watched as he dished up whatever he'd been stirring.

"Beef stew and crusty bread," he announced before setting a bowl in front of her.

"Thanks."

He'd done the job right. The stew was steaming hot. They ate in silence, watching each other. Zoe realized that they had more in common in that moment than either of them wished to admit.

"What?" Mercer questioned.

She shrugged. "Just noticing how alike we are in distrusting each other."

Amusement flickered in his dark eyes for a moment. She got up and took their dishes to the sink. "Your turn for a shower."

She felt him watching her. Would have sworn there was a shift in the air, a rise in temperature as his gaze touched her.

Nitwit . . . focus. He's on a mission.

Roni might have a few choice words about seizing the moment, but it felt like such a big risk.

Chicken.

Yeah, well, guilty as charged.

It was time to start playing it safe. Her walk on the wild side had left her with enough gouges to last her for quite some time.

Mercer waited until Zoe was asleep.

He listened to her breathing slow and deepen. She'd twisted a quilt around herself and rolled over onto her side. She looked so damn innocent.

He had to at least doubt her.

His life just might depend on it.

But that didn't stop him from feeling like he needed to focus more on protecting her.

His thoughts didn't make much sense but at least he could do something about defending them both. Or making sure their gear was secure. He made his way back into the garage, to where the bug-out gear was stored. He turned on a workshop light as he began to pull apart the packs, stripping them down completely.

Bug-out gear wasn't much good if there was a tracking device anywhere on it.

He worked for another couple of hours, using a scanner to check both of the bikes completely. When he made it back to the cabin, satisfaction settled on him for the first time.

True satisfaction.

He stretched out on the sofa, watching Zoe through the open doorway of the bedroom.

He could smell her.

The knowledge was a bit unsettling. He wasn't exactly inexperienced with sex, but this was something different. It was deeper. More tangible. Little details were more prominent, more memorable.

It was as if there was a connection between them, one he wanted to savor, hold close, and never let go of.

She stirred on the bed, drawing him back up to a sitting position. There was a tiny amount of light spilling out from the bathroom night-light. It was just enough for him to see the frown on her face and the way her jaw was clenched.

He was on his feet before he knew where he was going, crossing into the bedroom as she let out a whimper. The little sound was his undoing. There was no further thinking, only reaction.

He reached for her.

Pop.

Pop . . . pop . . .

How could such a soft sound be so terrifying?

Zoe strained against what was holding her down but she was trapped. She struggled, fighting as she felt the burning path of the bullet cutting its way across her flesh.

Pop . . .

She needed to run.

Escape.

The idea was pounding through her. Reenergizing her need to fight. She withered against the force holding her down, calling on all of her strength to break free.

"Zoe . . . wake up."

She opened her eyes with a gasp, swinging at the dark form leaning over her. There was the solid connection of flesh against flesh before pain snaked up her arm from the collision.

"Crap," she growled.

Mercer grunted, capturing her wrist. "You're dreaming, baby."

She blinked, feeling the nightmare lose its hold on her brain. It dissipated until it was just a lingering scent in the back of her mind.

"More like nightmare." She was suddenly grateful for the darkness, because her eyes stung with unshed tears. It was a good thing she was lying down, because her body was shaking. She'd tried to sound flippant, or at least mildly sarcastic, but her voice had failed her, betraying her crumbling composure. Deep in slumber, her mind had dropped all its defenses, leaving her at the mercy of her emotions. She was so completely done.

"I'm fine . . ."

She turned over, away from Mercer, because she honestly just couldn't deal with anything else.

Like how good he smells?

Yeah, like that.

Or how much she really wanted to fling herself at him

and just take solace in the way her hormones jumped the moment he touched her.

It would be pure indulgence.

Yeah, at the moment it sounded perfect. Right up until she realized that she'd be using him.

Two wrongs didn't make a right.

He released her wrist, and her breath caught at the parting. She slapped a hand over her mouth but too late. She heard him draw in a hard breath. He was just a shadow but she saw him reaching for her. Felt her skin tingle, her mouth go dry as anticipation gripped her.

"I can't . . ."

He cupped her shoulder and rolled her onto her back. She expected him to press down on her, craved it actually, but he hovered just out of contact, tempting her unbearably.

"Hoping I'll make it easy for you, Zoe?"

His voice was deep and husky, need and passion edging it.

"I want you," he declared.

It felt like something snapped inside her. She curled her fingers into the bedding to keep from reaching for what she wanted.

"And I've got as many doubts as you do," he continued. He was closer now, his breath teasing her lips, awakening all the little receptors on her delicate skin.

"So what are you doing, Mercer?" She forced the words past her crumbling resolve. "Waiting until I make a grab for the bait . . . again?"

The word *bait* shattered some of the need dulling her sense. She sat up, pushing him away from her. He sat on the edge of the bed, his face a study of angles.

"Maybe I was hoping you would since I'm out here, with you, my ass on the line. I'm not sorry about it."

"I'm glad you're here." She was ten kinds of a fool to confess her feelings to him, but the words just tumbled past her lips. She was talking to the man who had woken her from a nightmare. To the part of him that had freed something inside her, even if he'd been on a mission when he did it.

She just couldn't regret discovering that part of her sexuality. It was a gift, in its way. A knowledge that filled her with confidence and the understanding of the difference between being a girl and becoming a woman.

But that thought brought her up short. Mercer lifted an eyebrow when she stopped halfway across the bed to him. "I don't want to use you . . ."

"You're sweet, Zoe." It wasn't really a compliment. In fact, there was a definite ring of disappointment in his voice.

"But the thing is . . ." He reached across the space between them, hooking his arm around her waist and pulling her into contact with his hard body. "I like the way you use me, baby."

She shivered.

It was a full-body reaction. One that rose up from the connection with him as much as the sound of anticipation in his voice.

God, she wanted to rise to the challenge she heard in his tone.

It felt like something was uncoiling inside her. Stretching up, seeking him like some sort of life-giving force. She reached up, threading her fingers through his short hair. He arched his neck back, his lips curling away from his teeth as he sucked in a harsh breath.

"Yeah . . . like that . . . baby."

When she'd reached the back of his head, she pulled her fingers toward her, tipping his face down again so that she could lift herself up and kiss him. All of the reasons to refuse crumbled. In fact, every type of thinking came to a standstill. There was only impulse and action.

As she stretched up to kiss him he met her halfway, taking control of her head with a firm grip before claiming her mouth. He was pressing her down but she didn't want to go. Didn't want to yield so completely.

She wanted to take.

Their kiss was hard.

And wild.

And everything she craved.

Mercer growled, biting her lower lip. It was a soft nip, the sensation rippling down her body and raising goose bumps. He stroked her, running his hands down her arms and onto her thighs before he captured the bottom of her shirt and pulled it up.

She ended up being dumped back onto the bed as her arms went up with the removal of her clothing. The night air feeling like a relief because her skin was so warm.

"Nice . . ." he said as he reached out to cup her breasts. "So fucking . . . *nice* . . ."

Somehow, she'd never realized how much she liked having her breasts handled. Her eyes were slipping shut as pure bliss rolled through her.

"They taste good, too . . ." Mercer continued.

Zoe opened her eyes in time to see him targeting one of her nipples. He pushed her back, the bed rocking. He claimed the puckered point between his lips while capturing her wrist and stretching one of her arms above her head. Her other arm was useless because he was leaning over her and trapping it with his body.

That quickly, the power shifted between them. Her belly twisted with the knowledge and the feeling of being caught. She wiggled, unwilling to surrender. Mercer chuckled around her nipple. He raised his head, looking at her, showing her the smug, arrogant twist to his lips.

"Mine," he said slowly, softly. "All mine now."

It was a threat and a promise. One that made her shiver and lick her lips.

"It gives you a crazy kick . . . doesn't it, Zoe?"

He kept her still when she wiggled, teasing her wet nipple with his index finger while watching her. "Knowing I have you . . . knowing I'm going to touch you . . . play with you . . . take you . . ."

He trailed his finger down her body. Her skin was ultra-sensitive, tightening as he drew his hand across her body and down to her belly. He teased the soft skin there, rubbing it in a slow circle while she listened to her breathing become rough.

So bluntly sexual.

Honestly, it should have offended her sensibilities or bruised her personal sense of independence, but all that mattered was being suspended in the moment, enjoying the feeling of his fingers on her skin. Noticing the increased throbbing in her clit as he moved his hand lower, he caught the waistband of her pajama bottoms and dragged it down until he found her curls.

"Are you ready, Zoe?"

She arched. "Ready for more than teasing."

"There's my sassy bitch." He toyed with her curls, sending tingles of enjoyment through her passage.

"I don't think I'm done teasing you, though . . ." He pushed deeper, slipping into her folds. "You're not wet enough . . . *yet* . . ."

There was a hard promise in his voice. One he made good on immediately. She purred when he touched her clit. Her nipples puckered tighter as he rubbed the little bundle of nerve endings. Her thighs had parted for him, shamelessly eager.

Mercer caught her with a kiss, taking her mouth with a demand that stole her breath. The dual stimulation jerked her out of reality completely, tossing her into a realm where she twisted and strained toward the building climax his fingers were driving her into. She wanted to hold back. He rubbed her clit fast and harder, pushing her toward the end without giving her the chance to shatter his control.

She felt the climax breaking through her as he held her down, rubbing her clit. It was like the snap of a whip, sharp and stinging. The pleasure raced along her spine, up to her brain, where it exploded, blinding her while she lifted her hips to gain that last bit of pressure against her clit.

He was still fully clothed.

That was the first thought that made it through the haze clouding her brain.

And it wasn't right that he was so unaffected.

Not fucking right at all.

His grip had slackened, his guard lowered because he thought she was still dazed. She took advantage, twisting free and rolling over. His sweatpants pulled down easily, his cock springing free.

"My turn to drive you insane."

She'd never meant a statement more. It was like a burning need actually. She clasped his cock, enjoying the feel of his skin against her palm. Hot. Smooth. The damn thing was gorgeous, hard with distended veins running its length. She stroked it as he settled back, threading his fingers through her hair.

"No."

She looked up at him. He was propped up on a few pillows, one eyebrow raised. Zoe lifted herself up until she was on all fours and sat back on her haunches. His gaze slipped to her breasts, his lips thinning. She cupped them, rubbing her own nipples with her thumbs.

"You don't get to touch right now, Mercer." His attention rose to her face. "Only I do. Fair is fair."

He scoffed at her, looking every inch the badass she'd thought him to be when she first saw him.

"Told you before, Zoe." He had his fingers wrapped around her nape in a second, one of her breasts claimed by his free hand as he hovered over her lips. "I don't play fair."

"What makes you think *I'm* going to?"

She reclaimed his cock, stroking it from base to tip and teasing the slit on the top of it. A drop of fluid was already there, proving he was being pushed toward his limits, too.

"I'm going to suck you dry. Because I'm not a fucking baby doll."

He chuckled, the sound dark and untamed. "Give it your best shot."

He was cocky.

But she liked that trait of his personality.

Liked it way too much. Common sense had fallen victim to it completely, so there was only one thing left to do.

Make sure he suffered a similar fate.

She teased his length, stroking it, enjoying the feel of it in her hands before she leaned down and licked it. He groaned, the sound a soft boost to her confidence. It also whipped up the need to best him. She licked him again, this time trailing her tongue around the ridge of flesh that crowned his length.

"Fucking *incredible* . . ." He caught her head again.

"Hands off." She sounded bitchy and wasn't about to apologize for it. Mercer pressed his lips into a silent kiss before lifting his hand away.

"As the lady likes . . ."

"I'm not planning on being a lady."

"I hope not."

There was just enough yearning in his tone to satisfy her. She opened her mouth and sealed her lips around him, hollowing her cheeks as she cupped his balls.

He bucked beneath her.

"Oh . . . hell yeah . . ." he groaned.

She sucked harder, closing her fingers around his staff and pumping him as she used her tongue on the underside of his cock head. He was lifting his hips toward her now, thrusting up into her mouth as she worked her hands on the part of his cock that didn't fit. He wasn't content to sit back now, gripping her hair and holding her in place as he fucked her mouth.

But she didn't let him take complete control. She sucked him, making sure he felt her lips driving him toward the edge of reason. His breath was ragged, his grip hard enough to pull her hair. He was arching, his body beginning to twist. She opened her jaw wider and gripped his balls.

"Shit!"

His voice was guttural and harsh.

And perfect, because he was tumbling over the edge.

His cock pumped into her mouth, his cum wetting her tongue. She licked it away, sucking him hard until he finished.

"Now let's fuck."

There was a rawness to his words, a hard, blunt edge, which pleased something inside her. It was exactly what she craved.

He curled up off the bed, reaching over to open the side table drawer. There was a crinkle of foil before he was sheathing his cock. She tried to mount him but he shook his head.

"Not a chance, baby . . ." The bed rocked as he rose up and captured her hips. "I'm going to fuck you until you scream."

He turned her around, maintaining his grip on her hips. His cock was still hard, slipping easily between the wet folds of her sex. He pulled her back as he thrust forward, impaling her with a harsh grunt.

"You're going to take it, Zoe . . . Every last bit of it . . ."

He leaned over her back and pressed her shoulders down until she was on her elbows, completely caged by his body. He hadn't moved, hadn't pulled his length free. She felt stretched to her maximum, his cock almost too large.

"You've got a tight little pussy . . ."

He pulled free and pushed back in as he kept his lips next to her ear. "Makes me want to come again but that would be way too fast . . ."

"Um . . . *hum* . . ." It was more a whimper than an answer.

"Your turn to not move . . ." He caught her neck in a soft bite. The little nip sent a tingle of pleasure and pain down her spine. "Stay right . . . there."

He straightened up, drawing a groan from her because it felt like he was being ripped away.

"Don't worry, baby . . . I'm going to give you everything you need."

He held her hips hard as he started to move. It wasn't a fast-enough pace for the churning need inside her. She tried to push back into his thrusts, seeking more friction, but he held her ruthlessly in place.

"I'm doing the fucking, Zoe . . ." He plunged into her and held her there for a moment of pure agony. "And you're going to take it."

"Like hell I am." She shoved back, sinking his cock back into her.

He delivered a light slap to her butt in retaliation.

She gasped, surprise making her mute. The sting from the blow rippled over her cheek and mixed with the pulsing in her clit. A low moan escaped her lips before she realized she was going to make any sound at all.

There was an answering chuckle from Mercer. "Like hell you will . . ."

He unleashed a series of slaps on her backside. making her butt sting and her insides twist with hunger. She was grinding her teeth, the need to come driving her insane.

"So when are you planning on getting to the fucking part?" she demanded. "Maybe you should reconsider letting me be in the driver's seat since all you want to do is play."

He lifted her off his cock and flipped her over. She landed on her back in the middle of the bed. He loomed over her, catching one of her legs and pushing it over his shoulder as he came down on top of her.

"Baby dolls are made to be played with, Zoe."

She dug her fingernails into his shoulders in response, losing her train of thought when he sunk his cock back into her. Now that he was on top, his length was pressing against her clit. Two hard plunges and she was moaning. Another couple and she was straining up to meet him, her need a living, breathing thing inside her. It was so consuming, there wasn't room for anything but the desire to lift up toward his next plunge.

"And you like the way I play with you, sweetheart."

She was gasping, poised on the edge of another climax. This one was going to be deeper, harder. Her body was tightening with an unbearable tension. He was pushing her toward the boundary between pain and pleasure, the hard tempo of his hips making it impossible to avoid the next thrust.

And the next.

He was driving down into her, keeping her leg over his shoulder so she was spread wide for his use.

"Mercer . . . I'm . . . not sure . . ."

But her body was. She was lifting toward him, groaning as he hit some spot deep inside her that sent a new wave of sensation through her, white-hot and searing.

"Just let me make it happen, Zoe."

His voice was nearly unrecognizable, harsh and savage. She opened her eyes, staring transfixed at the tightness of his features. *Untamed* was the only word that suited the moment. The bed was rocking at a crazy pace, their bodies straining toward each other while she heard the wet sounds of her flesh as he rode her. He was harder than she'd ever felt. Larger. Stretching her with every thrust.

She was being driven someplace she'd never gone, some dark, hidden depth of need. It was all bunched up inside her. He was pounding into it, breaking it apart as she lifted up to make sure he had all of her.

She cried out, the sound low and long. Grabbing at the bedding, she locked her free leg around him. Pleasure was burning her from the inside out, flashing like a grenade, but in slow motion so that she felt herself being ripped to shreds.

"Oh . . . yeah . . . shit . . . *yeah* . . ." He was growling out his words, hammering into her as his cock jerked and began to spurt. She hated the condom in that moment, detested the barrier between them. She could feel his member jerking as it emptied, detect the change in temperature as his cum filled the latex.

But it was a tiny frustration. Her entire body was glowing with satisfaction. Mercer rolled off her, releasing her leg as they both gasped. Sleep reclaimed her as she was still wrapped in the high and she went willingly.

Honestly, she'd didn't have a scrap of strength left.

But she didn't need it. Mercer pulled the bedding over them. She tried to fend off slumber's hold for just a moment as she felt him pulling her into the curve of her body.

It felt so nice. So perfect. So much like something she needed even more than the physical release he'd just wrung out of her flesh.

There was some reason she needed to question it.

But there was no way she was going to find the strength to do it tonight.

So she didn't.

Which felt just about as perfect as the man holding her.

CHAPTER FIVE

"Wait a minute . . ."

It was impossible to tell what time of day it was in the cabin, but the chill in the air suggested it was morning. Her question startled her bed partner. Mercer jerked awake, rolling off the side of the bed before he was completely sure what was happening. He looked around the room, cocking his head to the side as he listened. The pistol was back in his hand, his finger over the trigger.

"I just thought of something," Zoe said.

Mercer rubbed a hand down his face before putting his gun back on the bedside table with a grunt. "You might consider giving me a little warning before you start in on me, Zoe."

She shrugged. "I'm a morning person."

He shot her an ominous look. She shrugged again in response.

"That intel you keep talking about, does it include the location where my brother and dad are at the moment?"

"I can't tell you that, Zoe." Mercer sat back down and punched the pillows up before laying his head back.

"Okay, but you know. So ask yourself this. If the intel includes their current location, wouldn't that be mega stupid? I mean, money isn't much good to a dead man. And if any of your teammates makes even the slightest reference to me not caring if my family comes home alive . . . there will be violence."

Mercer contemplated her for a long moment. It was a tad too long because it gave her time to realize he was wearing nothing but skin.

Oh man, did he look good in it, too.

He caught her watching him. His eyes narrowed in a purely sexual way, transforming his face into something sensual. "We need to have more sex."

Her mouth went dry. "Ah . . . why?"

He rolled onto his side and settled his elbow against the mattress so he could prop his head into his hand. "Because your thinking clears up when the sexual tension is relieved."

She swung a pillow at him, hitting him square in the face with a soft sound. She enjoyed a split second of satisfaction before Mercer surged toward her and pinned her to the bed. He was hot and hard and too damn strong. He settled just enough of his weight on her to keep her beneath him as he stretched her arms out above her head while holding her wrists.

"That was a sucky thing to say," she informed him.

He only looked mildly amused by her complaint.

"I'm not a piece of ass," she insisted.

He leaned down and pressed a kiss against her mouth. She turned her head away with a hiss, trying to dredge up

some determination to resist him. Or—more to the point—
his effect on her.

"You're a great piece of ass, Zoe."

She snapped her attention back to him, shooting him a
killing glare.

"You're sexy, baby." His voice had roughened. Maybe
his words were less than smooth, but something about his
tone hinted at emotional involvement.

"Confident," he continued.

"Get off me, Mercer."

He slowly shook his head. "You like me right . . . here."
He rubbed his bare chest against her breasts, holding his
weight off her so that she was left with nothing but the pure
bliss of having his skin in contact with hers.

"I'm sore." Her cheeks heated as she admitted it. His
lips twitched, rising into a grin that made her want to head-
butt him.

"Yeah, I'm feeling it, too." He rolled off her and onto
his feet again, giving her a superb view of his ass cheeks.

"Working out with you sure beats squats in the gym."

She chucked the pillow at him, half falling out of the
bed when he moved out of range. He disappeared into the
outer room, where his jeans were draped over the back of
the sofa that he'd started the night out on. The door swung
shut and she gave in to the urge to stick her tongue out
at him.

It didn't give her much satisfaction.

She ended up rolling out of the tangle of bedding. The
air was crisp, driving her back into her clothing before she
turned around and righted the bed. The foil packet was lying on the floor. She started to bend down to scoop it up
but got distracted by the partially open side table drawer.

She tugged it open farther, staring at the contents. There was the box of condoms, the top ripped off to allow for easy access. But that wasn't the end of the contents.

Not by far.

There were bottles of lubricants, tubes of KY jelly, and lots of toys. Dildos, rabbit vibrators, anal plugs, in different sizes and colors. All of them still in their packaging. Batteries were stocked in one corner, along with a selection of restraints, gags, and whips.

Roni would have called it a pleasure chest.

"Something get your attention, Zoe?"

Mercer was in the doorway, watching her from behind what she'd learned was his guarded expression. She offered him a lifted eyebrow.

"Why is this place outfitted with sex toys?"

Mercer didn't want to answer her. His lips were pressed into a hard line.

"Why don't you want to tell me?"

He ended up pegging her with a hard look. "Sure you want to know? The answer isn't pretty."

He walked into the room. It felt like there was a change in the temperature. Her awareness of him increased. She bit her lip and tightened her mental grip.

"I think I do want to know."

He walked in a circle around her, his steps slow and measured. Calculated.

"I get the bug-out gear, the fake windows, the whole ultra-secret hideout-house thing," she said as he crossed behind her. Standing her ground was harder than it should have been. Their midnight romp had done exactly what she'd suspected Saxon might have been plotting: It cultivated new trust between them.

Mercer stopped next to her. "It's about trust. You already called that right on the money. It loosens lips because it builds trust fast. Sex cuts through stress like nothing else. "

"So a hideout is outfitted with pleasure toys?" She pushed the drawer closed, feeling slightly offended. "Bet that one will never end up on a budget report the taxpayers see."

Mercer flashed her a wicked grin. "I doubt it." He looped an arm across her body and moved up behind her. "We can play later."

She wiggled but he held her in place. "Not interested. Thanks. I like a live show."

"Admit it. You want me to twist your insides." He held her when she would have stepped away, settling his chin next to her ear. "You won't find the sort of satisfaction I give you while you're in control, Zoe. It doesn't work that way. Nothing in life does. If you want a mega high, you have to take an extreme risk."

"How many times have you done this?" She didn't care for how wounded she sounded but she just couldn't seem to control the urge to ask him.

He kissed the side of her neck. "First time."

She snorted in disbelief. He let her go when she pushed on his arm. She made a beeline for the bedroom doorway, needing some space between herself, Mercer, and the drawer of toys. He'd reduced her to a cinder with his body; there was no way she'd survive dealing with him armed with power tools.

"Why is that so hard to believe?"

She stopped in the doorway and turned around to look back at him.

"I could just as easily assume you bar-hop with your girlfriend and pick up one-nighters all the time."

"I don't," she said.

"But it's the same logic, Zoe. I met you in a bar. Your friend was coming on to me. Birds of a feather flock together."

He had a point. She lifted her shoulders in a shrug. "Fine. You don't make a habit out of working girls over for evidence. I'm just a special case."

His expression tightened. "Actually, you are. I'm putting my neck on the line for you because I think you just might be telling the truth."

"I am."

"Good." He started toward her and she ended up in the other room. "Time to prove it."

He cupped her elbow and guided her around to the kitchen table. A laptop was set up.

"No one can navigate your system. Give up your encryption codes. We want full access to your hard drive."

She landed in the chair. Mercer flattened his palm on the tabletop as he leaned over her.

"Do it now, Zoe, or you're full of shit and I've risked my neck for nothing."

It felt like a gavel had landed, the sharp sound piercing her heart like a bullet.

"It's not a code."

The laptop had a shot of her home system on it. The sign-in screen so familiar, while the situation so very strange.

"Wrong answer." Mercer's tone had turned arctic. He reached behind him and pulled out the gun.

"I didn't say I wouldn't do it," she snapped as she typed

in her password. "I said it wasn't a code. I like puns and I'm a language gal. It's not like I'm the only one on the planet who keeps their personal computer protected."

The screen changed, opening up to her desktop. She hammered in a few more passwords before making it into the security settings. A window popped up on the upper right-hand side of the screen with Saxon's face on it.

"We're in. This will take some time."

The window closed.

It felt like something in her heart did, too. Which was stupid, because she knew better than to let Mercer get anywhere near her heart.

But it felt like he was making himself right at home.

"ETA?" Tyler was back on Saxon's phone, eighteen hours later.

Mercer's words rang very true and Saxon was having a hard time finding any reason to discredit them.

The logic was sound. There was more to the case than Saxon had on his data file.

"Are you dead or something?" Tyler demanded as the silence lengthened.

"No sir," Saxon answered out of habit.

"Estimated time on that hard drive intel?" Tyler pressed the issue.

"Couple of days."

Thais looked up, her eyebrows lowering: He'd just doubled the time she'd given him.

"The Magnus girl is a language specialist. At least six different languages are floating around in this thing. It's going to be labor-intensive."

"No one sleeps until it's done."

The line went dead. Thais was still watching him. Saxon shook his head. He stood up, taking a walk to the curb as he contemplated his misgivings.

Something was off. Zoe Magnus had given them access without a single delay tactic. Either the hard drive was wiped or she was innocent. He propped his foot on the retaining wall that ran along the driveway and leaned over as if he was tying his shoe. Instead he reached into his sock and pressed a button on a small cell phone he had Velcroed to his ankle.

His brother would know differently. The little microphone was a direct link to Vitus. The one Saxon had kept hidden since Vitus had been kicked to the curb.

They were still blood, and blood was thicker than anything else.

Saxon made his way back into the house. Thais had her nose stuck to her computer screen. She was scanning the hard drive off Zoe's home computer. He moved behind her and into the back rooms of the house. He felt only a momentary twinge of guilt before slipping through a false cabinet and out an escape tunnel.

Besides himself, only Vitus knew it was there.

It wasn't very big. He had to army-crawl through it, his elbows bruising long before he made it the four hundred feet to the end. Saxon surfaced behind a dense shrubbery in the side yard of the house at the base of the hill. The home owner was a senior citizen who was well known for his dislike of trespassers. But he was equally well known for his love of napping on his back porch. Off to his right, Saxon had a clear shot of the man's sneaker-clad feet.

Saxon slipped into the house and into the man's clothing before borrowing the mid-1970s sedan sitting in the driveway. Vintage cars had lots of things going for them when it came to espionage. Like no computer chips. Tracking had to be done from the license plate, and the ones on this car were so dirty, they likely wouldn't register. It also wasn't a vehicle assigned to his team.

It was time to make sure someone was watching his backside. Treason had a nasty history of running deep and into places no one thought to look. Was it as simple as the Magnus family?

Maybe.

Then again, he'd be ten kinds of a fool if he failed to factor in that two of his men were dead and the strike had come right after his more experienced men had left. That might have been a lucky accident for his experienced men or inside knowledge on just when the new kids would be taking a round of duty. He sure couldn't take a chance on it being just a lucky break for their sniper.

Vitus was the last one anyone would suspect of backing him up. The reason was simple: everyone thought Saxon was dedicated to his career. He and Vitus had decided to let it look like Saxon cut him off after Vitus messed up. Nothing was farther from the truth. Saxon was going to clear his brother's name, just as soon as he could prove it. But it looked like today he would be the one going to his brother for help.

Saxon had the feeling he was going to need that kind of an ace in the hole.

He didn't like the feeling at all.

"Why are you mad at me?"

Zoe looked up from the book she was reading. Mercer was watching her from the sofa. The air between them was full of tension and had been since that morning.

"I thought you wanted a chance to prove your family innocent," he went on, pressing the issue.

She sat up. "My wants have never factored into this situation."

His eyes flashed with a warning.

"On the business side," she clarified.

"Fine." He crossed his arms over his chest. "Still doesn't explain why you're giving me the silent treatment over letting us onto your hard drive."

"I object to you pulling your gun."

And she really wished she didn't. Because she was losing the battle against keeping the lines from blurring. Caring about things like the way he interrogated her. The guy was an agent, not her boyfriend. Being considerate had never been part of his MO. He wasn't a nice guy and she really needed to get her mind wrapped around that.

"Do you trust me, Zoe?"

His question caught her off guard. He offered her a half laugh. "Don't go blaming me for not doing something you aren't ready to do yourself yet. Trust takes time."

She picked the book back up but didn't really see the words. All she saw was the mess she seemed stuck in the middle of.

Life sucked.

"So you called me."

"Don't be a prick," Saxon warned his brother.

"Wouldn't dream of it," Vitus said as he joined Saxon in the underground fallout shelter. A grandfather of one of his buddies from high school had built it during the Cold War era. The house had burned down long ago, leaving an empty lot with decade-old fruit trees. Without a structure on it, the only people who ever crossed onto it were kids looking to grab a little fresh produce. No one ventured back far enough onto the rocky desert lot to notice that several of the boulders were fake and covering vents and access ports for the water and sanitation tanks. Best of all, no one could trace the ownership of it to him. It was still in his buddy's name. A friendship lost to the decades that separated him from the carefree youth he'd been. A relationship that had purposely been allowed to go dormant, so there wouldn't be a connection.

For a moment, he felt a bitter taste for how cold he'd managed to make his life. But his reasons kept him warm. Someone had to hold the line. Hold it against men who lived and breathed for greed. Men who didn't give a rat's ass for the blood spilled when they sold their classified information. They lived in glass towers. Drove exotic sports cars, and had women throwing themselves at them. All over the almighty dollar.

It sickened him.

It stoked up the fire in his belly. Looking around, he admired the plain interior of the fallout shelter. He preferred it to a penthouse. Preferred it to shallow companions who would hamstring him just as soon as it benefited them.

The shelter was maintained. Twenty feet underground, it was two hundred square feet of secret meeting place. Saxon settled back in a chair as the air-purifying system made a soft hum in the background. Vitus went to the tiny kitchen and helped himself to a cup of fresh coffee.

"What's rubbing you wrong?" Vitus asked over the rim of his mug.

"My dead men," Saxon started off. "New kids. Got capped ten minutes after shift change. Mercer brought up the fact that the sniper could have dropped him or Zoe a dozen times but waited until they were together. Seems like someone wants everyone silenced, which means this will all become a nice, neat, cold case."

Vitus drew off a sip of hot joe, waiting for more information.

"The Magnus family isn't striking me as the treason sort."

Vitus cocked his head to one side. "Agreed. Doesn't mean they aren't, though. We've been surprised before."

"True."

Saxon stopped talking. He toyed with the cup of coffee waiting on the small table next to him.

Vitus recognized his cue. "You wonder if someone isn't looking to cover their tracks."

Saxon nodded. "Someone high enough in the ranks to get orders handed down to me."

It wouldn't be the first time. Both of them knew it. One of the hardest parts of being on secret teams was the rather real fact that sometimes people liked to pin their dirty work on you. The plans tended to include death as a means of making sure you never got the chance to defend yourself. That possibility loomed over them both now like a hungry raven.

"Did you recover any evidence?"

Saxon shook his head. "Couple of hard drives. My team is working on them. Tyler gave me an ass kicking over getting it done pronto."

The air purification system was the only sound audible for several minutes.

"Move your team and the girl," Vitus said.

Saxon raised an eyebrow. Vitus put his mug down and shot him a hard look.

"Move the cheese, see who comes after it. That's where you'll find your answer."

"I need you for that," Saxon said. "Why do you think I'm here? I need to go off grid. See who has a problem with it."

Vitus rolled his eyes. "Could have cut to the chase, bro."

Saxon shrugged. "Wanted to make sure your brain still worked."

"Don't start," Vitus warned his brother. "I know what I did. Spend your time worrying about your boy Mercer. He's got it bad."

"I noticed," Saxon agreed. "The problem is, I need someone looking after her who won't mind being glued to her."

His brother scowled at him. "Don't you think you should let Mercer make his own choice about screwing his career?"

"Like you did?"

Vitus stuck a finger out at his sibling. "Warned you already. I fell for my target and she tossed me aside the second her rich and powerful daddy sent the limo to pick her up and take her home to Washington, DC. Difference between me and Mercer is you sent him into the chick's bed. So you owe your man honesty."

"You just didn't have the discipline to stay out of your mission's pants."

"My fuckup. I own it." Vitus shrugged. "Makes me rather useful now. Since no one remembers I'm alive."

"Yeah," Saxon agreed. "The useful part. I still think

people remember you. The respectable congressman doesn't strike me as the type to forget who snatched his precious daughter's cherry without his blessing. He's got plans for her. A man like him doesn't know how to do anything but use people. Family member or not."

"Well, she could have stayed with me but she left. So she can deal with her pops." Vitus tossed the remains of his coffee into the sink. "I'll get Mercer moving."

Saxon nodded. He lingered over his coffee, giving his brother half an hour to clear out of the area before he emerged from the shelter. The old man was finished with his nap by the time Saxon pulled the car back into the driveway. The owner never noticed, unable to see past the thick, overgrown bushes that grew in front of the house windows. Saxon tucked the keys back under the sun visor and disappeared down the access tunnel.

"We're moving."

Zoe looked up as Mercer appeared in the front room again. He shoved his cell phone into his pocket and gestured her toward him.

"You've got five minutes."

Her belly tightened, the tone of his voice making her suspicious.

"Your team couldn't have found anything on my hard drive. I'm not a spy."

Mercer stopped for a moment, looking surprised by her comment. She scooted off the bed, leaving the book where it had fallen.

"We're clearing out because Saxon is moving base camp."

She pushed her feet into her boots and tugged on the laces. "I'm hearing a tone in your voice that says there's some kind of significance to that. Care to share it with me?"

Mercer was checking his gun and looked at her over it. "Not right now."

Great. She wanted to argue but remembered the bikes. Bug-out gear . . .

Squandering her last few minutes with plumbing didn't seem like a wise choice.

She bit her lip and ran to the bathroom before her five minutes was up. She sort of hated him at the moment.

Yeah, well, that feeling will pass.

She didn't care for how sarcastic her inner voice was getting. Just because her willpower deserted her when the guy touched her was no reason for sarcasm.

Yes it is.

Shut it!

"Come on, Zoe."

Mercer hooked her biceps the moment she was close enough, pulling her through the door and out into the garage where the bikes were. He tossed one of the jackets at her before shrugging into the second one.

"Can you handle a bike?" he questioned her.

"Shouldn't you have asked me that a little sooner if this is our bug-out plan?"

He cut her a hard look. "Wasn't ready to trust you. Now the choice is being taken from me. Can you handle the bike?"

She nodded.

He'd picked up a helmet but froze with it in his hands. "I'm the only thing between you and a sniper, Zoe."

The helmet ended up perched on the seat of the bike. He wrapped his fingers around her elbow and pulled her close. "Don't ditch me. You've got nowhere to go. Call your brother and all he'll be able to do is worry about you."

"My brother has friends."

"And all of them are documented somewhere," Mercer replied, cutting through her argument. "Do you think Saxon didn't make sure he had all the information on your family before he started this operation?"

"I get it." She jerked against his hold. "Let's go."

He held her, pulling her closer. "I don't like it either, Zoe, but I'm here, trying to keep you alive."

There was a note of sincerity in his voice that touched something inside her that truly needed a little compassion. He wasn't the right person to seek it from. As in the *Way wrong person but beggars can't be choosers.*

She grabbed the helmet and put it on. Mercer watched her, uncertainty flickering in his eyes. Well, at least she had company. It was little comfort. He handed her one of the backpacks and opened just a panel on the garage door.

Her muscles tightened up as she started to follow her. The word *sniper* cracking through her head like thunder.

It was late afternoon, the shadows lengthening as the sun started to go down. Mercer stopped just outside the garage and swung his leg off the bike. He looked so damn confident. She kind of hated him at that moment because all she felt was a massive ball of tension burning a hole through her gut.

Suddenly, impulsive acts of sex seemed mighty insignificant compared with avoiding snipers.

He kicked the bike into life as she struggled to recall

how to work the controls. She clenched her jaw and felt the engine vibrate. Mercer looked back, watching her from behind the safety glass of his helmet. He gave her a half grin before taking off through the trees.

She didn't have to follow him.

Time felt like it froze while she pondered that fact. She was suspended in the moment, poised on the edge of making a decision that she knew would have a massive impact on her life.

Yeah . . . life.

Staying alive was what was important. Mercer looked really capable in the survival department. He might have used a dick move to get into her life but she couldn't very well explain away the sniper.

Even if she could, she had nothing to hide.

So she took off after him, dirt and pine needles flying up behind her.

Mercer headed up into the mountains. The rest of the daylight passed in a blur of dirt and weaving around trees. Mercer would stop and look at a compass from time to time while using a paper map that he kept tucked into the breast pocket of his jacket. It was tempting to laugh at the low-tech items until she thought about it and realized he was using them to avoid being on grid.

Apprehension rippled down her spine in response. It was blood chilling and too real to dismiss.

Call me if you notice anything suspicious.

Bram's call surfaced from her memory. He'd known something was up.

Or was she grasping at straws?

She snorted at herself as her joints felt like they were going to shatter from the constant vibration of the bike.

She was way past grasping at straws. Things were down-right desperate now. They were using a paper map.

Mercer didn't stop until the moon was up. Zoe was ready to beg for mercy but bit her lip when she got off the bike and her butt let her know exactly how bruised it was from the rough terrain.

"The bikes will draw too much attention if we run them late. Don't need any of the cabins up here to call in a noise complaint to the local forestry department."

She nodded, keeping her lips tightly sealed against the moan that wanted to slip out.

She wasn't going to wimp out.

Collapsing onto the ground was acceptable, though. She swore she could still feel the vibration of the bike.

Mercer pushed the bikes between some trees before sit-ting down near her and using a large boulder to lean back against. He started unzipping his pack and rummaging through the contents.

She ended up staring at him and embracing the fact that he was all she had. It wasn't a good feeling, and yet he was still the picture of strength. The sweat darkened his hair, looking good on him.

She preferred him untamed, his slacks-and-buttondown-shirt combo from the charity event striking her as ill fitting.

Of course at the moment, she really needed the badass side of his persona.

And when everything was over?

Well, that was when she could fall apart and decide if she really preferred good guys, because they were less likely to get her shot.

For the moment, Mercer's rough edges were perfect.

* * *

"Don't think I didn't notice."

Thais kept her voice low and her eyes on the screen in front of her. Saxon paused beside her, focusing his attention on the screen, but his mind was on her.

"Can't have you thinking it's that easy to pull one over on me," she continued. "What's happening?"

"Not sure yet," he answered her. "Do you have anything to report?"

"As far as I can tell, her system is clean. Not a hint of intel, not even a few scattered words. At this point, I'm more suspicious of the very detailed phone records. For a military family, I'd expect them to randomize their incoming locations. Buy a few hot cell phones on the street. Use some free Internet at the local coffee shop. The evidence is a little too easy to read at this point."

She turned to look at him. "I don't like it. Too easy translates into bait trail in my book."

Greer was listening in. Saxon exchanged a look with him before reaching past Thais to pick up the two hard drives sitting on her desk. He secured them in the zipper pockets of his jacket.

"Code Yeti."

There was a brief widening of Thais's eyes before she masked the reaction. He walked by her as Greer stood up and made a show of stretching his back. The newer members of the team were men assigned by Tyler. Saxon knew their files, but a file could be a fake.

Thais and Greer were his team.

He walked toward the room Harley was in. The parrot snapped his beak at him before Saxon picked him up and put him in his carrier.

"I've had enough of the bird." Saxon announced. "Going to take him to a parrot boarding place."

No one paid him much notice as he passed out of the house and into the driveway with the bird. Greer was already in the SUV. Thais wandered out a few minutes later.

"This might be a bad idea." Saxon gave them exactly two minutes to get out before he started the car and drove out of the driveway.

Harley let out a squawk as they entered the flow of traffic.

"Let's see who has a problem with us disappearing," Thais said.

"My thought exactly." Saxon confirmed.

And his gut told him, he wasn't going to like the answer.

"Party Time Rentals."

"What's happening, Tim?" Bram Magnus got straight to the point.

"Oh . . . yes," Tim Woodsy stammered. "Well, you see . . . there was some sort of fire at your sister's house a few days ago."

"How bad?"

"Rather minor, all things considered. The fire inspector says it can be saved. The house, that is. But I haven't seen your sister and Harley since. At first I thought she might have gone to a hotel but she hasn't answered any of my calls. Mind you, her cell phone might have been lost, but still, it has been some time. The police say they can't officially call her a missing person for another twelve hours. Still, it's highly unlike her," Tim rambled on. "I'm not really sure what you can do but I'm rather concerned—"

"I'll take care of it, Tim. Thanks for making contact."

Bram Magnus drew in a deep breath. He was fighting for control, battling the urge to let his emotions lead him around on a choke chain. When he straightened up, he was focused.

"Can I help you, Captain?"

Bram walked by the young enlisted man serving as assistant to Colonel Decains. "Sir? The colonel isn't expecting you.'"

"Sit back down," Bram told the young man. "This is going to be a private conversation."

He turned his back on the startled expression on the kid's face. Fresh out of boot camp, he was fattened up on the black-and-white rule book. In a few more years, he'd learn about the gray areas.

Decains looked up when Bram entered. Bram cut him a salute before stepping forward.

"I assume you had a reason for coming into my office, Captain?" the colonel asked when Bram didn't say anything.

Bram pegged him with a hard look. "My sister is missing, sir."

The colonel stiffened. He put down the tablet he'd been looking at and flattened his hands on the desktop. He was contemplating something, thinking it through long and hard.

"I know where she is. You aren't going to like it."

Bram lowered himself into a chair and waited for the explanation he'd hoped he wouldn't have to listen to.

But it looked like he did.

* * *

"What the fuck are you doing?" Tyler demanded when Tim answered the phone. "Calling Bram Magnus? That was stupid."

"I don't see it that way," Tim answered as he closed his office door shut so that his secretary wouldn't see the cell phone he was talking on. He'd bought it off a kid in the tougher part of town and paid him a lot of money to dig out the location chip. "Be a whole lot easier to wax him if he runs home to save little sis. Besides, I need him gone."

"You really did enlist," Tyler shot back. " 'Cause you don't know shit. I still have a man on the ground in Afghanistan. He is going to make sure the largest piece of Captain Magnus that makes it back to the States will fit inside a mason jar. If he ends up back on American soil, taking him out is going to draw the wrong sort of attention to this operation. Two members of the same family dead on opposite sides of the globe is bad luck. Them dying while there is an open investigation will raise eyebrows and questions I don't want to deal with."

"In that case, I guess you'd better get your man moving," Tim shot back. "Better remember that I brought the buyer to you."

"And you'd better remember that I didn't haul your ass in. This was my case, I put a lot on the line to keep you from getting caught," Tyler argued.

"Because you want the same thing I do," Tim growled. "You want more than table scraps. Well, I'm not sharing unless you give me what I want. It's taken me ten years to put this together, ten fucking years of licking the Magnus family boots. I want them silenced."

"They will be."

Tyler cut the line. Tim snickered but had to reach up and wipe his forehead with the back of his sleeve. There was no way he was going to let his new partner call all the shots. He really wasn't that stupid. Tyler could just have him killed and take all the money.

Well, he was going to make that hard. Damn brass, always thought they knew better than men like him, men who went the enlisted route. What the higher-ups never saw the value of was just how hungry a man like him got down on the bottom. He was getting his slice of pie. That was for damn sure.

"I want to call my brother."

Mercer looked up, his expression tightening. Zoe stared straight back at him. He crumpled up the paper package that had contained his dinner instead of answering her. Zoe left hers in her lap, the contents only half eaten. She had bigger fish to fry. Their makeshift campsite was under the cover of some low-hanging branches. The scent of pine needles was about the most pleasant thing she could think of. There was a thick mat of dead ones under her butt. At least her riding pants were thick enough to keep the ends from poking her. She had a sinking suspicion she was sitting on her bed. All the better to focus on a plan to get back to her life.

Normalcy had never been so attractive before.

"You challenged me to follow you today. To trust you."

He nodded once before he crossed his arms over his chest and waited for her to make her case. His stiff posture sure wasn't promising her much sympathy.

"So I'm serving that challenge right back at you. You've got my hard drives. Whatever is there, is there."

"True," he agreed. "Why did your brother call to warn you and not your dad?"

His eyes narrowed as he thought something through. "What did your brother call you about the night we met?"

Zoe looked away. It was just a reaction to having him peel away the layers of her life so easily. She felt exposed, the need to cover herself impossible to ignore.

"You started this trust conversation, Zoe," he said. "Don't chicken out."

She snapped her attention back to him. "It's not easy having my personal life dragged out for everyone to poke at."

He offered her a shrug. "A lot harder to have it presented as evidence at a trial."

"Stop threatening me. It's getting old."

Something that might have been regret flashed across his face for a whole second before it was covered up by the hard determination she'd come to expect from him.

"Bram called me and asked if everything was all right." She held up a finger when he started to interrupt her. "Only . . . it wasn't a normal 'how's it going' call. I know the difference. When my dad called, it was a normal, 'getting in touch with home' sort of call."

"But your brother was different?"

Zoe nodded. "He told me to call him if anything suspicious happened."

Mercer pressed his lips into a hard line. "You should have told me that."

"Before or after I was duct-taped to a chair?"

"Before would have been more comfortable for you." He didn't offer her any compassion.

She treated him to a stony silence and a single-finger salute.

He snorted at her. "I've got the phone disabled right now so no one can track us. Bugging out means I only check in every other day. Lowers the chances of us being tracked."

"Guess that buys you some time to make up your mind about trusting me or not," she said.

Mercer's lips curved. "Might give you a reason to stick close, too."

It was a less-than-satisfying conversation. And yet, part of her respected him for not giving in too easily.

She ended up choking on a laugh. Mercer raised an eyebrow.

"Didn't expect that reaction."

"Well . . ." she said. "Nice to know I'm not completely easy to work over."

The knowledge was little comfort. In fact, all it did was drive home how gullible she was. He knew it, too. So did Saxon.

She ended up looking at the night sky as her brain filled with the hard facts about her circumstances. They'd planned to put Mercer into her bed.

God, what a thought. What a personal space invasion.

Had there been meetings?

More than likely.

Her face caught fire as she made it to the next step in the thought chain.

Shit. Had there been a post meeting? A wrap-up of the particulars?

Was there going to be a report filed when Mercer made it back from their bugging out?

"What's on your mind, Zoe?"

Of course he was reading her body language. She ended up shooting him a glare full of resentment and bruised feelings. His expression tightened.

"Spit it out," he ordered her.

"Maybe I won't," she argued. "Maybe I don't feel like being so easy to push down your team's little planned-out mission path. Maybe . . . *maybe* . . . you can just discuss that when you all get around to talking about me again."

She looked away, trying to banish the hurt clawing at her. He didn't deserve a reaction from her. But damn it all, she really wanted him to be worth it.

"Why did you do it?" The question just slipped out, betraying how much she didn't want him to be a scumbag gigolo. She wanted him to be something more. Something she could respect.

Someone she could forgive.

"I have my reasons." His tone was tight, his lips pressed into a hard line.

"Well . . . they suck." She threw a rock at him. It was a small one and her aim wasn't any good. It ended up striking the boulder he was leaning on with a sharp little ping. "You suck."

A rock hit the bolder she was leaning against. She jumped and ended up locking gazes with Mercer. His black eyes were glittering.

"You're right, Zoe, I am fresh from the ranks. Want to know why I'm stateside? My entire team was taken out by insider information," he growled. "I went to every one of their funerals. Watched their flags be folded and handed over to their families. Sucks?" He chucked another rock toward her, the impact making her jump. "I know a lot about life sucking, Zoe. Five great guys. All gunned down because we were sold out. I only lived because there was so much blood, no one thought to make sure my wounds weren't fatal."

He shook his head, disgust twisting his features.

"Honestly, touching anyone who might be a traitor was the worst thing I could think of when Saxon tried to sell me on signing on to this mission. But I was wrong about that. It wasn't the worst thing that could happen." He was on his feet, the dry dirt crunching beneath his boots. He came closer, lowering himself until he was eye level with her.

The air became charged between them. The tiny hairs covering her body rose, her breath catching. But she noticed something else. She noticed the way his nostrils flared. His eyes narrowed with arousal.

"What was worse was enjoying the buzz you gave me the first time we met. You were nothing but a target. One there was enough evidence on to warrant action," he snarled softly. "Every one of my teammates deserved better than me being drawn into the way you smelled. You want to know the dirty deets? All those sex toys were at the safe house because more than one operation involves working between the sheets and sometimes, the agent just can't forget what sort of ugliness they're touching. It has a way of leaving a guy's cock cold no matter how much determination he's got to see the mission through. I wanted to think I was that kind of man, that I'd actually need the Viagra pills that were given to me."

Emotion edged his voice. It tore at her heart, ripping away the resentment that had been boiling inside her.

"But I didn't need them. I got a hard-on the second I smelled you, Zoe. My buddies deserved better than that."

He pushed back to his full height. "And I'd do it again.

Even thinking that you're just a mule, I'd take the assignment because there are good men out there who deserve to be safeguarded. Sucks? Sure does. But we're both going to have to deal with it because this is about more than just us. You say you're innocent? Fine. Suck it up and take one for the team."

He turned on his heel, leaving her behind as he disappeared into the darkness. Leaving her with her mouth hanging open in shock and nothing left to think about except that she agreed with him.

I wanted him to be something worth respecting . . .

Yeah, well she needed to be a whole lot more careful about what she decided she wanted.

Because now she had it.

"You'd better have a powerfully good reason for fingering your superior."

Saxon didn't let Kagan's tone get under his skin. It wasn't something many men could claim to be able to do. Kagan was massive, from his excessive height to a shoulder span that would have made several professional football players feel lacking.

"I'm not fingering anyone. Yet," Saxon clarified.

Kagan wasn't impressed. He gestured to the chair in front of his desk. "Make your point. And it had better be good. Tyler has already been on my tail demanding permission to set the dogs on your ass."

"Now I'm pointing my finger," Saxon said as he sat down.

Kagan drew in a stiff breath. "Why?"

"I've been off grid for exactly eight hours. Why is Tyler nursing a hard-on for me? When have I ever failed to bring in my target? What's his reason for doubting me this soon into the operation?"

Kagan's expression didn't change. "Interesting questions." His section leader leaned back as he plucked a pen from the desktop and started tapping it against his lips.

"Tyler claims he's concerned you're heading down the same path your brother took."

"Get off my brother's ass. He performed his mission. Got the girl back with nothing more than a few scratches on her."

The pen hit the desktop. "He screwed her, too."

Saxon shrugged. "It happens. Stop acting like it's the first time you've heard of it, or done it." Saxon shot his superior a hard look. Kagan's lips twitched in what could almost be called a grin. A cocky one. "The way I heard it, the girl didn't complain."

"Her daddy sure did and still is," Kagan shot back. "Personally, I couldn't care less about Vitus blowing off a little stress or whose thighs he does it between. But Congressman Ryland is of the opinion that his little girl would never be interested in anything like that."

"Right, and the good congressman has morals, like being faithful to his wife," Saxon answered.

Kagan had the pen back in his fingers and began tapping it against the armrest of his chair. "Thing is, the danger breeds a certain level of passion that is nearly impossible to ignore. You know it. So did your brother. The little snowbird? Well, she was an innocent. At best, Vitus failed to keep his perspective. That part he was guilty of. That girl had no idea how to handle an experienced operator like your brother."

Saxon had to nod in agreement.

"The punishment didn't fit the crime. It was a situational lapse. Not an uncommon one, either," Saxon said. "Hardly worth pulling a shield from a man with an impressive service record."

Kagan nodded. "Agreed. Except this was a high-profile target. Every man knows those politicians' daughters come with an additional set of rules. Jeb Ryland is a hopeful for the next vice-presidential nomination. His little girl can't be screwing the help."

The pen stopped. "I think that's what's pissing Tyler off. He knows you'll go to Vitus and together, you two won't be easy to pull in."

"Again, why the hurry to haul us in?"

"You have the hard drives," Kagan answered. "However, you've created an interesting situation by dropping off grid with the evidence."

"Exactly," Saxon said. "Someone took out my men. And went for my mole and the mule. Seems like a lot of people need to be silenced all of a sudden. I went off grid to see who had a problem with it and I'm in your office to prove that is the only reason."

The pen started tapping again. The office was silent until Kagan moved and the wheels on his desk chair ground against the tile floor.

"Dig in." He pulled a cell phone from his breast pocket. "There's a scrambler on this one, so watch your back because I won't be able to send in the cavalry. New location is in there, too. And pull your man in, keep that package secure."

Saxon looked up from reading the information on the phone. "You want the cheese and the mule in the same location?"

The pen went back to tapping. Saxon stared at Kagan, waiting for the man to finish thinking.

"The cheese was a setup. The intel is fake."

"What?" Saxon hissed. "I lost men on this operation. I don't do bullshit missions."

"Your team is activated when we need them to perform." Kagan spoke slowly. "The suspected leak was on the other side. A couple of the Defense Department civilian personal. Better fake intel than the real deal. We still need to plug the leak. Someone picked it up. I want to know who."

"I still question the order to bring my man in. His target might be the perpetrator."

Kagan let out a soft sound. "She was in your custody when the last batch was moved. Someone took out the cameras your team placed in her house. Tyler does have some explaining to do because someone is feeding inside information to the man picking up the intel. But the girl is a mule."

Saxon sat back.

"Don't scare me." Kagan was eyeing him critically. "You almost look relieved. She's a mark in an operation."

"She's innocent—"

"That's what I just said," Kagan cut in. "But something is still going on with the family. Her brother is making waves. Knows she's missing. I want to know how he found out. So pull your man in and get that information. Keep her muzzled while you do it. I'm reactivating your brother, unofficially. I want a man on this one who no one will think to keep an eye on."

"Yes sir."

Saxon walked through the nondescript office building toward the door. He didn't make eye contact with anyone working at the plain desks. Their computer screens had filters over them to blur the images, and it was possible the entire office would be moved by tomorrow. With Kagan, you were wise to expect nothing and anticipate the unexpected.

A healthy attitude for them all.

He stopped on the pavement outside to send a text message to Mercer. There was no reply, but he hadn't really expected one. Mercer had bugged out. He'd be off grid completely, only checking in every couple of days to make sure his location couldn't be pinpointed. Saxon walked around the building twice. Thais and Greer surfaced and joined him.

"Good news," he informed them. "We're not getting our shields pulled."

His team members' expressions tightened. Good news? Only when you didn't stop to consider the fact that Mercer's gut instinct had been right. Tyler was up to something.

And that was definitely bad news. The type that just might get them all toe tags when push came to shove and people started trying to cover their tracks.

Saxon selected a new vehicle from the ones left in the parking lot for teams to take.

He did enjoy a challenge.

Even one with deadly consequences.

"We need fuel."

Mercer pointed at a roadside gas station and snack shop. She was stretching a little to call it a snack shop. The entire building was covered in tin roof siding, all of it in different stages of rusting. It look like a giant patchwork quilt. If she couldn't peg it as scavenged, the piles sitting on the dirt nearby would clue her in. There was a dented pickup truck with a bed that had more exposed metal than paint left on it.

Mercer stared at her for a moment before he turned and rode down toward the station. It was just a stop on a rural road, somewhere in the middle of the state where there was nothing much but farms for hundreds of miles around.

A half-grown kid came out as they pulled up. The hems of his jeans were ripped and his T-shirt was in tatters.

"We need some gas," Mercer said.

"Cash only."

Mercer nodded and pulled a couple of twenties from his pocket. The kid shoved them into his own pocket before lifting one of the pumps up.

"Tamales?" a woman called from the doorway of the shop. "Fresh and hot. Best you ever tasted."

"Sure." Mercer looped an arm around Zoe and tried to guide her into the shop.

She sidestepped him. Something snapping inside her as he got too close. His eyes narrowed but she started walking toward the shop, refusing to give him any of her attention.

Ha! Like she could ignore him.

Well, she could at least not appear to be panting after him.

She was still no closer to thinking her way out of the mess she was in. The shop smelled amazing, distracting her at least for the moment. The woman patted a counter that looked like it had been lifted out of some soda shop from the 1940s. There were four bar stools in front of it, their cushion seats wrapped with duct tape.

She laid out a couple of place mats before serving up two plates of steaming-hot tamales.

"Gracias."

The woman flashed her a bright smile, showing off two silver crowned teeth. *"Se habla Español?"*

Zoe nodded. The woman went off in a peel of Spanish, happy to have someone to talk to.

"How about letting me join the conversation?"

The woman looked at Mercer and clicked her tongue. "That's a handsome man you have there," she said, still in Spanish.

"Just a friend," Zoe answered back.

The woman offered her a disbelieving look. "I'm not blind," she said.

They polished off the tamales and Mercer jerked his head toward the doorway. The woman smiled happily as she tucked the twenty-dollar bill Mercer gave her into her bra.

Zoe looked at her bike dubiously. Her backside was aching.

"We're not going far."

She looked up at Mercer hopefully. Hell, sure she was a little mad at the guy but her butt was killing her, so she'd take whatever escape she could from riding the bike. Even if it meant having a conversation with Mercer.

Of course that brought her face-to-face with just how mouthwatering he was. There was dark stubble on his chin now, making him look even more edgy. Damned if she didn't feel a stab of desire go through her.

I'm hopeless.

Nitwit.

Yeah, whatever. "What do you mean we're not going far?"

He swung his leg over the bike and revved up the engine. Zoe ground her teeth together as she did the same.

"My ass is killing me, too."

Whatever she'd expected him to say, that hadn't been it. Was he really commiserating with her? The sound of the bikes made further conversation impossible. Mercer peeled out of the station leaving her little choice but to follow him.

They rode through open land. It was dry desert. The cropland around them was fed by aqueducts but wherever humans hadn't interfered, there was just dry, rocky dirt, scrub brush, and the odd tumbleweed.

She followed him to the base of some hills. He pulled the bike up to a gully and left it there. Zoe yanked her helmet off and waited for him to explain. All he did was pull out the cell phone and look at the screen for a few moments.

The wind blew a dried-up tumbleweed past them as a couple of crows flew overhead. Something started buzzing off in the distance. Zoe lowered the water bottle she'd been drinking from and looked up.

"Our ride home," Mercer informed her.

In the distance, a pair of helicopters was hugging the line of hills.

"So, we're done bugging out?"

He nodded. It was a short, hard motion of his head. He'd slipped his mirrored sunglasses on again, making it impossible to judge his mood. The tamales were suddenly not sitting so well. Her belly knotted as the helicopters swooped in and hovered a foot off the ground.

Mercer cupped her nape, making sure she bent over as they approached the aircraft. The wind whipped up, dirt flying in her face as he guided her into the machine.

She stumbled into the backseat, fumbling with the body

harness as Mercer pulled on a pair of headphones and she watched his lips moving as he spoke to the pilot. He glanced back at her, checking to make certain she was buckled in.

And then . . . his attention was on the mission. Completely.

The observation hit her like a punch to her solar plexus.

From the moment she'd met him, she'd suspected what he was. Spent a lot of time mentally trying to pull his cover story back because she just knew it wasn't right.

This was right.

It was what he was.

There was a beauty in it and confirmation that their time together was limited.

Well, live in the moment, girl.

CHAPTER SIX

Harley let out a squawk when he saw her.

Zoe stepped away from Mercer, relieved to have a reason to pull her arm from his grip. The house they were in wasn't the Malibu Cliffside location. They were somewhere in the San Fernando Valley. But once inside the house, they might have been anywhere on the globe. Once again, the windows were dressed to look normal from the street—but they were nothing but plywood boxes on the inside, so that she couldn't see out. The artificial light lent a stale, prison-like feeling to the structure. The guns Saxon and his team members wore reinforced that feeling. She reached for the parrot cage door, desperate for affection, or at least some remnant of her life.

She opened Harley's cage and let him step up onto her hand. She shook as he rubbed beneath her chin.

"Told you he was a kitten."

It was Thais who spoke, her voice still as dusky and alluring as Zoe remembered. Even without makeup, the

femme fatale looked amazing. Zoe rubbed beneath
Harley's wing and felt grubby. She fought the urge to fuss
with her hair while Saxon and Greer were sizing her up.

"I get along with the bird just fine," Saxon informed his
teammate drily.

"If you call needing stitches just fine," Thais shot back
smoothly.

Zoe peered at the team leader, but Saxon only curled
his hand into a fist in response. "Enjoy your trip to the
mountains, Ms. Magnus?"

"Helped me tighten a few things up, that's for sure." Her
entire backside felt like stone.

He choked on a sound that might actually have been a
laugh. She wasn't 100 percent sure, though.

"We found the intel."

She felt like the blood was draining from her face.
"That's not possible."

He gestured her toward Thais, his expression confident.

Thais had turned a dining room into a workshop once
more. Zoe stared at it all, more than a little in awe of the
way the house had been so quickly transformed into a
technical command center. She slid into a chair and laid
her fingers on a mouse. The screens flickered to life, showing a complex digital display of the information on the
hard disk from Zoe's home computer.

"This hard drive is from your system. I had to bring in
a language specialist to help me with it but it's clean. Your
friend Roni is right, you need to get out more. You spend
an insane number of hours working."

"Like you clock out at five on the nose."

Thais sent her an amused look. "Point taken."

She clicked on one of the screens and brought up

another image. "Here's the hard disk from the parrot party laptop."

The screen was full of images of maps, broken up by pictures of Harley on kids' arms. It was a grotesque collage.

"Clever really," Thais said as she scanned the information on her screen. "See . . . right here . . . you can see where the information is and where the pictures began to be written over it. Graphic files take up a lot of storage. Since you're using this for parties, you delete files and write over the hard drive multiple times. Very clever way to try to cover up the tracks."

"Since the laptop was in the van, we missed it when we swept your house," Saxon said.

Zoe felt like someone had punched her in the gut. She needed air but couldn't seem to make her lungs work. All she could do was stare in horror at the screen.

Thais rubbed her eyes. "It's going to be a bitch to piece together. There are only fragments of the intel, but it's there."

"It . . . can't be . . ." Zoe muttered, her brain in complete denial. She felt the weight of Mercer's hard stare. His body had tightened up as he took in the information being displayed.

"Your prints weren't the only ones on the keys."

She snapped her head to look at Saxon. "Excuse me?"

The team leader was a very unlikely candidate for a savior. As in, never in a million years. Her brain just couldn't absorb it. She blinked, trying to understand him.

"Tim's were. He used the laptop."

"He doesn't do the parties," she blurted out, trying to think the situation through.

"We know."

Saxon's voice sounded like a gavel pounding. Of course they knew. Investigating was what they did. "Does he have a key to your house?" Saxon asked.

"Yes." Her brain was working at a frantic rate. Harley snapped at her when she rubbed him too hard. Zoe jumped and put the parrot down. "In case something happened to me and Harley needed to be taken care of. He and my dad go way back." She turned to stare at the screen again. "I . . . can't believe it."

"Not many others will believe it, either," Saxon said. "Not yet. This is circumstantial at best."

Zoe whipped around to stare at him. But it was Mercer who answered her stunned look.

"It still happened in your home, Zoe. Unless we get a confession out of Tim, you're as likely a suspect."

"Except that I was with you when the last intel was intercepted," she argued.

"Intel that surfaced while you were in custody," Saxon replied.

"What?" Zoe demanded, her brain finally shaking off its paralysis. "If that's the case, aren't things becoming sort of clear? In my favor?" She wished she could be happier, but she wasn't.

Saxon shook his head. "Might be a clever way for your partner to take the fall for you. An older guy would do that for the right person. Like a lover."

Her brain was right back to feeling like it couldn't deal with things again. Saxon offered her no mercy, studying her from behind a stony expression.

"You'll be staying here until we decide how to shift the fact from fiction. It's in your best interest to cooperate."

"Fine."

She tightened her jaw and straightened her back. There was no way she was going to let any of them know how defeated she felt. Saxon looked like he was trying to peel away her facades and didn't really care if she ended up a babbling mess on the floorboards.

Not that she could really blame him. She looked back at the screen, absorbing the harsh reality of lives being reduced to a dollar figure. It had to stop and her comfort wasn't more important.

She looked back at Saxon and Mercer. "So where do Harley and I bunk?"

That earned her a reprieve from the team leader's intense stare. "Third door on the right," he answered while shooting Harley a glare. "That thing throws more food on the ground than he eats."

"He hates to dine alone," she shot back.

The team leader's lips twitched before he turned away. "Your problem now."

Zoe grabbed the cage, intending to pull it down the hallway. Harley was still on top of the cage and didn't care for the unexpected motion. He opened his wings and beat the air while telling her what he thought about it. She picked him up and soothed him. Mercer pulled the cage down the hallway while she was dealing with the bird.

The bedroom was furnished only with the basics. A double bed and a single dresser with an overhead lamp. A door opened to a bathroom. At least the lack of furniture allowed lots of room for Harley's cage. Zoe put him down on the perch on top of the cage to let him get used to his new surroundings.

"You're still in custody, Zoe."

Mercer was watching her from the doorway. He'd

crossed his arms over his chest, the stubble on his chin making him look downright mean.

"I got that part," she said.

His jaw clenched but he had his shades on so she was left wondering what his mood was.

"We're protecting you, too."

"I need a shower."

The disgust in his tone from the night before was still ringing in her ears. It kept her from losing her focus and melting at his feet. Just another thing she'd wished for but wasn't so happy to be receiving.

She eased Harley into his cage and locked the door, checking it to make sure it was secure before turning her back on Mercer.

It hurt.

It shouldn't have.

Well, that about summed up her relationship with the man. So many things that shouldn't be and still were. She flipped on the shower and stood under the hot water, trying to let it wash away the tension eating at her. All she ended up doing was losing the battle against her emotions. Tears slid down her cheeks, the water washing them away.

Too bad it didn't make her feel any better.

She needed to call Bram.

Zoe woke up thinking about her brother and his call to her. Harley was greeting the morning and demanding that she take the blanket off his cage. Although with the way the windows were boarded up, the light of day was just a gray sort of haze inside the room.

"Your dad called it right. That bird does wake up at first light."

Zoe jumped and blinked at Mercer. He was leaning against the door frame, looking mouthwateringly good again. It really should have been impossible for anyone to look so damn fine in nothing but plain blue jeans. Mercer made her heart skip a beat. She felt like the air tightened in the room. Like some sort of a switch was being flipped inside her.

"What are you doing in here?" she demanded. "Wait. How did you know my dad said that about Harley?"

He didn't change his position or expression. She really should have been used to his over-the-top confidence but it still grated on her nerves. She was so sick of being his target while he was disgusted by her.

"We've got your cell phone transcripts," he said. "It's really for your own good."

"Yeah." She got out of bed, grateful for the fact that the only thing she'd found to sleep in was a man's sweatpants and T-shirt. She was swimming in them.

But she still felt exposed.

The first ripple was startling because of the intensity. It started at her nape and slid down her spine, awakening a hundred thousand nerve endings on its way to her tailbone.

"Don't be stubborn, Zoe." Mercer abandoned his lazy stance in the door frame. Although it was more of a position. He never did anything as normal as leaning. The damn man was calculating to the core.

And it turned her insides to molten lava.

"I didn't argue with you," she said, trying to rip her gaze away from the way he moved. He didn't really walk. His stride was more purposeful than that. It qualified as a prowl. Predatory.

And part of her was very interested in being his prey.

"I know your body language, baby."

Arrogance edged his tone. It resonated with her, striking a target deep inside her core. Heat was surging up from her belly, twisting through her veins as she fought to control it.

"I told you . . . don't call me that."

He was closing the distance between them. She felt him bearing down on her. Turning her back on him felt impossible, but sometimes the wiser choice was to avoid contact. She pivoted and headed for the bathroom.

Mercer shot his arm out, clotheslining her. She ran straight into it. He cupped her shoulder and turned her around so that he could flatten her back against the wall.

"What's wrong, Zoe? Afraid to be alone with me?" he asked softly.

She was caged between his arms, his hands flattened on the cream drywall. She had precious little left of her pride. Parting with it made her rebel. She worried her lower lip as she stuck her chin out at him. "Not interested in listening to you whine about me turning you on. Better retreat before I put you in the position of being disloyal to your buddies."

He sucked in his breath, his eyes narrowing as a muscle along his neck began to throb.

"Damned if your stubbornness doesn't make me want you even more," he said.

Want? Yeah, I like hearing him say he wants me.

Her insides twisted, the scent of his skin filling her senses. It was overwhelming. He cupped her chin when she started to look away. One last attempt at maintaining self-control.

The look in his eyes was her undoing.

A little moan got past her lips half a second before he claimed her mouth.

It was a hard domination. He took her lips, covering them with his own before unleashing a hard kiss that shattered her illusion of what kissing was.

But it wasn't bruising. He held her head, framing her face with one large hand and somehow managing to control his strength perfectly. It was aggressive without being biting. Controlling without crossing the boundary into force. It set her senses reeling and her thoughts scattering.

She reached for him, opening her mouth and kissing him back with a fury that singed her.

"My baby . . ." he growled against her lips. He held her back when she would have followed him, holding her prisoner for one spine-twinkling moment. "*Mine*. All mine."

There was a flash in his eyes that sent a jolt of anticipation through her. Zoe suddenly hated her clothing and his, too. She reached for his shirt, ripping at it until he chuckled and lifted his arms so she could drag it up and over his head. He had to slip to his knees so she could manage it. Which brought him eye level with her sex.

All she knew was that it was a relief when he hooked his hands into the waistband of the sweatpants and pulled them down her legs. He captured one ankle and lifted her foot free of the puddled fabric. He made a soft sound of male enjoyment as he lifted her leg and draped it over his shoulder. He rose back up, lifting her leg in the process and spreading her thighs in the same motion.

Yeah, it should have felt cheap.

But she was too busy gasping with anticipation. Her clit was throbbing. The first touch of his breath against her folds made her twist.

"All . . . mine . . ." he muttered before using his thumbs to spread her folds.

Her fingernail sank into the drywall but she didn't care. All of her attention was centered on the way Mercer took to eating her out. Calling it *oral sex* didn't cover what he was doing to her.

Not by half.

He sucked on her clit and drew his tongue across it. She withered against the wall, perspiration covering her skin. Pleasure was spiking through her, driven up into her core by the way he lashed his tongue across her clit. He would return to sucking it but stop when she whimpered, on the edge of climax.

"Mercer . . ."

Her voice was strained. Needy. Desperate.

"I'll take care of you, baby . . . never doubt it."

He claimed her clit again, sucking it hard as he pressed his thumb deep inside her. Her belly clenched, climax claiming her in a snap of brilliant ecstasy. It stole her breath, freezing her lungs as she twisted against his mouth, desperate to be closer to him.

She slumped against the wall, starting a slow slide down its surface as her body flatly refused to do anything but enjoy the pulse of rapture.

He pushed to his feet, scooping her up. He held her by the backs of her thighs, lifting her so that he could plunge his cock into her body.

"Oh yeah . . ." he groaned as he sank into her.

"When . . . when did you put the condom on?"

His lips split with satisfaction. "While you were whimpering, baby."

He turned around, carrying her to the bed. It rocked as

he lowered her onto it, following her down. She spread her thighs for him, cradling his hips between them as he drove deeply back into her spread body. It was the completion she craved. The missing component she yearned for. Details weren't important. Only the motion of his body on top of hers. She strained toward him, needing more friction. Mercer gave it to her. As he drove deep and hard into her spread body, her cravings rose, becoming more intense, more essential to her survival. Everything settled on the point of contact between them. He captured her wrists and pulled her arms above her head, pinning them to the surface of the bed as he hammered his cock into her.

She couldn't do anything but lift her hips to take the next plunge. It was all that mattered. Desire consumed her completely, transforming her into his willing prisoner.

Her body started tightening, an explosion beginning deep inside her.

"There it is, baby . . ." He was growling at her, his voice tight with his own need.

"Yes . . ." she hissed at him. "*Yes.*"

She was suddenly shattering into a million white-hot pieces, pleasure wringing every last bit of conscious thought from her. It jerked her away from reality, tossing her into a vortex that spun her around and around until she lost track of everything except him.

He ground himself into her, pumping through his pleasure as his grip tightened on her wrists, holding her in place. For a moment she was stretched out beneath him. His prize. His flesh still jerked inside her body. Satisfaction rolled through her as she filled her lungs and realized her thighs were cramping from holding him so tightly. She forced herself to unlock her legs and release him.

The bed jerked as Mercer rolled over and flopped back onto it. He ended up with a forearm across his eyes as his rapid breathing filled the room. "How in the hell do you do that to me?"

She wished she knew the answer. Wished she didn't hear the frustration in his tone.

But she did, and she slapped back into reality.

"Yeah, I know. You hate it. Guess I'm not the only one who has to take one for the team."

He jerked, curling up but she was already scrambling off the bed.

"Zoe—"

"Just . . . shut it." She stopped in the doorway to the bathroom and looked back at him. "I guess I'll just count myself fortunate you can get it up for me."

"That's not fair."

"It's as fair as you knowing everything about me and only telling me how much you hate the effect I have on you. Or that I need to have sex so I can think straight. Get out of my room."

He was off the bed, his open fly grating on her nerves even further because it would be super simple for him to finish up their encounter. His holster was still clipped to the waistband, the dark butt of the gun illuminating just how precarious her situation was.

He didn't want to be emotionally involved with her. No. But stress-releasing sex was fine. She was an idiot for forgetting how he thought about her.

Or maybe, she'd just hit rock bottom. Both options were pathetic to say the least.

Nitwit.

She stuck her finger toward the door.

"Out. Now!" She scooped his discarded T-shirt off the floor and chucked it at him. The soft fabric made a very unsatisfying missile. "You've done your rounds for the morning."

"We're not finished."

She went over to the bedroom door and yanked it open. "Out."

There was no way the other team members didn't hear her. Mercer's jaw tightened in response.

"Enjoy everyone knowing your private business for a change." It was a pissy thing to say but completely deserved.

"You win this round, Zoe." He buttoned his fly and shrugged into his shirt, moving across the space between them as she hid behind the door to cover her nakedness. He stopped in the doorway.

"But you can bet there is going to be a rematch."

There was hard promise in his voice. He sent her a look that reinforced his words before passing through the doorway.

Like hell there was. She was withdrawing from the game.

All she had to do was figure out how to get in touch with her brother. That would be a match point Mercer wouldn't see coming.

"I'm Servat."

Bram started to cut the man a salute but a tiny shake of his head stopped him. Bram ended up tugging his shades off his face to cover the aborted motion.

Servat offered him his hand. "Civilian ground, Captain. We like to blend in around here."

Bram clasped his hand and shook it. "Right. I'll adjust my thinking."

Servat shook his hand before pointing to the SUV behind them. "I don't have any good news to tell you."

Bram held his frustration in check as he tossed his duffel bag into the backseat of the vehicle and got into the passenger side of the front seat.

"The team that we believe has your sister has gone off grid."

"Someone knows where they are." Bram cut to the heart of the matter. "Or you wouldn't be referring to them as a team."

Servat held his silence as he pulled into traffic. "They are capable of safeguarding your sister."

"Assign me to them." Bram didn't spare a thought to what branch of the military any of them were. Special assignments meant working with the best resources.

Servat shook his head. "No one goes in or out. We're close to nabbing our perpetrator. Can't afford to spook him. You and I have our own objective to be concerned with. Colonel Decains needs us to be in position in case the point team can't handle things."

Bram wasn't happy. His jaw was tight as he struggled to maintain his professional detachment. He knew the ground rules for this type of operation. Emotional entanglements wouldn't be tolerated. His only chance to find Zoe was to work through the system.

And that wasn't going to be easy.

"I hope you're not going to tell me I flew halfway around the world to sit on my duff drinking coffee."

Servat cracked a grin. "Would hate to see you suffer like that, Captain." He slid him a look, one designed to assess him. "We need to box this dude in. Come up behind him while he's busy trying to get to your sister."

"Sounds good." Except that it didn't. Bram held his silence through years of discipline and a dash of desperation. He didn't need to hear that his sister was a target of any kind. But his personal feelings were going to have to wait.

"What's our first step?"

Servat chuckled ominously. "We need to start a fire and see who runs from it."

"I need the room, Ms. Magnus."

Saxon didn't even look back at her when he spoke.

Zoe bristled, earning a hard look from Mercer. She shot it right back at him. "I'd like to stay and hear what sort of plan there is for clearing this mess up."

Saxon turned to look at her. "Terrible idea."

Those two words seemed to be his way of dismissing her. She glared at him but Mercer stood up.

"You don't carry a shield, Zoe," he said as he crossed the room toward her. "This is a classified operation."

"Sitting around and waiting hasn't produced a resolution so far. So . . ." She walked farther into the work area. "Time for a new approach."

Thais looked her way, a soft smirk curving her lips. Greer simply shook his head and looked back at his computer screen. Mercer was leaning against a desk. He crossed his arms over his chest as he waited to see what his . . . well, whatever Saxon's title was would say to her.

"You don't want to try me, Ms. Magnus."

"My feelings exactly," she countered. "Except you sent someone after me and he brought me home. But hey, if you're sick of me, I'll be happy to take my dad's bird and go."

Saxon surprised her by chuckling. He stood up, the motion making the shirt he was wearing ride up, giving her a glimpse of his shoulder harness with his gun sitting in it.

"Need to get back to your partner?"

Time had clearly thickened her hide. She stared straight back at Saxon without flinching.

"Can the scare tactics," she said. "I'd already be discussing my plea options with my lawyer if you had a case against me."

"Don't be so certain that little scene won't be happening," Saxon continued.

"I'm feeling pretty confident it won't." She stood her ground. "So what are you planning to do about catching the real thief?"

"As I told you, classified."

"Fine." It really was about the farthest thing from fine there was, but she turned on her heel and headed back down the hallway. Harley squawked when she opened the bedroom door.

"Greer . . ."

Saxon had called out the name. Zoe hesitated with her foot in the air. She turned to look back at the dining room as Greer turned around and went to join his teammates.

No one was looking at her. She pulled the door shut while standing in the hallway and waited.

Nothing. Just the low rumble of voices in the front room of the house. Saxon used that room when he wanted to keep her from understanding what was being said.

She ducked through the kitchen and peeked around the doorway that opened into the dining room. Thais was in the front room as well. Zoe looked at the phone sitting on the desk. Her heart was hammering as she listened to the muffled voices. The desk was only three steps from the doorway but it looked like a hundred feet.

She tightened her resolve and stepped out of her shoes. The dining room had hardwood floors. She put her foot down gingerly, bracing for a creak that would blow her cover. There was only a faint groan. She took the next step and reached for the phone.

Zoe ended up back in the kitchen, the phone cradled against her chest. Her hands shook so badly, she feared she was going to fumble the damn thing. She pushed the TALK button and heard a faint buzz telling her the line was active.

Thank God for some of her dad's strange rules.

Like having to memorize family member phone numbers instead of relying on a cell phone to store them. She punched in her brother's number and lifted the phone to her ear. Time was slowing down again, feeling like every second was a tiny eternity. The line made some clicking noises while she waited with bated breath for it to connect. Relief washed through her as it rang. Once. Twice.

"Zoe?" Bram shouted into the receiver. "Are you there?"

She didn't dare answer him. She pressed one key on the number pad.

There was a short silence on the other end of the line. "Are you injured?"

Her brother knew the code. One for yes and two for no. She pressed a key twice.

"Put the phone down and walk away with the line open. I'm running a trace," Bram instructed her.

She pressed a key once.

Replacing the phone was more trouble than snatching

it from the desk. The meeting was still going on, but Saxon was pacing now, coming into view in the doorway before he moved out of sight. Zoe waited for him to disappear before taking the two steps back to Thais's desk. She left the phone out of its cradle and made it back to the kitchen.

Her heart rate started slowing down as she made it back to her bedroom. She opened the door only to see Mercer appear down the hallway.

"We're not finished. Stay in there."

She contemplated how he'd known she'd opened the door.

Of course!

Nitwit!

There was a sensor on the door, like stores typically had. She slid her hand around the doorway, pulling the chair over to stand on so that she could see on top.

Nothing.

Well, it was there.

And linked to their cell phones. She had no doubt about it.

Obviously they'd thought she was inside the room.

Well, they'd discover their error soon enough.

Bram Magnus was watching the computer screen. He was standing, his hands flattened on the desktop as he waited for the location of Zoe's call to pinpoint. The program was working. He leaned closer, anticipating an address.

The screen flickered and went black.

"What the fuck?"

"Sorry, Captain."

Bram straightened slowly, his body tensing as he turned to face Servat. His comrade was wearing a pair of slacks and a polo shirt that wasn't tucked in. Bram knew it was because he had a gun clipped to his belt.

"You've got some explaining to do." Bram was holding on to his calm by a thread.

Servat sat down on the edge of a desk. "Your sister is resourceful. Got to hand it to her. Hale is going to be steamed when he hears she managed to slip a call out."

"Who's Hale?"

Servat held silent for a moment. Bram stared him down.

"Saxon Hale. Special assignment agent. He's heading up the team on this project."

"My sister called me for help," Bram said slowly. "I plan to make sure she gets it."

"She is getting it," Servat abandoned his teasing tone. "She's tucked away because someone tried to kill her. I need her to stay in the hole we've stuffed her in. Otherwise, a sniper is going to put a round through her clever little head. Like he's tried to already . . . twice."

Bram crossed his arms over his chest. "Zoe wouldn't reach out to me if she felt safe. I can't ignore her."

"She's got her feathers ruffled, understandably."

Bram held up a single finger. "Explain."

Servat's expression became guarded. "The nature of the operation required a covert insertion of an undercover agent."

"Um-hummm . . ." Bram ended up gripping the sleeve of his shirt to keep his arms crossed across his chest. What he really wanted to do was smash his fist into Servat's jaw.

His fellow agent knew it, too.

"Not that I blame you for looking at me like that," Servat said. "But she isn't a baby. I've reviewed the intel. She liked the guy, a lot."

"That's my sister," Bram growled. "Did the colonel approve this?"

Servat shrugged. "He didn't have much choice. He'd already signed on to the operation."

"Because I suspected Tim was trying to use my father. I had to stop that from happening. And calling it *signed on* is a stretch. A big one. This was going down. My choice was to be able to join you and help or sit in Afghanistan and wait for the phone to ring—"

"Doesn't matter why," Servat interrupted. "Your sister was the most likely avenue for getting a man in on the ground. Tim's calling the shots."

"She would have cooperated."

"Except." Servat pegged him with a hard look. "It was always a possibility that she was involved."

"Like hell," Bram growled.

"The intel always moved when you and your dad were deployed. The only way to clearly pinpoint Tim was to keep her in the dark and see how she responded."

He needed to hit something.

Bram felt like his teeth might crack from the strain he had on them.

"My sister isn't a traitor." His tone was clipped.

"A proven fact now," Servat agreed. "But she's not going to live long enough to enjoy that if we don't keep her head down."

"Seems to me no one's explained the situation to her completely. Zoe isn't stupid. She made that call because your team leader is still keeping her in the dark."

"You're not stupid, either," Servat fired back smoothly. "You can see the merit of not exposing your cards until the operation is finished."

Bram was back to grinding his teeth. He wanted to argue further, but the fact was, there was solid sense coming out of Servat's mouth.

"If it wasn't your sister, you wouldn't take exception to the details."

Bram shook out his shoulders. "It is my sister. So let's get down to getting a net on Tim."

Servat nodded. "That's a request I can help you with."

"We need to talk," Tim informed Tyler.

"You're taking an unnecessary risk by calling me. If anyone establishes a link between us, this operation will fail."

"I need a boost of confidence." Tim looked at the personal message on his computer screen. "I'm meeting the buyer tomorrow."

"I know," Tyler answered. "Seal the deal and bring me my cut."

"Not until you share your plan for getting me out of the country."

There was silence on the other end of the line for a long moment. "That sounded like a threat. Are you that much of a dumb fuck? I don't take threats."

"It's a healthy move for me to make," Tim said. "I'm not going down for this. And I'm not wet behind the ears enough to tie up all the loose ends and leave you with all the evidence, while the blood is on my hands. If I sell the merchandise, it won't be hard to have me shot by your team while they were supposedly attempting to take me into custody."

"I'll have your exit passport and ticket waiting. No one else can get you a passport. We'll trade the passport for an account number."

"You'll wait until I'm out of the county and then I'll transfer the money," Tim countered.

"No deal," Tyler said. "I'll never hear from you again."

"If I give you the money, there is no reason for you not to flag the passport."

"Fine," Tyler said. "How about the hard drive? Without it, there isn't any hard evidence."

Tim was quiet for a moment. "Deal. But I've got to see the tie-up. I need to see the bodies."

"Don't expect me to do your wet work for you."

"I don't," Tim answered. "But you've got Zoe locked down. I need access."

"Let me see what I can do."

Tyler cussed as he severed the connection.

Wuss.

But he needed him to finish the operation. Tyler opened up the file on Zoe Magnus, looking for a way to make her jump.

"How in the hell did you get a call out?"

Zoe turned around in the kitchen. Mercer was furious with her. Saxon was right behind him.

She pointed through the doorway at the phone on Thais's desk.

Both men considered the information. She could see their minds working as Greer and Thais hovered in the background doing exactly the same thing.

Saxon finally grunted. "No one checked to see if she went into her room."

There was a short word of profanity from Greer.

"That was a stupid move," Mercer said.

Her eyes narrowed. "Like hell it was. I'm not going

down without a fight. I'm not guilty of anything and I sure as hell won't be sitting around while no one is doing anything about proving my family innocent. You're damn straight I placed a call to my brother."

She wasn't going to apologize for it. She stared at Mercer, refusing to crumble in the face of his disapproval.

"You need to listen to me, Zoe."

Oh no she didn't. Zoe flipped her hand in the air and went to brush past him.

Mercer let her make it to her bedroom before he hooked her biceps and flipped her around to face him, keeping her close with his greater strength. The door slammed shut.

"Let me go!" she hissed, flattening her hands on his chest. "I am sick of you telling me what to do."

"Too bad," he growled. "You're not in charge of this operation."

She smacked his chest, slapping at him when he wouldn't release her.

"No, I sure as shit ain't!" she shouted at him when he held her tight against him. "And I'm sick of taking orders." She was shaking with anger but being so close to him, all she wanted to do was let everything go and melt into his embrace.

He was just as immovable as always. Solid. Hard. In control, while she felt like the very fabric of her being was shredding. Just sharing airspace with him made her frickin' high. "Do you think I like being reduced to calling my brother? He's deployed. I should be able to be supportive of him. Instead I'm whining to him because my life got too complicated. You should understand. You've been deployed. You know what I'm talking about. As a family member, it's my duty to support my soldiers." She slapped his chest. "I hate you for doing that to me."

He released her. She ended up against the wall feeling miserable. Exposed and on display.

Damned if he didn't always reduce her to feeling weak.

She caught a momentary flash of something in his eyes that looked like compassion. Or at the least agreement. But he tightened his jaw and sent her a hard look.

"I can't protect you if you do stupid shit like that, Zoe."

"Stupid?"

He nodded. "Right. Stupid. You exposed your position and the rest of the team."

"I called in reinforcements," she argued. "You and your team are keeping me in the dark. How long did you expect me to just sit here taking it?"

One side of his mouth curved, just a tiny amount.

"This isn't your operation."

"You're damn right about that." She stepped toward him, pointing at him. "And I'm through being bait, or whatever other pathetic label your team leader wants to put on me. I called my brother and he's going to kick some ass and take some names but you can bet on one thing, Mercer, I am finished rolling over for you."

"Good."

His response surprised her. Mercer caught her against him while she was trying to process what he meant.

"I might have been sent after you, Zoe, but I enjoyed the hell out of you not rolling over for me."

She hissed at him and tried to push him away. "Yeah, you told me how much you liked me."

He held her, pushing her back until the wall was behind her. He cupped her nape and settled his lips next to her ear.

"But did you hear me, Zoe? I was telling you that I couldn't resist you. I still can't."

She shivered.

She just couldn't help it.

"And I'm just as fucking stubborn as you are, baby."

She jerked at the endearment. He massaged her nape in response. She tried to shut out how good it felt, biting into her lower lip to fend off the sensation. His tone was the one she remembered from their moments together. The passionate ones, where nothing else mattered but getting closer to him.

Mercer chuckled at her. He pulled his head back so they were face-to-face but kept his body pressed to hers. "Doesn't work . . . does it, baby? Trying to warn yourself against the pull between us."

"No," she said miserably, realizing there was no point in playing stupid. His cock was rock-hard, letting her know that he wasn't unmoved. "Just go away. I don't want to be your . . . sex partner."

"Yes you do." His tone was full of promise, the type that made her blood warm and her clit pulse. "You want me to push you, like no one else has ever pushed you before."

Her heart ached. "I mean it, Mercer. I can't do this anymore."

She was pathetic. A broken heap at his feet, just as she'd feared she'd end up. Her pride was nothing but a distant memory.

"I can't do any more of it. Bram can protect me."

"He's been on the team since the beginning."

Her blood chilled. "Step back, Mercer. I need to think."

He let out a clipped word of profanity but backed off.

"Guess I can't blame you for wanting an explanation for that."

"Bram knew you were going to try and . . . seduce me?" she asked bluntly.

Mercer shook his head. "This was always a sting operation, Zoe. Intel was moving from his side, and his commanding officer brought him."

"Bram knew your team was coming after my house?"

Mercer shook his head. "He knew we'd be watching the house."

Shock held her silent for a long moment. "I'm going to kick his ass when I see him."

The side of Mercer's mouth curled upward again.

"Well, that won't be anytime soon." His mouth was back in a firm line. "You'll have to trust me."

She was shaking her head. He reached out and cupped the side of her face. The connection was electric, jolting her all the way to her toes. She would have pulled away from a harder hold but he was cradling her face, giving her the support she so desperately needed.

"How?" She really shouldn't have asked. The question completed her fall to his feet.

His expression tightened. "By accepting what is." He slid his hand along her cheek, slowly sending a ripple of awareness across her skin.

So slow.

So intense.

He was closing the distance between them. Shutting out the rest of the world with his body.

It was bliss.

And everything she craved.

"No one chooses how they meet, Zoe." He'd claimed

her nape and angled her head up so their gazes fused. "Don't throw away the baby with the bathwater. I wanted to hate you. Was pissed at myself after that first night."

"You were . . ." The memory of him showing up with her cell phone replayed across her memory.

"But we still ended up on your kitchen counter because I just couldn't help myself."

She set her teeth into her lower lip. "You might just be really good at undercover work."

His lips thinned. "So what's my story now, Zoe?"

"I . . . don't know . . ." She pushed against his chest. "But I could figure it out if you'd just . . . back off for a second."

"I think I like you just like this." He leaned closer so that his breath teased her lips. A tiny sound escaped her. A needy sound. A breathless one.

"Yeah, I really like you like this . . . baby."

He muttered the last word against her lips, capturing her protest as he kissed her. She might have found the mental strength to resist a hard invasion of her mouth but this was a coaxing, the motion of enticement, sending a shiver down to her toes and curling them. It was extreme, which made her greedy for more. She craved him. Hungered for the intensity they produced together. It couldn't just be sex.

Because she'd had sex before.

This was something else.

There was a roaring in her ears as her heart accelerated. Her skin became hypersensitive, the need to rip her clothing away an absolute necessity.

Mercer helped her with that craving. Leaving off kissing her, he yanked her T-shirt over her head, but he twisted it around her wrists and pinned them to the wall.

She was stretched out for him, and he slid his dark gaze along her torso.

"I know what I'm asking for, Zoe." He found the front closure to her bra and flicked it open. The elastic band of the garment contracted, pulling the soft cups away from her breasts until they popped free. "I get that you're uncertain."

Her belly was twisting with it, and she'd be a liar if she didn't admit that the idea excited her. He was kissing one breast, planting soft, delicate compressions from his lips against the tender globe as her nipple contracted. It was a slow torment, one that her heightened senses made sure she felt every microsecond of. By the time he captured her nipple, she was twisting, seeking his erection. Her clit was throbbing incessantly, the need to climax already needling her.

"Our bodies trust each other, Zoe. Maybe we both need to listen."

Trust him?

Hell.

That opened a huge can of possibilities.

"Do you trust me?" she asked.

He pulled his attention back to her face.

"I can see the uncertainty in your eyes, Mercer."

It sent a sharp blade of regret through her.

"Same thing is in your eyes, Zoe. I could toss it in your face that I have to crowd you against the wall before you'll surrender to me or I could . . ."

She was suddenly free. Mercer was ripping his shirt off and tugging his gun off his waistband.

"Could . . . what?" she asked, feeling like part of her had been torn away.

He tossed the gun on the bedside table and popped the

buttons on his fly. His jeans ended up on the floor, leaving her biting her lower lip as she took in the magnificent sight of him in nothing but skin.

"Or I could invite you . . ." He backed up and sat on the bed. "To join me."

It was a hell of an invitation.

He was pure brawn. Temptation on a level she'd never encountered before. It was more than the sight of his chiseled body. Something pulled at her. The glitter in his eyes challenged her to step up and take what she wanted.

"You want to," he said bluntly.

"I do."

His lips curved. It was arrogant but there was also something else there. Something that hinted at him being on edge as he waited to hear her answer.

Being what he craved . . . now, that was something she was interested in.

She'd taken only a single step when he came at her, lunging like the animal she'd always thought he was. He tugged at her remaining clothing, pulling her jeans down her legs to bare her.

"I want you . . . naked." His tone was strained. He ended up dumping her on the bed as he pulled her underwear off. She bounced in a tangle of limbs and hair before rolling over and onto her knees.

Naked.

But not exposed.

No, what she felt was . . . freed.

And desired.

Mercer made a low sound in his throat. It was male and hard, just like him. His cock jutted out as he contemplated her.

"You look like a plate at a fancy restaurant, baby. Served up perfectly."

"There's plenty of life left in this dish," she informed him. "So don't expect me to let you devour me."

She placed one hand on the surface of the bed, starting to crawl toward him. She reached out, slipping her fingers around his cock. His face tightened, his neck cording.

"I might be interested in letting you have your way . . ."

"You're interested, all right." And strangely enough, so was she. Oral sex had always been more of a horse-trade sort of thing. Something she gave in order to receive.

With Mercer, it was different. She drew her fingers down his length, marveling at the smoothness of his skin. She'd never really liked a guy's cock before. But Mercer's, well, she wanted to play with it.

She scooted closer and gripped it at the base, teasing his balls with her fingertips for a moment before leaning over to lick the slit on its head.

"Shit," he hissed between clenched teeth. "That's hot, baby . . . scorching hot."

She was in complete agreement. Her clit was pulsing as she opened her mouth and sucked the head of his cock. They were connected in some strange way, the sounds coming from him whipping up the storm of anticipation brewing inside her. She sucked and hollowed her cheeks, working her hand up and down the portion of his length that she couldn't take inside her mouth. He was thrusting toward her, his hands in her hair, but he didn't take control. Didn't hold her in place and make her take more of him.

He was letting her drive him wherever she wanted.

The idea filled her with confidence. It was a new sort of intoxication, one that made her open her jaw and take more of him. His balls were tightening, his breathing rough. But it wasn't enough. She wanted him to lose it. Wanted to be the one who shoved him into mindless oblivion. His hips jerked, pumping into her mouth as she felt him start to lose control. Felt it in the way his body snapped, his fingers gripping her hair to hold her in place as his cum started hitting her tongue. She swallowed it and sucked harder, pulling more from his spasming cock.

"Holy Christ."

He swore softly, breathlessly. The bed rocked as he landed on it, falling backward and ending up on his back. She soaked up the moment. watching the way his chest heaved and his eyes remained closed while he was still caught in the grip of the climax.

He'd never let her see him so vulnerable. Never allowed himself to savor the moment while with her.

That was trust.

A deep sort. A kind she couldn't ignore.

He lifted his eyelids, opening them just a crack. "Enjoying your victory?"

"Yes." It was a soft admission, but not an prideful one.

His expression changed. The enjoyment shifting to something more . . . calculated.

"Good. Because now it's time for the flip side of this trust exercise."

There was a promise in his tone. She stiffened, feeling the power shift between them. He chuckled at her as he sat up. He reached out and stroked her cheek. It was so simple a touch, but she felt like flinching because it struck her as so intense.

"My turn to drive you insane."

She scoffed at him, shrugging and shifting back. "You've done that plenty of times."

He slipped his hand onto her nape and captured her. One moment his touch was teasing and light, the next, completely dominating. His dark eyes were lit with anticipation.

"No, baby. We collided before. Both of us spinning out of control from the impact." He teased her cheek with a kiss as she felt his body heat radiating out to stroke her bare torso. "Now you're going to let me take command."

It was the *let me* part that made her breath catch.

Submission.

Unmasking.

Things he'd done to her but he was right, she'd always struggled against allowing the tide to sweep her off her feet.

He knew what he was asking. She saw it glittering in his eyes. For a moment, she felt like she had to recoil, had to fall back to a protected position.

He teased one nipple in response. She jerked, sucking in a harsh breath of air as sensation spiked through her, taunting her with what highs were possible with him.

Extreme highs require extreme risks . . .

His words rose up from her memory.

"It isn't easy . . ." He swept his fingers along her nipple again.

Slowly.

So incredibly, insanely slowly.

She felt each fingertip. Anticipated every single one, too. He stopped with his thumb on top of the puckered point, tapping it while he watched her.

"I want to watch you give yourself over to me, Zoe."

She was biting her lower lip. He leaned forward and kissed her, using his lips to free hers. It had to be unjust, the way he kissed, because it sent her senses reeling. Soft motions increased in pressure and speed until he was kissing her with a demand that curled her toes.

He set her back, laying her out on the bed as he stretched her arms above her head, holding on to her wrists as he kissed her again.

But he left her there, sitting up to loom over her.

"Stay."

It was a command but one edged with promise. Her breath caught as she contemplated the look in his eyes. There was a flicker of enjoyment there. One she didn't want to rob him of.

"I want to see you . . ." He tapped her lips before trailing his fingers over her chin and down her neck. She arched beneath the touch, her eyes slipping closed so that there was only the sensation of his touch filling her thoughts.

"I want to watch you . . ."

He cupped her breasts, kneading them with expert motions.

"I think . . . I might actually need it, Zoe."

His voice had become raspy, hinting at a level of emotional involvement they'd never shared. She started to twist away, too uncertain to remain still.

Mercer caught her, hooking his arm beneath her knee and raising her leg so that he could press her back onto the bed with her thighs parted. Her breath caught, her insides twisting with excitement.

Oh yeah, she knew what it was. Couldn't ignore it.

He settled back down, trapping her leg beneath him as

he faced her on his side with one elbow pressing into the bed next to her ear.

"How do you pin me so fast?"

He offered her a smirk before pressing a hard kiss against her mouth. It was intoxicating, dulling her wits, making it easy to forget how exposed she was.

But he wasn't planning on forgetting what he'd started out to do. He raised his head, his gaze locked with hers as he slid his hand down her body. Her muscles were tightening. Goose bumps rose on the surface of her skin as he skimmed his way toward her spread sex.

She was caught up on the crest of a wave of anticipation, completely devoted to the path his fingers were taking. All the while he watched her, keeping her gaze locked with his, until that first touch hit her clit.

She moaned, arching beneath him.

"You're so honest with your reactions."

Zoe opened her eyes, his words shocking her, but it was damn hard to think with his fingers slipping through her slit.

He knew it, too. The moment their gaze connected, she witnessed the need in his eyes. It was a different sort of craving than she'd seen before. This was about building his confidence.

"When I'm inside you, I lose the ability to watch my effect on you."

He rimmed the opening to her body with his index fingertip. Her breath got stuck, her body straining toward him, but all he did was draw his finger up the center of her slit to where her clit was throbbing incessantly.

"I need to see."

She struggled against the tide of emotions urging her to surrender. Trying to maintain her grip on her dignity.

"Let go, Zoe. Trust me."

She wouldn't have done it for an order. But the request pushed her over the edge. She let her eyes flutter shut as he teased her clit, rubbing across its sensitive surface and driving her insane with the need to climax. She withered, arching up, seeking that last bit of pressure.

Mercer didn't give it to her. He teased her slit, rubbing the folds, trailing through the fluid that was flowing from her body. Leaning over her, the scent of his skin filled her senses. Taking his pleasure wasn't enough. He wanted to prove himself.

Part of her craved it as well.

Deep down inside her, where pride didn't matter, part of her was an animal that wanted to be pleased.

"Make me come." It was a demand, edged with the hunger he'd built with his fingers. "Now, damn you."

"Don't close your eyes," he countered, pushing his fingers into her sheath. She groaned, so close she felt like she was going to snap.

"Keep your eyes open, Zoe, and let me watch it happen . . ."

His voice was hypnotic, offering her satisfaction. She stared at him, yielding to his demand. His expression tightened, determination drawing his features into a setting that was primal. She was mesmerized by it, drawn in by the savage nature and the promise of satisfaction. His nostrils flared, his lips curling back as he leaned down and kissed her.

This time he claimed her mouth, taking her lips in a hard kiss of ownership as he shifted his fingers to her clit and rubbed it hard. She went spiraling out of control, the pleasure tearing through her as he lifted his lips off hers and hovered over her face, watching her fly into a million pieces.

He controlled her completely in that moment, mastering her body. It was wrenching and more intimate than anything she'd ever experienced. She looked away when it was over, feeling overly exposed.

He cupped her chin and brought her face back to his. There was a flicker of satisfaction but one born in accomplishment. It stirred something in her. She shifted, rolling over and coming up on top of him.

"Don't be too smug, Mercer . . ." She suddenly realized she didn't know his last name.

"It's St. Clair."

He cupped her hips, guiding her down onto his length. "Mercer Peter St. Clair."

It was more than a name. At least it felt far more significant. She lifted off him and lowered herself as he guided her. A soft hum of enjoyment passed her lips as she adjusted to being stretched by his cock. It was a deeper sort of pleasure, one that awakened a craving at the center of her core. She rode him, slowly building up to another eruption. He guided her hips, his fingers tightening as his cock hardened. He started to roll her beneath him.

"No," she insisted, clamping her thighs around him. "Not this time."

He bared his teeth at her, his breathing rough. She could see the desire to take command brightening his dark eyes. It was a fascinating view, the savage impulse mixing with the man who had decided to trust her.

Their gazes remained locked as she started to climax.

It was gripping, pounding through her deepest core. Mercer had been waiting for it. He surged upward, flipping her onto her back as he pistoned her through the waves of delight. His cock felt larger, harder. He arched back as he started coming. Hot spurts of cum hit her insides, setting off another ripple of enjoyment, deep inside her.

No condom.

She should have been able to dwell on that thought but she had no strength left. Mercer ground himself into her, his cock jerking a final time before the bed rocked violently when he collapsed beside her. She was too spent to move. But she didn't have to. He scooped her up, rolling her onto his chest as she surrendered to oblivion.

For just a moment, everything was perfect. She soaked it up, willingly ignoring everything else but the man holding her.

His heart rate had slowed down by the time she came back to her senses, but he was still stroking her back. She must have drifted off to sleep, lulled by the sound of his heart. A faint rapping on the wall woke her.

"Hummm?"

Zoe blinked as she tried to clear her head. Her brain was moving slowly, her thoughts fuzzy.

"Got to get back to work." Mercer rolled over and off the bed. He rubbed a hand over his face before beginning to dress.

Her thoughts crystalized with shocking clarity. She felt her cheeks catch fire as she realized that the other team members likely knew what was going on behind the closed door of the bedroom.

She witnessed a flicker of satisfaction in his eyes.

"Maybe I'm being a little bit of a dick, baby, but I want them to know that you're mine."

"Wait a second—"

He ducked out of the room while she was still formulating her argument, leaving her to struggle against the surge of enjoyment that washed through her in response. Really, she should be more . . . well . . . more something. More modern. More sophisticated than enjoying knowing a man was making a public declaration concerning her.

But she wasn't. In fact, she ended up hugging a pillow and hiding her smile against it.

"Been a long time," Kagan said.

Vitus only offered him a bland look in response.

Kagan slowly grinned. "Always did like the way you get straight to the point."

"Part of my charm."

Kagan sipped at his coffee, looking around the java joint. There were college kids in flip-flops and torn jeans and preppy moms sporting manicures. A few adults intent on being thrifty and using the free Internet offered by the café were dug in at various tables with their laptops. Vitus scrunched low in his seat, just a momentary flicker of annoyance with the poor posture making it into his eyes. Kagan propped an elbow on the bistro table in an effort to blend into their civilian setting.

"Don't you mean, part of your retaliation plan?" Kagan asked bluntly.

Vitus bared his teeth. "Tyler has it coming."

"You've been watching him for the last three years and there still isn't more than suspicion to support your opinion." Kagan was tapping his fingertips against the table.

"He was going to show his true colors at some point. Today is that day." Vitus flipped his tablet onto the table. The call record from Tim to Tyler was highlighted. Kagan stared at it for a moment.

"Bugging that party rental office was child's play," Vitus explained. "They used a burner phone but I've got both sides of the conversation. Tyler's gone soft, tossing in with someone like Tim."

Kagan nodded in agreement. "Tyler is just going to play the game. Tell us he was setting up the buyer."

"Fine." Vitus said. "Let's move forward. Let's see what Tyler does when that money hits his hand. I'm betting it's going to land somewhere with Saxon's name attached to it."

Kagan lifted his coffee cup and drew off a sip. "That's a stretch."

"Not when you and I both know Tyler has ties to Jeb Ryland. And Jeb Ryland is still screaming for vengeance. The man isn't even wise enough to do it quietly. He forgets that I have friends in Washington, too. Friends watching his ass, so they're stuck to it and hear a whole lot."

Kagan was sipping his coffee again. "You know I disagreed with Tyler taking your shield. But you stepped over a line, son. The kind of line you need to think twice about stepping over again."

"I didn't step over it alone. I completed my mission by bringing that girl back in one piece. The rest of it is none of your fucking business."

Kagan raised an eyebrow at the profanity but Vitus didn't give a damn. His superior ended up chuckling. It was darn near silent and his lips barely curved but on the face of his boss, it was like a crack in bulletproof glass.

"Another thing I like about you, no shame." Kagan looked at the tablet again. "Your plan?"

"Put the pressure on," Vitus answered.

Kagan raised an eyebrow.

"Tim wants that hard drive," Vitus said. "Tell Tyler it's coming in."

"He might just wait for it to arrive."

Vitus shook his head. "Loosen the chain on the mule. My bet is, he'll try to force her into bringing him the goods. Once she moves, Tyler will have to choose a course of action."

"That's mighty risky."

"Whole operation is. Saxon's ass is hanging out in the wind. One breath of a rumor on where he is and you're going to need a mop-up team and four flags, along with a mighty good explanation to Colonel Magnus about how his daughter ended up dead while in protective custody. Since she made that call out, we've lost the edge. Either we move or we run a high risk of getting blindsided."

Kagan was silent for a long moment, weighing the odds.

"I doubt your brother will agree to letting the civilian back into the line of fire."

Vitus drew in a deep breath. "Leave that part to me."

Kagan slowly smiled. "You're not planning on telling him."

Vitus shook his head. "I'm always on the level with Saxon. She's still a target. The mission needs to proceed. His life could depend on knowing if Tyler is a rat."

Kagan's expression grew pensive. "In that case, good luck. I think you're going to need it."

"Keep an eye on Tyler."

Kagan nodded before pushing his chair back and tossing

his cup into a nearby trash can. He winked at a college student on his way out the door and disappeared into the pedestrian foot traffic. A couple of moms with strollers eyed his table. Vitus shook his frame out before leaving it to them. Conversation flowed around him. He hid his emotions behind a practiced expression.

There was nothing about life that a man should ever turn his back on.

That was a one-way ticket to hell.

He knew the ride well.

"Ready for bed?" Mercer asked from the doorway.

The question caught her off guard. But then, so did the sight of him. He was once more the confident agent, watching her from behind an unreadable expression.

"Zoe?"

"Sure." She realized she'd been staring at him dumbfounded. "I mean, yes. I'm going to turn in."

"Got your teeth brushed?"

She curled her lips back, because one absurd question deserved an equally ridiculous answer. Maybe it was just her. She was still reeling from their encounter. The fact was, she had no idea how to feel.

He nodded, sweeping the room before coming through the doorway.

"What are you doing?" she asked.

He didn't answer her but made his way across the room to the other side of the bed. She heard his boots hit the floor before he swung his legs up and settled in beside her.

"Excuse me?" she asked. "Did I miss something?"

He settled back against the pillows, his expression cracking momentarily and turning sensuous. "You remember the whole thing, baby, but deny it all you like. I'll be happy to give a repeat performance. Are you saying you'll share your body with me but not your bed?"

Her cheeks heated. She looked away as she struggled to keep a grip on her composure.

Mercer struck in that moment, capturing her wrist. She felt the cold touch of metal and heard the handcuff click. She jerked her hand away but there was another click as he secured the second one to his own wrist.

"What do you think you're doing?" she demanded.

"Dealing with you." There was a soft whistle in the doorway. Saxon stood there, taking in the scene.

Her cheeks caught fire. Okay, so she'd accepted the fact that everyone in the house knew what she and Mercer were about when they were in the bedroom together, but that didn't mean she was ready to have the team leader watching them in bed. Even if their clothes were still on.

Saxon dangled a set of keys before dropping them into the breast pocket of his shirt. "Sleep tight."

"What is going on?" She pulled on their joined wrists but only ended up with Mercer's arm across her chest. "Unlock these."

He shook his head and settled back against the pillows. "Not a chance. I want to know exactly where you are for the next few hours."

She sent him a scathing look. "What are you trying to prove?"

"That it's time you started working with us." He rolled over onto his side and pegged her with a hard look. "You threw Greer under the bus today with that phone call. He was responsible for you at the time."

"I don't owe him anything. Or any of you."

"Really?" One dark eyebrow rose. "There are only the four of us. We're all taking turns pulling duty. Someone wants you dead, Zoe. That's why we're off grid. Greer didn't appreciate being shown up in front of his boss. So tonight, you're mine and I need some sleep. Cuffing you to the headboard leaves you slim opportunity to escape." His eyes glittered with determination. "Not on my watch."

Guilt stabbed into her. Mercer watched her face for a moment before he settled back against the pillows and closed his eyes.

"It isn't any easier for me, Zoe."

His voice was so low she blinked, thinking she'd imagined the words. But he opened his eyes a crack and shot her a look that was full of uncertainty.

"Both of us have to make a choice to trust each other."

"So when are you going to start sharing information?" she asked. "None of you would just sit around, waiting in the dark while everything you held dear was on the line."

He reached over and clasped her hand, the cuffs shifting and making a soft clinking sound. "I'm working on it."

He meant it. She heard the sincerity in his voice. It didn't cut through her frustration completely, but it made a good dent. Which left her settling back and closing her eyes.

Enough for one day.

CHAPTER SEVEN

Tim was nervous.

Bram knew the guy well enough to spot his habits. He tightened his grip on the binoculars he was watching his father's longtime friend through.

That was a big point of contention.

Friend.

Tim was a traitor.

Servat strolled up to the meeting place that Tim had changed three times in the last hour. This time, it was a jogging trail that stretched for twenty long miles along a flood-control channel. Servat lifted one of his feet and started retying his shoe. Bram switched from the binoculars to a camera with a telephoto lens on it. He started recording video as Servat offered Tim a small flash drive. Tim tucked it into his pocket as he pulled out a water bottle and unscrewed the cap. Tim got up and walked away. Servat collected the flash drive he'd left on the bench before jogging off in the opposite direction.

Bram itched to drag Tim off the trail.

But that wasn't going to happen.

At least not yet.

"You win."

Zoe looked up, but Mercer was hiding behind sunglasses. If that wasn't suspicious enough he tossed her cell phone onto the bed next to her. She had to scoop it up fast before Harley got ahold of it. The parrot squawked at her. Mercer held out his arm. Harley stepped up without hesitation.

"I don't get it," Zoe said as she stared at the cell phone. What had always been such a part of her life was now revealed in a new light.

Privilege. An everyday right that she'd taken for granted.

Mercer put Harley in his cage and checked the door lock twice before he turned back to face her.

"We want cooperation. You need to feel like a member of the team."

"All right. Makes sense."

He'd crossed his arms over his chest "Does it, Zoe?"

Her pride started to rear its head. She fought to contain it, craving information more than the need to blow off steam. She swallowed her temper.

"Explain." It was only a single word, but it was better than taking a dig at him.

"Explain what?"

She swung her legs over the side of the bed and faced him. Sensation rippled down her skin. She really sort of hated the reaction but the bed held too many fresh memories to ignore.

"What . . . you want me to do." She held the cell phone up. "I don't understand the rules. Explain them."

"The intel is set to be exchanged. It will be a hard hand turnover. We need that transaction to happen while you are in custody."

Understanding dawned instantly. "Got it."

"So . . . keep your head down."

"Why give this back to me?" she asked. "Sounds to me like you don't want me to use it."

"That's right. Maybe I'm giving you what you say you want, to see if you start whining about something else instead of accepting the facts." He grunted. "Maybe I'm just tired of sleeping handcuffed to you." He turned around and disappeared down the hallway.

Maybe that was a smoke screen.

At least, she had the feeling it was.

Part of her really hated admitting how much she didn't know about his world, and deep down inside she was sorry she didn't know him better.

She really wanted to.

Focus.

Yeah, focus. I'm heading for a crash-and-burn sort of letdown when he walks away from me. Untamed won't settle into being a house pet well.

All of her own frustration suddenly felt rash. The operation was going to end and when it did, Mercer would ride out of her life.

Maybe she should remember what Roni liked to say and spend a little more time living in the moment. She had a funny feeling that she was going to be hearing those sage words of advice for a long time to come.

Saxon was waiting for him when Mercer made it back into the living room. His team leader watched him from behind a set expression. It was one Mercer had seen countless times, but today it was pissing him off.

"You don't like it," Saxon said.

"She doesn't know how to navigate the pitfalls of a situation like this," Mercer responded. "I'd be unhappy about setting any innocent up—"

"Bull," Saxon cut him off softly. "You're personally involved."

"Even if that's true, it doesn't change the facts."

Saxon stared at him for a long moment. It was the closest thing Mercer was going to get to an agreement from him. Mercer cursed before staring at his computer screen again. The cold words sat there like salt in his wounds.

He flipped back around to face Saxon. "I am definitely personally involved."

It was a declaration. One that made Saxon's face darken.

"And it's done, so live with the fact that I am not happy about giving Zoe enough slack to get herself back into harm's way. I'm going to be hovering."

And that was all there was to it.

"How's the view?" Kagan asked.

Vitus was grateful to be talking on a cell phone because it afforded him the luxury of scowling. Not exactly a professional way to deal with someone of Kagan's rank and security clearance.

"I'll take that silence as confirmation of your enjoyment of being back in the saddle."

"Love it," Vitus confirmed. "Home sweet home. In a civilian foxhole."

He was stretched out on a thin mattress in the back of a battered pickup truck with a clamshell camper top on it.

He'd knocked his head against the top of it too many times to count as he shifted around in the confined space. The place was seedy to say the least, doubly so because circumstances afforded him only a brief, twenty-minute escape once a day, when he moved the truck to avoid suspicion or notice from the locals. The rest of the time, he was stuck watching the house Saxon was holed up in. But it did beat a foxhole in hostile territory.

"The mule is being given back her cell phone," Kagan informed him. "I'll be shaking the tree in another day, so stay sharp."

"Glad to hear it," Vitus said. "This situation stinks bad. Something's not right."

It was Vitus's turn to listen to a long silence on the other end of the phone. That chilled his blood. Kagan had a good head on his shoulders and a nose for shadow operations. If he was smelling a stink, there was a dead body coming their way. Maybe more than one.

"Stay on your post." Kagan said. "Mercer is your inside contact. Alert him to any movement from the target."

"Ten four."

Kagan cut the line, leaving Vitus alone with his thoughts and the time ticking away around him. The waiting game was the worst part of his job because it could wear a man down, dulling his senses with fatigue until a perpetrator found an opening to strike through.

"You hate the plan."

Bram glared at Servat. "Completely."

Servat nodded. "The colonel understands your objections, but you knew this was going to be a sticky situation from the beginning."

Bram's temper boiled over the lid he'd jammed down on top of it. "Stop making it sound like I have any choice in this."

"The colonel knows you didn't," Servat said. "We all know who started this mess and he's still on the loose. Tim brought this to your doorstep. Consider yourself fortunate to be able to help bring him down."

"There's nothing fortunate about my sister being caught up in this. I expected her to be locked down and kept out of the line of fire. Pissed but safe."

Servat sat on the edge of a desk. "A team had to be assigned that had no connections to the case. You know the reasons for that."

"Right," Bram grunted. "It's the only way to one hundred percent prove my family has no involvement."

Servat nodded. "They're a top-notch team. Experienced. Good record."

"They used a mole in her bed." Bram sliced through Servat's explanation.

Servat didn't offer him any compassion. "A proven tactic, and it beats waterboarding."

Bram grunted. "Fine. I get it. But she is my sister, so don't expect me to be happy about it."

"Professional will do."

"I've been that," Bram growled.

And it was chewing a hole in him. Sure, he understood. He also had a healthy respect for the special assignment teams. They dealt with the worst the planet had to offer and managed to hold the line fairly well considering they were up against slime who didn't have any compunctions about killing anyone in their path. They concerned themselves with profits and power. Blood was nothing more than the grease on the wheels of the machine.

But this was Zoe.

She was innocent.

She was also a whole lot like him and their dad. If he was being honest, a large part of his concern centered on the fact that he knew she wasn't going to sit quietly and hide.

No, she was a Magnus through and through. The plan needed her to stay put, and honestly he doubted if she would.

Which was going to ensure he had a lot of sleepless nights until the operation was complete.

It had been a while since she'd taken time to preen.

Not that she had much in the way of girlie essentials at hand.

Still, Zoe rummaged through her meager toiletry items and managed to bring her eyebrows back under control. She'd used her phone to add a little music to the moment, the single speaker like a lone candle flame in the otherwise quiet room. Even Harley fluffed up, enjoying the entertainment.

"Okay, you got me there." Mercer was back in the doorway. He'd cocked his head to one side, his lips curving slightly as he took in the sound. "It is a little stale in this place."

"Don't worry, I'm not streaming it."

He nodded before coming into the room. She still loved the way he moved. It was part prowl, part stride. A combination of brawn and control that was awe inspiring. Honestly, she could just stare at him, soaking up the primal perfection.

The soft jersey of his T-shirt let the chiseled condition of his abs show through. His jeans weren't tight. Nope. They were baggy enough for him to move in, and that had a whole different sort of sexiness to it. He didn't have to tell anyone he was a badass. All he had to do was walk into the room and you knew it, down deep in the pit of your stomach. Heat teased her, flicking to life as she felt the air between them thicken. She didn't shy away from it this time, just let it roll through her like the burn of an expensive brandy.

The sound of the handcuffs clinking against themselves drew her attention. They were looped through his belt, swaying as he moved.

He caught her looking at the handcuffs. She expected his expression to tighten but his lips curved instead, becoming a grin that was playful, in a man-eating tiger sort of way.

He tossed the cuffs onto the bed and unclipped his gun. "Should have given you that phone back days ago. You've loosened up."

She sat down on the bed and lay back against the pillows. "Think carefully about making any comments concerning stress-reduction methods."

Mercer settled beside her. "You're stubborn."

She sent him a harassed look. "Because I want to take care of myself? That's the pot calling the kettle black."

His expression became serious. "I'll take care of you, Zoe."

She felt each little word deep down inside that place in her heart that she'd been warning herself to keep him out of. He'd scratch it up with his powerful claws and leave her nursing the wounds when he prowled away.

"That's a little different tone than I've heard before."

She dropped the cuffs onto his chest and looked across the room with her hand waiting. "Not that I'm not appreciative of the change."

She heard the cuffs chink but it was as he sat them on the bedside table next to his gun. He captured her hand and rolled over until he was half on her.

Reaction was instant. Her belly tightened as heat flared up inside her. His gaze locked with hers, giving her an unobstructed view of desire flickering in his eyes.

"Promise me. Give me your word, Zoe."

His tone was thick with emotion. He maintained his grip on her wrist, his fingers feeling ten times stronger than the handcuffs had. The reason was simple. The cuffs were impersonal, something she might dismiss because she owed them nothing.

But this was Mercer. She cared what he thought of her. It was that simple and had roots that twisted deep inside her.

She nodded, her throat tightening because she realized he was reaching out to her. Trusting her when he wasn't a man who gave out confidence easily. His gaze burned into hers. She could feel him trying to read her thoughts, struggling to trust her.

"Saxon will call me a fool." He kissed her hand and rolled away from her. The bed rocked as he settled on his back, staring up at the ceiling.

She worried her lower lip, debating whether or not to keep her mouth shut. It would be the wiser course of action.

But not the one she wanted to take.

"Because of Vitus?" she asked.

Mercer turned his head so that he was looking at her. "What do you know about that?"

She shrugged. "Not much, just what I'm picking up by

being the silent observer. Vitus obviously used to do the same sort of work Saxon does. He had a good year's worth of hair on him that he cut off, surprising you. Clearly it's significant. He said he was back. That's got to mean he was on the bench, so to speak."

"They did work together." His expression tightened. "It was a woman who caused Vitus to lose his shield."

Mercer was torn. She could see the conflict in his dark eyes. It made her sick. He'd faced snipers without a single flinch, but trusting her was making him doubt.

She reached past him and grabbed the handcuffs, locking one around her wrist. He captured her hand before she got the second one around his wrist. He rolled over her again, pressing down until he claimed her mouth in a kiss.

She hummed with enjoyment.

It was possible she outright purred.

All she knew for certain was that it felt perfect to have his mouth on hers. She kissed him back, opening her lips as he pressed them apart. He tasted good. Hot. Virile. Like something she was addicted to.

And she wanted another hit.

There was no questioning the impulse. There was only need and hunger. He sat up, ripping his shirt off.

"Perfect . . ." She flattened her hands on his chest, sweeping her fingertips across the ridges of muscle. Her toes were curling, sensation rippling down her spine. There was a sense of being reunited with something that had been withheld from her for too long. She hadn't realized how much she longed for him.

"Your turn, baby." He didn't wait for her to move.

No, not Mercer. He took action, earning a soft sound of enjoyment from her as he tugged her shirt up and over her head. She settled back down on the bed, the cool night air touching her bare breasts as his gaze took her in.

"Now, that . . . is perfection . . . baby."

He came down, seeking out her nipples, first one and then the other. She gasped, arching up to offer them to him. The heat from his mouth felt like it traveled straight from her nipple to her clit. She was withering but also needy for more of him.

She grabbed his belt and worked it loose. He sat up, back on his haunches as she opened his fly and freed his cock. It sprang free the moment she popped the last button, swollen and hard and full of the promise of satisfaction.

"Like what you found?"

"I do." She drew her fingers along his length, delighting in the way his jaw tightened. His cock was silky smooth but hot.

"Good, because I plan to give it to you." His voice was rough. She shivered in response. He reached out and stroked her cheek.

"I love the way you tremble for me, baby . . ."

It wasn't the sort of polished compliment she'd been raised to expect—it was far better. More sincere, more honest. For a moment their gazes were fused, the need they stirred in each other flowing freely between them with no way for either of them to hide from it.

There was only surrender left.

To each other.

Mercer moved a second later, pulling her sweatpants down and tossing them over the side of the bed. He stood up and dropped his jeans, crawling back onto the bed like the predatory cat she often thought of him as.

The prowl was there.

The hunger for prey.

But he wasn't the only one with an appetite.

Zoe came up and met him in the middle of the bed, slipping her hands along his shoulders as he angled his head and claimed her mouth in a searing kiss once again. This time he captured the back of her head, holding her in place as he ravaged her mouth. Her thoughts scattered and she laughed in carefree abandonment.

He raised an eyebrow at her.

"I want to live in this moment."

Zoe cupped his shoulder and pulled him around. He decided to indulge her, settling back against the bed when she pushed him there.

"Just . . . feel . . ."

He wasn't willing to let her command the moment completely. He maintained his hold on her waist, cupping her hips and pulling her along with him as she pushed him down. She ended up straddling him, his cock pressing against the folds of her spread sex.

He curled his lips back in response, slipping his hands up to cup her breasts.

"Ride me."

It was a command, just as hard and action-packed as he was. Zoe lifted herself, feeling his cock spring up. He reached between them and nestled the head between her folds.

"I don't want to use a condom." His eyes were bright with need. "I want to feel our skin meeting . . ."

She quivered in response, lowering herself because thought was completely beyond her. There was only the promise of his hard flesh and the yearning driving her mad to have it lodged deeply inside her.

She gasped when she was seated, tilting her head back because she was already on the edge. She fought not to climax so quickly. She wanted to enjoy the ride.

"I know the feeling, baby . . ." He captured her hips and lifted her up. "Let's take our time tonight."

He thrust up into her, her body making a little wet sound. His cock felt harder, larger than she recalled, her body stretching to accommodate it.

She pressed down and he landed on the bed. His cock twitched inside her, his teeth showing as his lips curled back.

"Let's ride, baby . . ."

The bed rocked, the springs making a racket as she kept pace with him. He moved her hips in the motion he wanted. She clasped him between her thighs and plunged down onto his length as she tried to set the pace.

It was a constant battle, one that neither of them was willing to surrender to the other—but both were completely happy to try to best each other. Sweat covered them both, sensation twisting her into a knot that finally snapped. It tore her apart, the pleasure white-hot and searing. Mercer flipped her over in that moment, pounding into her body as the climax held her in its grip. She was suspended in the moment, unable to breathe or do anything except wither in ecstasy.

He rode her through it, hammering against her spread body, plunging deep and hard into her core until he growled and his cock jerked, starting to give up its load. His cum was hot, hitting the mouth of her womb and setting off another ripple of rapture that was so intense, she moaned. Just a deep sound, clawing its way up from the primal animal inside her that needed the assurance that her partner had reached his zenith.

Savage.

Maybe.

Stupid?

Possible.

But honestly, all she could do was cling to him as they panted. The darkness was a cloak that shielded them from things like rational, wise choices. They were someplace else. Someplace she'd dreamed about in her most private moments but always missed in her intimate encounters. Like a fabled ending that big girls had to accept as the stuff of fantasy. Never to be seen in real life.

In that moment, she was certain she felt it. Folded in Mercer's embrace, she was sure she was cherished. So certain, she drifted off into sleep, his scent filling her senses and her thoughts wrapped around the pure bliss of being in his arms.

Kagan fingered his cell phone, tracing the smooth case with the tip of his index finger.

"You're hesitating. Why?"

Kagan didn't take offense. "I learned a long time ago to identify when to dwell on a choice before rushing head-long into it."

Colonel Decains sniffed and nodded.

"Today's going to be a pisser," Kagan decided at last. He swiped his finger across the screen of the phone and selected a contact. The line started buzzing before he put the little bit of technology up to his ear.

"Tyler here."

"Kagan."

"Yes sir?" Tyler responded.

"I've got Saxon's team coming in with the hard drives.

They confirm they found the data. Process it and get me a full report."

"Sir." The single word was clipped.

"I'll be there to oversee the hard disk information retrieval," Kagan added.

"I can handle it, sir," Tyler said.

"Too sensitive. Got a few big dogs on my heels. But I'm a day away. Don't wait for me to start. I'll catch up when I make it to your location."

"Got it," Tyler said half a second before he killed the line.

"Now we see what runs from the fire," Decains said.

Across the room, two large one-way glass windows allowed them to see into interrogation rooms. They were concrete-floored cells with a single table and two chairs. In the middle of each table was a huge iron ring used to chain suspects. At the moment, there was a civilian contractor in each cell. They were both haggard, fatigue etched into their faces. The stink of fear permeated the air.

Kagan didn't have a morsel of compassion for either of them. At the moment, he was more occupied with being angry over the laws that prevented him from using anything more than time to loosen their lips.

"They're not going to talk," Decains said. "Someone has their mouths sealed tight."

"We'll see if time doesn't loosen them up," Kagan said. "Their faith might just grow thin when they start rotting in a cell and no one comes to set them free."

"Their boss might snuff them out before that can happen."

"Leave that to me." Kagan insisted. "I'm sending them off the prison grid. I'm going to bury them deep."

Decains's lips rose into a slight curve. "Hope it works. I really want to know who called the shots on this one."

"Me too. Maybe whatever comes out of the brush can help us with that."

"You know what's coming out of the brush," Decains said. "That's why you've put off making that call."

The colonel reached out and clasped Kagan on the shoulder. It was a motion only commanders understood, a squeeze that conveyed compassion for having one's trust betrayed in the shadow world they both operated in. It was a constant threat.

That didn't make it any easier to stomach.

Not one damn bit.

"Do you have my money?" Tyler demanded the moment Tim answered the phone.

"I thought you didn't want there to be any contact between us?" Tim sneered.

"The money?" Tyler cut back.

Tim grunted. "I got it. The transfer is going through now. What about Zoe? And the hard drive?"

"Saxon's team is coming in, with the girl and the hard drives. You're a dumb fuck for leaving that intel for them to find. Get her to meet you instead."

"How in the hell am I supposed to do that?" Tim demanded.

"She's got her cell. Get some bait. Set up an exchange. I'll be there to back you up."

Tim grunted. "You'd better be. The deal was full resettlement. The Magnus family has a lot of friends. I don't need to be looking over my shoulder."

"The money lands first. Second, you get the girl and the hard drives so I can clean them up without leaving a trail."

"Right," Tim agreed. "Give me an hour."

Kagan selected another contact and pressed it. Vitus answered before the line buzzed twice.

"I shook the tree. Keep your eye on the prize."

"Sounds like you don't have a lot of faith in my brother."

Kagan offered him a crusty sound of amusement. "That girl is a Magnus. If someone presses her, I expect she'll rise to the occasion. She's your prime target. Don't lose her. I expect action imminently."

"Got it."

Vitus ended the call and checked his gun before leaving the back of the pickup truck he'd been living in. Parked on the side of the road, it had a small shell that allowed him to keep an eye on the house Saxon was operating out of. He stretched his legs, looking like he was doing nothing more than enjoying the morning sun.

His body tingled, the waiting almost over. That much was a relief.

Of course, this was also the part where people started dying.

Mercer was gone when she woke.

Zoe stretched and tried to fend off the wave of loneliness that threatened to wash over her. She pulled the cover off Harley's cage. The parrot offered her a look.

"Yeah, I miss sunshine, too," she offered in an attempt to banish her negative attitude.

Live in the moment . . .

Right.

The house was always in a semi-gray sort of light, electric lighting on all the time. The clock on the wall was her only true way to keep tabs on the time.

Seven thirty sharp.

Zoe made her way down the hallway into the kitchen and poured herself a cup of coffee. There was a chill on the tile floor from the back door. Even without a window, there was still a thin line between the weather stripping and the doorjamb where the elements got in.

The coffee was hot and she grabbed a banana from the counter to share with Harley. She broke it in half and offered part of it to the parrot. He bobbed his head happily as he closed his talon around the fruit, then purred softly as he licked it.

"Good morning to you, too," she offered as she took a bite of the half she held.

The cell phone Mercer had given back to her rang. She turned around, questioning if the sound she'd heard had really come from it. The screen was flashing, the case vibrating against the end table, but the number was what caught her attention.

Roni.

She couldn't answer it.

Her fingers itched. That wave of loneliness she'd fought back when she woke up came at her and knocked her on her ass.

God, she wanted a girlfriend chat!

Needed it bad.

But she'd promised Mercer.

That stopped her. She curled her fingers into a fist as the call went to her voice mail.

Okay, so what she'd promised him was sort of undefined, but it was the concept that had her taking another bite of the banana instead of picking up her phone.

It vibrated again, this time with an incoming text message. She dropped the banana, scooping the phone up. Reading a text message wasn't breaking her word. It wasn't exactly the conversation she yearned for, either, but beggars couldn't be choosers.

If you want to see your friend alive, you will do as instructed.

A picture came through next. Zoe nearly dropped the phone as Tim's face filled the screen.

Call me. Make sure no one knows you're doing it.

The phone buzzed again, showing her a shot of Roni. There was a silver strip of duct tape across her mouth and a killing look in her eyes.

Horror nearly gagged her. The banana was suddenly not sitting very well in her stomach. She ended up in the bathroom, still clutching the phone. Her emotions were reeling as she tried to get a grip. The phone started buzzing again before she'd really come to any sort of decision. She swiped the screen without thinking, operating on pure adrenaline.

"Roni?"

"No, but she's right here." Tim sounded smug. A shiver went down her spine as her fingers tightened around the phone.

"Roni isn't part of this—"

"That's for me to say," Tim cut in. "If you don't want her to become a casualty, you are going to do exactly what I tell you."

There was a familiar note in Tim's voice. One that she'd so often listened to and taken solace in. That firm, "always

keeps his promises" tone that made her bite her lip today.
Disillusionment was a cold hard bitch. Zoe fought back
panic as she struggled to maintain her wits.

"I'm listening, Tim."

"Good," he answered. "You're going to bring me that
hard drive. Get out of the house alone."

"I want to talk to Roni," Zoe demanded. "You might
just have her cell phone and Photoshopped that picture."

There was a muffle on the other end of the line. "Don't
do anything this fucker says—"

"That's all you get." Tim was back on the line. "And I'm
not giving you much time. Bring me the evidence and you
get your friend. Don't forget, I served, too. Delay, and I'll
know you're trying to get your team in position. You have
five minutes to call me back. If you aren't outside, I'm going to kill your little friend here so that the next time I make
contact, you take me seriously. Your brother is right where
my contact can get at him. He's next. The clock starts now."

The call ended, leaving her staring at the blank screen
with Roni's number on it.

Roni.

They were all so stupid!

She was the worst for not thinking of her best friend.
Voices were coming through the bedroom door. Saxon and
his team were still discussing options. Desperation was
tearing at her insides. She was trembling but ordered herself to stop.

Think!

Mercer would know what to do.

Yeah, but Tim knew what he was doing, too. She had
three minutes left. Mercer would refuse to let her get in-

volved. She trusted now that he believed she was innocent. She'd never realized that might become a liability.

It sure was now. Tim had been friends with them for years. He knew their friends. Probably had a nice list of addresses, too. Not to mention a key to her house and the parrot party van.

So simple.

God, she wanted to kill him.

The rage came up from inside her, bubbling and churning its way past her common sense. Tim wanted a showdown? Fine. She would be more than happy to give it to him.

Tim had been using her gullibility and she was going to kick his teeth down his throat.

Zoe grabbed her credit card and a handful of cash. She stuffed them in her pocket before she opened the bedroom door and walked out. Mercer looked up, his dark gaze locking with hers.

"I need something to eat."

She brushed past them on her way to the kitchen. Thais was leaning in the doorway, focused on the discussion. Zoe grabbed something from the freezer and tossed it into the microwave. She turned it on before turning around and looking at the abandoned workstations in the dining room.

"He'll make you in about two minutes if you try that . . ." Thais said as she moved into the room the discussion was taking place in.

Zoe stepped up to the workstation, scooping up the hard drive from her computer. She left the one from the laptop on the desk. She peeled off the sticker that identified it and turned around while the microwave continued to buzz. She opened a cabinet door and took out a dish that she placed on the countertop with just enough force to add noise to the moment.

The back door opened without a sound as the microwave continued. She was down the steps and behind the garage before she really had time to think.

She hesitated for a moment, waiting for someone to yell. When the alarm didn't come, she forced herself to take a deep breath and walked along the exterior of the house. She made her way to the fence and used the planter to climb over it. Checking the time on the phone, she started walking up the block. She punched the redial.

"I'm out."

"Surprising." Tim replied. "Do you have the hard drive?"

"Yes."

She took delight in lying to him. Everything that had happened was his fault. It was going to be her pleasure to see him disappointed.

I wouldn't have met Mercer without him . . .

Yeah? And she'd be a whole lot better off, too.

Liar.

She didn't have time to deal with her personal feelings.

Just like Mercer.

Yeah, just like him.

She rounded the corner and found herself staring at a taxi. The driver was waiting outside a hotel, two more cabs in line behind him.

"Where you going?" he asked as she climbed in.

"I'm not agreeing to any plan that includes Zoe being in harm's way," Mercer said. "She's innocent."

"But we can't prove that yet," Saxon argued. "Right now it's going to blow up all over her and her family."

Mercer felt his phone vibrate. He almost ignored it, but some habits died hard. "Shit!" He ran into the kitchen but Vitus was right on the money as usual. "Zoe slipped out."

"How do you know?" Saxon demanded but he didn't wait for an answer. "Who else is working this case?"

"Vitus."

Saxon's complexion darkened. "And you didn't dial me into that bit of information?"

"Kagan made the call to him." Mercer was out of the door and heading for his bike. "He needed someone to watch Zoe who wouldn't have the distraction of answering to a team lead. A safety net."

"Kagan did what?"

Mercer stopped and gave Saxon his full attention. He owed him that.

Saxon bit back a word of profanity. His team leader proved his worth by adjusting quickly to the situation, shoving aside his wounded pride in favor of the most critical needs of the moment. "Where's she heading?" He was swinging his leg over his own bike.

"Into the line of fire," Mercer replied before peeling away from the curb.

Roni lived in a condo.

It didn't seem like the sort of place where someone might be held hostage or be in danger of being murdered. The building was new, the cars parked in front of it nice. No creepy, run-down house set back from the street to allow for criminal acts. There was traffic passing around it, even a guy walking his dog. It all felt surreal. Zoe stood on the doorstep for a long moment, trying to decide if she was locked inside some crazy nightmare.

Well, she was, and if she wanted out she was going to have to do something about it. Tim had been part of her nice, normal life. The deception stung.

Deeply.

She backed up and looked around. Spotting a planter, she dropped the hard drive in it with a satisfied nod.

She went to the front door and pushed the doorbell, hearing it buzz. It opened. "Come in, Zoe."

Tim stayed out of sight, leaving her facing the open doorway. It felt a whole lot like a giant mousetrap.

She stepped inside because she wasn't going to go out sniveling. And she wasn't going to abandon her friend.

Tim shut the door behind her. It was only a door but it felt like an iron cage had just been closed. She blinked, her eyes adjusting to the lower light level in the room. All the blinds were closed and the fireplace was on, making it hot and dark.

Roni growled at her from behind the duct tape.

"I think your friend was betting on you being a no-show." Tim appeared with a pistol in his grip. "What a disturbing lack of faith. But," he continued with a horrible smile on his lips that confirmed she had no clue who he really was, "you can never be sure who to trust."

"No kidding," Zoe fired back. She sidestepped away from him, not that a couple of feet was going to matter if he decided to shoot her. What she needed was to get him talking. Distract him so she had time to process the situation and formulate a plan.

Roni started up again as Tim held out his hand. "Let's have the hard drive."

"What? Do you think I walked in here with it?" Zoe

moved toward her friend but Tim grabbed her by the hair and yanked her to a stop.

"It's outside in the planter," she hissed at him. "Go get it."

There was a pleased snort from Roni.

Tim didn't release her. He tightened his hold on her hair and tucked the gun into his waistband.

He shoved her toward the opposite side of the room from Roni, pushing her down into a chair.

"Didn't you hear me?" Zoe demanded. She pointed toward the door. "It's right—"

"Shut your mouth, Zoe." Tim perched himself on the edge of Roni's sofa.

But her attention settled on the vest Tim was wearing. It was body armor, and that only meant one thing.

"The sniper was with you?" she demanded.

Tim offered her a snort. "Don't waste your time trying to figure out the details, baby girl. You don't have enough information. One of the reasons I picked you. With your brother and dad deployed, it was really a perfect match for this operation. Your dad gave me the fucking key to the door, for Christ's sake. I just had to wait until I had someone serving alongside your brother for me to be able to open up shop."

"My dad called you a friend. You served together," Zoe said.

"You mean under," Tim cut back. "Unlike your father, I didn't have a family who gave a crap about me. I was handed a high school diploma and a thirty-day eviction notice from my foster family. I was burning shit while your dad was learning to expect salutes from men like me."

"My dad treated you like a friend."

Tim shrugged. "Can't let that matter." He leaned toward her for a moment. "I've always been on my own with nothing to fall back on. You know what? I'm sick of licking everyone's testicles. From your dad to the whining parents who think their little brats need ten thousand dollars every time they twist their ankles in one of my bounce houses."

He reached over and picked up a helmet. The thing even had a neck guard. Tim buckled the chin strap, sending a chill down her spine. Roni felt it, too. Zoe looked at her friend and saw the shimmer of horror in her eyes. Time was slowly ticking away, helplessness pressing down harder and harder onto her shoulders.

"I'm going to get it, too. Enough to live on, with no one to answer to. A simple enough dream."

"But one you're going to have blood on your hands when you get it," Zoe argued. "If you were just an enlisted man, how could you sell information that puts others in the line of fire?"

"Simple. I don't owe them shit. No one ever gave me squat. Don't waste your breath trying to dust off my heart. It's been dead and buried since I was eight and some stupid social worker told me I had to leave the only home I'd ever known. Never mind the fact that my bio parents couldn't stay out of prison for more than a month at a time. Forget the fact that I didn't want to live in a constant state of uncertainty as I waited for the city to move me to another pair of jackasses self-righteous enough to think they were giving me stability. All they were doing was showing me how the world really worked. Everyone is out there for their own buck. I was income and an outlet to satisfy their power cravings."

"So you had a crappy childhood," she said. "Doesn't mean you—"

"Shut up," Tim snapped, pointing the gun at her head. "You mean shit to me. Do you have any idea how many times I've had to listen to your dad warn me about booking you in a shady part of town? But that's the brass for you. They can pick and choose where they get their bread. Not me. You're just a pampered princess. You've already had a better life than me ten times over. So you're going to be my ticket out of the gutter. Your dad's got it coming, too. About time he had to be on the receiving end of someone above him who wanted something done. You're just collateral damage. Don't really care if your dad and brother get lined up in front of a firing squad, either. They've sat back in a safe bunker and ordered plenty of other men like me out into the line of fire."

Her blood chilled. He meant every word he said. It was there in his expression. The calm set of his eyes. Why had she never noticed that he despised her? Her skin crawled as she realized how often she'd sat near him, trusting him.

Tim was waiting for something. Zoe pushed her disgust aside, trying to force her brain to function. The details were here, in the room. She had to read them. Had to do what Mercer would have done.

A memory surfaced of him lighting her curtains on fire. *Making his scope a little less reliable . . .*

Her attention flew back to the fireplace. Tim was perched in the corner nearest the flames. It was too warm in the room but he reached over and gave the gas a turn so the flames rose higher.

Her cell phone was still in her pocket. It suddenly felt red hot.

Mule . . .

Everyone had called her that. The knowledge was like a razor blade, slicing at her skin.

Tim stiffened. He reached up and pressed on a little rectangle hanging from a wire near his jaw, running beneath his helmet by his ear.

"Wait for them to enter. Remember the target priority," he said into the little silver rectangle before easing closer to the fireplace. He pulled the gun free and aimed it at her.

It felt like everything was happening in the distance. Like she was being forced to observe some horror, helpless to intervene while it unfolded right in front of her eyes.

I'm not helpless . . .

I'm a bloody Magnus . . .

She cast her gaze around the room, frantically looking for anything to use. Roni's eyes narrowed before her friend looked toward the front of the room.

"Come in and join us, Special Agent Mercer. I know you're there," Tim said.

There was a soft step in the hallway. Zoe cringed as Mercer entered the doorway. Her breath caught, lodging in her throat as his dark eyes locked with hers. Her world shifted off center as she wondered if this was their last moment in life.

She couldn't watch it unfold.

Couldn't watch him be gunned down. Tim's lips settled into a smug line as she shifted her attention to Mercer.

The moment of inattention felt as large as a barn door. Zoe surged out of her chair, lunging toward Tim with her hands out, reaching for the gun. She felt the cold metal as she shoved his arms upward like her dad had taught her, twisting her head to the side to get out of the line of fire.

The weapon discharged, making her ears ring as the bullet hit the ceiling and loosened a spray of drywall dust. She felt the burn of the discharge against her cheek as she smelled her hair burning.

Tim recoiled. Falling backward, he flailed his arms out wide, groping for something to help him recover his balance. He failed, landing in the fireplace. Zoe went tumbling headlong into the brick that edged it. Tim screamed as he scrambled out of the flames. His screaming seemed distant as pain exploded inside her skull from the collision with the brick. It felt like a sledgehammer had hit her, knocking her away from the scene.

Tim was howling, springing out of the flames and into the center of the room. His pants were on fire, the flames licking across the fabric as he hit the ground and rolled to snuff them out. Mercer dove after her as a whistle rent the air. There was a spray of stuffing from the sofa as the sniper's round cut deeply into it, coming through the doorway where Mercer had stood. He gathered the front of her shirt in a single fist, lifting her up in his grip.

Her head was spinning but she caught sight of Tim rolling into a sitting position behind Mercer. He raised the gun, the flicker of the fire dancing off the barrel.

Time was moving in slow motion, allowing her to notice every detail. Tim's face was twisted in a grimace of pain, his lips curled back to bare his teeth at her. She was fighting to gain her feet, her shoes finding traction on the carpet, letting her rise with the help of Mercer's strength. Her fingers curled around the fire poker that had been hanging from a polished brass holder on the side of the hearth. She dug in and pushed her body past Mercer, bringing the poker around in front of her like a spear. She never decided what to do. It was just there. An instinct. An action that she pushed herself into without taking time to think about the personal consequences.

All that mattered was Mercer.

She was airborne for a moment, sailing toward Tim with no way to stop herself. Mercer was a blur of motion behind her. There was a flash in the barrel of the gun. And then she was landing on Tim, the poker punching through his mouth. She wanted to recoil from the crunching sound of flesh being split. Wanted to escape from the feeling of blood gushing over her hands.

The metallic scent of it filled her senses. Mercer was yanking her off Tim as he convulsed, his body jerking beneath her as it fought to hold on to life. Zoe rolled to the side, suddenly lacking any strength whatsoever. Her entire shoulder was numb, a strange sort of electrical charge going down her spine. Her heart was suddenly racing, making her pant as she tried to keep up with it and not pass out. Her ears were still ringing and it felt like she was in the center of a bubble that was collapsing in on her.

"Zoe?" Mercer shoved his face into hers as she blinked and fought back unconsciousness. "Don't you fucking quit on me!"

He was right in her face, their noses an inch apart, if that much. He pressed on her shoulder and she gasped as pain went slicing through her, red-hot and searing.

There was another zip and then two more. She stared in fascination at the carpet. It looked like it jerked, tiny pieces of it making a little powder puff a few inches from her head.

"Someone drop that fucking sniper!" Mercer yelled into a handheld communications device.

"They're working on it," Saxon barked from across the room. He grabbed the chair Roni was strapped to and pulled it into the dining room. There was a horrifying grinding noise as the metal legs gouged tracks in the wooden floor. Roni made a sound that resembled a growl as she and Saxon disappeared from sight.

Zoe didn't get a chance to see much else. Mercer was pulling her up and slinging her over his shoulder. He didn't open the door. Instead he shot out the front window. The safety glass fell out of his way in a shower of tiny pebbles before he carried her through it.

She ended up crouched down in the middle of Roni's prized star lilies. The sweet smell engulfed them as the sound of a helicopter drowned out everything else.

"About time," Mercer growled. He grabbed a fistful of her shirt again and used it to sit her up against the side of the building. He was yanking his own shirt off and balling it up. A moment later, she gasped as he shoved it into the bullet wound on her shoulder. She arched up, trying to escape the agony.

"Not a chance, Zoe. I'm not letting you bleed out," he growled at her. "I warned you once. Not on my watch."

His watch.

That was right.

It was an operation.

They were the last thoughts that her brain managed to grip before the blackness she'd been fending off slammed into her with so much force, she lost the battle. It was better anyway.

Better that she wouldn't get the chance to see Mercer walk out of her life.

CHAPTER EIGHT

She'd never really understood pain before.

Zoe woke up feeling like she'd discovered a whole new definition of hurt. It was deep and hot and so intense, she wasn't sure opening her eyes was worth the effort. Sinking back into blissful unconsciousness was very attractive.

"Come on, Zoe . . . wake up."

"Bram?" She forced her eyelids up, looking around for her brother. He was sticking his head through the bodies of scrub-wearing people who were all busy poking her with various tubes and needles. They watched her through plastic glasses and had medical masks on.

"Big pinch now," one of them called out as a needle was pushed into her arm. Comparably, it was a drop in the bucket given the way her shoulder was on fire.

There was a soft ripping sound as her top was cut off her.

"Yeah, sis, it's me." Bram confirmed.

"Excuse me, sir." One of the medical people turned on her brother. "We need you to wait in the hall."

Zoe tried to sit up. "Wait . . . Bram . . . Where is Roni?"

She didn't get far. Someone pushed her back onto the bed as machines started beeping and chirping all around her. A blood pressure cuff was inflating around her arm, putting pressure on the biceps as someone pressed a cold stethoscope against her inner arm.

The pain was making her nauseous. The single foot that she'd managed to lift her head off the pillow was enough to make the room spin. She lay back down, fighting the urge to throw up. There was no way she was going to add public humiliation to the day's events.

Hell, it was the little things in life that counted . . . right?

"We're going to give you some pain medication, Ms. Magnus . . ."

The plunger was already being pushed as the doctor spoke. She looked up from where a glove-covered hand was holding the IV port stuck in her arm to see a doctor peering intently at the monitors above her.

"Right. Let's get her up to surgery."

Her thoughts went fuzzy as the bed started down the hallway. The iridescent lights above her looked like some kind of roller-coaster track. Bram poked his head in again as she felt herself being carried away on the wings of the drug. Behind him, she thought she saw Mercer, but wasn't really sure. Her vision was blurry, her grasp on facts slipping.

It didn't matter. He was waiting in her dreams for her. The nightmarish moments in Roni's condo replaying over and over again as she was held powerless by the pain medication to escape back into consciousness.

"This isn't over."

Saxon was kneeling on the floor of Roni's condo, taking in the scene. Vitus hunkered down near him, tracing the tracks of the bullets. There were little numbered flags dotting the area now. Flashes were still going off from cameras as evidence was collected. Tim's body lay where he'd drawn his last breath, his limbs contorted. The blood covering his chin was darkening. Time was dulling the facts.

"Why do you say that?" Kagan asked.

Vitus and Saxon pushed back up to their feet to greet their supervisor. Kagan was attired in his standard suit that covered his chest harness. Saxon and Vitus were still wearing their civilian jeans and T-shirts. Saxon had his badge clipped to his belt. Vitus had a SPECIAL AGENT sticker slapped onto his back to allow him into the crime scene. The uniformed police were stuck outside doing traffic duty as the term *classified* was used to keep them from getting a look at the scene.

"You know why," Saxon responded.

Kagan gave him a crusty laugh. "Just trying to compare notes. You might be brighter than I am."

"Some things don't change," Vitus observed, earning a raised eyebrow from Kagan. "You still play stupid when you want to know what someone else is thinking."

Kagan flashed him a grin. "Maybe I'm just humble."

"The word that comes to mind is . . . *calculating*," Vitus said.

His onetime superior enjoyed the compliment. His eyes brightened for a moment before he looked at Saxon, his

thoughts back on the case. Kagan nodded at the scene.
"What do you see?"

Saxon pointed at the corner Tim had taken refuge in.
"This was never about that hard drive. Tim used it as a way
to get Zoe in play."

"It was shit anyway," Vitus said. "Old data."

"That doesn't mean it wasn't being sold," Kagan said.
"I'd rather catch my bad guys with false bait than risk losing control of critical intel."

"True," Saxon agreed. "Bad data is still classified data.
But that doesn't explain the body armor and the sniper. The
perfect setting in the corner by the heat source. Bait placed
in the open area."

"This was a cross-fire kill zone," Vitus confirmed.

"It is." Kagan agreed. "Tight and almost effective.
Tyler wanted a whole lot of bodies on the ground. No
other reason for him to make Tim think he wanted in on
the deal. Tyler knew he could never touch that money, it
would be too simple to trace."

"And he assigned the case to me," Saxon concluded in
an ominous tone.

Kagan nodded. "I'd say it's a solid bet he had an ar-
rangement with the good Congressman Jeb Ryland."

"Can you prove it?" Vitus asked.

Kagan shook his head. "But I've got Tyler alive. Let's
see if anyone comes to his rescue."

"Ryland wouldn't be that stupid," Saxon said.

"I wouldn't be too sure about that," Kagan replied.
"Tyler isn't wet behind the ears. You can bet he's got some
deets on Ryland. Things that might really soil the man's
dreams of getting to the White House."

Kagan exchanged a hard look with Vitus.

The three men stood silent, surveying the evidence for a moment longer. Kagan slowly nodded. He pulled something out of his suit jacket and offered it to Vitus. The afternoon light reflected off the badge. Vitus hesitated, his eyes narrowing as his jaw tightened. He tightened his grip on his belt while Kagan considered his response.

"I never agreed a hundred percent with Tyler's handling of your case. Even if I did, I'd have to revisit the matter since he proved to be a rat's-assed traitor. Take your shield."

"Maybe I don't want it back," Vitus argued.

Kagan snorted. "You just don't want to reach for it. Don't blame you any for being a little steamed, either." He sobered. "Take your shield, man. We might all know Tyler was working for Ryland, but we're not going to take the good congressman down with our opinions. You need the resources the department can give you to keep yourselves alive. This isn't over."

Vitus took the badge and shook the hand Kagan offered him.

"Now, I know you've been working hard, but I need you to get up to the hospital and sit on Bryan Magnus's daughter. Can't have her getting smothered in her hospital bed."

"Mercer is up there," Saxon supplied.

"So is her brother," Vitus added.

"Bet that's a combustible combination. Sorry I won't get to see it." Kagan choked on a laugh. He offered them both a two-finger salute before disappearing through the kitchen of the condo.

Saxon took another look around the room.

"What are you thinking, brother?" Vitus asked.

"That we are going to have to deal with Ryland. As Kagan hinted."

Vitus declined to answer but that didn't change how much he agreed with his brother. "Well, today's challenge is keeping Zoe Magnus from getting smothered while Mercer is dealing with her brother."

"Why do you think I sent Greer and Maddox up there already?" Saxon supplied. "I've got enough paperwork to fill out without having to bail those two out of city jail."

Vitus clipped the shield to his belt and put his gun on his belt now that he was licensed to open-carry again. "In that case, let's get a move on it before we miss the fun."

The ICU nurses were accustomed to high emotions.

But they were getting nervous as Bram and Mercer took turns standing at Zoe's bedside. They changed places every fourteen and a half minutes, in strict accordance with the fifteen-minute visitation rule. It was those thirty seconds when they were passing each other that the air tightened and the nurses kept their hands hovering over the security panic button.

"We're going to talk," Bram said as he passed Mercer.

"You can count on that."

Bram pushed through the doors into the hallway and sent Greer a look warning the agent to clear the path. But that left him facing a ravishing female. She lifted her eyelids and flashed him a look that captivated him. A second later he was tripping over his own feet, his boot soles skidding on the polished tile floor. Disengaged from her stare, he shook off the fascination that had gripped him, giving him enough clear thought to realize what an idiot he'd just been.

"Agent Thais Sinclair." She was holding her hand out when he looked back at her.

Bram squelched the urge to take her hand and hold it

like . . . well, like he was going to kiss the back of it. But shaking it felt wrong. He finished after two short pumps and was pretty certain he caught a glint of amusement in her dark eyes. She oozed feminine . . . something or other. It was a hazy, undefined sort of awareness. He felt like he was about fourteen, at the first school dance and getting his first glance at dresses that reveled what school uniforms had been hiding.

"I was on the team assigned to your sister."

Mentioning Zoe cleared up his thinking instantly. "Really?"

"Of course," Thais responded in a tone that was honey-coated. The agent didn't appear to be attempting to cajole him, which made her seductiveness that much more effective. There was something about her that was a pure shot of captivation.

"An all-male team would have been inappropriate."

"You can leave off, Thais," Saxon said as he came around the hallway corner.

Agent Sinclair turned and considered her team leader but her attention shifted to the man walking beside him and the badge clipped to his belt.

"Very interesting," she said in that drawl before she turned and made her way down to the waiting room.

Bram felt his collar tightening as he watched her body move. Heat touched his cheeks when he shifted his attention back to Saxon and caught the man watching him with a knowing look in his eyes.

Which only flipped the switch of his temper.

"What kind of team do you run anyway, Hale?" Bram demanded.

"An effective one," was the cool reply.

Bram fought to keep his voice even. "So I've heard." He bit the words out, making it clear how much he wanted to smash his fist into Saxon's jaw.

"If you want to fight, I'm your man," Mercer said from behind him.

Bram twisted around, his fingers tightening into a fist.

"Zoe is worth it," Mercer said. "I'm not defending what I did and I'm not disappearing, either. So we might as well get the tension dealt with."

"We need to talk . . ." Saxon interrupted, stepping between the two men. "And get our professional back on."

Mercer stared at his team leader. "I held the line on the professional part of the operation. There is a personal part. One I mean to explore."

"Vitus . . . talk some sense into him."

Vitus only hooked his hands into his belt and considered Mercer for a long moment. He slowly shook his head. "Pointless. Besides, it's really up to the girl." He cast a look at Bram. "Do you clear your girlfriend choices through your sister?"

Bram's body tightened. "This isn't about me."

"No, it isn't," Mercer agreed. "I'm here to stay. Get used to it."

"Only if she'll have you," Bram fired back at him.

Mercer stood up to his hard glare before letting Saxon turn him away.

If she'll have you . . .

Yeah, that was the real problem.

He had no idea if she would.

"You can't touch me," Tyler said smugly. It was ballsy, considering he was handcuffed to the center of the table in the interrogation room, sealed inside a complex that officially did not exist. He was guarded by men who had orders to shoot first if the person didn't have the proper identification. They never asked questions. because knowing too much was the main reason prisoners ended up in the complex. People disappeared all the time inside the concrete-block walls. There was a chill in the air that was more than weather. It was the temperature of ice-cold orders being given out.

"That so?" Kagan asked softly.

Tyler shook his head. "You're not going to bait me into spilling my guts. You forget, I've seen you in action too many times."

"And now I've seen you in action," Kagan continued as he moved into the room and sat down opposite Tyler. "Rather interesting, too. Tell me, is it Decains? I wouldn't have fingered him but it makes sense. A man with his kind of rank wouldn't have to worry so much about taking a hit when the intel made it onto the black market."

Tyler stared back at him.

"The Hale brothers, then?" Kagan leaned forward, propping his elbows on the tabletop. "Did you really sell out one of your teams? Not that I haven't heard of it. Who's pissed at them? I can figure out a short list but I'd really like to know what kind of a price you're getting to wax one of your own. That carries a stink. One that clings to a man. Forever."

"You have your orders," Tyler said softly. "I know you do."

"Got that much faith in your contacts?" Kagan asked.

"I do," Tyler confirmed. "You were given explicit orders to not pursue this matter any further, and someone else has been read into this operation. If I disappear, your shield will be on the table."

He was sure, because he'd sold his soul for that sort of connection. Tyler refused to feel guilty about it. Every man chooses a side. Kagan was just trying to squeeze him into squealing so Kagan could get a slice of the pie.

"Maybe I care more about justice than a shield. Some of us are actually in this business because we believe in doing the right thing." He leaned across the table. "Take a good look at me. I am one of those men, and scum like you are the reason I put my neck on the line."

The cuffs chinked as Tyler moved his hands. It was just a tiny motion, but it betrayed how nervous he truly was. He was looking at Kagan and what he saw rattled him. His face went gray, his lips going bloodless.

"Lose your shield and your ass will be flapping in the wind with a target on it. You've got plenty of enemies. And I have powerful connections."

"But you'll be just as dead, and with your demise I'll have one less person to look for on my six," Kagan said with a touch of mirth.

"Then do it," Tyler goaded him. "It might be worth it to know you're going to be living in the gutter, like a fucking mutt, while you try to stay one step ahead of the hit man." He chuckled and swept Kagan with a knowing look. "You'll be eating out of Dumpsters and sleeping under piss-covered bushes, rubbing elbows with home-less meth addicts. All to keep drawing breath for one more night. There won't be a dingy motel you can crawl to that won't flag your location. Reach out to a contact, and their ass will be painted red, too. This world isn't the one our predecessors lived in. There are too many cameras, no way to hide for long. You'll get made and my contacts will make sure you watch everyone you care about die before they wax you. Welcome to the new age, Kagan. Make the powerful happy or get steamrolled when they don't get what they want." He flattened his hands on the table. "I've made my choice. Unlock me. I know you've been ordered to let me walk out of here."

Kagan slowly grinned. "Guess you're right. I can't touch you." Victory shone in Tyler's eyes but it turned to worry when Kagan rapped on the door for it to be opened.

"Unlock me," Tyler demanded. "You have orders to *unlock me*."

"Can't touch you," Kagan said ruefully. "My orders are to not touch you. Guess you can just sit there and wait for your connections to come and get you. I've been told to forget you exist." He tapped his temple. "Going . . . going . . . gone."

The door popped open, a guard standing back two feet with a high-powered machine gun trained on the open entrance. Kagan shot Tyler one last look before he left. "I can't wait to see who shows up to get you."

"Sure you want to know?" Tyler warned.

Kagan slowly smiled in response.

"You'll regret this," Tyler informed him.

"I already do," Kagan agreed. "But for a different reason than you're thinking."

Colonel Decains was still in the hallway, listening. The door shut, sealing Tyler inside the interrogation room.

"What's your reason?"

Kagan flashed Decains a somber look. "For my regret? Simple. I'm sorry I'm too much of a coward to put a bullet through that bastard's head. Dying for my principles I can do. Putting everyone who's ever cared about me in harm's way, I can't."

Decains nodded. "It's a hell of a world we work in. It sure isn't as simple as right and wrong."

"No, it isn't."

Harley squawked. This was followed by a series of mumblings from her father's prized companion, before she heard someone cuss.

"Don't touch him. He's going to bite . . . you," Zoe called out. She forced her eyes open with the aid of knowing that Harley was making ready to take a chomp out of whoever was being foolish enough to not respect his warning.

"No kidding." Mercer appeared in the doorway with Harley wrapped in a beach towel. The parrot glared at her and snapped his beak.

"He was warning you . . ." she said as she tried to recognize where she was.

"I respectfully disagree." Mercer came into the room. "He was trying to claim my boot as his new chew toy and cussed me out for not letting him have it."

She looked down and realized that Mercer's feet were bare and that he looked more laid-back than she'd ever seen him in a pair of shorts and T-shirt.

"I'm taking some personal time. With you." Harley squirmed. "And . . . Harley."

He unwrapped Harley and placed him on the perch that was in the room. The parrot climbed up, happy to be higher than everyone else. His dominant position reclaimed, he began to groom himself.

"What are you doing here?" The words slipped out as her brain started working. "Where's Roni?"

She bolted upright as the memory of her friend with silver duct tape over her mouth filled her thoughts. Mercer was suddenly there on the side of the bed, gripping her body when a jolt of pain pierced her from the too-quick motion.

She ended up gasping in his arms, unable to do anything but let him support her while she tried to force her lungs to work.

"Easy . . ." He was stroking her back, the firm touch of his hand so soothing, she felt tears burning her eyes.

"Roni . . ." She tried to focus her mind on her friend. She was such a rotten person for being so easily distracted by a simple touch.

Mercer has always affected me like that . . .

"She's fine." Mercer pulled back from her then reached behind her to stack up a bunch of pillows. Once she was settled he picked up a tablet and brought it to life with a sweep of his fingers. A picture of her friend was already loaded.

"I want to talk to her."

Mercer nodded. He pushed an icon on the tablet, and it started buzzing. The picture changed to a live one as her friend came onto the line.

"Zoe?" Roni peered intently at the screen. "You look rough, girl."

Zoe put a hand up to her face, realizing her hair was like a fuzzy cloud all around her head. "Ah . . . well . . . I wasn't thinking of my vanity when I woke up. Are you okay?"

Roni had settled back in her chair. "Sure am. But I'm having of a hell of a time choosing a new name. You need to help me when you're feeling better."

"Ah . . . what are you talking about?"

Mercer turned the tablet so Roni could see him. "She'll call you back."

"Bye, Zoe."

Roni's voice filled the air before Mercer tapped the screen to kill the call. He set the tablet aside.

"What was she talking about?"

"She's being relocated," Mercer explained. "As soon as you wake up a little more, you'll see the necessity."

"I'm awake."

He was watching her, his dark gaze as keen as always. Intuitive. Sharp. His lips set into a satisfied grin.

"That's right, Zoe." He flattened his hands on either side of her. "I'm right here, baby. And I'm not going anywhere."

He leaned in and pressed a kiss against her mouth. Maybe there were reasons why she shouldn't have kissed him back, but honestly, none of them got past the rush of sensation that flooded her. The scent of his skin was the missing component to her being able to truly rest. She reached for him, trying to pull him close, but her fingers were weak. A little whimper escaped her as she struggled to rise off the pillows and press herself into his embrace. She was desperate for the contact. So weary of being alone.

"I've got you, baby."

He shifted and turned, moving onto the bed and lying back so that she could lay her head on his shoulder. She sighed as she curled up against him, held securely to his side as the sound of his heart filled her head.

There.

That was so much better.

Sunlight.

Zoe was pretty sure she smelled it before she opened her eyes. She had to reach up and brush her tangled hair out of her face but the reward was a window full of sparkling sunshine. She smiled, relief slamming into her. She didn't know the details but obviously, things were sorting themselves out. No more secret hideout, and she wasn't in the prison wing of the hospital.

But her relief was short-lived.

She scanned the room, looking for any hint of Mercer. Nothing.

It hurt. She swallowed and crawled out of the bed. Her legs were a little weak but she made it into the bathroom.

She needed a shower.

And to shave her legs.

And . . . brush her teeth.

She forced herself to keep adding things to her list, to keep her mind occupied. Now wasn't the time to think. At least not about Mercer. She needed some coffee first.

In fact, she was thinking about it so hard, she smelled the java. Rich. Dark. Hot. She exited the shower and grabbed a towel, rubbing it over her skin before she opened the closet in search of something to wear. It wasn't going to be hard to find it, either. The double-wide closet only had three things in it. Hanging up were leggings, a lightweight tunic top, and a mystery bag that yielded underwear.

All in her size and favorite cut.

Well, she expected no less from such a covert team.

They really were the best.

She'd always known Mercer was too good to be sticking around.

"You coming out of there?"

She jumped, losing her balance and falling against the side of the closet with a thud.

The door went sliding all the way open, the sunlight hitting the back of a figure she was pretty sure she'd recognize when she was 103.

"I'm fine," she mumbled. "Just clumsy."

Zoe started to push away from the wall but stopped, trying to absorb the sight of him.

"Yeah, I'm still here."

He reached out and captured her hand, using the grip to gently pull her out of the closet.

"Um . . . I can see that." It was far from the poised response she wanted to make. As in, really far off. But the closet felt too confined with him in it. Her awareness of him was kicking in, as it always did.

There was a mug on the bathroom countertop with steam rising from it. She made a little hum of appreciation before lifting it to her lips and feeding her need for caffeine.

"Careful." Mercer took it from her before she'd taken more than a few sips. Zoe glared at him, pretty sure she was going to start pouting unless he gave it back. But her belly suddenly clenched, the coffee hitting her stomach like acid.

Mercer lifted the mug away. "You'll want to eat a little something before having any more coffee. You've been out for the better part of two days."

"Two days?" No wonder her brain felt frozen.

"Better than forever." Mercer sat the mug down and considered her. "Considering you charged into the line of fire."

His jaw tightened, disapproval flickering in his eyes. Zoe lifted her chin.

"If you think I'm going to apologize for going after Roni . . ."

"I'll settle for you recognizing how much danger it put you in."

She snorted at him and propped her hand onto her hip. "No. Don't know what you're talking about. I'm just such a naive little thing."

He didn't care for her flippant tone and she didn't like his glowering. She reached past him and captured the coffee mug off the counter. She took another sip from it as she walked out of the bathroom.

He was following her. Not that she heard him. Of course not. The damn man walked like a cat.

She'd made it into the kitchen with its breakfast nook before she snapped. Waking up to him gone was actually better than having him there. She'd expected him to be gone. Now she had to deal with just how deeply he affected her.

She had no clue where to start.

"Don't think I'm going to take a lecture from you," she warned him.

He was exactly where she'd expected him to be. On her six.

His expression was tight but his lips curved as her comment hit him. "Don't think I won't tell you how foolish it was for you to take on Tim without me."

"I couldn't take the chance. Not with Roni."

"You don't have to put up with him, sis."

She jerked her head away from Mercer and found Bram

standing in the doorway that connected the kitchen with the rest of the house.

"This team is staying right here, Magnus." Saxon's voice came through from the living room. Saxon was hunkered down on an edge of a pub highboy table, looking at the screen of a laptop. It was slightly ridiculous, given that she'd always seen him in a command center.

"Welcome to the new place," Bram said softly. "We sort of had to relocate you."

"Oh." She blinked and looked back at her brother, realizing she was missing what was important. "You're home."

She was suddenly hugging him, trying to crush him against her.

"I'm home," Bram said as he set her back a pace and considered her with a critical eye. "And none too soon, either."

The tone of his voice sparked a memory. "Wait. Did you know about all this?" She waved a hand around the room at Saxon and Mercer.

Bram let out a low sigh.

"What the . . ." She bit back the word of profanity as she recalled Harley was in the room. "Just: *What?*"

"I didn't know they were going to be utilizing the means they did." Bram scowled at Mercer.

"Too bad," Mercer shot back. "Here's another news flash for you. I'm not leaving."

"This is my family," Bram declared. "At least until my father gets back. Until then, I'll show you to the door if I want to."

"I think Zoe will be making the call on that."

Mercer stepped up and Bram met him happily. The pair

of them glowered at each other as the tension in the room tightened.

"I don't think so."

She was likely off her rocker but she stepped right between them, flattening her hands on each of them and shoving them back.

"You . . ." She pointed at Bram. "Are really late to the party. So stand back and wait for me to tell you how it's going to go down."

"And you . . ." Mercer had just started to smirk at Bram when she turned on him—but she felt her brain go blank, because he was still sinfully amazing to look at. Awareness was rippling through her, like a treasured memory or a song that just started up in her head.

"Did you say something about breakfast?"

It was a delay tactic. A cover-up for her lack of ability to think.

Liar.

I don't want to think.

Later, she sat over her finished breakfast plate and nursed her coffee mug. She felt the gazes of the men in the house, Mercer's most of all. She'd longed for him to be something she could respect, and fate had delivered just that.

So now what the fuck was she going to do?

Don't I mean, what is Mercer planning to do?

Yes. That was exactly what she was afraid of discovering.

"You had to move, too?"

Roni offered her a dry chuckle. "That Agent Hale is mighty sure the only opinion that matters is his."

"Oh yeah," Zoe replied as she watched Roni through the screen on the tablet. "I've discovered that."

"For what it's worth," Roni continued, "I appreciate you flipping him off and showing up to save me."

"I'm really sorry about that, Roni."

"Sorry for what?" Roni demanded. "I rather enjoyed seeing Tim get what was coming to him. Turd showed up, tracked mud across my living room, and taped me to a chair. Glad you dumped his tail into the fire. As for the condo, I've found another place. Special Agent Hale hooked me up with a good job, so all I need now is to pick out some new furniture." Roni smiled. "That's the fun part."

"So what's the name?"

"Le Cross." Roni rolled it off her tongue. "Debra Le Cross."

"Sis?"

Bram caught her investigating the kitchen. There were rosebushes beneath the kitchen window that had yellow roses on them. She'd been leaning over the large, farmhouse-style sink to look at them and enjoying the warm sun on her nose.

"Hope you like the house. I wanted to have it ready for you," Bram said.

She turned around and leaned against the countertop. "A house is nothing without family. I'm just glad you're home in one piece. I could have dealt with moving."

"You handled enough."

Bram had gotten their father's blue eyes. A deep blue, like a Caribbean lagoon.

"I'm fine." Her brother's attention settled on her shoulder. "It's not that bad, Bram. You aren't the only member of this family who can take one for the team."

"You weren't on the team, Zoe," Bram argued. "That's what's pissing me off. This guy . . ."

"Mercer." She supplied.

Her brother's eyes narrowed. "Let me kick him to the curb. I can handle looking out for you until this operation is mopped up."

"Thanks, but I'll look after myself." She held up a finger when Bram opened his mouth to argue. "You have no idea how much I mean that, Bram. I've spent too much time being looked after. It's my turn to deal with things my way."

"I'm home, Zoe."

And clearly feeling guilty. She bit back the first words that came to mind because she was just so damn happy to see her brother. But that didn't mean she was going to roll over.

"I'm fine, Bram," she said firmly. "And I will be dealing with Mercer."

"You were an assignment to him."

She flinched. Just couldn't help it. "Did he tell you that?"

Honestly, it wasn't any of her brother's business. But she needed to know.

"I was read into the operation report," Bram said.

Her cheeks heated. Report. Great. Just what she needed to know. She could have handled being mad. What made her turn around and head toward her bedroom was the fact that what she felt was hurt.

Deep, burning heartache.

"She doesn't need you."

Mercer was torn.

The need to follow Zoe was tearing at his insides.

Bram's voice, however, raised his hackles. He turned and faced off with Bram.

"It's her call. Not yours," he said.

"Excuse me, but this happens to be my family," Bram argued.

Mercer stepped up closer to Bram. He caught a glimpse of Saxon moving in, just in case things got ugly.

"Your sister would be very dead by now without me," Bram growled.

Mercer closed the gap even more so that they were almost nose-to-nose. "I won't kiss anyone's ass over my actions. My dedication runs as deep as yours, Captain. There was a job to do and it wasn't pretty. I stepped up because of duty but it was the best damn assignment I ever got. Because it brought me here."

"So take your pat on the shoulder, your glowing commendation, and pack out," Bram snapped.

"Like hell. I'm not going anywhere," Mercer bit back. "I might have gotten here by less-than-gentlemanly means but that doesn't mean I don't see what a gem your sister is. The reaction we have to each other is more than lust. I'm going to crawl on my knees if I have to but Zoe is going to listen to me."

Bram's face tightened. Mercer could see the man fighting back his temper. He suddenly turned and rammed his fist into the wall. The drywall didn't have a chance of holding. He cussed as he laid his forehead on the wall and pulled his fist free.

"Fine." He shook his head, still fighting his temper. "But what Zoe says, goes."

Bram looked through the doorway at Saxon. "And why are you still here?"

Saxon offered him a lazy shrug. "I could give you a half-assed answer or just admit I'm making sure my man gets his day."

Mercer looked at his team leader in surprise. Saxon offered him a half grin. "I might be guilty of having a stick up my ass, as Vitus claims, but I'm not a hundred percent dick."

"Never would have guessed it," Mercer said.

Saxon shrugged. "I know. Don't let my secret out." He pointed toward the bedroom Zoe had gone into. "Be a pal and get on with it. I really need a day off. Kagan's impressed by our performance, which means he's going to find some other case to stick us on."

"You might have to count me off."

Saxon nodded. "Another reason I'm hanging around."

Mercer started down the hallway as Bram faced off with Saxon.

"I'm not unreasonable. I would have let them make their own choices," Bram said, defending himself.

"You're her big brother who hasn't accepted the fact that she's not nineteen anymore. I'd threaten to kick your ass if it was my sister, just on principle."

"Don't threaten me with a good time if you're not going to step up," Bram growled.

A prickle of concern went through him but Mercer never faltered. His mission objective was ahead of him.

And he didn't intend to fail.

Mercer rapped on the door and gave her three seconds before he pushed it in. Zoe didn't have to turn around to see that it was him.

She knew it was him.

She felt it ripple across her skin. The awareness was like a sixth sense, there whether or not she wanted it to be. She was hardwired to notice him, to feel her knees go weak the second he entered the room.

"I didn't say I was choosing you."

Mercer shut the door firmly. The room instantly shrank. She raised her head, intent on fending off the sense of vulnerability trying to rattle her.

"I was just making sure Bram knows I won't be apologizing to him for making my own sexual decisions," she said smoothly. "Or you either, for that matter."

"Glad to hear it."

He was too damn poised. Just as confident and arrogant as the first time she'd seen him.

And I'm getting just as bothered by it, too . . .

"No I'm not."

His dark eyebrows rose. "You're not what, Zoe?"

She cringed as she realized she'd spoken out loud. "I'm . . . just not."

His lips twitched, but it wasn't a nice sort of smile.

It was menacing.

So full of the confidence she'd always felt radiating off him. Her insides twisted, her skin heating. "I need some space."

It was a last-ditch effort to hold on to her composure.

"Not a chance . . . baby." He moved closer, the air thickening between them. "We're going to have a discussion. One I've been waiting for you to be ready for."

"Okay . . ." She sidestepped, gaining a precious few feet of space. Sure, she was hedging.

Which wasn't retreating.

Oh right . . .

"Let's get married."

Her jaw dropped. She snapped it shut, trying not to look like an idiot. "I don't think that's . . . necessary."

He took a step toward her and a shiver shot down her spine.

Part of her felt it was very necessary.

"Besides . . ." she stuttered out when he started to close the gap between them again. "I thought you had trust issues with me giving you my word."

His expression tightened. "Don't pick a fight to avoid facing the personal relationship between us. I'm mad about you going off to meet Tim without me. That's a fact. It rips me up to think of you in any sort of situation that carries danger. The sight of you bleeding is branded into my memory, and that's exactly why I know I'll regret it for the rest of my life if I walk out of here. You're different. I don't know what the hell that means but I know being near you is like a punch in the gut."

She was backed up against the wall. "But . . ." She put her hands out as she struggled to make sense of the riot of emotions surging through her. As usual, her thoughts were crumbling, her body coming to life. Everything she thought was making way for what she craved from him.

"My brain stops working when you're this close."

"I know the problem." He cupped her jaw, raising her face so that their gazes met. Her belly twisted, her core heating with need so gripping, she trembled with it. "Do you think it's any easier for me?"

His question surprised her. "Actually, you've always struck me as being confident as hell. Cocky. Smug. And what frustrates me is that for the first time in my life, I can see those words being compliments when applied to you."

He chuckled at her, slipping his hand into her hair and gripping it. "Another point in favor of getting married. You understand me, Zoe."

He was so close, the scent of his skin filled her senses, intoxicating her, sending her speeding toward the high that would make it acceptable to yield to him.

"No, I don't," she said. "None of it makes any sense."

Actually, she wasn't making much sense. But he slowly grinned, leaning down until their lips were so close, his breath hit the sensitive surface of her mouth. She shivered and he massaged the back of her head in response.

"No, it doesn't," he agreed. "I hear that's the way love is."

"This isn't love."

She tried to wiggle away. He captured her hands and pulled them above her head, pinning them to the wall. It stunned her. The abrupt change in mood. The sudden tightening in tension. It made her gasp and started a pounding in her clit.

"I've had a lot of sex," he said bluntly, his eyes narrowing with the frank statement. "Good sex. Okay sex. Boring sex. Drunk—"

"I get it," she snapped and tried to yank free. The idea of him with other women was driving her insane. He held her in place and pressed his knee between her thighs. It felt like something snapped inside her. That pressure against her clit sent a shower of red-hot sparks up her core.

"Do you, baby?" he leaned down and whispered against her ear, his chest rubbing against her breasts. "Do you get how different you are? How the scent of your pussy is driving me insane right now? I've never wanted to get into a woman so bad. Never really noticed the way they smell."

He lifted his head so she could see his face again before he pressed his hips against her, giving her proof of just how hard his cock was.

"That's not love."

But it was what she craved.

"It's pure intensity," he bit back. "It's driving me insane. Shutting down my brain every time I see you. All I can do is think about touching you, driving you to the same edge you take me to when we're together. It's more than sex. I've had sex. With you, it's . . . intimate."

His eyes were bright with need. Her rational mind wanted to argue. Wanted to find some reason why his words didn't hold water.

"Nothing about you ever makes sense, Mercer."

He offered her a soft sound of amusement. "So stop thinking and feel."

He captured her argument beneath his kiss. Honestly, she wasn't sure what she'd intended to say. It dissipated beneath the hard motions of his mouth. She moaned, jerked into the vortex his touch always spawned.

And then all she wanted was more.

Just more.

She arched, rubbing against his thigh, kissing him back as need went twisting through her.

Intensity?

Hell yes. That was exactly what they brought out in each other. He left off kissing her mouth, working his way across her jawline to her neck, and she arched up, offering it to him. She felt the touch of air against her bare skin as she eased her shirt up and over her head. She felt the effort it cost him to be slow and gentle about it.

"I'm really okay," she said. Rolling her shoulder, making the bandage crinkle just a little, she reached forward and grabbed his shirt, yanking it up and over his shoulders to bare him. When she had it free, she balled it up and chucked it across the room before reaching out and cupping his jaw.

"I'm not a baby doll."

Their gazes were locked, giving her a prime view of the way her words hit him. Passion brightened his eyes, flickering in the darks orbs before he tilted his head and pressed his lips to hers.

This time, he claimed her mouth like a prize, tasting her lips with the pure intention of devouring her. He was hard and hot, pressing her against the wall as he cupped the back of her head and continued to ravage her mouth. She twisted against him, needing to be closer. It was a desperate motion, one she couldn't have controlled if she'd tried.

Once again, there was only need and the satisfaction his body promised.

He lifted his head, looking at her for a moment. "I like you like this. Panting for more. I'm going to give it to you, Zoe. Give it to you while I watch."

Her bra went sailing over his shoulder. His gaze slipped down to her breasts as he reached out to cup them.

"You're beautiful, baby."

He was cupping her breasts, the contact sending her back into the storm of sensation. He leaned over and licked one nipple. It drew tighter, puckering into a hard nub that he sucked into his mouth. It was as if the sensitive tip were connected to her clit. The little bundle of nerve endings hidden between the folds of her sex started to throb and beg for the same treatment.

"You're getting wetter," he whispered next to her ear. Her cheeks heated and he laughed as he felt the blush with his own cheek.

"It's sexy, Zoe."

"No, it's not," she argued.

"Look at me." His tone was raspy but just as full of authority as always. She raised her gaze to his. He waited until their eyes met before he pressed forward, flattening his body on top of hers. The hard presence of his erection made her breath catch and then release in a low sound of need.

"I can compliment you all day with pretty words, but feeling how hard my cock is tells you I find you attractive more than a thousand polished comments. Doesn't it?"

She was nodding, feeling like he could read how aroused she was just through eye contact.

He slid his hand down her arms, sending a new rush of delight through her. She was twisting in his grip as she felt him close his fingers around her wrists, capturing her. Her eyes had started to close as she sank into bliss but she forced them open and discovered him watching her, his eyes burning with need.

The need to take.

The need to conquer.

The need to claim.

Her mouth went dry. She wanted that, wanted it so badly.

He pulled her arms up, doing it slowly as he watched her face. His jaw was tight as he controlled himself. When he pressed her wrists to the wall above her head, he leaned against her for a long moment, letting her sense him claim-

ing her. She shifted, making him feel the hard points of
her nipples.

He sucked in his breath, baring his teeth at her.

"I'm going to play with you, baby." He leaned down and
nipped her ear. "Like my own personal toy."

He transferred her wrists into one hand and slipped
his other one down her body, teasing a path toward
her sex. She knew that was his destination, the knowledge
tormenting her with anticipation. The soft waistband of
the leggings wasn't much of a barrier. He pulled it down
as he found her curls and teased them.

She was wet.

So wet, his fingers slipped easily into her folds. She
moaned, a half breath away from climax.

"God I love the way you heat up for me, baby." He
teased her folds. Stroking her as he opened her thighs
wide with his knee.

"I like you like this." His tone was razor-edged. "I want
to take you. Hold you in place and watch you while I touch
you."

"Just . . . touch me . . ." She was pretty sure she wouldn't
survive if he didn't.

"Look at me, Zoe."

She opened her eyes, ready to do anything he asked.

"I'm going to make you come."

There was determination in his eyes. Flickering there.
Warning her. Promising her.

"You'd better." She tossed out the challenge, knew that
was what she was doing. In fact, she fully intended to push
him. She bared her teeth at him and watched him smile in
satisfaction.

He made a soft sound of amusement, his face drawing tight as he plunged his fingers into her folds to where her clit was throbbing madly. She gasped, pleasure spiking straight into her core. She twisted, arching toward his hand, seeking out what she needed from him.

"Is this the spot you want stroked?" he demanded bluntly.

Her mouth was dry, her eyes trying to close as rapture was taking hold of her.

"Look at me," he demanded. "And tell me . . ." He rubbed her clit, just hard enough to feel like climax was within reach. "Is this the way you like me to touch you?"

"Yes." Her voice was a hollow sound of yearning. "Harder."

"Sometimes, I'll give you what you need, baby . . ." His nostrils flared, his fingers pressing against her clit just a fraction harder. "And watch you enjoy satisfaction . . ." His jaw was set, his teeth bared. The grip on her hands tightened as he pushed her that last bit with his fingers, holding her still while he rubbed her into an orgasm. "Satisfaction from my touch."

She jerked, something snapping inside her. It was harsh and slammed her back into the wall. She withered, feeling like she was being wrung. He rubbed her through it, easing off the pressure as the moment subsided. He held her as she clung to his shoulders, her heart hammering.

"And sometimes . . ." She was suddenly free, sagging against the wall because her knees were jelly. He paused for a moment, drinking in the sight of her, enjoying what he'd reduced her to.

"Sometimes . . . You'll drive me to the brink of madness . . ."

He opened his fly, popping the buttons to free his cock. It sprang into sight, swollen, hard, and exactly what she craved. He closed his fingers around it, pumping his hand up and down the large staff while he backed away from her.

"I'm going to enjoy letting you take everything I see you craving from me."

"You bet your ass you will."

She sprang after him, pushing him onto the bed. The frame made a groaning sound as they both bounced on the mattress in a tangle of limbs. Mercer closed his arms around her, taking the brunt of the fall, his chest vibrating with his amusement.

But that wasn't what she wanted from him.

Hell no.

She pushed herself up and grabbed his pants, hooking her fingers into the soft denim and ripping it, baring him as she pulled the pants off him. Yanking his shoes off when she made it to his ankles, she left him lying on the bed in nothing but glorious skin.

And he was perfection. She purred and stripped out of her leggings before she flattened her hands on the bed as she crawled up and over him. She sat down on his cock, not letting him penetrate her but resting his staff between the folds of her sex. He sucked his breath in, jerking beneath her before he tightened his control. She flattened her hands on his chest, petting him, stroking him as she enjoyed having his hard flesh waiting for her whim.

"That's it, play with me."

She looked up and caught the look of anticipation on his face. It was savage and it sent victory surging through her.

"Sex with me will never be boring . . ." she said.

He slowly shook his head. Zoe curled her fingers into talons and drew them down his chest, stopping at his nipples to tease them.

"And I don't ever want to hear about how much other sex you've had," she instructed him.

"Yes you do," he argued. Reaching up to cup her breasts, he massaged the tender globes, shifting the power between them as he teased her nipples with his thumbs. "You want to know I compare you to them and find you something altogether different."

He wrapped his arms around her, curling up off the bed and holding her still as he thrust. His cock slid against her clit. She yelped at the intensity of the sensation, reeling from the spike.

"I'll remember them because it will confirm why I have no reason to ever stray from your bed, Zoe."

"You bet your ass you won't stray," she hissed.

She rose up and mounted him. Lowering herself onto his cock, she groaned as her body stretched to accommodate it. "Because I'm a bitch and I don't share my meat."

"Ride me . . . show me why I don't have a reason to stray, baby."

She opened her eyes and shot him a hard look, but she realized that he wasn't demanding. He was just as needy as she'd been.

Still was, really.

Hunger drew his lips back, baring his teeth as he cupped her breasts, massaging them gently, reverently. He was hers in that moment. Completely devoted to her. She was the object of his desire. The look in his eyes filled her with confidence, the surge of power that she'd only ever felt with him. There was no awkwardness. Only an enjoyment of the way they fit together, like it was meant to be. So natural, so right, she could focus completely on the motion of the ride.

And she did.

She braced her hands on either side of his head as she rose and fell, but it wasn't enough. She stretched up, her thighs burning with the effort, and rode him with her hands in the air and her head thrown back.

"Hell yes . . ." He had her hips in his hands, the grip tightening as his cock felt like it was hardening even further. He was bucking beneath her, filling her as she came down. Their bodies slapped together while the bed rocked at a frantic motion.

"*Hell . . .*" He was growling, grunting as his cock started to pump spurts of hot fluid into her. He wanted to flip her over; she could see the need in his eyes. She rolled, gripping him with her legs as he followed her and hammered himself into her spread body.

"Yes!" he snarled, fucking her until she felt her body dissolving into another climax. It came out of the swirling vortex of sensation being in contact with him produced. One moment she was enjoying the hard motions of his body as he pumped her through his climax and the next, her clit was twisting, her core clenching, and her pussy milking his cock.

The intensity was off the scale, burning through her with enough force to shatter her. It was a fate she willingly gave herself up to, the idea of surrender attractive as it yielded complete rapture.

She cried out, arching up to take the last few thrusts, jerking as pleasure tore through her and dropped her back onto the surface of the bed, more spent than she'd ever been. Moving was out of the question. Her muscles were nothing more than jelly.

Mercer smoothed her hair back from her face, kissing her temple before he rolled over and took her with him. He folded her into his embrace as he settled her against his side with her head pillowed on his chest. She shifted closer, rubbing against him as she tried to absorb every last detail of the moment.

She'd never felt cherished. Not until now. She might have noticed how much it frightened her if she had any ability left to think at all.

She didn't.

There was only the feeling of his arms around her and the scent of his skin. Everything else was a blur on the horizon. Too far away to concern herself with.

No, for the moment, she was going to just feel.

Just savor.

Someone cussed in the kitchen.

Zoe lifted her head, frowning as she came fully awake. She was rolling out of the bed before she thought about it. She paused for a moment as her body protested being in motion. Mercer was still stretched out in the bed, giving her a prime view of just why she was sore.

He was an animal.

Lean, cut, untamed.

And she loved it.

Shit.

She did love him. The admission left her feeling vulnerable. As in her ass hanging out in the wind. He could crush her heart. She knew it. Had to embrace the reality of that truth.

What I need to do is decide to trust him and live in the moment.

She shied away from her inner voice, plucking her clothing up from where it had fallen and dressing. She opened the door slowly and sneaked out with one last look back at Mercer to make sure he was still sleeping.

Chicken.

Guilty as charged. But in her defense, marriage was something she really should think about.

Chicken.

Her inner voice was screaming at her.

So was Roni's notable advice to live in the moment and enjoy the ride while it was available.

Zoe ended up in the hallway, admitting to herself that she was the one with trust issues. But another word of profanity came from the kitchen, giving her an excuse to shove her thoughts aside.

"No cussing in the house." She was already dishing out her opinion when she arrived in the kitchen and took in the scene.

Saxon was leaning against the counter, a longneck beer in his hand. His knuckles were bloody and when he lifted the bottle to his lips, she noticed that his lower one was split. He lowered the beer before leveling a hard look at her. "Why not?"

"Ah?" She'd lost her train of thought and stood staring at him while she tried to decide what she'd said to him to begin with.

"No cussing in the house because Harley might pick up the profanity," Bram answered for her.

He was sitting at the kitchen table, holding another

longneck beer bottle to the side of his face, which was turning purple.

"What in the hell has been going on out here?" she demanded despite it being obvious.

Her brother grinned at her, showing her bloody teeth. "We were coming to an understanding."

"Like you and Mercer were," Saxon stated.

Bram had been drinking from his beer and sputtered. "Not the same way at all," he insisted.

Saxon shrugged. "We exchanged bodily fluids." He toasted her with the bottle before offering her a knowing smirk.

Her cheeks caught fire.

Bram snorted. "Get a girlfriend."

Saxon grunted. "I bite."

"Some girls like that sort of thing." Mercer was suddenly there, draping an arm across her body when she tried to move away from him. He surveyed the scene. "Seems we missed the party." He nuzzled her neck. "I suddenly see the error of my thinking. Nap time isn't just for toddlers. I could become a habitual napper with you, baby."

She tried to shrug his arm off but he held tight. His lazy demeanor was only a facade. "Excuse us."

He scooped her off her feet and took her back down the hallway.

"Mercer . . ."

He paid her no mind, carrying her through the doorway of the bedroom and kicking the door shut before turning her loose. She backed away from him as he squared off with her.

"Don't accuse me of having trust issues, baby, when you have similar ones."

He was right. That admission brought her up short. She ended up worrying her lower lip as she contemplated him.

He was just so perfect.

"Do you trust me?" She needed to know.

His expression tightened, just a fraction, but it was enough to pierce the bubble of growing elation inside her.

"I trust that you're innocent, Zoe," he answered. "Are you still holding a grudge against me for how we met?"

"It isn't a grudge," she said. "At least, that's a mighty judgmental word under the circumstances."

"I'll agree with judgmental." His eyes were narrowed. "You support your family one hundred percent for the service they give but not me? I was laying it on the line to protect them."

"I know," she snapped. "But you . . . you—"

"Used sex?" He interrupted her bluntly. "Is that somehow worse than trying to scare the information out of you? Would you rather have been stuffed in the back of a van and hauled into some dank cell where you would have been broken down until you confessed? Waited to see what would happen."

"You pushed your way into my private space."

His lips twitched. "And you loved every second of it." He suddenly lost his firm hold on his confidence. Uncertainty swam through his eyes. "So did I. Maybe I'm the fool for trying to hold on to that. Vitus sure thinks so."

He let out a slow breath. "I need one of those beers."

The door closed behind him, leaving her facing the situation she'd always assumed would arrive.

He would leave her.

Except this time, she'd pointed him toward the door.

The urge to follow him was strong. Stronger than the

desire to hold on to her self-respect and reject him because of the way he'd used her, but both emotions were valid. She was caught between them, being pulled by both sides like a tug-of-war rope.

She didn't have to end up in pieces. All she had to do was trust.

So why did that feel so impossible?

Congressman Jeb Ryland sat back in his oversized office chair. His desk was a treasured antique that dominated the office. It was situated perfectly to afford him a view of the south side of his estate. The grounds were expertly manicured, but he scowled.

"I warned you what my expectations were," he said.

The man sitting in front of him didn't show any reaction. He sat there, stone-faced and silent.

This was another expectation Jeb had for those who worked for him. He was the master and they'd better remember it.

"Special Agent Vitus Hale is owed a reckoning. Losing his brother would have been a good place to begin. Were my expectations in any way unclear?"

The man sitting in front of him shook his head.

"Then why isn't the man mourning his sibling?" Jeb surged forward and flattened his hands on the surface of the desk. "He has his shield back!"

"Killing him straight out wouldn't have been too hard. The fact that you wanted him caught with dirt on his hands made it a lot harder. Saxon has a record. A good, solid one. I took a lot of chances trying to set him up."

"You used the wrong family," Jeb insisted. "A colonel

and a captain? Bryan Magnus has a long-standing commitment of service to his country. That was an idiotic choice."

"It was a good one," Tyler said, defending himself. "Saxon is no fool. He'd have sniffed out a trap if intel like that mysteriously appeared in the hands of some random civilian. You wanted too much by insisting he be disgraced. I could have taken him out and left his brother without his shield."

"That wasn't enough. Not nearly enough!" Jeb hissed. "He soiled my daughter. I want his family name dragged through the gutter! I want his family wiped off the face of this planet. I want his friends to see what happens to anyone who forgets who their betters are. And I want to make sure she knows what happens when she defies me."

Tyler took a deep breath. "You're not my better. Keep talking like that and you're on your own."

"Perhaps you're not smart enough to work for me," Jeb threatened. "I can replace you."

"Do it. I don't need this petty revenge crap. So what if your daughter screwed someone who wasn't on your approved list? She's back under control."

"And Damascus will stay there!" Jeb jabbed his index finger into the desktop. "My daughter won't be taking up with a member of her escort, even one who saved her life. That was his job. She's learning the error of her judgment. Now I want the Hale brothers to learn it, too. I know you special agents have a brotherhood. When this matter is dealt with, others will take note."

"They might also close ranks against you."

Jeb slapped the top of the desk. "I could have left you chained in that interrogation room."

"And I could have sung high and low to Kagan, telling him how you misled me into believing I was following legitimate orders."

Tyler enjoyed the way the congressman's eyes widened.

"Don't think I'm not covering my ass with enough documentation to drag you down with me if you try hamstringing me," Tyler insisted. "I'm in this to be a part of your administration. Don't forget what you've promised me. I won't."

"Find another way," Jeb ordered. "Saxon Hale likes shadow ops too much to retire from them. Concoct another operation to trap him. I want him disgraced and dead. In that order. Vitus doesn't deserve a clean death." Jeb pointed at Tyler. "I want that bastard Vitus to know his family is being taken out in both blood and name before I kill him. Damascus will learn just what happens when she steps outside the boundaries I set."

There was a glow in the man's eyes that made Tyler uneasy. Not a simple task. Tyler was getting a bad feeling about just how unstable the senator's sanity might be.

Not that he had any real choice. He was in too deep to fold now. So what if the guy had illusions about what his precious daughter should be doing with her lily-white body?

"It won't be easy," Tyler said.

"I pay you too much for easy work. You want to be one of my head people when I'm vice president? Get used to tough assignments. Get out."

Jeb pushed a button on the underside of his desk. There was a buzz as the door to the office opened. He resumed looking out over the grounds of his home as his business associate left. His daughter Damascus came into view, running down the side steps and onto the walking path.

He pressed his lips into a tight line at the running sportswear she had on.

So damn masculine. She knew he detested the sight of her in it.

She took off to the side of the house, keeping to the area she was allowed in. Two of his personal security men trotted along behind her. But she'd made sure she ran past his sight. Of course, she might have some flimsy excuse, but he suspected she was needling him. He wasn't sure of her. Sometime between her meeting with Vitus Hale and her return she'd learned to hide her feelings from him. Now she presented a calm, collected exterior at all times.

Which was why he doubted her sincerity. The night he'd taken her back, she'd been too full of passion for it to have cooled so completely.

Another reason why the Hale brothers needed to die. There could be no going back for Damascus. His daughter needed the additional lesson of understanding what would happen to anyone she foolishly grew attached to that he did not approve of.

He'd be the master of his home.

Maybe his daughter's cool demeanor was a wise choice on her part to accept his rule.

Possibly.

Then again, perhaps she was making sure he glimpsed her in her athletic attire because she knew it was the only way to strike back at him. That would fit with the daughter who had so brazenly told him she was going to marry Vitus Hale.

She'd signed his death warrant with that statement. The daughter of Congressman Jeb Ryland would never be wed to a mongrel dog of war like Special Agent Vitus Hale.

Even if she had foolishly played at being the man's bitch.

He clenched his fingers into fists as his temper surged.

At least she was keeping in shape. He had uses for that. Men who wanted a wife with connections and a good figure. Jeb planned to exploit their desires. Very soon, he'd make his move. Which only brought his temper back to a slow boil.

He'd needed his revenge now, while the media wasn't focused on him. While the facts might be buried along with the Hale brothers.

But he wasn't giving it up. No. Vitus Hale wasn't going to walk away free.

Not from Jeb Ryland.

No one walked away clean after crossing Jeb Ryland.

"You're being an idiot."

Mercer lowered his beer and glared at Vitus.

"You are," Vitus confirmed. "Getting drunk when the case isn't closed."

"It's closed," Mercer confirmed.

Vitus shook his head. "She didn't kick you out. Didn't run to her big brother to help kick you to the curb." Vitus nodded. "Case is still . . . open."

"I asked her to marry me."

Vitus raised an eyebrow. "And?"

Mercer tipped his longneck back once more. Vitus reached over and pulled it out of his fingers.

"What the fuck do you want from me, Vitus?" Mercer demanded. "I'm sitting here, behaving like a gentleman. Giving her . . . space."

Vitus snorted. And then snickered. "She didn't fall for a nice guy. She liked all your rough edges a whole lot from what I saw. So stop being a dumb ass by turning into the poster boy for society's idea of what relationships should be. If she wanted that, she'd have a ring on her finger and a couple of kids. That woman has her father's need for a good challenge in her. You two will fight as much as you fuck."

Mercer felt like his ears were ringing from that truth. It knocked him upside his head and left him staring at Vitus. It was a harsh analysis.

And so on point, he was ready to agree that he'd been a dumb ass. He stood up and grabbed a coffee mug. The pot was sitting on warm. He poured half a mugful and downed it.

"Thanks for the kick in the ass."

Vitus lifted his beer bottle to him in response.

The walk down the hallway twisted his insides but he liked it.

Because it was go-time.

Mercer closed the door behind him silently. It was more startling than if he'd slammed it. She turned around and surveyed him, taking in the set expression on his face, the warning flickering in his eyes.

"I'm thinking," she said.

He shrugged out of his jacket and tossed it over the top of one of her bedposts.

"No, Zoe, you're avoiding the truth."

She propped her hand onto her hip. "Oh really?" She tossed her hair back and sent him a warning look. "Came down here just to tell me what I'm doing wrong?"

He slowly grinned, his lips parting and flashing his teeth at her. But it wasn't a nice expression. Nope. Far from it. The guy was downright menacing now. "You wouldn't have me any other way, baby."

She shifted, feeling his words as much as she heard them, which didn't make any sense.

As if her dealings with Mercer ever made any sense.

"Enough of the pushing into my space," she warned him. "Your operation is over."

"It's over, all right," he agreed. "But I'm far from finished with being in your space."

"That's not for you to say."

He tilted his head to the side, offering her a partial shrug. "Oh, I think it really is for me to say, Zoe. In fact, I'm waiting for you to stop being such a good little girl. The one Tim was so sure it would be easy to pull one over on."

"Yeah, well, I schooled him, didn't I?" she shot back.

"You did. Your dad and brother aren't the only ones with grit."

Mercer was smiling at her now, the expression one of approval. It warmed her because she knew without a doubt he wasn't a man to hand out praise to the undeserving. Or unworthy. The feeling spreading through her was great because it was something she'd earned.

"So, when are you going to stop trying to crawl back into the shell of your old life?"

The question brought her up short. "I'm not sure what you're getting at."

He unfolded his arms and closed the distance between them, slowly stalking her. Her insides twisted, but she stood her ground and it felt damn good.

"I was sitting out in the kitchen, giving you space . . . like a nice guy."

She wrinkled her nose at the phrase. Mercer chuckled.

"Yeah, that's when Vitus hit me upside the head with a richly deserved ass kick." The amusement faded from his face. His eyes filled with yearning. It reached out across the space between them, feeling like a live current connected to the swirling need driving her insane. Everything was so incredibly impossible and yet pathetically simple.

"You don't want a nice guy, baby."

I don't.

The admission was just there, bubbling up from inside her. She looked away because she was pretty certain he'd read it right off her face.

"And I love the way you come out of your shell for me," he continued, his voice deepening, becoming husky.

Sexy beyond belief.

He was reaching for her, his fingertips stroking across her jaw and lifting her face so their gazes could fuse again.

The connection was restored. Full-strength current surged between them, making her feel like she was coming fully alive. It was fucking intense and she gritted her teeth to avoid purring.

"Where's my bitch?" he demanded.

She shook off his touch, rising to the challenge in his voice. "Be careful what you wish for, Mercer."

He opened his arms wide. "Hit me with your best shot, baby. I'll let you know if I'm impressed."

"Oh, you will be," she warned, sticking her finger out and poking him in the chest. "I can handle you, Mr. Special Agent Man. Untamed or not. Don't think you're going to steamroll over me. I am not a good little girl."

"You're sitting in your room like one."

Her eyes narrowed. He was smirking at her. Expectation surged through her veins as she recognized the look in his eyes. He was lowering his attention to her lips, making ready to kiss her. She wanted him to. Craved the connection and the mind-numbing reaction she knew would follow.

But that was letting him take control.

She stepped back. He raised an eyebrow in question.

"You're not going to kiss me senseless."

He bared his teeth at her. "Yes I am."

She stepped back and shook her head. His eyes brightened, practically glowing with anticipation. Her belly twisted in response, a surge of confidence flooding her as she drank in the way she made him look so hungry.

Her.

She did that.

To him.

That's right . . .

It was a heady feeling, an aphrodisiac.

"I want you naked," she declared. "Stripped down to skin."

"Is that a fact?" he asked smoothly. "What makes you think I'm going to jump?"

It was her turn to flash him a grin. "You wanted a bitch. Well, that means I'm going to be mouthy. Very mouthy."

He offered her a sound that was half grunt, half chuckle. It was very male and loaded with promise. Her clit started throbbing in response, the heat surging up from her core as he backed up and ripped his shirt off.

"Like this, baby?"

She nodded, making a little sound of enjoyment under her breath. "But it could be so much better."

"Let me see if I can improve my performance . . ." He

kicked his shoes free and popped the waistband button on his jeans.

Her mouth went dry, her attention on his fingers as he worked the buttons on his fly. Time slowed down, her heart accelerating. He finished and his cock sprang into sight, already swollen. She reached for it, curling her fingers around the stiff staff and enjoying the slide of his soft skin against her palm.

But he pulled back, leaving her with only the sight of him again.

"Not enough, is it, Zoe?" he asked as he shucked his jeans completely. "Just watching isn't enough."

"No. It's not." She didn't really think about her response. It was pure reaction.

As always.

She reached down to grasp the bottom of her tunic top and pull it up her body. When she cleared her head, she caught sight of Mercer watching her. Every inch of him was hard. Every detail still striking her as untamed.

But he was looking at her.

She let her thoughts scatter, let all the reasons just dissipate into a vapor as passion filled her. He was her haven. His embrace the place she needed to be to prove herself and take solace. It was explosive and the embers kept her warm when they were both spent.

Fuck tomorrow.

She was living in the moment.

Kagan felt his company arrive. The veteran agent didn't look up because he didn't need to. Servat settled down near him, scanning the area in front of them.

"You're looking for me," Servat said.

Kagan nodded. "And you know why."

Servat was silent for a long moment. A gust of wind blew a scattering of dried leaves past his feet.

"We all have orders," Servat said.

"Who told you about Tyler?"

Kagan's poise slipped just a bit, exposing his temper.

"You weren't really going to leave him chained to that table," Servat said, defending himself.

Kagan turned to look at him. "Who?"

Servat held his tongue for a long moment. "General Presson."

Kagan pressed his lips into a hard line.

"It's a complication," Servat continued. "Tyler is being moved out of your sphere of activity. Your orders still stand."

Kagan got up and strolled away. A car slid up to the curb and he opened the door and got in. The people moving down the sidewalk never took much notice of him.

Kagan had devoted his life to preserving their way of living.

And he had a feeling that fight was about to get very complicated.

"Daddy's home!"

Zoe lifted her head, hitting Mercer in the chin. He grunted, his arms tightening out of reflex around her. She pushed against him as she heard her father's footfalls coming down the hallway.

She was suddenly feeling seventeen.

"My dad . . ."

"Is home," her father announced in a booming voice.

Colonel Bryan Magnus stood in the doorway, still in his fatigues. Mercer was wide awake now but he held her still, only moving to tug the comforter up to cover her shoulder. Her father had planted himself in the doorway, slowly tugging his glasses off as he caught Mercer with a razor-sharp look.

"Morning, sir."

Her father pegged Mercer with a hard look. "Get some shorts on, son. You're burning daylight and I need some coffee."

Her dad winked at her before turning neatly on his heel and letting the bedroom door close.

Zoe groaned.

Mercer chuckled. He was already out of bed and stepping into his jeans. She lifted her face from the bed and shot him a look.

"My dad is going—"

"To bust my balls," Mercer finished for her.

"Ah, pretty much," she agreed.

He shrugged into a T-shirt and winked at her. "I'm looking forward to it."

Zoe pushed herself up and onto her knees. "You are?"

He leaned over and pressed a hard kiss against her lips. "Sure am." His eyes flashed a warning at her. "Because as soon as I get him on my side, I'm going to drag you down to the courthouse."

"I didn't say I was going to marry you."

Mercer stopped with his hand on the doorknob. He turned and gave her a wink. "Why do you think I need your dad on my side? He's got to hold the shotgun. While I hold on to you."

"Mercer . . ."

She ended up staring at the closed bedroom door and laughing.

At herself.

"Who's my fluffy baby . . ."

Saxon and Mercer turned around slowly. Mercer pulled his shades off his face as he stared at her father in dumbfounded shock.

Zoe smothered her amusement behind her hand.

"Sweet little birdie . . ."

Her father was cradling Harley like an infant. The scarlet-winged macaw was lying contently on his back in her father's arms with most of his feathers fluffed up.

"That's wrong," Saxon said.

"What's wrong about it?" her father demanded as he rocked Harley gently. The parrot had his beak open, looking for all the world like he was the happiest creature alive. "Don't tell me my little girl didn't explain that Harley is her baby brother?"

Mercer cut her a look. "The hatch-day cake?"

"Yup," Zoe answered. "From scratch. Every year."

Her father rolled Harley over so that the parrot was perched on his hand. The bird started nuzzling him under his chin as he rubbed him. "No store-bought cakes for family members in this house."

Saxon reached out and patted Mercer on the shoulder. "She's all yours. This family is completely crazy. And those birds live forever. You're going to be dealing with it when you're sixty."

"Maybe I haven't agreed to be his," Zoe said.

"Harley, Daddy needs to put you down so he can get his shotgun."

"That's not funny, Dad."

Mercer winked at her. "Yes it is. Real funny, because I get to watch you be pushed around for a change."

Mercer dropped his arms around her from behind, kissing her temple before nuzzling her neck.

"You know you're going to marry me."

"Do I?" she asked as she melted against him. "Why?"

"Because I love you."

She was pretty sure she was wearing a smile. It still felt strange, the lack of tension, the feeling of him against her when none of the odds had favored them.

Mercer leaned down and whispered in her ear. "I love you, Zoe Magnus. So marry me and I'll help you bake that cake for Harley."

"You've got a deal."

But she was the one who had gotten the real deal.

The golden-ticket type.

"They'll come for you next," Saxon said.

Kagan nodded. He was looking at his computer screen, a NO MATCH FOUND message flashing on it.

No match found for one Tyler Martin.

No service record. No shield number. No arrest record. Nothing.

"This runs deep," Kagan said at last. "Better make sure your ass is covered. Double time."

He doubted there was any way to avoid the storm that was coming. Someone had come for Tyler all right. A someone with mighty deep connections. In its way, it was interesting to note. A strangely fascinating type of puzzle that he enjoyed because he couldn't figure it out.

But that was also his Achilles' heel.

A man who knew too much was a liability.

No one liked having those around.

In this case, whoever was on the other end of getting Tyler released was going to try to clean the slate. He knew it because that would be his own next move.

So he'd just have to make sure he was a harder target to hit.

Read on for an excerpt from Dawn Ryder's
upcoming novel

DARE YOU TO RUN

Coming soon from St. Martin's Paperbacks

He was home.

Damascus felt him. Call that what you may, but she was sure she felt his presence registering on her skin. The air in the house fairly crackled as she felt him drawing closer. She sat still, keeping her chin up and her hands on her knees. Her breath was caught in her throat as she caught the first sight of him, just a quarter of his face as he looked around the doorframe and down the barrel of his handgun. He had his finger on the trigger, his left hand cupping the butt of it. His bare forearms allowed her to see the definition that proved he was just as hard and deadly as she recalled.

She bit her lower lip to keep from talking, her composure flying to pieces like it was being hit by a tornado. All the resolve and self-discipline she'd spent the last three years cultivating were being ripped away in chunks and strips by this sheer force of nature. He finished checking the house before coming back to stare at her. She felt his glare, felt like it was burning away the layers of the façade she'd built after realizing she had to leave him.

"You wanted my attention?" he asked at last, his voice a low rumble that suited the nearly dark room. The only light was coming from a red light. It had turned on the moment she entered the room, allowing her to see without killing her night vision.

"Actually, that's my line," she said as she stood. He'd stopped across the room from her, the gun tucked against his center, behind his belt.

His brows lowered. "I don't follow."

"Well, your brother is trailing me," she countered. "Don't bother to deny it. You bugged my dragonfly, didn't you?"

Surprise widened his eyes. It was a momentary loss of control, one he masked quickly but not before she saw it.

"I knew it," she said. "That was a low thing to do. The dragonfly belonged to my grandmother. It's important to me."

Which was why he'd used it, she realized that as the words were sailing out of her mouth like some sort of plea for an apology. What the hell was wrong with her? Vitus sure wouldn't be sparing much empathy for her bruised feelings.

"I did place a bug in the dragonfly." He lifted a finger and pointed at her. "As a safeguard, when you were my responsibility. I haven't used it since."

"Well, your brother is now. I caught him today, at the university." She shot his attempt to dodge the issue out of the air. "And Saxon wouldn't be watching me unless you were in on it."

"You're guessing, Princess."

There was arrogance in his tone. One that she wanted

to hate, but she knew it was earned and that just pissed her off even more because there were unknown factors. But, it also wasn't a denial; he was dodging the question and trying to distract her.

"I'm not guessing that I saw him and there was no way he would have known where I was unless he had a tracking beacon." She looked away from him, realizing she was saying too much. Her association with Colonel Magnus had to remain secret. She drew in a deep breath and turned to face him again. "Well, I'm here to tell you to stop."

"Saxon has a reason to keep an eye on your father. That doesn't mean he'd trail you."

"He was with me at the university," she said confidently. "And you have to stop before—"

She shut her mouth with a click of her teeth. A second later, Vitus had her by the forearms, his seemingly relaxed stance in the doorway nothing but a smokescreen to keep her at ease and spilling her guts.

"You took a damned stupid risk coming here by yourself. Thank God I had the system enabled to let you in or you'd have been stuck on the step like a sitting duck for who the hell knows how long. Don't be stupid like that, Princess. Your father has a lot of enemies."

He was hissing through clenched teeth. She tried to recoil from his temper, slapping at his chest when he held her without any real effort. Somehow, she'd forgotten just how bloody strong he was.

"Well, I did do it," she shot back. "You and your brother aren't the only ones who know how to play shadow games. And no one taught me how to do it."

She was suddenly free and ended up stumbling back a few paces, finally coming to rest against the wall.

"You shouldn't have to learn," Vitus said softly. So softly she might have missed the sympathy in his tone.

But she didn't and she lifted her chin, needing to be more than the helpless creature she'd been the last time she'd been inside his house. "You think I want to be the princess you always called me?" She shook her head. "I'm not a little girl."

His lips twitched, curving sensuously as his eyes narrowed in a purely male way. It had been three long years since she'd seen that look on his face, but she recognized it instantly, sensation rippling across the surface of her skin in response. There was no thinking, no deciding what she felt; there was only him and the way her body sprang to life when he was close enough to touch her.

"I have never. . . ." He stepped closer, her senses so keen, she head the soft sounds of his boots connecting with the wooden floor. "Never . . . thought of you as a little girl." All the tiny hairs on her skin were standing straight up as he closed the space so that he could flatten his hands against the wall on either side of her face. "But I sure as hell tried to."

His eyes were closed now as he leaned down and inhaled against her hair.

"I tried so damned hard to think of you as a little girl. . . . instead of the woman I wanted to touch. . . ."

She heard the desire in his voice, felt it wash through her like a flash flood, sweeping everything else aside in the blink of an eye.

"*Touch me.* . . ." She couldn't have held the words back if she'd tried. There was no way to silence the cravings she had for him, she'd tried.

"Don't say that." He growled. "I need to get you back. . . ."

"Screw that." It felt like every fiber in her being rejected the idea. What she wanted was right there. She could smell him, feel his body heat, and all she wanted was a taste to go with it all, to send her into sensory overload where reality could just fucking drown.

She reached out, finished with waiting and being cautious. He was too close, too real to be ignored in favor of doing the wise thing. His chest felt as good as she recalled. Hard and sculpted, and her fingertips were suddenly ultrasensitive. The T-shirt he had on was a thin barrier that nevertheless frustrated her because it kept her from what she craved.

So she dug her fingers into the soft jersey and yanked it up. The tail of it came free from his belt, rising up to give her exactly what she wanted, bare skin.

"Agreed. Fuck it and everything else but this. . . ." he said, reaching down to take control of his shirt. There was a rustle of motion, a bunching of his abdominal muscles as he pulled the shirt up and over his head, chucking it across the room with a motion that was full of barely controlled strength. He was breathing as hard as she was, both of them a hair's-breadth from some sort of explosion. Damascus felt it building inside her, and she licked her lips with anticipation.

His face tightened as his gaze settled on her tongue as it made the journey across her lower lip. She was fingering the fabric of her dress and suddenly couldn't bear the impediment of it between them. She tugged it up, pulling it above her head before she felt him grasp it and finish the job.

The cool air brushed against her overheated skin, but only for a moment before he caught her up against him. He captured her mouth in a searing kiss. She moaned softly, unable to contain all the sensation inside her anymore. He pressed her lips apart, licking across her lower lip before threading his hands into her hair and holding her head and thrusting his tongue into her mouth to stroke hers.

She shuddered, the bluntness of it making her clit pulse. Her heart was hammering with a crazy rhythm, but she didn't care if it burst; the only thing on her mind was to get closer to him. She reached for his belt, fumbling with it as she struggled to free what she craved.

"Fuck . . . no," he growled as he put her at arm's length. "Too fast."

His voice was raspy and his face looked like it was etched in solid stone. There was a fury in his eyes that should have scared her, but the only thing she had room for in her brain was the need to get back in contact with him.

Vitus wasn't letting her decide anything, though. He scooped her off her feet like she weighed as much as a pillow, cradling her against his chest as he carried her through the dark house to his bed. Her belly tightened as she realized what he was doing, excitement curling her toes even as she fought off a twinge of frustration for the way he was taking command.

She couldn't expect anything less from him, but he wasn't the only one with desires. She flipped over and rose onto her knees the moment he tossed her onto the mattress. It bounced, the springs groaning as she reached behind her and unhooked the flimsy bra she'd bought. Her cash fluttered down as she enjoyed the way Vitus had frozen, his gaze riveted on her breasts, his mouth a thin line of hunger.

"Shit," he groaned, his voice thick with need. His fly was only half open but he leaned across the bed and fastened his lips around one nipple, drawing on the point like he was starving.

She gasped, sensation flowing from that connection down to her clit. He crawled right over her, slipping his knees on either side of her hips as he closed his arms around her and sucked on her tit. She arched back, offering it to him, offering every bit of herself to him.

His. . . . she just wanted to be his.